Educated in Australia and England, the author started travelling the world as a young man and essentially never stopped. He has served in the Royal Navy and the Merchant Marine prior to his long-time career as an accountant in the field of international telecommunications. He has lived and worked in every corner of the globe.

Whilst none of his books are autobiographical, they reflect his deep understanding of human nature and frailty.

Also by G. K. Robinson:

A Time to Live

G. K. Robinson

The Munich Pursuit

AUSTIN MACAULEY PUBLISHERS™
LONDON • CAMBRIDGE • NEW YORK • SHARJAH

A CIP catalogue record for this title is available from the British Library.

ISBN 9781528905619 (Paperback)
ISBN 9781528905626 (Hardback)
ISBN 9781528905633 (Kindle e-book)
ISBN 9781528958035 (ePub e-book)

www.austinmacauley.com

First Published (2019)
Austin Macauley Publishers Ltd
25 Canada Square
Canary Wharf
London
E14 5LQ

Chapter One

David Coulter looked gloomily into the street from the foyer of his office building; the rain still as heavy as when he'd travelled to work that morning. The clouds low and dark and showing no signs of lifting. Nevertheless, when he'd telephoned the local metrological office earlier that morning at Speke airfield, close to Liverpool, a few miles from where he was in Chester, they'd given him a little hope, forecasting a possible clearer afternoon.

He was a member of the Royal Air Force Volunteer Reserve in his spare time. The origin of the Royal Air Force Volunteer Reserve, or to give it its official title Royal Auxiliary Air Force, goes back to an idea of Lord Trenchard in the early 1920s. He had a vision of an elite corps of civilians who would serve their country in flying squadrons in their spare time. Instituted by Order in Council on 9th October 1924, the first Auxiliary Air Force Squadrons were formed the following year. On the formation of a squadron, although most of the aircrew would be reserve personnel, the ground crews were invariably regular Royal Air Force personnel, who then trained reserve personnel to gradually take over. By 1938 most squadrons were 50 per cent regular personnel and 50 per cent reserve personnel and nearly all pilots were reserve personnel, and 610 Squadron (City of Chester), David Coulter's squadron, was no different.

David Coulter was a pilot with the local 610 (City of Chester) Squadron, flying Blenheim twin-engine light bombers. He'd joined the R.A.F. Reserve in 1936, shortly after the local squadron had been formed, having learnt to fly whilst at the university. After joining the R.A.F.V.R., he trained on Avro Tutor and Hawker Hart aircraft, then was commissioned as a Pilot Officer in the air crew branch of the Volunteer Reserve.

He converted to Blenheim bombers when the squadron was re-equipped in late 1937. Rumour had it that they were shortly going to convert again, this time either into a fighter squadron in keeping with the R.A.F.'s expansion programme – this was announced by the government in January 1937, the previous year, or into Fairey Battle light bombers. It was thought they were more likely to convert to the Fairey Battle, which would be more in keeping with their current training.

Now in March 1938, the government had authorised spending to increase the number of airfields. The government was keen to build up the fighter defences to meet the threat from the totalitarian states, in particular Adolf Hitler's Germany. In keeping with this expansion, the facilities at the airfield that 610 Squadron used were currently being upgraded.

The squadron's home airfield was at Hooton Park, Cheshire, in what had been the grounds of a large country house, Hooton Hall. The main house had been demolished in 1932, only what was the stable block remained. The estate dated back to early 1300 and passing through various hands, ended up with Ministry of Defence.

Hooton Hall and Park were located about two to three miles north-east of the small Wirral Peninsula village of Eastham. This was just off the main Birkenhead to Chester Road, between this road and the River Mersey, which was about two miles to the north. Across the River Mersey from Hooton again to the north was Speke airfield, with a full-time metrological department, whilst Hooton only had a part time one, hence him telephoning Speke airfield that morning.

The squadron also at times used an airfield about 15 miles to the west, near a small Welsh town of Hawarden, close to a factory producing one of the new fighter aircraft recently ordered by the Air Ministry as part of the R.A.F. expansion programme. Another airfield the squadron used when operating in co-operation with the army was at Shobdon, about one hundred miles south of Chester and about 15 miles north-west of Hereford.

He had hoped to be able to spend that afternoon putting in some flying hours and had arranged to meet with Peter Jones, his sergeant co-pilot. The Blenheim normally carried a crew of three, the third man being an air gunner, who manned the upper turret but for the purposes of putting in flying hours for the pilots, he wasn't needed.

The squadron, apart from training as a conventional day light bomber squadron, had also been working with the Western Command of the British Army in close support of infantry units. In this respect they had been training in conjunction with the Herefordshire Regiment of the Shropshire Light Infantry, using the army training grounds in mid Wales. Hence their use of Shobdon airfield, about 40 miles from the Brecon Beacons army training ground.

The tactics they were trying to develop had previously drawn a certain amount of criticism from some of the senior officers in the War Office, whose minds were still fighting using The Great War tactics and trench warfare. Not that the minds of senior officers in the Air Ministry were receptive to close co-operation with the army. They were in fact a little terrified of any close co-operation.

They had fought hard in the early 1920s to keep the Air Force a separate service and therefore, were a little wary of being too close to the Army when it came to developing tactics. Their preferred strategy was to mass bomb any enemy into submission; ground troops would only be required to mop up afterwards.

There were people in Britain, notably Captain B. H. Liddell Hart and J.C.F. ('Boney') Fuller, chief staff officer of the British Tank Corps in 1918 and others (unfortunately, not many in the key areas of the Ministry of Defence), who could see that the next war would be a very fluid affair, using motorised columns and close aircraft support in the place of artillery.

These methods had been explored by various nations in the years following the end of The Great War but chiefly by the Germans, who were in the process of trying them out in Spain during the civil war currently raging there.

Tactics of a similar nature had been tried out by the British Army during manoeuvres on Salisbury Plain in 1934. The entrenched cavalry diehards made sure that the exercise had been shamelessly rigged to discredit the armoured formations taking part. Other factors contributing to the failure of the trial were firstly, at that time a reliable air to ground radio was not available, and secondly, there was not a suitable aircraft available in the Royal Air Force to co-operate closely with the ground forces.

What was really required was a dive bomber of the type used by the American Colonel Billy Mitchell when he demonstrated after The Great War how dive bombers could sink battleships.

Although the current Master of General Ordnance, Hugh Elles, (the first commander of the Royal Tank Corps in The Great War) and other senior officers had lost faith in tanks other than for infantry support, there were those in the Western Command of the British Army who could see a role for aircraft working in close co-operation with the ground forces and willing to persevere and experiment.

Therefore, within their limited means, they were trying to develop this close co-operation, hence the connection between 610 Squadron and the Herefordshire Regiment. The Herefordshire Regiment was a Territorial Regiment, also which meant both were outside the mainstream of military control being territorial reserve units, and therefore, could be a little more flexible in their approach to tactics, although having only limited financial means.

This co-operation was the result of the commanding officer of 610 Squadron, Donald Selby, and the colonel in charge of the Herefordshire Regiment, Henry Marsden, first discussing it when they had met at a family get-together. The two men were married to sisters, the colonel slightly older than the C.O. of 610 Squadron. The discussion had first started when the two men talked about the Italian campaign in Abyssinia and the rumours that the Germans were assisting the Italians. They had gone on to talk about the German Army and the re-arming of the German military machine; from there had lamented the fact that both the War Office in London and the Air Ministry were preparing for a future war based on the tactics of the last war.

Whilst Donald Selby had been far too young to take part in the 1914 – 1918 War, the 'Great War', Henry Marsden had seen service as a private soldier in the closing days of the war and had been horrified firstly by the casualties and secondly by the methods used when attacking.

Both men agreed to talk to their respective superiors to see if they could unofficially co-operate on Army and Air Force close support, this they had both done and reluctant approval had been given.

The type of aircraft 610 Squadron was using was really unsuitable for the task of close support. The 610 Squadron was equipped with the twin-engined Bristol Blenheim bomber. Officially classed as a day bomber with a maximum bomb load of 1000lbs, it had one fixed .303 inch Browning machine gun firing forward and one .303 inch Vickers K machine gun in the upper dorsal turret. The Blenheim's unsuitability was the reason for most personnel believing they would convert to Fairey Battle light bombers – a single-engined light bomber carrying a similar bomb load as the Blenheim at a similar speed, although having a slightly lower ceiling, but more suitable to be used as a dive bomber for army support.

The German Army, on the other hand, was using a Junkers 87 Dive Bomber, which carried a bomb load of 4 x 500lb bombs and had two machine guns firing forward and two machine guns in the rear upper turret, all firing 7.92mm ammunition, slightly smaller calibre than the .303 British machine gun. This aeroplane was specifically designed for close infantry support.

Another factor that made the co-operation between the two units somewhat difficult was that the Herefordshire Regiment was an infantry unit and not an armoured unit equipped with either tanks or armoured cars. The unit was equipped with a small number of Bren Gun Carriers; principally an infantry support vehicle, although for the purpose of developing tactics a suitable substitute for conventional armoured fighting vehicles. The Bren gun was a light machine gun, developed in answer to the German MG 34. The German gun was a very versatile and reliable light machine gun.

The Bren gun was considered by many to be superior to the German weapon and had just come into service with the Territorial Army units, in a ratio of about one gun to every eight infantrymen, whilst in the Regular Army the ratio was one to four men.

The Bren Gun Carrier or Bren Carrier was developed as a fast, tracked, infantry support armoured personnel carrier, designed to move quickly in support of and to carry infantry across denied ground, but also act as a reconnaissance vehicle, a forerunner to the later armoured personnel carriers.

The Bren Carrier was an open-topped vehicle, powered by a Ford V8 water-cooled engine, carrying a maximum of five men and armed with a .303 Bren gun and in addition sometimes a Boyes Anti-Tank rifle. The armour plate was about half an inch thick, and the vehicle could travel on a good surface at around 30 to 40 miles per hour. It was fully tracked and therefore, could move across rough terrain at a reasonable speed.

Peter Jones, David's co-pilot, was employed by the Chester City Council as a surveyor, so David Coulter decided to walk down the street to the Chester City Council Offices and discuss with Peter what he thought they should do. Should they go out to Hooton Park or cancel the trip and wait for a forecasted better day? The trouble was that he couldn't see a free day for himself for about a fortnight, even at weekends.

Making his way with an umbrella and raincoat, he walked to Peter Jones' office. Peter, a fresh-faced light-brown-haired young man, was standing by the window looking out as David walked in; he turned and pointed with a backward use of a thumb.

"Not much good for flying today, David. I would have thought we could have had better weather than this in March."

"When I talked to Speke earlier, they thought there might be a better afternoon in store. Come on, let's take a chance. I'll get my car and pick you up, say in ten minutes."

"OK, let's go. I didn't like what I was doing anyway."

David Coulter walked back through the driving rain to the rear of his building, where he had parked his car, a small MG sports saloon, a model much loved by young men. The car he'd bought second-hand shortly after becoming articled to Kimberley and Spooner, the firm of Chartered Accountants. He'd borrowed the money from his parents, who were greatly relieved he didn't show any interest in a motorcycles, which they considered to be too dangerous.

The two men drove off along the Birkenhead road north, turning into a narrow lane shortly after going through Eastham village and then between some imposing gate pillars, the remnants of the old Hooton Park entrance. The trip took about half an hour and by the time they got to the airfield, the clouds seemed to have lifted slightly, showing promise of a better afternoon later. David had called the airfield before they left and had advised the sergeant in charge of their ground crew of their intention. The airfield had a nucleus of regular R.A.F. ground personnel under the control of an engineering branch officer to service the planes, apart from training R.A.F.V.R. ground staff.

They drove to the hangar where their plane was located, leaving the car to one side of the open hangar door. Just inside the wide doorway, they met the flight sergeant in charge of their ground crew.

"I think it might clear later, but later could be after about four or five, sir, the cloud ceiling is only about six hundred feet, too low for anything safe. In fact, at times it has barely cleared those trees over there," pointing to a clump of Scotch pines to the right of the hangar. The time now was shortly after two, the two men looked at each other. David nodded to the sergeant.

"I think we'll wait for a while and see how the weather develops, Flight. Thank you. We'll be over in the flight mess."

The facilities at Hooton were slightly different from a Regular Air Force airfield. The regular or permanent Air Force bases had separate messes for commissioned and non-commissioned officers. The class distinction between commissioned and non-commissioned ranks in the regular Air Force was stricter than in the Auxiliary Air Force. In the regular Air Force, non-commissioned ranks were expected to undertake ground duties as well as flying duties, whilst the commissioned officers of the flying branch only undertook flying duties. In fact, some martinet warrant officers in charge of the non-commissioned officers on some of the regular Air Force stations were particularly heavy-handed when it came to apportioning out ground duties to non-commissioned flight crews on the basis that flying was something they should do in their spare time.

At Hooton, whilst the eating and recreational facilities were separate for commissioned and non-commissioned officers, the flight crews also had a mess or room where they could meet together whilst waiting to be summoned for flying and the non-commissioned aircrew personnel did not undertake ground duties.

Going back to their car, the two men drove around the runway perimeter track to a group of buildings on the far side of the airfield, where the flying mess was situated. The building had been the old stables of Hooton Hall, left when

Hooton Hall itself was demolished in 1932. These had been converted into the squadron offices and messes for the commissioned and non-commissioned ranks.

The rest of the buildings on the airfield, apart from the two aircraft hangars and civilian workshops, were 16ft by 18ft Nissen huts, a corrugated iron-hooped shape building used for offices, stores and accommodation. The Nissen hut was originally designed in the Great War and used extensively by all the British services. Built on a concrete base, quick to erect, cheap and if used as accommodation, usually fitted with a stove in the middle. Currently, there were no arrangements for accommodation for the auxiliary Air Force personnel on the airfield, although the small number of regular Air Force personnel under a Warrant Officer were accommodated in Nissen huts. The Commissioned Officer in charge was living with his family in an Air Ministry rented house in the village of Eastham, just over a mile away. Also located on the airfield site were two light aircraft manufacturers and an aircraft repair company.

The 610 Squadron planes were housed in two Belfast Truss hangars, the design of which had been established during the Great War and was used extensively by R.A.F. airfields throughout the United Kingdom. These two hangars had been left over from the use of the airfield by the military during the Great War as a training ground for the Royal Flying Corps, the forerunner of the Royal Air Force.

The two men went across to the flight mess using the perimeter track and noted that the contractor building the third hangar was well advanced in his work.

Entering the flight mess, they were met in the doorway by Donald Selby, their commanding officer, and a fresh-faced dark-haired man of 30, a solicitor from Liverpool and one of the founder members of the 610 Squadron in 1935. Older than the majority of the Squadron flyers, David Coulter being 22 and Peter Jones 21, the rest of the pilots were of similar age to themselves.

"Hello, you two, I suppose you're on the same thing as me, trying to get some hours in, and this weather isn't helping."

"Yes Don, it's supposed to lift soon, but I can't say I'm hopeful."

The squadron leader nodded. "I'm about to call it a day, I'll give it another half an hour." He walked across to one of the battered armchairs and slumped into it.

"Any news yet of our change of aircraft, as rumour has it, sir?"

"Not yet, Peter, although I did hear the other day talking to George Williams at Group H.Q. that they were expecting an allocation of Fairey Battles, that new light bomber, single-engined job, which sounded highly suspicious to me but he denied we were being considered for a change."

"I read about that plane in the 'Flying Now' magazine, the performance seemed to be very similar to our Blenheims, except ours have two engines. Lot safer if you lose one, with one engine you've nothing left." David Coulter gave a short laugh.

The three men talked generally about the performance of their Blenheim aircraft, then Peter Jones made another reference to the 'Flying Now' magazine, a weekly magazine more or less compulsory reading for anyone interested in flying.

"Did you see that article in last week's 'Flying Now' on a new engine being developed which will take planes to speeds over 500 mph?" The Blenheim they were flying, if all things were favourable, could reach a top speed of 280mph, so a fighter plane flying at speeds of over 500mph would be able to run rings around them.

"Oh, that's nothing new; I think I saw a similar article last year," replied Donald Selby. "I think it will come eventually, but I think they're a long way off getting an engine to use in an aircraft; the theory is there but the practical application is missing. No one has yet made the connection."

"Well, this article said that there was a company called Power Jets which had actually made a model that had run last year. Not in an aircraft but certainly on a test bed. In fact, it said the Air Ministry was funding further development, because it had been such a success."

"There's a lot of difference between running an engine on a test bed and fitting it into an aircraft, Peter. I would think it'll take a few years."

"The writer seemed to think one could be ready by the end of this year, at the latest early next year. He also said that a German, Hans Von Ohain, had developed a very similar engine."

"Y'know Peter, if this engine is really as good as that paper said it is, the Air Ministry wouldn't have allowed anything to be written and published, in case it gives the Germans an insight into what we're up to, y'know secrets and such."

"What sort of an engine is it?" David Coulter interjected.

"It's an engine that doesn't drive a kite along with propellers, it sort of sucks air in one end and blows it out the other, bit like a turbine on a ship, or a vacuum cleaner, if you know what I mean. Apparently, there's a R.A.F. officer who has designed one of these things, he calls it a Power Jet. The man's name is Whittle, Frank Whittle, but like I said, it's common knowledge in aviation engine circles. I think these engineer types have been looking for something like this for years. A piston engine would thrash itself to bits trying to go at the sort of high speeds they're thinking of for the future."

Donald Selby laughed. "And like I've said, it's going to take a long time before they get the thing off the test bed. Can you imagine the sort of aircraft they'd need to travel at over five hundred miles per hour, the strength and shape, apart from the strain on the pilot, particularly in some of those tight turns? It would bring on all sorts of problems."

"I know, Don, but you know as well as I do that technology doesn't stand still. The Germans are claiming they have a death ray or at least something that stops an aeroplane from flying, you know, cuts the engine off," this last from David Coulter.

"And I think that's a load of hog wash. I know we've a sort of system that can detect a kite in the distance, about ten miles I think, and not by sound. Anyway, you chaps, I don't think I'll wait any longer but I'll go, this weather doesn't seem to be clearing. You take my advice and don't wait."

With that Donald Selby heaved himself from the chair and reached for his raincoat. "I'm off."

After David Selby had left, the other two men sat and talked a little about the new aero engine, neither really believing that such a thing would come into general use for a few years. Eventually, by about four o'clock, although the rain had eased considerably, the cloud ceiling was far too low and they decided to call it a day.

The two men set off back to Chester.

"Have we had any news yet of when the summer camp has been set for, David?" This was the annual two weeks training that all territorial formations, (i.e. Royal Navy Volunteer Reserves, Territorial Army, and R.A.F.V.R.), had to attend on a full-time basis usually in summer, apart from their weekend training. It was usually called a 'camp' because the accommodation was normally tented, either on an Air Force base or, in the case of the army, close to an army barracks, and not very comfortable.

"Not yet, Pete, but I expect it will be in August sometime, at least I hope so. I've agreed with Tom Wadsworth I'll go with him to Germany in September for a couple of weeks. If we can get a date for the camp and it's early August, we may go late August. But we've not arranged anything firm as yet."

"Sounds good. Any idea where you'll go?"

"Well, I think Tom wants to go via the old battlefields and then onto the Rhine, he's got some idea of sailing down the Rhine on one of the steamers, but really we've nothing like firm plans as yet."

"Are you taking a car?"

"Not sure, if we're going to sail down the Rhine, a car will be in the way and there's a particular good rail system in Germany which we could use. But as I say, we've no firm plans as yet, just thoughts as to what we'd like to do."

"I understand their road systems are very good, autobahns I think they call them, no speed limits, just a road between point A and point B with no side roads."

"Yep, I've heard about them, but I think Tom is a little bit romantically inclined and wants to see a Rhine maiden, but I've no idea where he'll see one. I think he's seen too many pictures of those castles on the Rhine and expects there's a blonde-haired maiden in every window just waiting for him. I'll try and talk him out of the Rhine trip and stay with the car."

Peter laughed. "I think you'll have a great time. Anyway, think of all that beer you'll get at. But I believe the German police are very strict. You can drink as much as you like but don't wander around the streets drunk."

"Are you going anywhere?"

"I suppose I'll go with my parents, we've a cottage on the North Wales coast not far from Conway, towards Penmanmar, on what they call the Morfa. As long as the weather is good, it's quite nice. We usually get down there for a good deal of the summer; Dad and I commute, leave early Monday and stay in the house in Chester Monday night to Friday morning, then back there for the weekend. Depending on when 'camp' is, I'll take my fortnight's holiday there. If the summer is rotten, we then usually come home. But the last two summers have been great."

They were now entering Chester, and David threaded his way through the traffic towards Peter's office. The rain had eased a little but the clouds were still very low and the wind had freshened considerably.

"Just as well we called it a day, Peter, looks as if this won't stop until later tonight."

"Yeah, what time is it? Do you feel like a pint before you go home?"

"Don't mind if I do, let me drop you and I'll park the car and meet you in the bar of the Grosvenor." The Grosvenor was an old established Chester hotel. The pilots of 610 Squadron had more or less formed a habit of meeting there for drinks in a sort of ad hoc arrangement during the week, most of them being from the Chester area, apart from their squadron leader who lived in West Kirby, a small dormitory village for Liverpool on the estuary of the River Dee, along with one other pilot who lived in Heswall, another village further up the Dee estuary towards Chester.

David Coulter parked his car close to the cathedral square and walked back down to the Grosvenor Hotel and into the small bar towards the rear. Once inside he was greeted by two of the other pilots, along with Peter Jones. Peter had ordered up a pint for him, and the four pilots commandeered their usual table in the corner and sat talking flying.

The group was typical of the young people of that time who joined the military reserves, mostly young in either late teens or early twenties. The Commissioned Officers were grammar, public school or secondary school educated and employed in a profession of some sort and usually having been to a university. Most of the 'other ranks' were usually tradesmen, semi-skilled or labourers, having left elementary school at 14 with a good all-round education, which made them independent thinkers.

They were all aware that sooner rather than later their country would have to go to war. Their parents were of a generation that was still in shock from the 1914–1918 War and the size of the casualty lists; nevertheless, the makings of a fresh conflict were on the horizon.

The group at the table asked David if he'd heard any further news of their possible conversion to fighters. One of them produced one of the newspapers of that day, which contained a report of the sitting of Parliament the day before. The Secretary of State for Air had announced that day in the House of Lords that the government intended to increase the number of airfields for the R.A.F. by 20 and expand some of the existing airfields. In the current government of the day, the Secretary of State for Air was Viscount Swinton and he sat in the House of Lords. (This arrangement was changed in May 1938, when Sir Howard Kingsley Wood was appointed in the House of Commons to enable members of Parliament to have a closer contact in relation to Royal Air Force matters.)

David voiced his opinion that he was a little sceptical about their being transferred into a fighter squadron because of their involvement with the army in Herefordshire. Another thing which pointed to them not being transferred to the fighter wing was that they had recently taken delivery of an Army co-operation Lysander aircraft, a specialist aircraft capable of landing and taking off from a very limited space.

"I think we'll remain a bomber squadron, maybe a fighter-bomber squadron if we take delivery, as the latest rumour suggests, of the Fairey Battle bomber."

One pointed out that the co-operation with the army was not official policy.

The group sat and discussed the pros and cons of any change from bomber aircraft to fighters. Like all young men of their day, the four seemed to be in favour of re-mustering as fighter pilots, thinking of the prestige, a fighter pilot being a very glamorous figure. Bomber pilots were considered to be staid and not very adventurous.

Other members of the squadron dropped in and soon the group had grown to about 15 young men, all noisily arguing over the future of the squadron. The consensus of opinion seemed to be in favour of a fighter squadron.

Eventually, David Coulter said he had to go; Pete Jones went with him, the two bidding goodnight to the crowd walked out into the street.

"Can I give you a lift, Pete?"

"No thanks, I appreciate it, but I'm meeting a chap at the Duck," naming a pub further down the street. "I'm going to look at his car, it's a three-wheeler Morgan, only a couple of years old, he's wanting to get rid of it. Might be a bargain."

"OK, see you next weekend."

David walked off towards his car, thinking as he walked of the noisy argument in the Grosvenor. He personally didn't care which way they went, fighter or bomber, as long as he could fly, then his thoughts turned to the talk earlier about the propeller-less engine, the jet engine, was it possible? He thought he'd see what he could find in the way of information. There was a good reference library attached to the main Chester City Council run library, so he thought he'd pay a call there during the next day or so; another source of information was maybe Brian Wilson, the engineering officer in charge of their mechanics on the airfield.

As he entered the driveway of their house, he saw his father had just arrived and was getting out of his car; the rain by now had stopped but the cloud was still low.

His father waited until he stopped his car alongside his and had climbed out.

"Hello, Dave, you wouldn't have got much flying in today."

He'd mentioned to his parents as he was leaving that morning he might be a little late in getting home, because he intended to try and fly that afternoon.

David smiled ruefully. "No, we went out but the cloud ceiling was too low. It would have been sheer madness to try. I may get a shot at it at the weekend."

As they walked towards the house, his father, who needed to travel extensively throughout Cheshire and that part of Shropshire north of Shrewsbury which bordered on the Cheshire boundary as part of his job as area manager for a cattle food company, said he'd heard that the R.A.F. was busy expanding rapidly. Several of the farmers around the airfield at Shawbury had been approached by the Air Ministry in regard to having some of their fields prepared as emergency landing strips in case Shawbury was put out of action by enemy bombers, and they had agreed to keep them as grassland.

"Well, Dad, the minister did make an announcement in the Commons the other day that they were doubling the size of the current Air Force. They're busy extending Hooton at the moment."

His father nodded. "Mmmm, I don't think that this man Hitler will risk it. The Germans took a hammering in the last one, and I can't really see them having a go again. Maybe in another ten years. What do your people think?"

"Don Selby, the C.O., seems to think it's all pretty imminent; well, not sort of like next week but either later this year or next. He says the Krauts will have a go just so as not to lose face. He says with these new fighters and bombers coming on stream this year and the next, the government will draw a line and say to the Krauts, stop or else. He thinks air power will have a big influence in the next war and on any decision regarding when it starts."

The two of them entered the house and went through into the kitchen, where Mary Coulter, David's mother, was preparing their dinner, helped by his sister Catherine. His other sister Therese was currently on duty at the Chester Royal Infirmary, studying to be a Pathology technician and had a late shift. His mother had a daily help during the day but did most of the cooking herself.

"Hello, you two, both late as usual, haven't you heard of a telephone?"

"Now, now Mary, I got stuck out at Frodsham with Tom Shields, he had a problem with some calves, and I'm sure Dave has a reasonable explanation." Turning to David, "Don't you?"

David laughed. "Yes."

Catherine his sister sniffed. "He smells of beer, I bet he's been with that bunch of tearaways he calls his squadron companions." Although talking disparagingly about his weekend flying most of the time, secretly she was proud of her elder brother.

His father asked how long it would be before they ate, and his mother said he had about ten minutes.

"I just need to make phone call."

"Don't take all day, John," his mother called as his father went back into the hall towards the telephone.

The meal was lively, with his father continuing along the theme he and David had been talking about as they had walked in, about the darkening storm clouds over the political scene in Europe.

Chester being a garrison town and headquarters for the Cheshire Regiment, they had friends amongst the soldiers and therefore, were also aware of the increased activity amongst the military apart from David's input.

Listening to the two men talk, Mary Coulter joined in every now and again.

"Peter Smith's wife was saying at the meeting last week her husband thought there would be trouble this summer. The Germans were getting ready to invade Czechoslovakia."

John Coulter nodded. "Most of the political commentators seem to think so, also, Hitler wouldn't be making such a noise about the Sudetenland Germans if he didn't have designs on the Czechs. He needs to expand, otherwise Germany will sink into a depression again. Although on the surface Germany looks prosperous, she's desperately short of raw materials and the legitimate means of acquiring them. So Hitler has his eyes on the Czech iron and coal, amongst other things, including their manufacturing facilities. Particularly their Skoda Armament factory at Brno, where one of our lightweight machine guns, the Bren, was developed." Turning to David,

"When were you and Tom thinking of going to the continent, but you're not thinking of Germany, are you?"

"Tom wants to do the 14–18 battlefields in France and then go down the Rhine, but I wanted to go to Germany to see if I can get a look at some of their aircraft, just out of curiosity. I don't think we can go before September anyway, because of our 'camp'. The situation should be pretty clear by then."

"Most likely, but I'd give it a lot of thought and first see how the situation develops, and certainly, obtain the blessing of your superiors in the R.A.F."

Chapter Two

Towards the end of May 1938 the editor of 'Flying Now' magazine received a request from an apparently similar magazine devoted to flying in Germany for several back articles they had published on the development of a jet engine.

The request intrigued the editor, because in October 1936, he'd had occasion to be in Stuttgart, staying in the 'Hotel Graf Zeppelin' prior to an invited visit to the Heinkel factory located just outside Stuttgart. His visit was in relation to Heinkel passenger planes, in particular the Heinkel HE70, a high speed airliner. When he'd first made the request to visit the Heinkel plant, he thought he would get an invite to go to Warnemunde on the Baltic and was surprised to be invited to the plant at Stuttgart, which he wasn't aware existed.

Whilst sitting in the lounge room of the Graf Zeppelin Hotel in Stuttgart, as a fluent German speaker, he'd been in a position to overhear a conversation between two men he thought must be from the Heinkel factory, discussing experiments in relation to a turbo-jet engine.

Well aware that the British Thompson-Houston factory near Rugby was already experimenting along the same lines, when he visited the Heinkel factory the next day, he asked about the engine.

Now none of the British experiments were classified as secret, although the Royal Air Force were involved and had even subsidised some of the work, but most of it was being done commercially. He was greatly surprised the next day at the Heinkel factory when he asked about the 'jet' engine and the public relations man he asked denied all knowledge of it and questioned him as to where his information came from. He quite openly said he'd heard two people talking in the hotel, referring to some experiments at this factory. The man said he must have been mistaken and denied there were any such experiments to his knowledge taking place in Germany.

He was only in Stuttgart for one day and was leaving the next day for France; for some reason he felt very uneasy, almost as if he was under surveillance. As he walked through the hotel lounge to the bar, he was aware of a man getting up and following him into the bar, though he thought nothing of it. The same man was in the dining room with a male companion when he ate his dinner later and as he left the room, one of the men left at the same time.

Waiting for his train the next morning and looking around the platform, he was sure that one of the faces he saw was in the hotel dining room the previous evening. He dismissed this as pure coincidence that the man just happened to be travelling the same as himself. As he boarded the train for Strasbourg and onto France, the same man joined the train also.

When the train reached the border with France, the same man watched him board the French train and waited until it left.

On arriving back in England, he wondered if he should report his experience to someone but was at a loss to know whom he should approach. After all, most of it was conjecture or even imagination on his part, except for the conversation between the two Germans in the hotel.

Therefore, the receiving of this request intrigued him. Were the Germans experimenting or even thinking about experimenting with a 'jet' engine?

During a reception held at Farnborough to demonstrate a new commercial aeroplane from the Airspeed Company of York, the Airspeed Oxford, in June the previous year, he'd found himself talking to a group captain from the Royal Air Force. During the course of their conversation, they seemed to get on to talking about the emergence of the new German Air Force, the Luftwaffe. The group captain had said that the Air Ministry would be receptive to any information that came by him in the course of his editing 'Flying Now' magazine that he thought the Air Force might be interested in, and gave him his card.

The editor had thought nothing of this at that time but now thinking back to 1936 and then this request, he thought he'd mention something to this Group Captain. He searched around his desk and came up with the Group Captain's card and telephone number. All the card showed was his name and rank in the centre and at the bottom right-hand side was a telephone number and 'Air Ministry' alongside it.

He telephoned the number and a female voice answered. "Air Ministry, DDI Department."

Giving his name and who he was, he asked to speak to the Group Captain, Group Captain Thompson, and explained where he'd met him.

The woman asked him to wait and then came back to him saying she was connecting him. After a short wait and a couple of clicks, a male voice came through.

"Thompson, Mr Wilson, how are you?"

"Good, thank you, Group Captain."

"What can I do for you?"

"When we met at Farnborough, you mentioned that if I came across something you might be interested in, to give you a call."

"That's right, have you something?"

"I've had a request from a German flying magazine for some information on jet engines. That in itself is not anything special but it connects with a trip I made to Germany in 1936."

"I see, maybe we should meet and discuss it further, the telephone's not really the medium for this. I could come around to your offices if you like. How about tomorrow at about ten?"

"OK, no problem." Peter Wilson gave his address just off Trafalgar Square. "I'll look forward to seeing you."

Next morning Gerald Thompson was ushered into Peter Wilson's office promptly at ten. He was a man of about 50, tall, grey-haired and walked with a slight limp, the result of a war wound.

The two men shook hands, and Gerald Thompson opened the meeting with a brief description of his role in the Air Ministry; he worked for Air Marshal Burridge, who was the Deputy Director of Intelligence and his specific job was to monitor foreign Air Force engine and aeroplane developments. Over coffee Peter Wilson showed the request he'd received from the German magazine. It was written in German and he offered to translate, but Gerald Thompson shook his head and replied in perfect German that he would manage.

"What makes you think that there's something odd about this, Mr Wilson?"

Peter Wilson recounted his experience when he visited the Heinkel factory at Stuttgart, where they had denied any knowledge of experiments with jet engines.

The Group Captain smiled. "The Germans get a little paranoid when you touch an area that they consider sensitive. The jet aero-engine project here is not classified in the Secrets Act sense, but we certainly don't like to let any rivals to know where we are up to in the development but this really in a commercial sense. We in the R.A.F. are helping with the development and Frank Whittle, I think you've heard of him, is expecting to achieve something by the end of this year. The principle of a jet engine is not new; in fact, it goes back to the early twenties. The information we are getting out of Germany indicates that both at Stuttgart with Heinkel and the Messerschmitt factory at Augsburg they are trying to develop something along aero jet lines. Heinkel's main factory is at Warnemunde on the Baltic, although they have a small production plant at Stuttgart; we think for engines. We're not sure, and we are finding it hard to get confirmation. Your information adds another piece to the puzzle, although I'm surprised they invited you to there."

"I was surprised to start with. My enquiry with Heinkel was in relation to their HE70 airliner and apparently, Stuttgart handles the sales side of it. Warnemunde, on the Baltic, is only for their one eleven bomber, y'know. It is considered to be too remote from the main European markets in France, England and others in the region. Anyway, after telephoning you, I did some checking and found that an engineer, Hans von Ohain had taken out a patent in 1937 on using the exhaust from a gas turbine as a method of propulsion. I think when I was in Stuttgart that was the name of one of the men talking in the hotel lounge. I'm sure I heard one of the men use that name when addressing the other man."

"Yes, we were aware of that patent. Our problem is finding out how far the Germans have got with their development and if they have anything that they can use in a plane or even getting a plane to fly."

"I can't help there; I get a lot of my information from technical manuals originating in other countries, except what I dig out here in the UK first-hand doing the rounds of the Embassies. The German technical manuals are not much help; it's almost as if they have been censored. My foray into Germany was the first I'd done for a few years, and I didn't like it. I wanted to go because of the lack of information in their manuals."

"I agree; it's not very pleasant there at the moment. The Secret State Police, Geheime Staatspolizei in German, we know them as the Gestapo, it's derived from Geheime Staatspolizei-Amt or in a short form GeStaPA as they call themselves, are very intrusive and brutal at times. Not nice at all."

"The other odd thing is that we are an English magazine, printed and published in England, we are totally English, I'm English, any requests we get from foreign magazines are always in English. Now this request from a German magazine was written, as you can see, in German. How did they know I could read and understand German? The only people who would have noted I spoke German were at Heinkel's in Stuttgart. This magazine is a Berlin-based magazine. How did they know I spoke German? Someone passed the information on, so I don't think this is a genuine request from a magazine, it's from somewhere else."

The two men sat silent for a moment, then Peter said,

"What I could do is a follow up at the German Embassy on this request, it might bring something out. I'll say I'm checking the authenticity of the publication."

"Not a bad idea, although a bit slim, but try it. Anyway, I agree with you the whole thing is a bit rum. What do you think they are after?"

"I think this is a fishing expedition, they've got so far with their engine development and have hit a problem of some sort. They know we are doing similar developments, and they haven't kept up with our publication of progress so far. So they want back numbers to see if they can get a clue from our articles."

"But all your articles are of a general nature, you don't go into detail. Have you ever reported on problems encountered?"

"No, never; in fact, the only problem I was aware of and certainly didn't report on was in April last year at Rugby, when they were testing an engine and it kept racing out of control but they managed to find a solution."

"Maybe the Germans have similar problem, although we haven't heard of any problems. Try the embassy and see what comes up. You know where it is?"

"Yes, Carlton House Terrace, behind Pall Mall."

"That's right. The ambassador is Herbert Von Dirksen, not a bad chap, bit better than the other fellow that was there until last January, Von Ribbentrop. Rabid Nazi if ever there was one. The Times called him Von Brickendrop; he dropped a few boners whilst he was here. Nasty piece of work, gave His Majesty the Nazi salute when they met."

"Oh, I usually meet with the military attaché; I think his name is Kitschmann."

"That's right; he's been there a long time. I must be going, give me a call when you've been, let me know how you go."

The Group Captain then took his leave.

Peter Wilson telephoned the German Embassy next morning and explained he had a request from a German flying magazine requesting some information and he wanted to authenticate the magazine before passing on any information. The woman who took the call took his name and telephone number and said she would contact the appropriate person and have them call him.

He didn't hear anything for two days, and then a German calling himself the press secretary telephoned him and made an appointment for him to visit him at the embassy the next morning. Peter Wilson telephoned Group Captain Thompson, advising him what was happening and asking if there was anything special he should ask about.

"I don't think so Mr Wilson; although any information you can get on the German progress with the jet engine would help, but I doubt you'd be able to even ask that sort of a question. Play it by ear, and if we get anything all well and good, if not don't worry."

After Peter Wilson had rung off, Gerald Thompson walked across to a filing cabinet in the corner of his office, selecting a key from his key ring, he opened the cabinet taking out a file marked 'Operation Luftwaffe Jet'.

Sitting back behind his desk, he opened the file and studied the contents. He almost knew them by heart, starting with the 1936 patent taken out by Hans von Ohain and continued by the Heinkel factory; there was also information regarding the 1935 development by Messerschmitt, which was far behind that of Heinkel.

He'd had word about three weeks ago that their man in Germany, to be correct MI6's man in Germany working on this project, had been betrayed to the German counter intelligence people and had been arrested. His whereabouts were unknown but MI6 were very pessimistic of his chances of survival, therefore they needed to have someone else getting information to them.

The speed these jet engines would give to a plane would make the R.A.F.'s newest fighter obsolete. The R.A.F.'s latest fighter, the Spitfire, only just coming off the production lines, had a top speed of around 350mph, higher than most fighter planes at the moment, whereas the projected speeds of an aeroplane fitted with the German engine would be in the region of 500mph, according to their unfortunate informant.

Group Captain Thompson badly wanted more information as to how far the Germans had progressed and whether they were ready to go into mass production of an aircraft.

In mid-March Germany annexed Austria, calling it the unification of Germany; the war clouds were getting closer.

A few days later Thompson paid a visit to the MI6 offices, hidden in a nondescript building in the Haymarket, but they were unable to give much help, getting a new agent in position would take time. They promised to keep him informed of any further developments.

Walking back along the Strand from MI6 to his office in York House, Kingsway, Group Captain Thompson wondered how he might get the information he required. If he could come up with something solid regarding the German planes, his superior would have ample scope to assist the Air Ministry in obtaining more funding to expedite the Frank Whittle jet engine. After years of procrastination, the government in 1937 had made a grant of £6000, spread in instalments into 1938, to assist in the development but more funding was badly needed. A case had to be made before more funds would be made available.

He would have liked to have gone to Germany himself but recognised that the Germans probably knew who he was and his position in the R.A.F. What was required was someone who would be unknown and preferably with knowledge of aircraft to enable them to recognise a jet-engined plane if they saw one. Regular Air Force officers wouldn't be any use, a regular military man can be spotted a mile away, apart from the fact the Germans would be on their guard in the areas where any of these planes would be operating. He was pretty sure the Germans were still at the experimental stage, otherwise information would have leaked out.

He put the problem at the back of his mind until after he had heard from Wilson regarding his visit to the embassy.

Peter Wilson presented himself at the German Embassy a few minutes before 10 AM; going in through the door, he walked towards the desk located to one side of the foyer. The desk was staffed by a young blonde girl and a young uniformed man wearing the grey-green uniform of the German Army; Wilson noted he had the insignia of a captain (Hauptmann), his collar had white flashes, which Wilson was to know later indicated the man was from one of the Schutzstaffel Regiments, commonly known as the S.S., the Hitler Praetorian Guard.

All the major German Embassies from early 1937 onwards were given a staff of S.S. specifically to vet all visitors and generally to take over internal policing of the embassies; this was recommended by Heinrich Himmler and approved by Adolf Hitler.

Peter Wilson proffered his card to the young woman, who in turn handed it to the man, who asked her in German if Wilson had an appointment and whom with.

Before she could answer, Peter Wilson answered instead in German, giving the name of the man he was to meet; the captain smiled.

"Ah, so, Mr Wilson, you speak very good German."

"Yes, Captain, I studied it, firstly at school and then at my university."

"You are to be congratulated."

The captain rang a bell and a uniformed attendant arrived; the captain ordered him to escort Peter Wilson to the office of the press attaché. The attendant took Peter Wilson upstairs to an office just beyond the head of the stairs and knocked on the door. At the command 'enter', the attendant opened the door and held it for Peter Wilson to go in.

The office contained two men seated behind a large desk with very few papers on it; a single chair was in front of the desk. One man, about 40 years old, fresh-faced, balding, in a brown suit sat in the centre on the other side of the desk; the second man a beefy red-faced man, looked as if he was going to fat, in his mid-thirties, dark suit, small indistinguishable badge in his lapel, striped tie, close cropped dark hair, what little there was brushed straight back, was seated to one side.

The man in the centre stood as Peter entered and held his hand out, speaking in English.

"Welcome, Mr Wilson, sit down," indicating the chair. The second man didn't move or say anything, just looked at him with flat expressionless eyes.

Peter sat down, the man looked expectantly at him, then spoke again, "What can I do for you?"

Peter spoke in German. "Good morning, Herr Brandt, I am the editor – as you know – of 'Flying Now' magazine, and as I explained to the woman I first spoke to the other day, I've received a request from a German magazine for copies of some articles published in some of our previous issues.

"I wasn't aware of this magazine, the name I'd not heard of and couldn't find any trace of it in any of my reference books, so before I sent the articles, I wanted to check on the authenticity of the magazine. I could have done this over the telephone but the woman said I should come and see you."

"Ah, yes, we like to make sure to whom we are talking to, you see, Mr Wilson. Have you got the request with you?"

Peter Wilson produced the letter from the small leather document case he had with him. Herr Brandt looked at the letter and then passed it to the other man. So far Herr Brandt had made no effort to introduce him, and the man hadn't spoken. The man took a cursory glance at the letter and handed it back to Herr Brandt.

"This magazine is a Luftwaffe magazine, it has a limited circulation within the Luftwaffe and therefore, you wouldn't find it in any of your reference books."

Peter Wilson knew this was a lie, one of the books he had looked in contained all the official, semi-official magazines and publishers specialising in the various military publications around the world; if it was official, it would have been there, there were several German publications, including one for the Luftwaffe, so the man was lying.

"Herr Wilson, when you were in Stuttgart just over 12 months ago, you were asking about the German developments on the jet engine. Why was this?" This question came from the other man.

Peter Wilson was silent for a moment, then looking at the man, said,

"Why are you asking such a question? That was long ago and certainly has nothing to do with my visit here now."

The man gave an icy smile. "Herr Wilson, please answer the question."

Herr Brandt looked a little uneasy. He looked as if he was about to say something else but the other man again spoke.

"Herr Wilson, answer the question; if you've nothing to hide the answer, must be simple."

Peter Wilson's mind went back to his Stuttgart visit, and he tried to remember what he'd said.

"I was in the lounge of the Graf Zeppelin Hotel, and I heard the name Ohain mentioned by two men talking close by. I knew that Hans von Ohain had taken a patent out on a jet engine development and they mentioned the Heinkel factory. We had just published an article on jet engine development, so I was interested, hence my question when I was at the factory."

"What was their answer, Herr Wilson?"

"They said they didn't know anything about a jet engine. Anyway, who are you to ask such a question?"

"Are you sure that was the only reason you asked?"

Peter Wilson looked across at Herr Brandt.

"Who is this man, why should I answer his questions? I wouldn't be here if this magazine hadn't requested information. I might ask you, Herr Brandt, why does a supposed German Air Force magazine want to look at past articles about jet engines?"

Herr Brandt was looking decidedly uneasy, he didn't answer Peter Wilson's question but turned to look at the other man.

"You haven't answered my question, Herr Wilson. Are you sure you weren't trying to pry into classified secret developments of the Reich for the British intelligence department?"

"Don't be ridiculous, I happened to see the two men purely by accident. Your line of questioning is stupid, I wasn't in Germany to enquire about jet engines, I was there to discuss the passenger airliner that Heinkel make."

"Ah so, but you did ask about jet engines."

"This whole discussion is stupid. Jet engines in this country and their development are not classified as secret. The patents are there for anyone to see, their development is openly discussed and the Air Ministry welcome questions, so why all the fuss in Germany?"

Then Peter Wilson stood up. "I refuse to take part in this interrogation any further, and you can tell your friends in the Luftwaffe they will have to go to another source for their information." He started to walk towards the door.

The public relations man stood up, the other man still sat, his face expressionless and stony.

"Goodbye, Herr Wilson, I'm sorry you have adopted this attitude, we were only trying to clarify a small matter."

Peter Wilson walked out of the room, down the stairs, out of the building, into the street back to his office.

Back in his own office, he telephoned Group Captain Thompson; the Group Captain was not there so he left a message for him to call him.

Later that day the Group Captain returned his call and listened in silence whilst Peter Wilson recounted his experience in the German Embassy.

"That other man would be Paul Muller, he's supposedly their military attaché in place of Horst Kitschmann, but we think he's a member of the Geheime Staatspolizei, the Gestapo. Nevertheless, what you say confirms to me that the Germans are certainly experimenting with jet engines and are wanting to keep it secret for some reason, which is a little bit silly, considering what is known about the engine."

"Not really, if they have it to a stage where they can fit it into an aircraft, and this no one else has reached, they have a strategic advantage and would want to keep it secret for the time being."

This thought had already crossed the Group Captain's mind when Peter Wilson had originally told him about the enquiry at their meeting. The two things the Germans would want to check on were how far had the opposition got to and did the opposition suspect or had knowledge of where the German scientists had reached with their experiments? They would, therefore, explore all avenues they were aware of, and their reason for getting Peter Wilson in to see them was that he was an obvious choice, being the editor of the foremost flying magazine in England and already publishing articles on jet engines. The request for past articles was a red herring, all they wanted to do was get Peter Wilson into the embassy and question him, but the Gestapo man had blown the interview with his heavy-handed approach.

"Yes, good thinking, Mr Wilson, I think you might be right there, I'd dearly like to find out. Anyway, thank you for your call; if you come across anything you think might help us, I'd appreciate you letting us know. Don't hesitate."

After the call Group Captain Thompson sat thinking about the various aspects of the problem and decided to talk it over with his superior, Air Marshal Cowley, the Deputy Director of Intelligence, at the first opportunity. At the back of his mind he had the idea of using someone either not connected to the Air Force or only slightly connected but who had knowledge of aeroplanes, but to do this he needed the permission of his superior, unless MI6 came in with something in the meantime.

The opportunity arose the following week, he was called in to a meeting to give a briefing to senior politicians on the German air effort in the Spanish Civil War; afterwards, he stayed behind with Air Marshal Cowley and briefed him on the jet engine position.

He outlined the position of English developments and how far the English team had got in relation to designing an engine which could be used in an aircraft. That they were still a long way off having a viable aircraft engine, and he then went on to outline what they knew about the German effort, most of it obtained before the MI6 man was taken.

The German aircraft company Heinkel had an engine that could be fitted into an aircraft and were actually at the present time designing an aircraft around this engine, the aircraft to be known as the Heinkel 178. Unfortunately, the MI6 man had been betrayed and taken by the Germans, so the source of information had dried up.

He described the recent visit to the German Embassy of the editor of 'Flying Now' and his questioning. He said he thought it was safe to assume that the Germans were fairly close to flying an aircraft equipped with a jet engine and the British Government and Air Force needed to be aware of the capability.

He went on to say they needed to get someone into Germany to try and evaluate the readiness of the aircraft; preferably, someone with knowledge of aeroplanes.

The Air Marshal looked thoughtful.

"What do you suggest, Gerry, you must have given it some thought."

"Yes sir, we can't send any of our regular pilots or officers, they'd be too easy to spot, someone like the editor of 'Flying Now' would be ideal but he's been once. He's already under suspicion and it would be risky sending him again. We need someone under service discipline, an ordinary civilian wouldn't do. Maybe ground staff, but we would need to be careful in our selection."

"How about one of these Volunteer Reserve people, they nearly all look like and act as civilians, yet we can lock them in with the Official Secrets Act. What do you think?"

"Sounds as if it might do, that's if we can find a good man. How about funding, sir?"

"I don't think that's a problem, we've just had increased monies for expansion, and I'm sure old Percy wot not of Finance can find a few pounds for this. Leave it to me and I'll let you know. You find the right man."

Gerald Thompson went off a satisfied man with the need to find someone to undertake the task.

When he got back to his office, Gerald Thompson checked against the organisation manual and found that there were 18 Auxiliary Air Force Squadrons located in various parts of the country and two more were to be formed the next year (1939).

Over the next few days, he gave the problem of finding a suitable man a lot of thought and eventually contacted a friend from his old Royal Flying Corps squadron, who – like himself – had been wounded and now had a desk job looking after the logistics for the Auxiliary Air Force Squadrons.

He arranged to have lunch with him and over the meal, without going into too much detail, outlined what he wanted. A young officer, preferably a pilot from one of the Auxiliary Squadrons, to go to Germany for them and snoop around to see if he could find anything out about the Heinkel jet plane. He would need to be mature for his age; most pilots were in their early twenties or below and inclined to be a little hare-brained. The selected man needed to be very discreet, because of the German sensitivity of the subject and the brutality of their counter-intelligence units.

His friend was intrigued and promised to try and find a list of possible young men for Gerald Thompson to personally vet. The vetting could be done by sending Gerald Thompson around in the guise of someone inspecting the progress of the expansion and upgrading of the airfields under the new government programme. He asked for a few weeks to come up with his list.

At his next meeting with the Air Marshal Cowley, Gerald Thompson outlined how far he had got with the project of finding a man. The Air Marshal approved but thought he should discuss the proposal with MI6, and said that funding had been found to finance the trip. Old Percy had come up trumps.

Gerald telephoned MI6 and arranged a meeting with the appropriate man, Aubrey Evans, who had been responsible for the flow of information until his agent had been caught.

At first Aubrey Evans was against the idea of an amateur being sent into the field, since it was a dangerous field and he could easily lose his life, apart from being an embarrassment to H. M. Government.

Gerald Thompson explained all he wanted the man to do was to spend time watching the area around the Heinkel factory near Stuttgart to see if the Germans had a plane. He wouldn't be trying to act as an agent; his would be a watching brief. Aircraft once in the air cannot be hidden and can be seen from a long way off, the man needn't get anywhere close to an aerodrome on the ground, as long as he was two or three miles away, he would see any aircraft in the air.

The MI6 man reluctantly agreed as long as he could see the man before he went, to try and educate him in some of the pitfalls of the trade.

Gerald Thompson left MI6 not too happy, this was his baby and he didn't really like to share it with anyone else, except that his superior had said he should discuss it with MI6, which he had done.

All he could do now was wait for the list of possibles to be given to him and then vet them and make a selection.

Getting back to his office, he sat down and wrote a report for the air marshal, giving details of how far he was with the project and the outcome of his meeting with MI6.

He didn't hear anything for about six weeks, and then his friend with the Auxiliary Air Force responsibility telephoned him saying he had a list of about ten people who could be considered suitable and could they meet?

Chapter Three

Elizabeth Austell, a 23-year-old nurse at St George's Hospital, Hyde Park Corner in central London, finished her night shift at 6 AM. The morning was a fine April morning, prior to going to the nurses' home to get some sleep, Elizabeth walked across the hospital courtyard to the matron's office.

Tapping on the door she heard the quiet "Come in" and entering, saw the person behind the desk was Julia Smith, the Deputy Matron. Not that she'd expected the Matron there at that time but her Ward Sister had said she was required at the Matron's office before she went home after finishing her duties.

She'd been expecting the call for a few days. She'd sat her final examinations in February, and the results were due out about now, so she anticipated this was the reason for the summons to the Matron's office.

Julia Smith looked up as the young girl entered, seeing the fresh-faced, rather pretty dark-haired slim girl for the first time. Julia Smith had been recently appointed as Deputy Matron and therefore, hadn't met all the trainee nurses at the hospital.

"Good morning, ma'am, I'm Elizabeth Austell, I understand you wanted to see me."

Julia Smith smiled broadly, "Yes, Elizabeth, and congratulations, you have passed your Finals."

Elizabeth smiled. "Thank goodness, although I didn't think I'd done too badly, but one can never tell."

The two women chatted, Elizabeth wanting to know about the other girls in her year and Julia wanting to know what, if any, plans she had for the future.

"Daddy promised me a trip to the Continent if I passed as a celebration."

"Any idea where you'd go?"

"No, not really, but I expect France and Germany would be part of it."

"Off you go, you get some sleep."

"Thank you, ma'am." With that Elizabeth left the office and went out of the building to the nurses' home, stopping in the foyer at the bank of public telephones to call her parents in Raynes Park, London, to tell them the good news.

After talking to her parents she headed for her room to get some sleep, and then intended to go home for her three-day break following her week's stint of night duty, which finished that morning.

Later that day after a few hours' sleep, she showered and went down to the Common Room of the Home; some of the girls from her year were there and all were excited by the results, all in the class had passed.

Going back up to her room, she packed a small bag and left to get the Underground train out to her home and parents in Raynes Park.

Arriving home, she found that her mother had arranged a small family party consisting of her father, brother and mother in celebration.

During the course of which her father brought up the subject of the promised trip to Europe and where she would like to go, and which countries she wanted to visit.

Her father had served in The Great War and was therefore, keen on visiting the old battlefields of Flanders, but was not keen on Germany, because of the current problems there.

Her brother, two years older and a French language teacher at the local Grammar School, was also keen to stay in France, she and her mother didn't have any set ideas, although both of them wanted to visit Germany and the Black Forest area. Another factor they had to consider was whether they would travel by their car or by rail, their father was of the opinion their car would be the best because it gave them a lot of flexibility.

They decided to leave any decision for another month by which time she would have decided what she was going to do, either stay at St George's Hospital or find work at another hospital to broaden her experience.

After her three-day break Elizabeth reported back to the hospital, checking the duty roster she found she was up in the operating theatres, which pleased her greatly, she always liked the work there.

Talking to some of the girls in the Nurses' Home Common Room, it appeared that a few of them were contemplating joining the Queen Alexandra's Nursing Corps. Elizabeth didn't really know much about the organisation other than it was the nursing arm of the British Army.

The general consensus of opinion was that there was going to be a war in the near future, and they might as well get in from the start.

Elizabeth was well aware that the international situation was deteriorating badly and, like most young people of her day, recognised she'd probably be one of those called upon to serve her country. The talk was that everyone would be involved this time, civilians included. She wasn't too enamoured by the Army nursing service, having heard her father talk about The Great War and the mud and blood. She was also aware that the Air Force had a nursing service, Princess Mary's Nursing Service and thought maybe that that would be a better organisation, no mud and blood there.

The resolving of a wartime position could wait, the country wasn't at war yet; therefore, the decision could go on the back burner until war was imminent.

During May her father started to plan their trip and with taking the car in his mind, he made enquiries about the ferries from Dover to Calais and also Ostend to Harwich.

There was a very popular ferry service for people wishing to take their cars onto Europe.

In talking to the Royal Automobile Club Foreign Travel section, he found that nearly 25,000 people had taken their cars to France in 1937. The cars were loaded onto the ferries by crane, a very efficient operation; so taking the family car wouldn't appear to be a problem.

He was very reluctant to go to Germany because of the political situation and thought that if he gave his wife and daughter a trip to Strasburg and a look at the Rhine, it might suffice. Then checking with Thomas Cook's office in Wimbledon, he found that they offered a day trip from Strasburg to Freiburg in the Black Forest and returning via Colmar, France, and he thought that might be enough. They then could drive from Strasburg along the German frontier, taking in the Rhine and Moselle rivers and then the 1914–1918 battlefields along the Belgium frontier, then returning home via Belgium.

The family had agreed that by mid-May they would all have made up their minds regarding the route they preferred to take and make a final decision then.

At the Heinkel factory near Plieningen, just a few miles from Stuttgart, Dr Klaus Brendel, the young 25-year-old leader of the Heinkel Jet Engine Project Team, was talking to the head of security at the Heinkel factory, Erich Linhard, a 47-year-old ex-policeman.

They were standing by the perimeter fence of the factory, looking at the airstrip used by planes when they tested a new engine.

The airstrip was a grass strip, enclosed within a perimeter fence of chain link about six feet high, topped by four strands of barbed wire, at the foot of which a coil of razor wire snaked along the whole fence. An inside road also followed the fence around the airstrip.

To their right were the factory buildings built in groups, the first of which had an aircraft hangar amongst them and in front of the hangar was a patch of hard standing tarmac about one hundred feet square. To their left, the other side of the perimeter fence about three hundred feet away, was the public road between Denkendorf in the east, the village of Echterdingen and Sindelfingen.

Shielding the airstrip from the road was a thick belt of pine trees and undergrowth.

Klaus Brendel was talking.

"The contractor's men come in on Monday to re-lay the runway with concrete to take the weight of planes in all weathers because of the heavier weight of this new jet engine. You need to make sure that we don't have any spectators when we start our tests, which should be in about two months. I don't like the way anyone can come off the road to the perimeter fence, I'd sooner have that fence closer to the road than the screen of trees. Is that possible? Who owns that strip of land the trees are on between the road and the fence?"

"I don't know, Herr Docktor, but maybe the legal department can help you. If we can obtain permission we could move the fence."

"The owner shouldn't complain or obstruct us; this project is for the glory of the Third Reich. Security is your responsibility, I therefore expect you to make the necessary enquiries and arrange the move."

Erich Linhard was a kindly man of 47, more a village policeman than a head of security, but until the engine project had come to the factory, he was ideally suited to the atmosphere of the country district where the Heinkel factory was situated. But he was also well-aware of the type of person that the good doctor was typical of, and who seemed to be gaining the upper hand in Germany these days.

Single-minded in achieving success in the task in which they were employed on, and heaven help anyone who got in their way.

"Ja, Herr Docktor, I'll look into it immediately."

After being dismissed by Klaus Brendel following an inspection of the hangar doors regarding security, Erich Linhard went first to the legal department, where he discussed the ownership of the land alongside the perimeter fence.

It appeared that the land belonged to the Municipality of Stuttgart, the airstrip itself was only rented from the municipality; this was land earmarked for the expansion of the existing Stuttgart Airport, previously known as the Stuttgart-Echterdingen Airport. The head of the legal department was willing to try and obtain permission to move the fence on the basis they would restore it to its original position when the security requirements changed.

Erich Linhard then, using one of the Heinkel factory's light trucks and driver, went several times up and down the Sindelfingen road to see what could be seen by a casual passer-by. Coming from Sindelfingen the first thing sighted were the factory buildings, then the entrance to the gates, then a solid fringe of trees, only in one place was the airstrip itself seen where the screen of trees was thin. Coming from the opposite direction about a half mile from the end of the airstrip was a small rise in the road, which gave anyone a quick glimpse of the airstrip, and then the screen of trees blocked out the view.

Then driving slowly along the line of trees, there were places where a driver to get his vehicle off the road and cross to the perimeter fence on foot, but that would require a deliberate action on the part of a person.

He then gave his attention to the other sides of the airstrip.

At the western end of the airstrip a narrow road, roughly north-south ran from the village of Bernhausen to Plieningen, this gave an uninterrupted view of the airstrip to the east. The pine trees had been cleared from between the road and the fence to give aircraft using the strip a safe landing and take-off route without having to lift over trees immediately on take-off. At the eastern end of the runway was just farmland, he supposed a determined person could walk on the farmland to see the airstrip but would be easily seen. The only alteration he would recommend would be a guard hut at the end plus regular motorised patrols along the perimeter road.

In the south there weren't any roads in close proximity to the airstrip and a belt of trees stopped anyone from seeing anything.

Beyond the eastern end of the airstrip the Stuttgart-Echterdingen airport runways were located, Erich Linhard presumed it was only a question of time before the Heinkel airstrip and the Stuttgart airstrip were joined, but right now nothing could be seen looking towards the Heinkel strip from the closest road to the Stuttgart strip.

Sitting back in his office in the factory, Erich Linhard examined his notes and commenced to draft a report to his superiors, giving his assessment of the security situation for the perimeter. He had decided to write this report in view of the remarks made by Klaus Brendel when they had been standing outside, he didn't want any come-back should anything happen, he wanted everyone in the picture.

Before he finalised his report, he again went along to the legal department to see if they had anything new. Talking to the head of the legal department, he found apart from the Municipality of Stuttgart being involved, the Ministry of Security in Berlin had an interest, together with the Roads Ministry.

Apparently, the new autobahn running across country from Nurnberg to Karlsruhe was scheduled to run close to the Stuttgart airport along the northern boundary. Work was to be commenced in the area shortly, the autobahn was considerably advanced out of both Karlsruhe and the other end at Nurnberg and therefore, they were not prepared to allow any change in the fence. In fact, there was a suggestion they would lose some of their land to facilitate the building of the autobahn.

The project had been given priority by the Fuhrer on the grounds of national security.

Furthermore, the road from Bernhausen to Plieningen had already been blocked at both ends to facilitate the construction of an underpass where the new autobahn would cross over. At the moment discussions were also taking place to include an extension to the autobahn bridging to take extensions to the Stuttgart Airport runway to join the Heinkel runway to the east.

This was to make an extension to the Stuttgart airfield for the Luftwaffe.

Erich Linhard returned to his office a satisfied man and completed his report. In essence the report stated that he'd inspected and assessed the security of the perimeter and he made the following recommendations.

1. The airstrip could be observed briefly from the Sindelfingen road by a person travelling towards Denkendorf.
2. Going the other way towards Sindelfingen, a person would need to come off the road and penetrate the screen of pine trees and scrub and this was easy in places. Unfortunately, the fence could not be moved to the other side of the trees, the road side, because of reasons of national security originating from Berlin. (He put it this way knowing no one would question such a phrase.)
3. At the western end the road from Bernhausen to Plieningen had already been blocked off; therefore, it didn't present a problem.
4. He recommended a guard hut at the eastern end and provision made for regular motorised patrols to circle the perimeter road, highlighting the need for more personnel and vehicles.

His report was accepted, approved and the necessary personnel and vehicles provided.

Whilst the general improvement of the security pleased Klaus Brendel, but the fact that the fence couldn't be moved he considered was a serious lapse and that it would lead to leakage of the project to the outside world. He completely overlooked the fact that once in the air, all and sundry in the area would see the plane.

In early June 1938 Gruppenfuhrer (Air Vice Marshal) Gerhard Diemer, head of the Luftwaffe Aircraft development section, his assistant Standartenfuhrer (Group Captain) Erhard Gromer, Klaus Brendel and his assistant, along with the general manager of the Heinkel factory met at the factory for a briefing on the progress made on the jet engine project.

Dr Klaus Brendel was able to confirm that the prototype of the engine had almost finished the second series of tests, the first series completed in 1937, and they were in a position the install the engine in a test aeroplane as soon as it was received from the Heinkel factory at Warnemunde.

The engine to be fitted was the third generation of the HeS Turbo jet, capable of propelling the aircraft at approximately 500 mph. The aeroplane had been designated as the He 178 and as a prototype was to be fitted with a single turbo jet. This engine had been successfully tested in 1937, and a decision had been taken to build an aircraft for it.

The aeroplane had been specifically designed around the Von Ohain engine, which burnt diesel fuel. The He 178 had an all metal fuselage with high mounted wooden wings; the jet intake was in the nose, and the aircraft was fitted with a tail dragger type of undercarriage, the main landing gear was fixed.

The He 178 had a crew of one, was 24ft long and had a wingspan of 23ft. It would weigh on take-off approximately 4400lbs and because of this the airstrip runway was being totally concreted.

Two aeroplanes minus the engines were anticipated to be delivered by the end of the month.

It was intended to fit one first and then make the modifications on the second as required after the tests on the first one.

They first intended to have the aircraft taxi up and down the runway, then make two or three short hops prior to a full flight. Security around the area had been considerably tightened.

The test pilot allocated for the flight was Sturmbannfuhrer (Squadron Leader) Max Dietz, a veteran of the Spanish conflict and with many years of Luftwaffe experience.

It was thought that the first flight would possibly be made around August.

"Not before August, Herr Brendel?"

"No, Gruppenfuhrer, we have first to receive the aircraft, and then fit the engine, and then run the engine up with the aircraft stationary. All this prior to having it taxi around the airfield. We will then have two or three short hops down the runway before a complete take-off."

"Ah, so, I understand but we will have to convince the Fuhrer and the Reich Marshal Goering of the reason for the delay. We did promise them an aircraft ready for combat early next year."

"Impossible, Gruppenfuhrer."

"Our problem is that Field Marshal Von Brauchitsch has obtained funding and the Fuhrer's attention for the development of rocket-assisted anti-aircraft missiles. He's closed the rocket training experimental school at Karlshafen and the Kummersdorf Army research centre and is transferring them to a new facility at Peenmunde on the Baltic coast. He has convinced the Fuhrer that this is the way to go rather than a jet aircraft. We need something solid to show the Fuhrer before Von Brauchitsch's facility can become established."

"I understand, Gruppenfuhrer, but we have to be careful, a failure due to haste would make the whole project look bad in the eyes of the Fuhrer and Reich Marshal Goering. I am convinced given time, we can have an operational aircraft in production that will fly at speeds in excess of 500mph. Far outstripping anything the French and English have at this time."

"But aren't the English developing a similar engine? Have they an aeroplane flying yet?"

"I am aware of an Englishman Whittle who has developed a similar engine, but as far as I know, they haven't yet developed an aircraft to take the engine.

"We should be monitoring their progress, if possible. We had the editor of their foremost flying magazine here a year or so ago, he asked about our development of the jet engine, claiming he'd heard two men talking in his hotel about it. So I reported it to Franz Schaab, of the Staatspolizei in Stuttgart, who put him under surveillance but the man left Germany the next day. Earlier this year I was getting worried about the lack of information of about the British progress and so I talked to Franz Schaab again, trying to find out who I could use in England to obtain information. He said he'd talk to their man in the German Embassy in England but in the meantime, he would send a letter to the editor of the flying magazine and try and get information that way, but I don't think that's the way we should go. Anyway, I didn't hear anything.

"We really need some input from the Abwehr (German Intelligence Service); they should be trying to get some information. I did speak to Wolf Landsberg in Berlin in May, he's the Abwehr section head for England, and I asked him to try and get information, but again I haven't heard."

"Leave it with me; I'll have a talk with someone."

"Ja, thank you, Gruppenfuhrer."

Gerhard Diemer turned to his assistant. "Make a note for me to talk to Admiral Canaris or his Deputy Heinrich Haslop of the Abwehr when we get back to Berlin. We'll ask how far they've got in obtaining information for us." Then turning back to Klaus Brendel,

"I expect you to have the engine in a plane and starting to test by the end of June, you understand, Herr Brendel."

"Yes, Gruppenfuhrer, I think we should be able to do that." Making a mental note that it was nearly impossible but he'd drive his people as hard as he could.

On arriving back in Berlin, Gerhard Diemer telephoned the Abwehr Headquarters and asked to speak to either Admiral Canaris or Heinrich Haslop, his deputy, only to be advised that they were currently in Austria.

He had to be satisfied with talking to Wolf Landsberg, the section head responsible for the English area of operations. In giving his request for as much information as possible they could obtain in relation to the development of an English jet engine. He said he wanted maximum priority on it and said he would talk to Admiral Canaris on the admiral's return from Austria.

Admiral Canaris was in Austria, following the German occupation the previous April, setting up an organisation to monitor the various Austrian ministries which were still going to function as separate entities until the country was properly incorporated in the Reich.

Wolf Landsberg telephoned Heinrich Haslop to obtain permission to try and gather the information that Gruppenfuhrer Diemer had requested.

Wolf Landsberg was under strict orders not to deviate from his written brief regarding the gathering of information in England. If he wished to deviate, he had to obtain permission from firstly Heinrich Haslop, who if need be would refer it to Admiral Canaris, the head of the Abwehr.

When Dr Klaus Brendel had first approached him with the request to seek out information regarding jet aircraft in England, he'd ignored it, that was not part of his brief and Admiral Canaris was away. The request from Gruppenfuhrer Diemer was a different kettle of fish, it couldn't be ignored. So Wolf Landsberg placed a telephone call to Heinrich Haslop at the Abwehr office in Vienna; he was connected immediately.

By 1938 both Rear Admiral Wilhelm Canaris, director of the Abwehr and Heinrich Haslop, his deputy, had realised that Adolf Hitler's plans and policies, aided and abetted by the thugs who had risen to the top within the Nazi party, would end in disaster for Germany and suffering for the German people. In a discussion, more by suggestion and innuendo than direct reference, Heinrich Haslop would take the lead in any actions to sabotage the policies of Adolf Hitler. It was agreed that Admiral Canaris would assist where possible.

To this end Heinrich Haslop had issued strict limits as to how the Abwehr operations in England were to be conducted, explaining that the Fuhrer had cautioned Admiral Canaris personally not to antagonise the English with unnecessary actions. Hence his directive to Wolf Landsberg regarding the need to obtain permission to deviate from his instructions.

When connected Wolf Landsberg outlined the request from Gruppenfuhrer Diemer and requested permission to proceed using their man, Heinz Kern, in the London Embassy. Heinrich Haslop listened in silence to Wolf Landsberg, then agreed he could go ahead but should have their man come to Germany to be briefed on the perimeters of his enquiries.

Kern's last report had given an outline of the clumsy attempt – which shouldn't have taken place – by Paul Muller to obtain information, which had ended in disaster. The English editor left the embassy without telling them anything and must have alerted the English intelligence authorities. Haslop intended to bring Kern back to Germany next week and in the meantime prepare instructions in detail as how he should go about his task. He would brief Admiral Canaris and get him to speak to Gruppenfuhrer Diemer to assure him they would try and obtain the information.

Following his conversation with Heinrich Haslop, Wolf Landsberg sent a coded cable to Heinz Kern, ordering him back to Berlin for discussions without giving him specific details. Wolf Landsberg then did a little research in their files to refresh his memory of their knowledge of the jet engine projects in England and the areas which would prove lucrative for Kern to trawl for information.

He found that apart from some early references to the jet technology in the 1920s, an English Royal Air Force officer Frank Whittle had filed a patent in 1932 for a jet engine. Then in 1936, along with another man, formed a company called 'Power Jets' to develop the Whittle Jet Engine.

In conjunction with the English company British Thomson-Houston at Rugby in the English Midlands, a test-bed had been set up in 1937 to run the engine. As far as was known, the English Air Ministry were not involved and surprisingly, according to their information, hadn't provided any funding. Their file ended there, so the starting point for Kern was at the British Thomson-Houston factory at Rugby and then to follow any leads to aircraft manufacturers he was able to uncover.

Heinz Kern arrived in Berlin a few days later and spent the morning with Wolf Landsberg. In the afternoon they met with Heinrich Haslop, now returned from Austria, who emphasised that during the course of their information gathering, if at any time they felt that the English authorities had been alerted, they should cease the operation. The Fuhrer was adamant he didn't want the English to be upset at any cost. This wasn't true, of course, the Fuhrer hadn't issued those instructions, it was Heinrich Haslop's idea and part of his strategy for undermining the Hitler regime. The strongest opposition to Germany would come from the British Empire; therefore, he should covertly support the British by keeping the German military machine ignorant of the British intentions and activities.

After his briefing Heinz Kern returned to London and made contact via a letter with one of his informants in Bristol in the west of England.

His informant, William Foulkes, was a 50-year-old electrical fitter, thin-faced and sparse-haired, bearing a grudge against the world and the British Empire in particular. His father had been a South African Boer and was killed in the fight against the British at the turn of the century. His mother, an Englishwoman, had died in a camp in South Africa and he'd been brought up by his maternal grandparents in England and had adopted their name, his father's name had been Van Doork.

He'd approached the German Embassy a few years before, offering to help them with information, and had been used by Kern a few times, obtaining minor information within the West Country area. He was currently working for the Bristol City Corporation and had a freedom of movement within that area but could also take days off to move into the surrounding areas, such as the naval base at Plymouth and army locations around Salisbury.

Heinz Kern met William Foulkes in the Paddington Railway station refreshment bar and commissioned him to make enquiries around the British Thompson-Houston works at Rugby in relation to jet engine development and any aircraft associated with it. It was a little out of Foulkes area but he said he could manage it, anyway Kern didn't have anyone else to use in that general area.

Using the train, Foulkes went to the BTH works at Rugby and applied for a job there. He represented himself as an electrical fitter who wished to change his employer. During the course of conversation with the employment office clerk, he found that the jet engine facility had moved from there to the BTH Ladywood Works at Lutterworth in Leicestershire a few miles to the north of Rugby.

The British armament industry was working flat out on government contracts now that Parliament had made available funding for re-armament and skilled tradesmen were in great demand, so he was tentatively offered employment at both the main BTH works in Rugby and also at the BTH Ladywood works, subject to satisfactory interviews with the foremen of the respective works.

In keeping with his assignment, he told the interviewing clerk he would prefer to be outside of Rugby, claiming he had relatives in the Lutterworth area with whom he could lodge. The personnel department of the main BTH plant in Rugby also handled personnel for the Ladywood works, so the personnel department clerk arranged for him to be interviewed by the foreman electrical fitter at Ladywood, giving Foulkes his bus fare and directions of how to get there from Rugby.

The bus dropped Foulkes in Market Street, and he crossed the busy street to a small pub opposite to think things out.

In thinking about it he could see two problems which were connected. Firstly, he didn't wish to draw attention to himself unduly, therefore he needed to go into the Ladywood works and talk to the foreman. If he didn't turn up, it might look odd and raise their suspicions. Secondly, he needed to find a reasonable excuse as to why he wouldn't take any job offered, again without raising their suspicions because with the shortage of skilled tradesmen, he was sure he would be approved by the foreman.

Sitting there in the pub bar, nursing a half pint of Trent ale, he thought about his next move. He realised he needed to go in and be interviewed, which would enable him to ask the foreman questions regarding the type of work carried on in the works, pretending he'd like to know to help him make a decision.

This he did and fortunately, the foreman was of the type who can't help telling all they know to show how important they are in their field of operations.

The foreman, in giving him a list of products produced and activities at the Ladywood works, also added the additional information that they'd had trouble with the jet engine racing out of control when running and it required further development. They anticipated having an engine ready in September, when the airframe would be ready at the Gloster Aircraft works at Gloucester. The foreman, after further discussion with Foulkes, agreed to employ him and sent him back to the personnel department at the main works.

Arriving back at the main personnel office, Foulkes saw the clerk he'd seen before and discussed terms and conditions of employment, he gave the clerk his address in Bristol and said he'd need to think about any written offer they would make because he still had a few other companies to visit. The clerk didn't seem to think it odd he'd requested an offer in writing, he said they always confirmed their employment offers in writing.

Foulkes returned to Bristol and the following day took the day off work to visit Gloucester, about 40 miles away, travelling by train again. Before setting out he'd visited the Bristol Council Library, in the reference section, and had looked up the whereabouts of the Gloster Aircraft Company. Finding it was located at the small village of Hucclecote, just outside of Gloucester, more or less a suburb on an airfield the company had purchased in 1928, following the company's move into all metal airframe construction.

On leaving the Gloucester railway station, his first move was to go to the local government labour exchange, explaining to the clerk he was having to move to the Gloucester and Cheltenham area because of the ill health of his parents who lived in Cheltenham. He was currently employed in Bristol but would like a job in the Gloucester and Cheltenham area.

The clerk in the employment exchange was able to offer him several positions as an electrical fitter, including one at the Gloster Aircraft Company. Foulkes pretended he selected the Gloster Aircraft Company vacancy on the grounds that the company's location at Hucclecote was on the Gloucester to Cheltenham road and would be easier for him to get there from Cheltenham. The clerk arranged for him to have an interview that afternoon.

Foulkes travelled out by bus to Hucclecote village shortly before midday, and then walked out to the edge of the village where the airfield was located to orientate himself with the area. The works were located at the far side of the airfield from the road and so all he could see were the buildings and hangars, in front of which were a number of biplanes, which he assumed were the Gloster Gladiator biplane fighter aircraft more or less obsolete now that the monoplane fighters were starting to dominate the skies around the world.

He thought he needed to brush up on his aircraft recognition if he was going to get more of this type of assignment from the Germans.

He walked back to the village and entered the first public house he came to on the basis that at lunchtime anyone from the Gloster works would use it for lunch, and he might hear some gossip. He was right, a few of the overalled workers from the Gloster works came in, but all he overheard were references to the Gladiator aeroplane.

Presenting himself at the personnel department at the appropriate time, after the formality of filling out an application form, he was then interviewed by a clerk. The clerk listed a range of positions which he thought might interest Foulkes. The company, apart from designing and manufacturing aeroplanes, also had manufactured a wide variety of products during the depression of the early thirties, although most of these products had been phased out such as milk churns, fish fryers and steel roll-up shop fronts. Their main product currently was the Gloster Gladiator, of which the company produced about two hundred or more a year, but no mention was made of an airframe for the jet engine. Foulkes agreed to be interviewed by the foreman of the maintenance department of the works for a position similar to the one he occupied with Bristol Corporation.

He waited in the personnel department waiting room and eventually a young boy of about sixteen came for him and took him off to meet the factory maintenance foreman. On the way to his office, they passed through the building housing the production line for the Gladiator. Skirting the Gladiator production line, they passed a bay with several metal aircraft frames in various stages of completion, one almost fully completed, except for the engine which looked as if it would be fitted into the nose cone; these were different from the Gladiator frames.

Indicating these different airframes Foulkes asked the boy what was the name of the aircraft. The boy told him some were for the Gloster Whittle E28 and awaiting a new type of engine, and the ones at the back had been for the Gloster F5, which he thought had been discontinued.

The foreman questioned Foulkes about his training, experience and where he was at present and then offered him a place. Foulkes said he had been to Rugby to the British Thompson-Houston works and had been promised an offer from them but agreed he'd sooner work nearer Cheltenham in keeping with his cover story.

When he mentioned BTH the foreman said that they as a company worked with BTH on producing an aircraft with a revolutionary type of engine, the airframe was ready but they were awaiting the engine. He said he didn't know what the engine looked like but understood from people on the shop floor it could make the aircraft travel very fast, far faster than any known aeroplane currently in service.

Foulkes was then returned to the personnel office and he was advised they'd be in touch.

He received an offer in the mail about two days later and threw it away.

Chapter Four

Early in June on a mid-week evening, Thomas Wadsworth, a second lieutenant in the Herefordshire Regiment of the Shropshire Light Infantry, a Territorial Army Regiment of the British Army, arranged to meet with David Coulter in Dorrington. A point midway between their respective homes.

Tom Wadsworth in civil life was a chartered surveyor with a firm of civil engineers, McPherson and Townes in Hereford. His father was a local bank manager and the family were long established in Hereford. He'd gone to school at the local grammar school and then on to Birmingham University. At 26 he was the eldest of four children; his brother Bill at 24; sister, Margaret, known as Peggy, 22; and the youngest, Paul, 16.

He'd arranged to meet with David Coulter to discuss two things. One was their proposed trip to the Continent later that year, and secondly their respective Territorial unit's training 'camp' dates also later that year. He'd received the dates of the Herefordshire Regiment's fortnight camp, and David Coulter had promised to find out and meet with him armed with the 610 Squadron dates. The two men were the prime movers in the co-operation between the two units, although both commanding officers were very keen also to support the Army Western Command initiative on Army Air Force co-operation.

The two men met regularly, it had initially commenced at Army and R.A.F. meetings to establish operating procedures during the combined R.A.F. and Army exercises held on the Brecon Beacon military firing range. The two men had hit it off together immediately and had established a rapport, seeing each other and visiting each other's families on a regular basis, with David Coulter slightly interested in Tom Wadsworth's sister, Peggy, having taken her out a few times.

They had arranged to meet in the little village of Dorrington, just south of Shrewsbury on the A49 main road, which ran between Birkenhead on the Wirral Peninsula and Ross on Wye in Herefordshire, one of the main roads north to south on the western side of England.

Tom Wadsworth arrived first and pulled off the main road into the small car park of the village inn. Going inside he ordered a pint of the local ale and sat at one of the tables in the small saloon bar to await David Coulter and listened idly to the conversations going on around him amongst the small groups of local people. Most of it was about farming, this being a predominately farming community, although a group in the corner consisting of three middle-aged men, about the age of his father, were arguing about the current situation in Czechoslovakia and the Sudeten German problem, one insisting that the only course of action that England could take to uphold its honour was to warn the Germans off.

He'd been waiting for about 15 minutes when David Coulter came in. He waved to attract his attention; David nodded and went across to the bar first, bringing over a pint of beer and then sitting down opposite to him.

"How's things, Tom, family all well?"

"OK, Dave and you?"

"Yup, OK," taking a slurp of his beer.

"Anything about your new planes?"

"Nothing as yet, although we've just taken delivery of a Lysander Army Co-operation job. It all seems to indicate we'll stay as an army co-operation squadron, more so if we get those Fairey Battle bombers. They're specifically designed for close work with the army. But a lot of the chaps are plumping for a fighter squadron."

"Pity, I was reading an article in the Combined Services mag over the weekend; an article by a man who'd just got back from Spain. The Germans are there with a group called the Condor Legion and using similar tactics to the ones we're trying to develop if those dinosaurs in the War office will let us. He wrote that the instigator is a German General Heinz Guderian, working with the full backing of the German General Staff. Apparently, every time the German armour supported by infantry encounters an area of resistance, they use the planes as mobile artillery and blast their way through. They try and move at high speed and the co-operation between the planes and ground forces is maintained by radio. By moving at speed they keep the enemy off balance, a bit like the cavalry used to try and do, like the Boer tactics of mounted infantry during the Boer War."

"Y'know Tom, there are one or two people here who advocate those sorts of tactics but unfortunately, they haven't much influence in the cobwebby areas of the military hierarchy. We know there's likely to be another one with Germany if the politicians have any guts but unless they change their ways in the War Office, we'll lose it. But you can't tell with politicians, they'll look after their own skins and what they call their legacy."

"What do you mean?"

"Trying to make their actions look good when future generations look back. Even if it means abjectly crawling to someone, like with Hitler and Mussolini now, instead of telling them to stop or else, you've gone far enough."

"Stop philosophising and let's get down to business. Have you got any dates yet?"

"Yes Tom, our dates are the middle two weeks of August, which means we can head for the Continent sometime in the last week of August for three weeks. How about yours?"

"The same two weeks, I think the powers that be are setting us up for a joint exercise."

"OK, I think we ought to go by train, that way we can do the Rhine trip, Tom, you want to do that."

"Are you sure, Dave? It would be easier by car, we'd be more flexible and I'm sure there's somewhere we could leave the car just to go down the Rhine and back. I'll look into it. Get your passport sorted early, and you'll need your C.O.'s permission, being an officer in His Majesty's Service."

"Permission? Will I, are you sure, Tom?" David Coulter took another pull at his beer.

"Yup, I was talking to the adjutant, old Bill Fothergill, and telling him about our proposed trip, and he said it was mandatory to get your C.O.'s permission. It's in the King's Regulations."

"OK, I'll talk to Don Selby, have you talked to your colonel yet?"

"Yes, I saw him the other night, and he didn't think there would be a problem. But I've got to submit it in writing. He said he'd approve the application and forward it to our H.Q., and he didn't think there'd be any trouble getting permission."

David Coulter consulted his pocket diary regarding dates. That year the last full week in August commenced Monday 22, August which didn't give them much time between coming from their respective 'camps' and leaving England. So they decided to take their holiday starting the following week, Monday 29 August to 17 September, about three weeks.

They then agreed to travel in David's car and sort something out when they got to Germany regarding the trip down the Rhine.

David was to sort out the travel arrangements for the car, permissions and insurance and the like, each would look after his own passport application and visas for France and Germany.

The two friends talked on for a while, mainly in relation to the exercises scheduled for the following weekend; after another beer each they parted, returning to their homes.

The following week David Coulter spoke to his C.O., Donald Selby, about the proposed trip and produced a written application for permission, which Don Selby forwarded to their Group H.Q. at Watnall in Nottinghamshire for their permission. The application lay on the desk of the Regular Wing Commander in charge of personnel for a week. When he came to read it, he remembered a communication he'd received from a Group Captain in the Air Ministry Intelligence department asking to be notified of any officers travelling to Europe during that summer.

He forwarded David Coulter's application to the Group Captain in the Intelligence Department, advising Don Selby of what he'd done.

Gerald Thompson met with his Auxiliary Air Force contact and received the list of names, along with details of the men on the list. Talking together and examining the service details of the men after Gerald Thompson had outlined the profile of the man he was looking for, they eliminated all bar three on the list. One from Scotland, 603 City of Edinburgh Squadron, one from the Home Counties 604 Squadron and one man with 610 City of Chester Squadron.

Gerald Thompson knew he'd have to tread very carefully at the next stage of his project. The air vice marshals in charge of the two R.A.F. Groups, 11 and 12, under whose command the squadrons were located, were both very irascible men and needed to be treated with kid gloves. Gerald Thompson had been in the service long enough to have a few friends around and therefore, first approached a friend with 12 Group H.Q. on the basis that two of the men were in squadrons in that group and he may not need to search further.

His contact within 12 Group smoothed the way for him, and he received permission to approach the two men.

He travelled up to Scotland by train and spent two days in Edinburgh evaluating covertly the likely candidate, a charming solicitor who had been with the R.A.F.V.R. Squadron since its formation. Gerald Thompson was using the cover previously agreed that he would be inspecting progress on the updating of the airfields and the expansion of squadrons.

The man didn't have any knowledge of German, but he and his wife were travelling to the Rhine area and spending three weeks in that area looking at the vineyards. The man was bright, a sharp mind and full of enthusiasm, a natural self-starter. His project in Germany, although initially in the Rhine area, could easily be expanded to take in the Stuttgart area, where on the hills around Stuttgart were several vineyards.

At the end of his two days there Gerald Thompson took the train to Liverpool after making arrangements on the telephone to meet with Squadron Leader Selby, C.O. of 610 Squadron.

He had made a booking at the Adelphi Hotel in Liverpool and met with Donald Selby there, still using the guise of inspecting expansion plans and progress, and agreed with him to be collected the following day, Saturday, and be taken out to the airfield across the river south of Birkenhead.

Don Selby arranged with Eric Payne, the Engineering Branch Flight Lieutenant, to have the Group Captain collected from the Adelphi the next day.

Around 9am in the morning Eric Payne collected Gerald Thompson from the Adelphi Hotel and drove out to the Hooton airfield; the day was bright with a promise of showers. Most of the Auxiliary Air Force members were there, and they met with the Group Captain in the officer's mess for drinks prior to lunch.

Gerald Thompson was able to talk with David Coulter prior to lunch and also kept a covert eye on him throughout the meal, then after the meal had a general chat with Don Selby about service in the squadron. He'd more or less formed an opinion that David Coulter was probably the type of person he was searching for in relation to the task. Whether Aubrey Evans of MI6 would agree was a different matter.

The following day, Sunday, some of the squadron, David Coulter included, were meeting up with the Army people of the Herefordshire Regiment at an airfield in the south, so at the end of the day Gerald Thompson took his leave from them.

The next week he telephoned the commanding officer of 604 Squadron to see if he could visit with them the following weekend. The squadron was based at North Weald in Essex which it shared with two Regular Royal Air Force squadrons, so he made arrangements with his contact in the Auxiliary Air Force to be part of his organisation and collecting some personnel service records on his behalf, which his friend would return the following week, one of the records was the subject of his visit.

His visit was a reasonable success and he met with his man; he was eminently suitable for the role, spoke fluent German and therefore it was a toss-up between him and David Coulter. The 604 squadron man would be in the Stuttgart area visiting friends at Ulm, about 50 miles to the west, the problem would be how he'd explain to his friends why he wanted to visit Stuttgart and hang about for a period of time, particularly the way Germans were these days paranoid about security. They were spying on each other and reporting anything remotely suspicious to the Gestapo, therefore even if his hosts didn't report him, some other German neighbour might. It was too risky.

It looked as if things were bending towards David Coulter, one problem was that he only spoke a little German, maybe it could be remedied with a little quick schooling; they had about three months. Travelling back to London he gave the matter some thought and decided he ought to talk to Aubrey Evans as soon as possible, anyway Evans wanted to meet with the man picked to give him a briefing.

The following morning, he telephoned Aubrey Evans and arranged a meeting that afternoon. Later that day he entered the unmarked building in Victoria Street, giving his name to the receptionist, and was escorted upstairs to Aubrey Evans' office.

Here he produced the service record for David Coulter and gave a brief description of his search and how he'd arrived at the selection of David Coulter.

"Bit hit or miss, wasn't it?" Aubrey Evans growled.

"Well, I suppose so but I think we've got a good man. Very level-headed, a pilot, therefore used to making quick decisions under stress. He's been in the service about four years and therefore covered by the Official Secrets Act. One problem is that he only speaks a little German."

"We can remedy that, how long have we got?"

"He and an Army friend are thinking of going to Germany late August or early September, which gives us about three months."

"You better get in touch and brief him on what we'd like, bring his commanding officer into the picture but nobody else. I'll organise some German lessons, we've one or two German-speaking refugees in that area we can call on to help, he'll need to give us the time. At least four hours a week. After you've spoken to him and got his agreement, I'd like word with him to make an assessment before we go further."

"I'll try and get both him and his commanding officer down here next weekend, being territorials they have weekday jobs, so it'll need to be at the weekend."

"Do that but I don't think we want to see the commanding officer, talk to him on the phone. I'll organise the German lessons in the Chester area, and I'll see him next weekend. Keep me in touch."

Gerald Thompson went back to his office, talked to Air Marshal Cowley bringing him up to date, then rang Group 12 Headquarters and talked to his contact advising him what was about to happen. His contact agreed to cover with the various people in Group 12 who needed to know but to keep the list as small as possible, because of the danger involved for David Coulter should anything leak out.

Thinking about it again, Gerald Thompson decided rather than talk to Don Selby on the phone, he'd go and see him.

The following day Don Selby received a telegram from the Air Ministry at his office in Dale Street, Liverpool advising him that Group Captain Gerald Thompson would be visiting him the next day on an urgent matter regarding his squadron, also notifying him his Group Commander had been informed already and given permission.

Don Selby wondered what the permission was for and what it was all about, thinking perhaps it was in reference to their change of aircraft.

The following day Gerald Thompson arrived in Liverpool mid-morning by train, taking a taxi to Dale Street to meet with Don Selby at his office.

Don Selby recognised the Group Captain from his previous visit, although from the telegram of the previous day, he hadn't made the connection.

Without any delay Gerald Thompson got to the subject of his visit.

"Mr Selby, I must make you aware that what I am about to discuss with you comes under the Official Secrets Act and therefore, I caution you that anything I say must not be discussed with anyone else other than other participants in this matter. You understand?"

"Certainly, sir."

"My position within the Air Ministry is that of an Intelligence Officer, working under Air Marshal Burridge, and my current task is to evaluate the progress made by other nations in the field of development of aircraft, particularly engines."

He then went on to explain the Air Ministry concern about the development of the jet engine and in particular, the German development. He said that up to the beginning of that year they were getting very good intelligence information concerning Heinkel, but unfortunately, their source had been exposed to the German authorities and the information had dried up. They had reason to believe the Germans were very advanced with the development of their engine and close to flying an aircraft using one. One of the problems associated with gathering information was that the Germans were a little paranoid regarding their development, whereas because the patents were public knowledge, the British Air Ministry were more open.

"You mean we're developing an engine here, sir? I always thought that was pie in the sky stuff. One of my chaps was talking about it a while ago, but I didn't really think it was possible, maybe in the future."

"No, it's not, we're pretty well advanced, but to maintain a lead it requires proper government funding. We need to be able to quote to the politicians just where the opposition are with their development. The main opposition being the

Germans, if they get an engine to use in a plane before us, they'll blow us out of the skies in the event of war. We just won't be able to compete."

"OK. I understand, but where do we come into this?"

"We need to have someone to scout around the Stuttgart area. This is where we know Heinkel's developing the engine, and will make a test flight somewhere there. This project has the full approval of Air Force hierarchy, I can assure you. Now you have a young officer who fits the profile we've been looking for, and we are aware that he is contemplating a trip to Germany this summer. You forwarded an application from him for permission for him to leave the country."

"Yes, correct, David Coulter; he's going with a friend from Hereford."

"We'd like him to visit the Stuttgart area and see if he could observe anything in regard to the Heinkel experiments. I use the word 'observe' with care, we don't expect anything more than to have a look at the Heinkel factory and airstrip, not to try and get information from any other source. We'd be willing to meet his expenses."

"You better talk with him yourself. He might not be going anywhere near Stuttgart."

"I agree, but wherever he is going in Germany a visit to the Stuttgart area could be included, and we would meet the cost, even for both of them. Who's the friend from Hereford, have you any idea?"

"Yes, I think the man's an officer with an Army unit we work with from time to time. Anyway, David would fill you in with the detail."

The information that the companion of their man was also one of His Majesty's Army officers was also very satisfactory for Gerald Thompson, at a pinch they could bring him in under the Official Secrets Act.

"Can I see Coulter today, d'you think?"

"Probably, let me see if I can reach him, you may have to wait until this evening, will that suit?"

Gerald Thompson gave it a quick thought; he may need a hotel room, but he'd wait until he found out when he could see the young man.

He nodded. "Try, I'd like to see him today, if possible."

Don Selby spoke to his secretary, asking her to see if she could get David Coulter on the phone. As they sat there waiting, they discussed the problems in Europe and in particular Czechoslovakia and the Sudeten German problem.

"D'you think the Krauts mean business? This fella Hitler seems to be pushing hard."

"I think so, Mr Selby, I'm afraid we'll be up against them again soon, sooner than most people think. That is if the politicians hold their nerve and don't cave in."

"What's your idea of soon, Sir?"

"End of this year, maybe next, traditionally Europe goes to war after the harvesting in August or September, look at the last show, early August, I don't think the next one will be any different."

"Do you think we'll be ready? There's a lot to do in our service, I'm pretty sure the Army is the same, they're only just getting the new weapons, and a lot of our Air Force squadrons haven't been fully equipped."

"Yes, we need another year if possible, but I doubt whether we're going to get that breathing space, and if we do will the powers that be, the politicians, use it to get us ready? I doubt it."

Donald Selby's intercom unit on his desk buzzed; picking the handset up, he spoke to his secretary.

"Put him on." Then speaking,

"Hello, Dave, I was wondering if we could meet this afternoon at the airfield, there's a couple of things that need to be discussed, I've had word about your trip from the Wing H.Q." There was a silence.

"You can, good, see you about three."

He put the receiver down, and then looked across at Gerald Thompson.

"Arranged, he'll meet us about three at Hooton. Now how about a spot of lunch?"

"Something light, Mr Selby."

"Yes, we can go to the Cornmarket, it's a small pub, type of buffet, you can have what you like. Then I'll take you to Hooton."

The Cornmarket turned out to be a city pub just like many others in English cities. Very busy during the lunchtime trade and no doubt very quiet at night, a slight variation on the London eating houses. This had long bench-like tables running down the centre of a large room, against the walls were sideboards full of food, drinks were ordered from the waiters, paid for when brought, and patrons then helped themselves to the food. The intriguing part was that on the way out one stopped by a woman sat at a desk and told her what you had eaten and were charged accordingly.

The two men arrived at the airfield early afternoon and found David Coulter waiting for them. Borrowing Don Selby's office, Gerald Thompson sat a rather apprehensive David Coulter opposite him across the desk.

Producing David Coulter's application for permission to visit Germany and France endorsed by Don Selby and the Wing HQ, he looked across at David and smiled.

"No doubt you wonder what on earth this is all about and quite rightly so, let me explain. Firstly, what we are going to discuss comes within the Official Secrets Act and therefore, you can't discuss this with anyone other than people who are directly involved, that means not with your family, brother officers, except your commanding officer and even your travelling companion."

He then went into similar detail of their requirements, roughly the same way he'd approached Don Selby. "So you see, we think maybe you could help us whilst on your trip to Germany. Whereabouts in Germany had you thought of visiting?"

"My friend and I thought we'd visit the battlefields in Northern France then go on to the Rhine, he's keen on a trip down the Rhine. We had thought of heading to Karlsruhe and finding a boat, we're not too clear and would play it by ear when we got there."

"That sounds fine; Karlsruhe isn't that far from Stuttgart, about 40 miles. A little diversion wouldn't look too unusual, there's a place close to Stuttgart, Ludwigsburg, the seat of a mad king. Very often visited by tourists, beautiful palace and gardens, so it wouldn't be out of the context of a tourist trip."

David looked a little doubtful, thinking about Tom and how he'd need to put it to Tom.

Gerald Thompson went on, "Now about the expenses, we wouldn't expect you to undertake something like this and be out of pocket, and I have the authority to make available monies to cover the cost of the trip for yourself and companion. You'll be taking a car, I presume, and we can help with that, the paperwork is a little complicated."

"I think I'd need to bring my travelling companion into this, otherwise it would be a little difficult explaining the diversion. He's a second lieutenant with the Herefordshire Regiment, it's a Territorial Regiment, we often do exercises with them, it was how we met, and he's a surveyor, so he could be studying landscapes or palaces or something."

"I'd need to meet him, but I think we can give you cover before you go. You'll need to meet with a man in another government department before you go, I'll set that up but after I've met your friend. Give me his name and how I can contact him, meanwhile don't say anything to him; I need to get this cleared with the appropriate authorities. But you'll participate in our little project?"

"Yes, sir." David then wrote down Tom Wadsworth's name, address and telephone number and gave it to Gerald Thompson.

"Good man, I'll just talk to Squadron Leader Selby again before I go, but thank you, and I'll get clearance to make contact with your friend and we'll be in touch."

David Coulter then left him and Don Selby came in, Gerald Thompson moved to the other side of the desk to allow Don to sit in his own chair.

"I've had a satisfactory chat with young Coulter and he's willing to participate. He's given me the name and contact point of his friend. First, I need to clear this contact with the powers that be before we proceed, otherwise all is well. I've warned him not to talk about this because between you and me, should this leak out his life would be in danger in Germany. These Germans stop at nothing to keep things hidden, the last man was liquidated. Now if you could get me to Liverpool, I'll make the five o'clock Euston train and be back in London by nine."

The next morning Gerald Thompson made two telephone calls, one was to Aubrey Evans, bringing him up to date on the David Coulter situation and arranging to meet him that afternoon. The other call was to Air Marshal Burridge, his superior, requesting permission to approach the War Office in relation to talking to Thomas Wadsworth and the German trip.

Given that approval, he talked to his opposite number in the War Office, a Colonel Williams, making an appointment for later that morning.

Arriving at Bill William's office at the War Office, he came straight to the point.

"Bill, MI6 was feeding us with information regarding the Krauts' progress on a semi-secret project and their asset managed to get liquidated. We've been blind since but I'm setting up a team to go and see what they can find out in an unobtrusive way and how far the Krauts have got with their project."

He went on to explain what he had in mind and the relationship of David Coulter and his military friend to the project.

"What I would like is to be able to approach this Territorial officer and brief him with the situation to enlist his help, with the War Office's permission, of course. Otherwise it's going to be difficult for Coulter to get to the Stuttgart area without Wadsworth being fully in the picture."

"I don't see a problem, Gerry; I'll have a word with our people here and then talk to his commanding officer. I'll let you know as soon as everything is cleared. You look a bit doubtful?"

"We need to keep this with as few people as necessary."

"I must talk to his commanding officer, also with Charlie Horrock, who's assistant to the director of Army intelligence, General Wilkinson. They'll all need to put their blessing on it."

"Yeees, I understand, but also we must remember because young Coulter and his friend are amateurs at this game, we need to be doubly careful of leaks at our end."

"Leave it with me, Gerry, we'll be careful; I'll restrict it to just the director and his assistant, and the boy's commanding officer with a strict Top Secret Classification, that'll button it down tight. I'll call you later today and let you know how I've gone on."

Gerald Thompson then left and went on to Aubrey Evans of MI6, with whom he'd spoken to earlier.

Sitting with Aubrey, Gerald Thompson outlined where he reached with the project.

"A slight complication turned up, Aubrey, but I think I've overcome it. Young Coulter, whom I'd selected, apparently is going to Germany with an Army friend, to get him into the Stuttgart area means we have to also bring the Military into the picture. I don't like it but there's no satisfactory alternative."

"No doubt the Military want the thing laid out in triplicate, with all and sundry giving their blessing."

Gerald Thompson laughed, the antagonism and hostility between the two organisations was well known. One side regarded the other as a bunch of dinosaurs, whilst they regarded MI6 as a bunch of brothel-creeping old poufs peddling useless information.

"No, not quite, and I did extract a promise to keep it as low a profile as possible. Young Coulter is on board, and I hope to see his travelling companion sometime this week, then we can get them up here next weekend or the one after at the latest."

"OK, it suits me; I can then brief them on some of the major man-traps around in Germany these days."

More or less satisfied with his morning's work, Gerald Thompson returned to his office; there were one or two things he needed to clear up on the project, such as the amount of funding and how he needed to go about obtaining it. Arming himself with Air Marshal Burridge's letter of authority, giving him approval to administer funds for the project code named 'Swann', he visited with his opposite number in the pay department.

The Squadron Leader in charge suggested he came up with a figure for the project, and then the funds would be made available in a special bank account, to be drawn on as required and paid as he directed and to whom he wanted reimbursed.

Gerald Thompson was aware that Volunteer Reserve officers received a stipend along with all other Territorial Service personnel, some were paid quarterly, some twice a year, others only received a lump sum annually. It appeared that the Royal Air Force officers received theirs twice a year. A payment had been made to them at the beginning of April; the next one was due in September, a little late to help them with their trip if advance payments were needed. He felt he should conceal within Coulter's normal stipend the fact monies were being paid to him for the trip rather than make a separate payment at an odd time.

Thanking the pay Squadron Leader, he went back to his office to think out what he should do; although the first thing he needed to do was get the two officers up to London for a briefing with Aubrey Evans.

The following morning Bill Williams telephoned him to say that all was well, he'd spoken to all concerned, including the young man's commanding officer, and it was in order for him to approach the young officer. The best way was for him to go to Hereford and see the man there.

Bill Williams gave him a contact telephone number for Henry Marsden, Colonel of the Herefordshire Regiment, who lived and farmed at Church Stretton, about 40 miles north of Hereford.

Gerald Thompson telephoned Henry Marsden and agreed to meet him the following day in the Green Dragon Hotel in Hereford. Checking Bradshaw's Rail Timetable, he found it would probably be better for him to motor across to Hereford and accordingly, arranged to set off about six in the morning, much to the chagrin of his wife, although she was used to the disruptions of service life.

He arrived in Hereford shortly after midday and parked his car around the rear of the hotel in the assigned parking area. He'd made a booking for that night in the hotel and checked in; after a clean-up in his room, he returned downstairs to await Henry Marsden, first advising the receptionist where he'd be in the lounge room.

He didn't have to wait long before a pageboy brought a tweed-suited fit-looking man of about 40 to him.

They shook hands and introduced each other; Gerald Thompson suggested a drink prior to their lunch, and the two of them moved to the bar next to the dining room.

Over their meal the two men sized each other up and asking each other exploratory questions, filled in their backgrounds.

Each had seen service in The Great War; Gerald Thompson as an infantry officer prior to his service with the Flying Corps, the forerunner of the Royal Air Force. Henry Marsden as a private soldier, underage when he went in 1917 and had been commissioned just at the end of hostilities, apart from being a part-time soldier as a Territorial Colonel, he was farming just outside Church Stretton in Shropshire. His family had been in that area for a few hundred years but had also a long connection with the Herefordshire Regiment.

After lunch Henry Marsden took Gerald Thompson along to the headquarters of the regiment in Harold Street, and sitting in Colonel Marsden's office Gerald Thompson outlined what he required from Tom Wadsworth.

"I don't see a problem, Group Captain; it all seems to be a fairly simple observation job, no cloak and dagger work, and if the two of them are careful where they go, they shouldn't get into trouble.

"Young Wadsworth should be here shortly, I asked him to get here about four; and then I'll leave you with him."

Shortly after he'd spoken there was a knock on the door and a fresh-faced young dark-haired man entered. Colonel Marsden made the introductions and left, agreeing with Gerald Thompson they'd talk later on the phone.

Gerald Thompson gestured to Tom Wadsworth to sit where he'd been sitting and he moved around to sit opposite.

"You must be wondering what all this is about, let me explain."

He then went into a short explanation of the jet engine project and what was happening, what had happened and what he hoped they'd achieve.

"What you and David Coulter shouldn't do is put yourselves at risk by some action other than observation, is that understood? The German security authorities are particularly brutal these days and show very little mercy in cases of doubt. Virtually everyone spies on everyone else."

"Yes, sir, I understand."

"Now you should come up to London next weekend, there's someone there you should meet. Here's the address, and you'll be booked in to the Imperial Hotel, Russell Square, for Friday and Saturday nights. Telephone this number when you get to the hotel." He gave Tom Wadsworth a slip of paper with the MI6 address and a telephone number on it.

Chapter Five

Joan Healey arrived home in early June from Cambridge University, where she was studying Science, to start her long summer break.

After being at home for a few days, she decided she would like to get a job during the summer. Her father was none too happy about this when she voiced it one night at the dinner table. Her mother thought it a good idea, so her father backed off and allowed himself to be over-ruled by the two females.

Their home was close to Knutsford, Cheshire; her father having a solicitor's practice in Altringham, following his father's footsteps. They'd moved to Knutsford a few years previously from Altringham to a large Georgian house on the outskirts of Knutsford, the house having a few acres of land on which to keep a horse, her father being keen on hunting with the Cheshire Hunt.

Joan Healey had passed her driving licence a few months earlier. This driving test had been made compulsory in 1935 by the then minister of Transport Leslie Hore-Belisha but first advocated by his predecessor Oliver Stanley. In the first year of testing the government of the day claimed that death toll on the road had been brought down by a thousand. Whether this was true or not is doubtful because the majority of the drivers on the road at that time weren't required to take the test, only new drivers.

Her father had bought her a small car, an Austin Seven 'Nippy', popular with young people, a small two-seater sports vehicle in a bright yellow paint, so she was reasonably mobile.

She and her mother discussed what sort of temporary summer job she should look for; she didn't want purely office work, otherwise she could work in her father's office.

The two women spent most of her first week at home talking through various options available for her and eventually, her mother came up with a suggestion.

"I was talking to Moira Wilson at our Townswomen's Guild Meeting last night; her brother operates a small travel agency in Chester, he mainly arranges small escorted tours to France and Germany, it's a new thing and apparently, he's always searching for energetic young people to assist his senior tour guides, you know, people of the right calibre (what her mother really meant was people of the right social background). You speak German and have knowledge of French and have been with us to France several times. When I was telling her about you, she said she'd speak to her brother about you. It would be better than being cooped up in an office all day. What do you think?"

"I think I'd like it, sounds great."

The following day Moira Wilson telephoned to say her brother was interested in seeing Joan and she should telephone him either that day or the next. This Joan did and arranged to meet him in his office. At the interview Edward Smith, Moira's brother tested her knowledge of German and French and was satisfied and offered her a position as assistant tour guide starting the following Monday, which Joan accepted.

Before leaving Chester she made arrangements for lodgings with a woman her mother knew. Her first two weeks were spent orientating herself with the type of tours the agency arranged and the methods of travel they used.

She was to be working with a very experienced guide, a man who had started at the turn of the century escorting groups of immigrants from various parts of Eastern Europe to the northern French and German ports for shipping companies to take to the United States. He spoke several European languages fluently; the man, Hans Van Dyke, was a man of about 60, of Dutch-British parentage, having been born in England of an English mother and Dutch father, educated in England and with a natural flair for languages. As Joan was to find out, his ancestry made him totally unflappable and a pillar of strength in adversity.

Joan Healey learnt a lot from him during the short time they worked together prior to their first trip taking a group of middle-aged English ladies on a tour of the Flanders battlefields, most of the ladies having lost a relative during The Great War in the areas to be visited. The trip would take about 14 days, commencing in London and ending in London.

Her first tour was a success, and Hans Van Dyke reported favourably on her manner and attitude with the difficult group of middle-aged ladies. On her second tour they took a mixed party again of middle-aged people to Paris for a week of sightseeing, again she proved invaluable to Hans Van Dyke for problems encountered with some of the ladies on the tour. Their third tour together was escorting a group around the Black Forest area of Germany, then returning via Switzerland, spending a few days in Geneva.

In between the tours on the Continent, she had the occasional trip around England with a group, usually Americans. The routine for the United Kingdom tour was to meet the group in Southampton on the arrival of their vessel, help them through immigration and customs formalities, get them onto the boat train to London, and settle them in their London hotel, depending on the type of tour.

Edward Smith was developing and offered three tours; one called 'Rural England', commencing in London, travelling by train to Chester, spending three days in the Chester area visiting cheese-making farms, Welsh hill farms and various mixed farms; and then the tour moved up to Carlisle and spent three days up there visiting farms. Returning down through the Yorkshire moors and dales, it finished in London, usually taking about three weeks. A second tour spent all the time in the West Country, Devon and Cornwall, and the third was in conjunction with a London agency, spending all the time in London. These tours were increasingly popular with the American market and the demand was growing.

By the end of the summer Joan was an accomplished tour guide and Edward Smith promised the following year she could handle tours as the senior guide.

Their final tour that year was to be another visit with a group to the Black Forest, a visit to Basle in Switzerland and then a trip down the Rhine from Basle to Karlsruhe by boat, but the boat trip was cancelled due to the political situation.

In mid-July Joan, along with Hans Van Dyke, had collected a party of Americans in London who had spent a week there sightseeing and brought them up to Chester for the Rural England Tour. They had already spent two nights in Chester at The Grosvenor Hotel, the night of their arrival and then the next day was spent in the Cheshire area around Frodsham visiting cheese farms. Their second day was in North Wales in the Llangollen valley on two hill farms. They were then scheduled to leave the following morning for the Border country between England and Scotland, a slight variation to the usual Rural England Tour.

Later that evening Hans Van Dyke and Joan were just sitting having a quiet drink in a corner of the large foyer prior to going home, Joan to her lodgings and Hans to his home at Upton, a village near Chester. A group of about ten boisterous young men exited the bar, with much noise and loud talk; the doorway of the bar was close to where Hans and Joan were sitting, one of the young men brushed against Hans' chair, causing him to spill his drink. The young man was a little under the weather, attempting to apologise but having difficulty with the words. One of his friends turned and came back, then pulled at him and at the same time apologised for his friend.

Telling his friend to go, the young man – he looked about Joan's age – insisted on getting a replacement drink for Hans, apologising all the time.

Calling the waiter over, the young man asked for a replacement drink for Hans. He was obviously well-known; the waiter immediately went off and returned with the drink, the young man told him to put on his bill. "Yes, Mr Coulter." Hans protested saying there was no damage, the young man held up his hands and muttered something about his friend being clumsy.

Then the pleasant fresh-faced sandy-haired man smiled at them and apologised once again and went off, following his friend. Joan thought he was rather nice and wondered where they were from; she had noticed them before in the hotel bar, all rather noisy but not objectionably so.

She and Hans finished their drinks and walked towards the door into Eastgate Street, she was intending to drop Hans off in Upton and then return to her lodgings at Newton Heath using the recently completed Chester bypass road, both places slightly to the north, on the outskirts of Chester. She had parked her car in St John's Street, the next street off Eastgate Street towards the east. As they got to the door the front desk manager called across to Hans.

"I'll be leaving in a minute, Mr Van Dyke, let me give you a lift home, it's pouring down out there." The man lived close to Hans and had given him a lift home before. Hans looked at Joan.

"Save you going out of your way, Joan," he called back. "Thank you, I'll wait over here."

Joan, after saying goodnight to Hans, walked out into the wet street, then turning right walked towards where her car was parked. As she turned into St John's Street, the rain was sheeting down and shining wet on the pavements, she saw the young man from the hotel standing under an umbrella looking at what must be his car. She then saw the front near side wheel had a puncture; he turned as she came along and recognising her, smiled ruefully.

"You have troubles?"

He nodded. "I'm just trying to make up my mind what I should do. Stop and get soaked changing the wheel or telephone home for a lift and come back tomorrow to change it in the hope that the weather will be kinder."

"Where do you live?"

"Christleton, you know it?"

"I think so; look, my car is just along here, why don't I drop you off? It'll be better than getting wet and also save you getting someone out on a night like this."

"Are you sure, will it be taking you out of your way?"

"Not really, I live in Newton Heath, just off the new bypass."

"That's about two miles away from Christleton. It's getting late, will your family wonder where you are?"

"No, I'm in lodgings with a family friend and I often have to work late, my times are a little erratic, so they won't mind. Come on, I'm just down here, all we'll do is get wet standing here."

She led him to her car.

"Here we are the yellow peril, or so my father says."

The young man laughed and waited for her to open his door lock, then climbed in beside her.

She started the car and moved off, out into the nearly deserted Eastgate Street, turning right to get to Foregate Street and then join the new bypass about a half mile away. As they drove, he asked her what she did.

"Well, I'm actually at uni but during the summer break I've been working for Bluebird Travel, sort of helping the tour guides. It's interesting and better than straight office work. Where are you?"

"Oh, I'm articled with Kimberly and Spooner, accountants, do you know them?"

"Nope, I'm more or less a stranger to Chester, my home is in Knutsford. The group of you in the hotel, I've seen you all there before; are they all accountants?"

He laughed. "Far from it, no, we sort of meet there, we're all members of an R.A.F. Auxiliary Squadron, but we live in this area, so we meet up there in the Grosvenor. We haven't a proper mess at the base but we should have soon."

"Where's your base?"

"At a place called Hooton, down the Wirral towards Birkenhead."

"Don't know it; I don't remember ever going down that way at all."

As they drove along he was half turned towards her and caught a glimpse of her features every now and again by the light of the street lamps. He'd not really had a good look at the girl in the hotel; he'd been more occupied in apologising for the clumsiness of that half-drunken Pete Gregory. She seemed a pleasant-faced girl, much about his age, dark hair, a raincoat more or less hid her figure.

"You'll have to direct me when we get to the bypass; I know I need to turn right."

"Yep, when we get onto the bypass, we can either carry straight on through the roundabouts and join the Whitchurch Road or turn the roundabout before the Whitchurch Road and get onto the Tarvin Road; either way is just as quick."

She opted to turn onto the Tarvin Road and turned left at the next roundabout. He then directed her from then on into the driveway of their house and the large gravel patch by the front door.

"Thank you, incidentally, my name is David Coulter."

She giggled a little self-consciously, saying. "I'm Joan Healey."

It had almost stopped raining as he got out of her car: leaning in he smiled.

"Thank you again, Miss Healy, it was very kind of you to do this."

"No, not at all. I'm off tomorrow up north but when I come back, we may see each other in The Grosvenor some time."

"A friend and I are in the process of planning a trip to France and Germany, late August into September, we thought we'd go by car. If you don't mind, I'll give you a call, and maybe we could meet up and have a chat regarding pitfalls and such travelling in France and Germany."

"I should be back in two weeks, so give me a call at Bluebird Travel, the number's in the book. I'm not that experienced but the man I work with has been doing it for years. He'd help you, I'm sure. Call me and I'm sure we can fix something." He closed the car door and stood back as she made a half circle in the drive and went off back into the road.

He walked slowly into the house and thought what a nice obliging girl, she had an attractive face and lively eyes, and he looked forward to meeting her again.

She, on her drive back to her lodgings in Newton Heath, thought he was rather nice.

The next day David Coulter received a call from Gerald Thompson asking him to come up to London the following weekend. He was given directions to the hotel in Russell Square and was informed that Tom Wadsworth would be there as well.

The two men met on the Friday evening in the bar of the Imperial Hotel and exchanged details of their interviews with Gerald Thompson. David Coulter then recounted his meeting with Joan Healey.

"She's a travel guide with an agency in Chester; she hasn't been doing it long but the man she works with is very experienced. I said I'd give her a call and we'd appreciate having a chat with them both, you could come and stay with us one weekend."

"Sounds great, anyway, what do you think this lot will say to us tomorrow? It all seems a bit odd to me. Have you talked to your C.O. about it?"

"No, I was waiting for him to say something but he didn't, even when I told him I was having to come up to London this weekend to the Air Ministry. He didn't even ask why."

"Same with me. When I asked Harry Marsden about it after your man had gone, all he did was grunt and change the subject."

"All a bit odd."

"Well, what's the form for tomorrow?"

"We are to meet with Group Captain Thompson in the Air Ministry, his office in Kingsway, it's just down the road from here; and after that I've no idea what will happen. I don't even know what we're here for really."

The two friends had a few more drinks and then a meal in the hotel dining room and went off to bed early.

Next morning, after a hearty breakfast the two men walked down Southampton Row into Kingsway to the Air Ministry offices. Entering the foyer they handed in their visiting cards to the uniformed receptionist, who indicated they should sit down on a settee on the other side of the room.

After a short wait, Group Captain Thompson came down the stairs and across to them.

"Nice to see you both. Now we have to go and see someone else, I've a car outside, it'll be quicker. Did you both have a good night?"

"Yes, sir."

Gerald Thompson led the way outside to a waiting black Humber, once in, the two young men in the back and he in the front, he gave an address to the driver.

Neither of the two young men had any idea of locations in London and where they had been taken, which was the MI6 office in the Haymarket.

They entered the building and were obviously expected and taken straight up to a first-floor office. On entering his secretary's room, the girl looked at Gerald Thompson and told him to go straight in.

Aubrey Evans watched as the three men entered. He studied the two young men as they came in, he'd already had their service records a couple of days before and was satisfied with what he'd read.

After all had settled down, coffee had been served, with the two young men facing Aubrey Evans and Gerald Thompson across the desk, Aubrey Evans smiled.

"I suppose you two are wondering what this is all about. I think the Group Captain here has given you an outline of what we'd like but let me fill you in with a little background. So that you know what to expect and how the Krauts operate these days."

He then went on to explain that the main Heinkel plant was at Warnemunde on the Baltic coast but in late 1936 had joined with the Hirth aero-engine company to develop a jet engine based on a design patented by the German engineer Hans Von Ohain, who successfully demonstrated his first engine in 1934.

Heinkel decided in late 1937 to transfer their engine development to near Stuttgart. These changes were followed closely by an agent they had within the Heinkel organisation, and they received regular reports. Unfortunately, their man was discovered in an area of the factory where he was not authorised to enter and was arrested. The latest information was that he had been sent to a prison camp at Dachau, a place notorious for cruelty and the extermination of inmates.

"Therefore, you two must be very careful with your actions. The Germans are very sensitive about their military developments; if an area has signs forbidding entry, do not under any circumstances try and enter the area. Do not ask questions other than those a normal tourist would ask. Do not take photographs close to airfields and other military installations. Always obey any directions or orders given to you by a person in uniform, even if it sounds silly, do not argue with them. In other words, keep a low profile, do not attract attention. Your passports will show your civilian occupations, so you've no need at any time to reveal you are with any sort of military organisations. Hotel registers are daily inspected by the police in Germany to see who is staying there and where they have come from.

"Should you get into difficulties, you should immediately ask for contact with a British consular official; we will be alerting the various consular people that you will be in Germany and France, but only on the basis of the 'Old Boy's Network'; in other words, your families have strong political connections and you should be given extra help if needed."

What he didn't tell them was that the MI6 man in the British Embassy in Berlin had been alerted that two assets would be in the Stuttgart area and he had to keep his ear to the ground.

"Any questions so far?"

"We were going to a local travel agent to get the various details of the trip sorted, such as arrangements to take our car across and the odd hotel booking, should we require one, but most of the time we were going to take pot luck regarding where we stay." As he said this, David wondered if he shouldn't have kept quiet about Joan Healey.

"Good idea, don't change things, it then looks as if you're just tourists if anyone wants to check back, which I doubt. You said you were going to look at the battlefields first. Start in the north around Ypres, then move toward Verdun and from there across to Strasbourg and into Germany. Drive along the Rhine to Karlsruhe and then across to Stuttgart, take about ten days to get there.

"Spend a couple of days in the Stuttgart area, plenty to see, palaces and such. Act as if you are resting after a week or so constantly on the move, from there go through Ulm to Munich, pretend you're looking for the beer festival in Munich. It's a big thing there but you'll be about two weeks too early, it's usually the beginning of October, but say you'd heard about it and wondered what it was all about. Then from there drive south-west to Switzerland, Zurich and back through France. Now in the Stuttgart area, try and get close to the Heinkel factory, the airstrip is next door and you may see something. Group Captain

Thompson will give you a map, memorise it but under no circumstances are you to take it with you. Understood? Any questions?"

David started to say something but Tom cut in.

"If we do strike a problem, what would be the action of a normal tourist, who would they contact?"

"Good question. When you go and talk to your travel agency people, ask them for a contact number or person should you have difficulties. They'll give you one and when they do, let Group Captain Thompson know who and what the contact is; he'll advise us and we'll make indirect contact in Germany with them so that if you do flag them, we'll know as well.

"You were about to say something, Mr Coulter?"

"Your contact in the Heinkel factory. Did he have any family or anyone we could make contact with in case there is still information he hadn't passed on?"

"Yes and no, he did have family but they were over in Rostock, close to Warnemunde, but we've managed to get them out without exciting any suspicion. His wife was Polish and as soon as we realised what had happened, we moved her back to Poland; but unusual for the Krauts, although we've been watching his house they haven't been near it. We think he hasn't confessed to where he's from, the papers he had showed he was from Stuttgart and made no mention of Rostock. She, therefore, didn't have any immediate contact with him, and whilst the Gestapo will have made a thorough search of his lodgings in Stuttgart, he was professional enough not to have anything there to lead them back to Rostock."

"Any more questions?" This from Group Captain Thompson.

David Coulter and Tom Wadsworth looked at each other then back to the other two men. David answered for both,

"Not for the moment, no doubt something will crop up and I'll speak to you," looking across at Group Captain Thompson.

"Good, now if you two wait downstairs, I'll just have a word with Mr Evans. We want you to have a talk with our German expert so you'll know what to expect there, and a secondary item is we'd like you, David, to brush up your German, but we'll arrange that for when you go back to Chester."

In the secretary's room a uniformed security guard was waiting, and he escorted them to the foyer, where they sat and waited for someone to take them to their next meeting.

Upstairs the two older men sat and talked.

"What do you think, Aubrey, will they do?"

"Better than nothing; they may come in with something. It's pretty certain the Krauts are advanced with their engine, so there should be something on the tarmac of the airstrip."

"Now how about brushing up that boy's German."

"Yes, I'll give you the name and contact point of someone in the Chester area who'll help. As you know, we've absorbed a lot of refugees from Germany, who're only too keen to help. I'll sell it on the basis that we're trying to build up a pool of German speakers in our forces. Let me talk to Josef Mecklinger first, he can talk to them next, I've already spoken to him and he's waiting."

Aubrey Evans picked his telephone up, dialled a number and then spoke rapidly in German, grunted a few times and then hung up.

He then took a notebook from a desk drawer and wrote a name, address and telephone number from it on a slip of paper, then handed it to Gerald Thompson, who glanced at it.

The name was Rebecca Wurtz, although the surname wasn't Jewish the Christian name certainly was, the address was a Chester address.

"She's German, escaped with her family from Germany last year; she's living with her family and works for a Jewish organisation which specialises in helping Jews who come from Germany and wish to settle in England. I'll telephone her today, then I suggest you telephone her about Tuesday next, and come to some arrangement regarding a fee and then get young Coulter to contact her."

Downstairs the two young men waited and eventually, a small grey-haired slightly built man came into the foyer and walked across to them. In heavily accented English, he introduced himself.

"I'm Josef Mecklinger, could you two gentlemen come this way please?" leading the two men out into a corridor and on to a small office on the ground floor.

Gesturing for them to sit in two chairs in front of a desk, he sat down facing them.

"So you two are going to Germany, yes?"

Both men nodded.

"I think Herr Evans has already said a little about the situation in Germany at the present time."

Both men nodded again.

"I understand you are going as tourists, and in the course of your trip you will be reporting anything unusual you see. What you must remember all the time is that Germany is almost an armed camp. Germans everywhere have to report anything suspicious that they see, even of their neighbours and of course, strangers even more so. Amongst certain sections of the population Adolf Hitler is a god, usually the younger people; Jews are persecuted and denied freedom of any sort. The German Government does not allow anyone to express an opinion contrary to the government's view, and anyone found expressing such an opinion at the best is taken to the local Gestapo headquarters and kept overnight with maybe the odd beating, and at the worst is shipped off to prison or worse still one of these new concentration camps where they are worked to death. So therefore, gentlemen, although you will be tourists, firstly, you must guard your tongues."

Tom cut in,

"Surely, there are some decent Germans about; they can't all be as you describe them?"

"Yes, there are, but unfortunately most of them daren't protest or say anything. You will see for yourself the adulation given to Adolf Hitler. When the Germans marched into Austria in April, the population turned out to a man and welcomed them waving, Heil Hitlering with joy in their eyes."

David Coulter nodded. "I saw some of that on the newsreels last month."

"Yes, so above all, guard your tongues even with people who express opinions contrary to government thinking and distance yourself from them as quickly as possible. The person could be an agent provocateur trying to trap you. You are going to the Stuttgart area; Stuttgart is a small town surrounded by hills covered with vineyards, stay in the Graf Zeppelin hotel, a nice hotel opposite to the railway station, in German the Bahnhof on Bahnhof Street. They have an excellent garage, safe. Now from the hotel you need to take the Dagerloch Road towards Echterdingen, this will bring you to the airport. You come out of the hotel garage and turn left, head towards the hill you will see in front of you, the road bends a little and you will see the sign, Stuttgart Flughafen, so take that road which climbs up a twisty hill and through the village of Degerloch. Should you be stopped you can say you were looking for the Prince Rupert Hunting Lodge, which is in that area. Look."

He reached into a drawer and produced a small-scale map of the Stuttgart area and traced the roads out for them.

"I've marked the route to the hunting lodge, but if you miss that right turn there and go straight on, you will end up passing the airport. Then should someone stop you, wave the map at them and say that you are looking for the hunting lodge which figured in a big scandal of the 1900s."

He briefly told them of the suicide of the Crown Prince and his commoner mistress, a scandal that rocked German society just before the Great War.

"Now do not accept anything from anyone to carry something out of Germany for them."

"What do you mean?" David asked.

"Apart from Jews there are German nationals who are trying to escape from Germany. I doubt whether any Jews will approach you, but you may get a German national who wants to leave Germany surreptitiously. Firstly, he's restricted on what he can take in the way of valuables, money etc. if he does get permission to leave; secondly, if he hasn't got permission to leave officially other than go on a holiday, to carry a lot of valuables would give his game away that he was not intending to come back.

"Jews can't take a thing, and both sets of people try and get someone to carry say jewellery or gold coins out for them, someone like you. They use any pretence to use people as couriers, and then again the Gestapo are not above trying to trap people by pretending to be one of those sorts of people. So under no circumstances do you agree to carry a package for anyone. Understood?"

Both young men nodded.

"Now have you any questions?"

David thought for a moment and then asked, "Do you have any photographs of the various police and Gestapo and other uniformed officials we might meet so that we would recognise them? You know, the type of their uniforms."

"Good question; let me see what we have." Josef walked across to a filing cabinet and took out a bulky file, coming back to his desk he leafed through it and produced a series of cards, mostly in colour, showing people in various uniforms, frontal and side views. The two young men studied them whilst he gave a brief description of their duties and place in the hierarchy of the German scene and a brief history of each organisation.

He said that the Gestapo was by far the most dangerous organisation to contend with, and to fall foul of it was tantamount to committing suicide.

Laws passed in 1935 effectively gave the Gestapo *carte blanche* to operate without judicial oversight. It had been stated that as long as the Gestapo was carrying out the will of the leadership, it was acting legally. The power of the Gestapo most open to misuse was called Schutzhaft – protective custody – a euphemism for the power to imprison people without judicial proceedings, which was often used. People just disappeared, never to be heard of again, their bodies never even found or given back to their relatives.

A second organisation which was gradually coming into prominence was the Schutzstaffel or SS; it was a major military organisation which had grown from a small paramilitary force to an elite organisation and served as Adolf Hitler's 'Praetorian Guard', again very brutal in their methods of detaining people.

The German civil police merely handled civil crimes such as burglary and the like and stood smartly aside should the Gestapo or SS become involved.

He then spent time showing them the various uniforms and insignia of the German security forces.

When he finished and they couldn't think of any more questions, he led them back to the foyer and left them to await Gerald Thompson.

Back in the Air Ministry building and Gerald Thompson's office in Kingsway, Gerald Thompson put the blunt question to the two young men,

"Having heard how things are in Germany, do you two wish to continue?"

The young men first looked at each other and nodded, then turning to Gerald Thompson, more or less in unison, said, "We do, sir."

"Good, go back and make arrangements for your trip as if you were normal tourists. I'll arrange finance through your normal territorial allowances, so as soon as you have it arranged," looking at David Coulter, "let me know the amount and I'll forward it to you."

Chapter Six

The Austell family hadn't got very far in making firm plans for the family trip to the Continent, apart from Tom Austell finding out that there were reasonable methods of taking a car.

The family had previously shelved the formulating of any final plans until June. June had come around but from early May onwards, Tom Austell had become very busy with a large-scale building project in central London, and it was the beginning of July before he could eventually turn his mind to the subject and get the family together for a council of war on any sort of a trip to France.

So the first Sunday in July, the 3rd of July, the family sat together in the warm sunshine in their garden after lunch to finalise their plans. They all realised it was very late to be fixing details for a summer holiday in France but this was the first time they had all been able to sit together as a group.

Originally, they had intended to take their car and Tom Austell had obtained details of the services available but on the previous Friday, in making further enquiries in anticipation of their meeting, found that the car ferry service was fully booked, either they went on a waiting list or they would have to travel by train as the next best alternative.

Another limiting factor was Brian Austell, Tom and Mary Austell's 25-year-old son, was only available for certain dates for the holiday; whereas Tom Austell and daughter Elizabeth were not restricted to a return date. Brian had to be back in England no later than the 5th of September for the first day of the autumn term at the school where he was employed.

They agreed to be back in England about the second or 3rd of September, a Friday and Saturday respectively. Then working back from that, depending on the availability of trains and hotels, they decided to leave England around the 13th or 14th of August, which would give them about three weeks away on holiday.

To meet the wishes of Tom Austell, who wanted to re-visit areas he'd been in roughly 20 years before during his war service, they agreed to start at Arras, spending a week there. They then would move to Rheims and across to Metz, with a side trip to Verdun, ending for the last week in Strasbourg for a quick trip across to the Black Forest area of Germany to meet the wishes of Brian. The return from France would be directly from Strasbourg to Paris and the 'Golden Arrow'.

Brian Austell agreed to undertake the research into the detail of the rail journeys and come up with a schedule which would meet these requirements, and then after getting family agreement make the necessary bookings.

To this end he spent all of the following Monday researching the Bradshaw Railway Guides for both England and Europe. Then commencing with the 'Golden Arrow' Continental Express out of Victoria to the Dover Marine station, changing onto the steamer 'Canterbury' which would take them to Calais, and the French 'Golden Arrow' or 'Fleche D'Or' for the onward journey to the Paris Gare du Nord. Then he plotted their journey as they'd had agreed, first to Arras, spending a week there, on to Rheims, then Metz, finishing in Paris and back onto the 'Golden Arrow' again for England.

The following day, taking his schedule with him, he went into the Thomas Cook office in the Strand and spent a good two hours sitting with one of the clerks, confirming the dates, travel times and trains and hotels in their various stopovers until he had a fairly firm and costed itinerary to present to the rest of the family. At the travel agency he was able to get details of battlefield conducted tours, including one to Verdun out of Metz.

Upon talking with the family that night, they seemed impressed with the results of his labours and agreed for him to proceed to make firm bookings.

In early July, Wolf Landsberg, section head for UK in the Abwehr, received the report from the German Embassy in London, giving the result of the investigation by their man in the field. The report gave details of where the jet engines were being developed and where the matching airframes were being manufactured but didn't give much of a picture regarding timing of when the two components would be put together to make a viable aircraft. Reading the report several times, he realised the report would not do, it showed them in a bad light as if they had failed. Thinking about it, he eventually decided to fudge some of the information, using the fudge to gain more time for their man to obtain better information, if possible.

By this time Heinrich Haslop was back in Berlin in his office, and bearing in mind the strict instructions regarding information from England before releasing the report to Gruppenfuhrer Diemer, Wolf Landsberg went to talk to him and discuss the proposed fudge with him.

Sitting Haslop's office he produced the report received from London. Knowing the deputy director had received a copy, he launched right into the subject.

"Sir, this report on the jet engine and plane, whilst it contains good information, doesn't contain any timescale for the completion of the British project. It seems to indicate that the British are not as advanced as we are."

"No, Wolf, our Gruppenfuhrer will not be too pleased. He needs the British completion date for his own ends to convince the Fuhrer that funds should be allocated to his project to get ahead of the British and edge Field Marshal Von Brauchitsch out of the way."

"Ja, ja, I submit then, we really have only one road open for us. I propose we should massage it slightly to give us more time. We could add, to the best of our knowledge the two components, the engine and the airframe, are almost ready but need more work to solve some minor problems and therefore, a test flight wouldn't be made for some time. That we are still trying to get a firm date for the fight tests. In the meantime, we could send an instruction to our man to try and ferret the information out."

Haslop giggled, thinking of the confusion such a report would cause in Air Force circles. The report would indicate that the British were more or less in the same position as themselves, neither side in a commanding position but suggesting the British were possibly behind them.

Heinrich Haslop gave his permission for the doctored report to be forwarded to Gruppenfuhrer Diemer but gave instructions that the Abwehr English office should use every effort to find a date. He also made sure a copy landed on the desk of Field Marshal Von Brauchitsch, the head of the anti-aircraft missile project, who was vying for funding against the jet-fighter group.

Heinz Kern left the German Embassy a few mornings later, following a coded cable from Wolf Landsberg using the Abwehr inter-office code. He was on his way to rendezvous with William Foulkes in Hyde Park, not far from the Albert Memorial. As he walked through Hyde Park towards the Serpentine, he made sure he was not under surveillance, often stopping to admire the flower beds and covertly studying those around him; seeing nothing to alarm him, he continued on his way.

At the foot of the Albert Memorial he spotted William Foulkes sitting on a seat; slowly walking past him, he turned and walked back towards the Serpentine and stopped on the bridge carrying the Carriageway Drive across it and looked over the side at the water. Turning he pulled a map from his pocket and opened it as if he was studying the area to match against the map. William Foulkes came up and stopped, pointing at the map; the two men looked at the map together as if William Foulkes was helping him.

"You know these trips to meet you cost money, I need more."

Heinz Kern nodded but ignoring the question of money, for the moment outlined what Berlin wanted.

"It is imperative that we try and find a date the British anticipate they will be ready for first flight of the jet plane, Berlin require this information."

"I don't think it's possible for me to obtain it. I've no direct contact with the Gloster people or the engine people for that matter."

The two men stood looking down at the map, the gentle breeze blowing every now and again catching the map and making it lift slightly.

"I'm sure Berlin will pay handsomely for the information. There must be some way of getting it."

William Foulkes thought for a moment.

"Maybe the British haven't set a date when they intend the trials to be made. If they have problems, they wouldn't be able to set a date, although from what I saw at the Gloster factory, the airframe was ready for the engine so a test wouldn't be far off."

He fell silent again, turning over in his mind what he could do, the prospect of some more money interesting him.

"Look," he said, turning to the German, "I'll go and spend weekends and any week time I can get around that area, and I may strike an acquaintance with someone who works there. Leave it with me and I'll try hard, but I'll have to be careful not to make anyone suspicious."

Heinz Kern nodded, he'd obviously interested the man with the extra money bait he'd dangled.

"Good, I'll await your information." Shaking hands with Foulkes, he walked off towards Park Lane.

Foulkes walked off in the opposite direction, turning onto Kensington Road and walking towards Hyde Park corner, then down Grosvenor Place to the Victoria Coach station to catch a long-distance bus back to Bristol; this had been his cheapest way to get to London. The journey would take him about six hours, with two stops on the way.

Sitting in the Art Deco coach station, which had been opened only six years previously, awaiting his bus he thought about how he could achieve what the Germans wanted.

A sure way was for him to take a job with the Gloster Aircraft company, but he didn't want to do that; it would restrict any movements in the future. His current job with the Bristol Corporation gave him a flexibility and independence he liked. If he went to work for the Gloster Company, once he obtained the information, he could see the Germans would drop him like a hot cake. He liked the extra money the Germans paid him for the various tasks he undertook for them, apart from sticking it to the English. These tasks would cease if he didn't have the flexibility to get about, and he certainly wouldn't have any freedom of movement with the Gloster Company.

Although with all this talk about war being imminent, if war did break out, he'd cease getting money from the Germans anyway.

He wondered if he could make contact with someone living in the area around the Gloster works or even in the city of Gloucester itself. Casting his mind around his acquaintances and friends, he couldn't come up with anyone he knew with connections in that area.

Leaving the coach in Bristol late that evening, he still hadn't come up with a solution.

After their visit to London, David Coulter and Tom Wadsworth met again the following weekend and agreed on the dates for their trip. They also agreed that David Coulter would make the arrangements through a Chester travel office, Gerald Thompson had said to use a local travel office, and then he should make contact with Gerald Thompson for re-imbursement.

So in late July David Coulter located Bluebird Travel in Foregate Street, Chester, and telephoned to see if he could contact Joan Healey.

After a short wait Joan Healey came on the line, and he made an appointment to call at their office the following afternoon.

David Coulter's office was located in Watergate Street, which meant he had about a five-minute walk to the Bluebird Travel office, not far from the cinema on the corner of Foregate Street and Love Street. As he walked towards the Bluebird Travel office in the warm late July sunshine, he thought about the girl and wondered if his first impressions of her on that wet, dark night would hold good in the daylight.

Entering their office he gave his name to the young girl at the counter, she smiled and led him through to an office towards the rear.

Tapping on the door, a voice bade them enter; she opened the door and motioned him to go in.

Entering he found himself facing a man of about 60 behind a desk facing the door; to the side he saw the girl, Joan Healey, sitting at another desk.

Seeing her for the first time in a good light, he saw she was dark-haired, with a pleasant and attractive face, generous mouth and dark eyes – a slim full-bodied girl of about his age.

The man at the desk looked vaguely familiar.

She stood and smiled in greeting.

"Hello again, this is Hans Van Dyke," gesturing with her hand towards the man at the desk.

"Hans, this is David, isn't it? Coulter, the airman I was telling you about. You remember him from the Grosvenor incident?"

Hans Van Dyke stood and held out his hand. "Welcome, Mr Coulter. I remember you, thank you again."

David blushed. "Not at all, my friend was clumsy."

Hans Van Dyke gestured to a chair in front of his desk. "Please sit down, Mr Coulter. Joan tells me you are thinking of a trip to France and Germany?" His voice was almost accentless, if anything a little overlay of Dutch.

"Yes, myself and a friend."

"What can we do for you?"

"We want to go to France, my friend wants to see some of the Western Front old battlefields, and I wanted to go to Germany, more out of general interest than anything. I'd read a very interesting book about the mad king of Ludwigsburg and thought a quick visit there could be made just before returning home. We thought we could take about three weeks, late August into September."

"Would you travel by train?"

"No, we thought we would take a car."

Hans Van Dyke looked a bit pensive pursing his lips.

"Mmmm, a bit late in the season to take a car by the ferry. Most of the spaces will be booked up by now. I doubt whether there's any room left. We could try for you. Anyway, sit with Joan and give her your itinerary, and we'll see what we can do."

David blushed again.

"All I've really got are dates of leaving and returning. Nothing else."

Hans Van Dyke roared with laughter.

"No problem, the pair of you work out a schedule of sorts, we can leave it fairly flexible if that suits you, but you'd probably need to take pot luck with hotels. We can give you names of reasonable places at each stop, and you can try them either now or when you get there. Now I have to go out for about half an hour, and we can talk when I get back."

Hans Van Dyke then left the office.

Joan Healey and David Coulter then sat and with the start date and end date, worked out a rough schedule, assuming the two men would be travelling by car.

The route they plotted roughly was London to Dover, ferry across to Calais, then to Arras. Arras to Le Cateau for the British Army Guards Brigade's last ditch stand in 1914, from there to Chateau Thierry for the American Army blooding in 1918, then to Verdun to see where the French Army held the Germans in 1915 and 1916. Thence to Nancy, Strasbourg, Karlsruhe, Stuttgart, Heidelberg, Saarbrucken, Metz, Rheims, Amiens and Calais. Most places had a one-night stop, except about seven places, which were given a two-night stop to enable a day of sightseeing to take place.

Sitting with the girl David Coulter gradually realised how attractive she was and occasionally caught the slight aroma of her perfume. She was very business-like; using reference books, she quickly produced a list of about three small hotels for each stop.

Hans Van Dyke was away about an hour, and they had just completed the list when he returned.

"Have you finished?"

Joan Healey nodded and handed him the list. "Only just, and pretty rough."

Hans Van Dyke read the list, then reached for the telephone and asked for a number in London; putting the handset back on its cradle to await his call, he turned to David.

"You've left the booking of the ferry crossing a little late, there may be no spaces available, but we can try. Another thing, how important is it that you go back to France via Saarbrucken?"

"It's not important really; we just picked that route because it was direct from the area we intend to visit in Germany. Why?"

"Amongst the foreign papers I read is a German one, and I saw recently that areas around Saarbrucken are blocked off and visiting these areas is banned. In Germany these days it's better to avoid such places, if possible, because you could get into a sensitive area by mistake and find yourself in trouble. I understand the German Army are constructing a defensive line of fortifications, calling it the Siegfried Line."

"We can change that then and go further south through Strasbourg."

Hans Van Dyke nodded in agreement; just then his telephone rang and picking up the receiver, he identified himself and asked about space on the ferry on their start date. He fell silent, then grunted a few times finishing, saying. "Do that and let us know as soon as possible," putting the receiver down.

Turning to David Coulter, "That was the ferry booking office in Victoria, London. They haven't any space at the moment for that date of yours, they're fully booked, but will give us the first cancellation. The return date of 17 September is good and confirmed."

"How about those hotels, Hans?" This from Joan Healey.

"They look all right, Joan, they're all pretty reasonable, and if you don't get in one, you'll be bound to get in another."

Looking at David, "I don't see any point in making bookings at any of the hotels, it all depends on the ferry date, and you may have to switch your travel dates up or down if you can. The ferry people may offer you another date. So let's wait until we hear from the ferry people."

David Coulter took his leave, Joan Healey promising to telephone him as soon as they had any news from the ferry people.

Hans Van Dyke and Joan Healey, following their trip around England in July, had a scheduled trip in early August, taking a group of Americans on a two-week visit to Ireland and Scotland, all the group having relatives who originated in one or both countries.

They were then scheduled to collect a group of Americans arriving in Southampton on 31st August on the Cunard liner 'RMS Antonia', travel with them up to London by train, shepherd them around London for two nights and leave on 2nd September for Brussels by train, collecting a coach there to be used for most of the rest of the trip.

Then leave from Brussels on 4th September for Paris, leaving Paris 8th September for Strasbourg, then 9th September for Geneva via the Black Forest area of Germany, entering Switzerland through Basel. After two nights in Geneva, they were to travel to Paris for a stay of five nights. In Paris they would leave the coach and travel back to England by the boat train. Originally a trip down the Rhine had been included.

Back in his office David Coulter thought about the ferry problem and decided to see if Group Captain Thompson could help, otherwise they might be a little restricted in movement if they couldn't have a motor vehicle with them. He checked his address book and picking up the telephone handset, placed a call with the operator to Group Captain Thompson's number in London.

After waiting for about an hour, his telephone rang and Group Captain Thompson came on the line.

"Good afternoon, sir."

"Afternoon, Coulter."

"Sorry to bother you, sir, but we seem to have struck a problem. I've just returned from the travel agent, and they're having difficulty in getting us a booking to take our car across to France on the ferry. It seems the ferry is fully booked for the time we wanted to travel; we are waiting for them to get back to us. The return date is good. The alternatives are for us to travel by rail, which will limit our flexibility to move around freely, or wait until the ferry situation clears, which might be not until the end of September."

Gerald Thompson thought quickly; firstly, the two men needed to be independent and have flexibility of movement, and secondly, end September was too late. The information was required as soon as possible; if war broke out, the Air Force needed to know how close the Germans were to achieving jet-powered flight.

"Leave it with me, Coulter, and I'll see what I can do. In the meantime, if you hear anything more, let me know. Incidentally, I did mention that you should brush up your German. Make contact with this young woman and arrange lessons."

He then dictated the name and address of Rebecca Wurtz.

After he'd replaced his telephone handset, Gerald Thompson sat and thought. He didn't know anyone in the Townsend Car Ferry organisation but he was on very good terms with a director of the Southern Railway, which ran the Golden Arrow rail service to the Continent; maybe he could help, one organisation may help the other out at times.

Telephoning his contact without going into detail, he said he was looking for a place on the car ferry for two Air Force officers who were needed on the Continent. He was aware that Southern Railway didn't handle cars, but was it possible to have a little help with the Townsend Car Ferry people?

His contact called him back within half an hour, giving him the name and telephone number of a man to call who handled the car ferry bookings and would be expecting his call.

Gerald Thompson telephoned David Coulter and obtained the name of the travel agent before he called the man.

He then called the number his contact had given him. The Townsend Car Ferry executive took the details and said to leave it with him, later calling Gerald Thompson back to say it had been arranged.

The following morning David Coulter heard from Joan Healey that a space had been found for them and their car on the car ferry leaving the evening of Monday, 29th August, which meant they could travel to Dover during the day on the Monday.

Joan Healey said it was a surprise, they were very lucky; some of their clients had been waiting two or three weeks and hadn't heard yet, the demand for places were great that year.

David Coulter called Group Captain Thompson and advised him of the news from the travel agent; Gerald Thompson then arranged to meet with the two officers the week before they went to give them the latest information he had from Germany.

Later that week Gerald Thompson attended an inter-services Intelligence briefing in Whitehall and during the coffee break in the morning, he stood talking with Aubrey Evans of MI6 and bringing him up to date on the position of David Coulter. Aubrey Evans said they'd received a warning that the German Intelligence Service, the Abwehr, were actively seeking information about the British jet engine programme.

"You know, Gerry, you Air Force people should put that programme into the realms of the Official Secrets Act. Our Berlin desk received word from one of their most reliable contacts that Heinz Kern, the Abwehr man in the embassy here, had been briefed to find out at what stage the R.A.F. programme for that jet engine had reached. Our man talked to the counter espionage section of MI5 to see if they had any knowledge of anyone ferreting around, but they'd heard nothing. What it really means is that the programme in Germany is very alive, and they want to know how far they are either ahead or behind you people."

"Why would classifying the programme help? Most of the information on our jet engine is in the public domain. Frank Whittle's company is a private civilian company, and anyone can read about the developments in 'Flying Now' magazine."

"Putting it under the Official Secrets Act would then stop any more publication of information; anyone who's approached for information would have to report the incident, and we maybe could get a handle on who's working for the Germans here. It would help the United Kingdom general intelligence situation a great deal. One of our problems is that there are so many refugees here from Germany, there has to be some German agents amongst them, even though they're vetted before being allowed in."

"You don't think the Germans have turned to using some home-grown spies, you know people with a chip on their shoulders, like some of the Irish?"

"That's possible, but the other scenario is more likely. Someone imported, so to speak."

"How good is your information out of Germany?"

"Very good. We don't really know the originator but every now and again we get a tip off that such and such is about to happen and sure enough, it does. We think whoever is passing on the information is very high up in the Abwehr but so far has not revealed himself directly to us."

"How do you get the information? Surely, how you get it must give you a clue to whoever the informant is."

"That's the strange thing. It comes in various ways. Usually a typed note, either through the mail to our embassy in Berlin or one of the other cities in Europe. When the letter is opened, there's always another envelope addressed to Frank Lloyd on our MI6 German desk inside it. We've alerted all our embassies that as soon as one of these letters arrives, to courier it to us immediately. In fact, it was a bit comic last year, our ambassador in Berlin was at a reception in the house of one of the German ministers and on leaving he felt in his overcoat pocket and found one of these envelopes. Most amusing."

"How do you know it's the Abwehr?"

"That's a guess on our part. The first two or three notes, which incidentally only started last year, came on Abwehr paper, since then the paper has been a good quality plain paper. A good quality English-made paper, and only the higher ups can get that sort of paper in Germany."

"Interesting. All right, Aubrey, I'll talk to the deputy director and see what he wants to do about it."

The following week Gerald Thompson was having his weekly meeting with Air Marshal Burridge, deputy director of Royal Air Force Intelligence, and brought up the subject of the jet engine programme and the Official Secrets Act.

"I was with Aubrey Evans of MI6 last week, sir, and they've had information from Germany that the German intelligence organisation, the Abwehr, is actively seeking information here regarding our jet engine programme. Theirs, as you know, is very much alive and being pushed by the Luftwaffe. Evans thinks they want to know where we stand in relation to them. As you are aware, Evans lost his operative in the Stuttgart area and we've taken steps to try and fill the hole. Evans suggested that we might think about putting our programme under the Official Secrets Act. He felt it would drive any German informant here out of the woodwork, apart from confusing the Hun if he couldn't get any information."

The Air Marshal swung his chair sideways and looked out of the window for a few minutes and turning back to Gerald Thompson.

"What's your idea, Gerry, you're closer to these things than I am? I'm aware of their contact and the information is extremely accurate."

"I think it might be a good idea. Frank Whittle's people won't have any trouble over it. Peter Wilson of 'Flying Now' magazine is already feeding us information. Pretty sharp man he is, he spotted something a few months back, if you remember? Aubrey Evans thinks it might drive any German agent into the open if people have to report any suspicious enquiries they get or anyone snooping around."

"Yes, all right, make out the formal application, and I'll have the minister sign the order and then I'll get it issued and circulated. But you better talk to the engineering people yourself; they are bound to be upset. Talk to them at Halton." (R.A.F. Halton was the HQ for the Air Force engineering branch).

Going back to his own office, Gerald Thompson wrote out the official request, had it typed up and sent to the Deputy Director. He then contacted his opposite number in the engineering branch of the Royal Air Force based at the Royal Air Force Engineering Apprentice School at Halton and advised him what he'd done and why.

The Group Captain in charge of the engineering branch was far from happy.

"Gerry, we're not at war, the information has been in the public domain for years, as far back as 1922. All it will do is hinder the development of the engine."

"I know but that's not the point. We are fully aware that most of the information has been in the public domain for a long time. What isn't in the public domain is the extent of the Air Force's involvement and how we intend to use the engine, in what sort of kite. Our information leads us to believe that the Krauts are actively seeking that sort of information. We must be careful and on our guard. We realise that it may hinder people, but any suspicious actions should be reported immediately and I hope you'll warn your people accordingly."

The engineering Group Captain grumbled on and finally agreed that under the circumstances it was probably the wisest thing to do.

Following his meeting in London with Heinz Kern, William Foulkes spent a week thinking how he could obtain the information required. The thought did cross his mind that he could fake it. The way things were developing there could be a war between England and Germany soon, so if he gave a date sufficiently far in advance, if it didn't come off, the declaration of war between the two countries may have overtaken the date. On the other hand, if war wasn't declared, he would be in trouble even if he blamed an informant. Faking it was not an option. The extra money was an attraction.

He remembered from his visit to the Gloster Works at Hucclecote that at the Hucclecote end of the Hucclecote-Brockworth airfield there were several housing estates close by along with several public houses. He reasoned that there must be a few employees from the aircraft factory living in that area and wondered if he frequented the pubs, could he strike an acquaintance with someone working in the aircraft factory. He thought it worth a try, better than not doing anything. He also thought either Friday or Saturday nights would be the best time, although there was plenty of money around these days, not like during the Depression, they'd only go out on Friday and Saturday nights.

The first weekend he tried two of the public houses without any luck, although they were crowded, but he didn't hear any reference to the airfield nor when he asked someone about it did he get an encouraging reply. He knew he was on a long shot and was doubtful if the way he was trying would succeed.

The next week he was sent by Bristol Corporation along with some electrical fitters to install a new electrical substation at the village of Filton, on the northern outskirts of Bristol. The significance of the place dawned on him when he arrived there.

At the beginning of the 20th century, Filton was a sleepy farming village on the edge of Bristol, close to the Bristol to South Wales railway. In 1910 a large railway station was built when the railway from London to South Wales was completed. The area was developed as a manufacturing area during the early 1900s, and the Bristol Tramway Company moved there in 1908. In 1910 these facilities were taken over by British and Colonial Aeroplane Company, later known as the Bristol Aeroplane Company, for the manufacture of aeroplanes. During the 1914 – 1918 War, thousands of 'Bristol' fighter planes were manufactured there and the premises expanded. The Royal Flying Corps established an aerodrome in fields at the bottom of Filton Hill, and in 1922 the manufacture of aero engines started on the site as well.

The British Government's re-armament programme commenced in 1935 meant that the manufacturing facilities needed to be extended. Bristol City Corporation was responsible for the electricity supply in the area. Consequently, in late July William Foulkes and some electrical fitters were sent to Filton as part of this expansion programme to improve the electrical supply by the installation of a new substation.

The new substation was located on Gloucester Road North and apparently connected with new factories being built for the manufacture of aero engines.

The installing of the substation was going to take a period of a few weeks, so the Bristol Corporation negotiated with the Bristol Aeroplane Company for William Foulkes and his associates to have the use of the Bristol work's canteen at the aeroplane factory.

During the course of the next two weeks, William Foulkes was able to make friends with several of the Bristol Aeroplane Company employees. In talking to several of the Bristol Aeroplane Company employees and listening to others talking, he was able to establish that there had been an interchange of employees with the Gloster factory and also that some of the employees in the Bristol factory had relatives and friends working in the Gloster factory.

During the Depression in the early thirties, as one company laid people off, it so happened the other company took them on and vice versa, so there was an invisible link between the two aircraft manufacturers in the use of a pool of skilled aircraft builders within the district.

Now with the re-armament program in full flow, there was a shortage of skilled people.

William Foulkes took advantage of this shortage and when talking to one of the men gave his experience at Gloster when he'd applied for a job. He gave a fanciful story of how he'd been put off from agreeing to accept employment there because of the attitude of one of the people who had interviewed him but had wanted a job there because of family problems in Gloucester.

The man he talked to offered to introduce him to one of the foremen at Gloster and he said he was sure Foulkes would like the man and that they were desperately short of qualified engineers and electricians.

A bonus for working at the Bristol Aeroplane location was he was able to see the types of aircraft manufactured and make notes, which he forwarded to the German Embassy, giving as much detail as he could ascertain from the people he talked to without arousing their suspicions.

He also advised the German Embassy that he probably would be able to give them details of the British position in their jet engine trials soon.

In Germany, Admiral Canaris' deputy, Heinrich Haslop, read the reports coming in from the German Embassy in London and decided to slow things down a little, their informant in England was being too successful.

In London, the German desk of MI6 passed a message to the Counter Intelligence Agency of MI5 and the director of intelligence at the Air Ministry to the effect that they had received information from a reliable source in Germany that an Abwehr agent was now working in the Bristol aircraft factory. Passing information back to the Abwehr agent in the German Embassy, Heinz Kern was in pursuit of the jet engine information.

The information specifically stated that details of current aircraft manufacture and possible jet engine manufacture had been passed back to Germany.

At a subsequent all services counter-intelligence meeting, Scotland Yard Special Branch were authorised to place maximum surveillance on Heinz Kern to see if they could uncover his contact in the Bristol aircraft works. The information regarding the jet engine manufacture puzzled Gerald Thompson when he received the report. The Bristol people weren't involved in the manufacture in any way nor were they producing an aircraft or intending to produce an aircraft fitted with a jet engine. He thought a visit to the Bristol aircraft factory might help to give him a clearer view of the jet engine part of the message. He was aware that factories were being built in that area to manufacture engines specifically for aircraft, but as far as he knew, not jet engines and yet it could be possible.

Chapter Seven

In July when the Austell family had agreed on the dates for their trip, Elizabeth Austell applied for leave of absence for the period Sunday 7th of August to Saturday 3rd of September.

The hospital personnel department was not too sure that they would be able to release her on the 7th of August but would look into the nurse's holiday roster and let her know. The end date of 3rd of September was good, the difficulty with the start date was that she'd left it a little late, and August was a popular month for people to go on holiday and a number of people had applied before her.

The hospital authorities eventually came back to her saying that the best they could manage was a commence date of the 28th of August to mid-September, which gave all the Austell family a problem.

Her brother Brian had to be back no later than 3rd of September; he gallantly said he'd go with them for that first week and then leave, in the end they compromised and agreed for Father, Mother and Brian to go Sunday, 20th of August, and Elizabeth to join them a week later in Rheims and then Brian to leave to make his date on the 3rd.

David Coulter telephoned the number that Gerald Thompson had given him regarding the German language lessons, and the woman who answered gave him an address on the outskirts of Chester and arranged to see him that evening. The address turned out to be a small house with a small gold lettered plaque by the door – 'The Jewish Refugee Centre'.

A small slightly-built dark-haired woman, mid-thirties, opened the door and smiling invited him in, taking him into a downstairs room furnished like an office.

"Your Group Captain Thompson telephoned me, you wish to, as you say, brush up your German, yes?"

"Yes. Ma'am, we…my friend and I, are visiting Germany in September, and Group Captain Thompson thought it better if I improved my German."

"Firstly, young man, call me Rebecca, now let us speak some German so I can find out how good or bad (she smiled, her eyes twinkling) you are."

She broke into German, and he replied as best he could, although he was able to understand most of what she said. At the end of it she said his German was reasonable but needed some work on his vocabulary and accent. She said they must always converse in German, she would give him some homework, and he should visit with her three times a week for sessions of about an hour. After about an hour she gave him some books and exercises to do and said that he should visit her the day after next, at that time in the evening, with the work she had given him completed.

The next morning Rebecca Wurtz telephoned Gerald Thompson and reported her assessment of David Coulter's proficiency in German.

"Group Captain, your young man doesn't need a lot of work, his German would be adequate for a tourist, but he needs to brush up his vocabulary and accent. He'll be all right but won't pass off as a German."

"I understand, Miss Wurtz, but, how shall I put it, he's not really a tourist but then he's not trying to pass himself off as a German. He's an airman, therefore I think if his vocabulary is slanted in that direction, it would help."

"Yes, Group Captain, I'll move the emphasis in that direction."

After finishing the call Gerald Thompson placed a call to a contact in MI5, he'd been giving the information they had received about a German agent in the Bristol Aeroplane Company's facilities a little thought and wondered if any progress had been made in finding the German agent.

His MI5 contact returned his call after about an hour. Charles Ferguson was the head of the counter intelligence operation in the West of England for MI5. Gerald Thompson raised the issue of the German agent in Bristol.

"Ferguson here, what can I do for you, Gerry?"

"I was thinking about the information we've received regarding the possibility of a German agent in the Bristol Aeroplane Company's operation. We've known for a time that the Germans have been trying to establish where we have reached in regard to the development of one of our aircraft engines, but the Bristol Company isn't connected to that development. The information said that the German agent was passing information back in regard to aircraft manufacture at Bristol, which is understandable. The puzzling part is he or she was also passing information back about engine developments."

"Yes, but the Ministry of Defence is building three new factories at Filton for the production of aircraft, tank and motor torpedo boat engines."

"I agree, the aircraft engine is the Rolls Royce Merlin. That's used in the new fighter aircraft, the Spitfire, but that's not the engine information the Germans are after, from what I can gather."

"Oh, just a minute, let me look at the MI6 report. This says 'possible jet engine production'."

"That's right, and the production of that is a hundred or so miles away at the British Thompson Houston plant in Leicestershire. Incidentally, any information regarding that engine is now the subject of Top Secret Restrictions under the Official Secrets Act."

"Yes, I saw the notice. I assume the production of the engine will be linked to an aeroplane, and where's that going to be produced? A Bristol plane or haven't you got that far?"

"Mmmm, I see what you're driving at; well, the engine at the moment is scheduled to be used in a Gloster aircraft. They're produced just outside Gloucester, at a place called Hucclecote, here again that's about 40 miles from Bristol. I don't see the connection."

“If their agent has somehow made a mistake and thinks the jet engine will be used in a Bristol aircraft, that would account for him being in Bristol. Anyway, the information is pretty specific; that there is an agent in Bristol and he has said he’ll have information on the jet engine.”

Gerald Thompson thought quickly, then it came to him in a flash. If the German agent was in the Bristol factory, the Germans were looking for what we are looking for; that is, are we at the stage of marrying a jet engine with an airframe and making test flights? So they are checking all aircraft manufacturing factories, and as a bonus passing on Bristol aircraft information.

Gerald Thompson quickly gave his thoughts to Charles Ferguson, MI5 comptroller for the west of England.

“Fergie, if they are checking all aircraft factories, what you should be looking for is someone who, apart from working in the Bristol factory, is also making enquiries about the Gloster factory. I’m pretty sure the Krauts are after the same information as us.”

“What’s that, Gerry?”

“Which country is ahead in having an aircraft fitted with a jet engine?”

“OK. I’ll talk to Robert Wilson, who is handling this for the Special Branch.” Charles Ferguson didn’t sound very convinced.

“I’ll leave it with you, but I’ll go down and see the Bristol people as well. Ask Wilson to have his people contact me whilst I’m down there. Probably next week.”

“I’ll do that, Gerry, talk to you again.” Charles Ferguson rang off and made a note to talk to Robert Wilson of the Special Branch.

Later that day Charles Ferguson telephoned Robert Wilson, the Special Branch inspector, asking about progress over in the Bristol area.

“None so far. My men have only been down there two days, they contacted the local force, who, understandably hadn’t come across anything overtly suspicious. Then they went and interviewed the management at the Bristol factory, alerting them to possibilities. Bit like looking for a needle in a haystack. They’ve taken on a lot of new men recently, and so my men are looking at the personnel records of new hires to see if there’s anything suspicious in their backgrounds.”

“I agree, a needle in a haystack about sums up the situation, it could even be a sleeper that’s been there for years. What we think is happening is that the Germans are searching to establish where we are with developing a jet-powered aircraft, possibly checking all aircraft manufacturers. Whilst the development of the jet engine up until recently has been public knowledge, the location of an aircraft to use the finished product has not. So they’re looking to establish where we are in the development. Anyway, Group Captain Thompson of R.A.F. Intelligence is going down there one day next week; he wants to talk to your people. Alert them to watch out for him, if you wouldn’t mind.”

“Very good, Mr Ferguson. I’ll do that.”

Intermittently since the end of The Great War, the R.A.F. had stationed at the Filton Aerodrome a detachment of personnel, depending on circumstances, to monitor the output from the Bristol factory. This usually consisted of a test pilot and several members of the engineering branch; the pilot would test the flight performance of an aeroplane selected at random as it came off the production line, the engineering personnel would monitor the production.

Making enquiries, Group Captain Thompson found that the detachment at R.A.F. Filton was currently eight men under the command of an Engineering Branch Squadron Leader. Their main task was to monitor the production of the 200 Blenheim Fighter Bombers currently ordered by the Air Ministry. They were also monitoring the prototype tests of the Bristol Beaufort Torpedo bomber, due in service in 1939, along with the Bristol Beaufighter, a twin-engined fighter also due in service in 1939, at the same time, provisional orders having been placed.

Group Captain Thompson telephoned the admin offices at R.A.F. Filton and spoke with a clerk, asking to be met at Bristol Temple Meads railway station the following morning.

The following morning Group Captain Thompson boarded the early morning train to Bristol, and shortly before eleven o'clock went through the ticket barrier at Temple Meads station. Looking around he spotted an R.A.F. uniformed corporal standing to one side; he signalled to the man, who briskly marched over to him to take his small overnight bag and briefcase.

"Morning, sir, Squadron Leader Wilson offers his apology, sir. He was unable to meet you himself due to a prior arrangement with the design team at the Bristol factory."

"Thank you, Corporal."

They walked to the Humber staff car outside in the station forecourt.

"Do wish to go to the air field first, sir?"

"No, Corporal, I'd like to go to the aeroplane factory, I have a meeting arranged with some people there."

The corporal opened the door for Gerald Thompson, saw him seated and then climbed behind the wheel.

The drive took about half an hour travelling through the city then along the main Gloucester road, the A38, towards Filton village. As they neared the factory, they passed the airfield; Gerald Thompson noted that it was a grass field and probably unsuited for the heavier jet-engined aircraft, when the runway would need to be concrete. The driver pulled up at the main entrance to the factory and opened the car door for him.

"Shall I wait, sir?"

"No, I don't think so, Corporal, they'll find transportation for me from here. But if I do have difficulties, I'll call the admin offices for help. Thank you."

Entering the offices he handed his visiting card to the receptionist, telling her was expected.

The receptionist, a pretty girl in her twenties, smiled.

"Yes, sir, Mr Hodge, our security manager, is expecting you; it you'll take a seat, I'll give him a call to say you've arrived."

The girl made a telephone call and within a few minutes a steel-grey-haired man, about mid-fifties, appeared and walked across to Gerald Thompson, holding out his hand.

"Paul Hodge, Group Captain. Robert Wilson told me you were coming. If you could come this way, sir, we'll be more comfortable in my office." He led the way through into a corridor and across the top of an open-plan office with about three rows of desks, then through another door into a short corridor, turning into an office halfway down.

The office window overlooked the road outside; the office itself was sparsely furnished. Plain oak furniture, a desk, a table to the left-hand side, a swivel chair behind the desk, two plain wooden chairs in front of the desk and a couple of filing cabinets in the corner.

"Sit down, Group Captain, would you like coffee or something?"

"Yes, coffee, please, Mr Hodge." Paul Hodge spoke into a small intercom set, asking for coffee.

"Now, Group Captain, what can I do for you? Mr Wilson of the London Special Branch was a little bit reticent when he said you wanted to visit. We already have some of his people here going through our records."

"Mr Hodge, I'm sorry about that but he was acting correctly. My responsibilities in the R.A.F. Intelligence Branch cover the monitoring of the progress other countries are making in the developing of aircraft, methods of propulsion and such matters. As a secondary responsibility, I also am responsible for making sure that any of our aero developments covered by the Official Secrets Act are protected correctly. We have reason to believe that the Germans are actively seeking information regarding the development of jet-propelled aircraft in this country. This information leads us also to believe that there is someone in the Bristol Aeroplane Company area passing information back to Germany. I, therefore, caution you that our conversation is covered by the Official Secrets Act and should remain confidential between you and I."

"Yes, I understand, sir. We already have two of the Special Branch men here; they are currently examining the personnel records of the new hires we've taken on recently. So far they've not come up with anything to give them cause for alarm."

"I think I'd like to talk to them, just to see how far they've got."

"No problem, I think we should go the office where they are working, that'll be for the best."

Paul Hodge stood up and led the way from his office down the corridor to a small office further along, opening the door he went in.

"Tony, this is Group Captain Thompson from R.A.F. Intelligence in London; Group captain, Sergeant Tony Rudd in charge of the Special Branch team."

A young man in his late twenties stood up from the desk he was working at, along with another younger man, who glanced up but kept reading the document he had in his hand.

Gerald Thompson extended his hand and grasped the young man's hand.

"I won't keep you long, Sergeant, we're more than a little concerned over the report we received of the German agent supposed to be here. I thought I'd pop down just to have a look at the situation myself, not that I can add much to your search. What's the position? I understand from Mr Hodge nothing has surfaced as yet."

Tony Rudd had been previously warned of the visit by Robert Wilson in London. He guessed that the Group Captain was covering his backside by visiting Bristol; he'd be able to tell his superiors he'd been to the area.

"No, sir, we've nearly completed all the personnel files for the recent new entrants, nothing suspicious amongst them."

"Any with Irish connections?"

"No sir, we've checked that out, nothing apparent. There are a few Irish labourers working on the building sites over the other side of the road where the new factories are being built, but we've really discounted them. This fellow we're looking for has to have a slightly technical background; secondly, the thought crossed my mind that he might also be seeking connections with the Gloster factory, and they make aircraft as well."

"Smart thinking, Sergeant, my thoughts have been along those lines. I personally think that he is fishing, wanting to know where this new development is taking place. He knows where the engines are made, so he wants to know where the airframes are going to come from and be married to the engine, and when this is likely to happen. I think the most important information he's looking for is something that will tell him where we are with the development of an aircraft to compare with his own development."

Turning to Paul Hodge, Gerald Thompson brought him into the conversation.

"Do you have any sub-contractors working here, I can't see any agent taking a permanent job here, and it's got to be someone with capability to move around various sites, y'know, covering all bases so to speak. We are aware the Germans haven't a lot of full-time agents in this country, so they'll only be using one man or woman for that matter to try and obtain this information."

Paul Hodge thought for a moment.

"We have two or three sub-contractors but not actually working on the site here, they operate from their own premises and only deliver parts here, they've no personnel working here. The most that happens is that we get the occasional visit but that's to the design office by their design people. But we mostly put out tenders for specific parts and then make a selection."

"So that really rules the sub-contractors out."

"Certainly, sir."

Gerald Thompson smiled at Anthony Rudd. "Well, keep searching, when you've finished trawling through those records, what's your next move?"

"I think we'll put an undercover man on the shop floor, maybe two, and see if they can come up with something."

Turning to Paul Hodge again, "I realise that it's logical to assume that the informant is a recent arrival but what say he's a sleeper in your regular staff and only been activated for this specific task?"

Paul Hodge laughed. "When we first got the information, I talked to all the departmental heads and put the question to them. Most have them have known their regular staff for many years, nearly all going back to The Great War, and none of them had any suspicions about any of their regular people. So I think if he's anywhere, he's going to be found amongst the newcomers."

Anthony Rudd cut in, "I think another line to pursue is the pubs and clubs in the surrounding area, see if anyone has been nosing around there for information."

Gerald Thompson was well satisfied that the Special Branch men had the situation under control and were no fools, so would cover all possible areas.

After a further short discussion with Paul Hodge, he took his leave and got a lift across to the R.A.F. administration building for a discussion with the Engineering Branch people on their findings in regard to the general efficiency of the Bristol Aeroplane Company people. From the favourable report he received, he deduced that their security people would no doubt be just as efficient.

After lunch at a local pub with the Engineering Branch Squadron Leader, he had them arrange a lift to Temple Meads Railway station and caught the mid-afternoon train back to Paddington, arriving around seven in the evening.

The following morning from the rough notes he'd made of his visit whilst on the train, he compiled a report for the Deputy Director, covering the main points of his visit. The report was pretty thin but at least it showed he was actively engaged assisting the Special Branch.

He then telephoned Robert Wilson of the Special branch in London.

"Mr Wilson, Gerald Thompson here. Just a brief word about my visit yesterday to Bristol. Your people seem to be on top of things down there. That young man Rudd came over to me as being very capable and on the ball, I've said so in my report to the Deputy Director."

"Thank you, Group Captain, I've every confidence in him; he's been with me for a number of years. His work has always been excellent."

After a little more chatting about the general intelligence situation, the two men hung up.

Putting the receiver down Bob Wilson smiled to himself, thinking that Gerald Thompson was a typical desk-bound warrior covering his backside. He'd no need to go to Bristol, but it would make it look as if he was part of the operation if things went well; and if things didn't go well, he could always say he went and saw what was being done himself.

Heinz Kern left the flat he rented in Pimlico for the German Embassy building. He wondered how William Foulkes was making out in his search for information concerning the jet engine development of the British. He'd not heard from him for over a week, whereas two weeks previously he'd received from him information giving details of some new British aircraft being developed by the Bristol people almost on a daily basis. As he walked in the warm early morning August sunshine along Rochester Row towards Victoria Street, he watched warily to see if he was being followed. He wondered if the British kept an eye on the so-called military attachés of potential enemy embassies. He'd often watched other days and was sure he hadn't been followed, this was one of the reasons he liked to walk to the embassy. It was easy to spot a follower as one walked rather than ride on public transport.

He turned into Victoria Street and stopped to look in the windows of a departmental store, stopping several times to watch passers-by and look at the other side of the street through the reflection in the plate glass windows. Sure enough a figure across the street looked very familiar, he was a man who'd been further down the street when he came out of the door of his flat. The man was standing facing across Victoria Street, looking at a piece of paper as if to look for an address.

Heinz Kern turned and walked on, crossing the street and turning into Broadway towards Birdcage Walk and the Horse Guards. As he turned into Broadway, he spotted the man again walking down Victoria Street towards him; he quickly went along Broadway through the twisting streets to the Horse Guards, walking up towards the Mall. As he walked along the Horse Guards and neared the Parade Ground, he half turned and sure enough, the man was behind him. That settled it, he was being followed, so would have to be very careful in future in meeting their clandestine agents, particularly William Foulkes. Heinz Kern was sure the British were aware of some of their informants but he was sure they had no idea about the existence of William Foulkes.

Once in his office he wrote a note addressed to William Foulkes at the newsagent they used as a postal drop, telling him to keep in contact by mail posted somewhere other than in Bristol and on no account to contact the embassy, either by telephone or in person.

William Foulkes called in at the newsagents twice a week for his mail, the newsagent was a German married to an Englishwoman and had settled there before the Great War. During the Great War he'd been interned but resumed working his small shop following the Armistice in 1918, filled with resentment for his treatment as a German internee during the war. He'd contacted the German Embassy in early 1925 to see if he could assist the German nation in any way at all; his offer had been passed from military attaché to military attaché, until Heinz Kern had arrived and took advantage of it to use the shop as a useful drop for contacting agents.

That week William Foulkes collected the letter, addressed to his alias 'Michael Mulroney' and cursed at the contents. He needed more money and had been about to make contact himself; the letter told him to lay low for a while and that the English counter-intelligence operatives were active, although not necessarily in his area. William Foulkes replied with a letter he posted in Bath, asking for more money but also passing on the information that he had heard and was about to check out that the British anticipated making a flight with a jet-engined plane in a month. This last piece of information was fabricated, William Foulkes wanted more money, he could see that in the near future England and Germany would be at war and his source of income would dry up. In peacetime he stood a chance of getting away with a little espionage, even if caught, he'd probably just get a prison sentence; in wartime it was the death penalty, and that he was not prepared to risk.

In London, Robert Wilson, Special Branch police inspector, was discussing the German leaked intelligence report with his superior, Andrew Carter, deputy controller, Special Branch.

Andrew Carter had looked in on Robert Wilson to ask if any progress had been made towards locating the German agent in the Bristol area.

"No, sir, Rudd hasn't had any luck so far. His people have vetted most of the new hires and all seem to be clean."

"Mmmm, I was thinking, Bob, this man in the embassy must be the conduit for passing the information on. He must make contact somehow with the man or woman in Bristol."

"Yes, sir, we've put a tail on him for the past week. We think he spotted us, he's a pretty canny operative, and anyway so far he hasn't made any contacts with outsiders."

"Nunno, I don't expect he'd make physical contact. It'll be done by drops, by the post most likely. I know diplomatic mail is untouchable, but G.P.O. mail isn't. The only way he can get in touch apart from telephone – and I'm sure he won't do that – is by letter. Put someone in the Mount Pleasant sorting office to check the postmarks of mail into the German Embassy, anything from the Bristol area should be opened and read before re-sealing and sending on. Get assistance from MI5, they're experts at that sort of stuff."

Robert Wilson looked a little surprised at such a suggestion.

"But with all due respect, sir…"

"I know what you're going to say, Bob, it's not cricket, and we need to get permission. Look, Bob, the Germans right now are murdering people without compunction, some of them our people, some women and children. In the near future, maybe not next week but most likely within the next few months, at the outside next year, we'll be at war, we're really at war now. They have a man passing on vital information to them regarding this country's military information; it's our duty to use every avenue to get him or her."

"You keep saying her? Do you think it's a woman?"

"No, but we need to cover everything. Contact MI5 today." With that Andrew Carter left Robert Wilson's office; as he did so, Robert Wilson picked up the telephone and asked to talk to Charles Ferguson, MI5 comptroller for the west of England.

He was connected fairly quickly.

"Bob Wilson here, sir."

"Yes, Bob, have you news from Bristol?"

"No, sir, but I'd like to ask for a favour that is connected. The Deputy Commissioner wants the German Embassy mail checked out at the Mount Pleasant sorting office. All mail with a Bristol area postmark is to be opened and read and re-sealed. He thinks that'll be the method used by the Germans to contact their man. We've had their man in the embassy under surveillance for a week, but we think he's on to us, so we don't think he'll make physical contact with his agent. He won't want to make telephone contact because of tapping."

"I don't see a problem, Bob, I take it you'd have to get permission for you people to do it?"

Robert Wilson was silent for a few seconds. "Well, yes, we'd need to go to a magistrate and obtain an authority, there'd be all sorts of places for a leak to develop, even the newspapers might find out. Imagine the row. The politicians might also get in the act, saying it's an infringement of diplomatic protocol."

"All right, leave it with me; we've a man in there full-time so it won't be a problem."

Charles Ferguson made a note and after a few more words rang off. He then dictated a confidential memo, copying his superior and Aubrey Evans of MI6, of his intention to monitor and read items of the German Embassy mail deliveries from Bristol, the Bristol area and nearby towns. His justification was that they were trying to track down a German agent in that area. He reasoned that the German Embassy wouldn't get much mail from the south-west of England anyway.

He was correct in his assumption, during the first week there were only three letters to the German Embassy from that area, all from Bristol. Two were regarding visa requirements and a third contained advertising material relating to carpet manufacture.

In the second week there were five letters, three from Bristol, one from Gloucester and one from Bath. The Bath one was the interesting one, a single sheet of paper requesting payment of an account, signed by a Michael Mulroney, giving no return address and also saying the information required would be available the following week regarding the jet-plane flight. The letter confirmed two things, one, that an agent was operating in the Bristol area, and secondly, that the Germans wanted to know the position of the British jet-aeroplane project.

The letter and envelope were photographed and the letter resealed. The letter and envelope were both handwritten and in ink, the paper and envelope were of the cheap variety that could be bought anywhere. Copies were sent to the Special Branch, on receipt Inspector Robert Wilson telephoned Charles Ferguson of MI5.

"I've received a copy of the letter you photographed. It's obviously what we are looking for but doesn't help much. No return address, not necessarily from someone in Bath and the name of course could be a phoney. But it does confirm the report out of Germany that there is an agent down there."

"Yes, I agree, Mr Wilson but we'll keep up the surveillance, they may slip up, you can never tell. It indicates the man is working for money and not just a zealous dissident. Mind you, I'd never had any doubt about the authenticity of the German report; the fellow, whoever he is, has always been very accurate."

"You mean you don't know who the man is in Germany?"

"We don't here in MI5 but I'm quite sure our friends in MI6 know who he is. That's their patch, and they wouldn't pass anything on that they didn't know the provenance of. It would be too risky to pass on, then find you've egg all over your face. I sent the letter to our handwriting expert to see if he could give us a profile. He came back with some interesting information. He placed the man's age at about late 40 but most likely 50, something to do with how he slanted his writing, and educated in this country, and also male. Pity we couldn't keep the original, we maybe could have had a good set of prints off it."

"Have we anyway of getting at the mail out of the German Embassy?"

"Not really, they seem to post most of their non-diplomatic mail in any old post box, the diplomatic mail of course we can't touch. Anyway, the mail to this Irishman wouldn't be diplomatic and short of having everyone followed out of the embassy to see who drops what where, which would be an impossible task, we've no way of getting at them."

"It's a little frustrating, we know what's going on but can't get a handle on the players. I suppose all we have left is that Heinz Kern will slip up and relax his guard."

"I agree, Mr Wilson, keep up the surveillance."

Following the conversation with Robert Wilson, Charles Ferguson telephoned Group Captain Gerald Thompson, R.A.F. Intelligence, and briefed him on the letter.

"Well, Gerry, the letter does confirm what you've thought for a while that Germany wants to know where we are with the design of the jet fighter. But we're no closer to getting the man down in Bristol, according to Wilson of the Special Branch."

"I think it's a bit like looking for a needle in a haystack, Fergie, the best we can hope for is that the man in the Bristol area will make a mistake because that man in the embassy seems a wily bird to me, and he's certainly on to us so he'll be very careful, not wanting to violate his diplomatic status with an espionage charge. Getting back to the character in the Bristol area, he's lying; we don't even know ourselves when the jet engine will be fitted into a plane, we've a good idea but nothing concrete. If he's short of money, and won't get paid until he turns in the jet engine information, he might get a little careless trying to get something which will satisfy his masters."

After a few more words on the subject, the two men rang off.

At Filton William Foulkes stopped asking questions as instructed by his contact in the German Embassy. Shortly after he'd received this instruction, he was sitting in the Bristol factory canteen and the man he was with, whom he'd struck up friendship with, pointed to two men walking across the far side coming from the executive dining room.

"Those two over there are from the Special Branch Police; they've been here for about three weeks. It's said they're looking for a German spy."

"How do you know?" William Foulkes asked.

"My daughter works in the personnel department, and she says they've been checking on the records of people employed here."

"I didn't know we had people in this country such as them."

“Well, we do, bit like Nazi Germany.” The man laughed. “Anyway, do you want to come to Gloucester with me on Friday night? I’ve got to go with the darts team; we’ve got a coach laid on, 6 PM here. Be a good night, and you could meet that foreman I was telling you about. The darts game is in their canteen, it’s quite nice there.”

William Foulkes thought for a few minutes and agreed to go with him. He thought, *I may find something out and can send it by letter to them and might get some money.*

“OK, I’ll go, a night out will do me good.”

Chapter Eight

The three weeks prior to their leaving had been a busy time for the Austell family, although with Brian, their son, a school teacher, a lot of the arrangements had been left with him. He'd gone round the French and German Embassies and had obtained visas for them all. He firmed up with the seats on the train for himself and his parents leaving on the 'Golden Arrow' from Victoria station on the 20th of August and a seat for Elizabeth following them on the 27th of August.

The morning of Saturday, 20th August, saw the Austell family in a frenzy of last-minute packing; Elizabeth had been able to arrange a day off to help get them away. On the insistence of Father, the whole family had been up around 6 AM, breakfasted and completed their packing before 8.30 AM.

A taxi had been ordered for 10 AM to get them from Raynes Park to Victoria station and the 'Golden Arrow'. Elizabeth had offered to drive them in the family car, but her father thought the parking around Victoria would be difficult at that time in the morning.

The taxi journey was uneventful but slow, and they eventually arrived at the main entrance to Victoria station in Terminus Place at 10.30 AM.

Tom Austell called across a porter, and the man shepherded them into the station and to the main departure platform on the eastern side of the station, where the 'Golden Arrow' was awaiting. At that time the platform was thronged with a mass of people, consisting of people leaving, porters with their baggage, relatives and friends seeing people off going to all corners of Europe.

Paris to a lot of people was a mere stepping stone to more distant parts of Europe, maybe Switzerland and the Alps, maybe to the Riviera on the Mediterranean coast, maybe to catch the 'Orient Express' for the Near East, maybe to Marseilles to catch a fast steamer to Egypt. The whole platform had an air of excitement about it and a certain foreignness, which contrasted sharply with the English voices and the London outside the station.

Both Tom Austell and his wife Mary were giving instructions to Elizabeth, Tom on last-minute travel 'dos and don'ts' and his wife Mary on last minute household details, although their daily maid would be there whilst they were away.

Elizabeth was scheduled to join them in Arras on the 27th of August, shortly before brother Brian had to leave on 3rd September to be back in time for the start of the school autumn term at the school where he was teaching.

Their schedule took them to Rheims from Arras, visiting various vineyards and nearby battlefields. After a stay of a week, they were to go on to Metz for a few days, visiting the area around Verdun, the scene of a stubborn French resistance during the war.

The family sorted their seats out and saw their luggage on-board, then went back onto the platform to say goodbye to Elizabeth. The family were travelling first-class and their coach was at the rear of the train, just beyond the baggage cars and behind the restaurant cars. Ahead of the restaurant cars and next to engine were the second-class cars.

Promptly at 11 AM the guard blew his whistle, waved the green flag and the train slowly started to pull away, and the 77-mile journey had begun to Dover and its rendezvous with the passenger ferry SS Canterbury, a specially built steamer for the service.

As the train pulled away, Elizabeth saw the rear baggage car, or truck as it was called, with its rows of small containers fastened to the flat-bed vehicle by chains. Her father had explained that these containers were for the luggage of passengers who were not staying in France, and the luggage would be sealed in the container and not opened until the country of destination was reached, having been transhipped in Paris to the appropriate train of the passenger. It saved the time consuming and somewhat wearying task of having to go through customs formalities at every frontier.

As the train pulled out of sight, Elizabeth slowly walked across the station concourse to the entrance to the tube and the start of her journey back to Raynes Park and the empty house.

On the train the Austell family settled down for the journey, the train was slow at first across the Thames and then started to gather speed across the other side but wouldn't reach its potential high speed until about 20 miles out of London, the first part of the journey being a little uphill.

After a journey of just over an hour and a half, the train pulled into Dover Marine station.

The Austell family disembarked and boarded the cross channel steamer SS Canterbury.

They watched from on deck as the shunting engine brought the luggage vans alongside, and the containers loaded into the steamer in a matter of minutes. The steamer sounded its horn ready to depart, the scheduled time being 1 PM. Tom Austell looked at his watch and saw that the time was five minutes to one; it had taken only 20 minutes to empty the train of luggage and passengers.

The trip across the channel was relatively smooth, the family watching the white cliffs of Dover receding into the distance whilst the coastline of France drew nearer and nearer. The towers of Calais appeared, and the steamer turned stern towards the quay and reversed to enter the twin breakwaters into Calais harbour.

At Calais they were transferred to the Paris Express, as they boarded the Pullman cars, Tom Austell noticed they had arrows of gold painted on them, the fabled 'Fleche D'Or', some of the cars were labelled Rome and others were labelled 'Blue Train', which were to be part of the famous express running down to the Riviera once they reached Paris.

The family settled in to make the journey to the Gare du Nord in Paris; on reaching Paris, the family were staying one night in a small family hotel on the Rue La Fayette.

The hotel was close to the Gare de L'Est, from where they would leave for Arras, staying in Arras until the 28th of August and joined by Elizabeth on 27th August. They were to leave there on Sunday, 28th August for Rheims.

On arrival in Paris the family took a taxi to their hotel, Tom Austell leaving the haggling regarding the fare to Brian, whose French whilst not perfect was adequate. Their hotel turned out to be small family hotel and very comfortable.

The following morning the family made their way to the Gare de L'Est railway station for the train to Arras.

Tom Austell was familiar with the area around the station, having gone through it many times during the war. The station itself, whilst being familiar, had also changed a lot from how he remembered it; according to a plaque at the station entrance, it had been refurbished and extended in 1931.

They boarded the train for the two-hour journey to Arras, a route Tom Austell knew well. Here again the hotel turned out to be a small family hotel near the Grande Place. Tom Austell had spent several months in the area in 1917 with his artillery unit, which had been attached to the Canadian army and took part in their attack on Vimy Ridge, just north of the town, lending supporting fire during the several months of battle.

The day after their arrival, whilst his wife and son went sightseeing in the town, Tom Austell joined a group visiting the Carriere Wellington museum in the suburbs and, in particular, the vast network of tunnels used as a shelter by himself and comrades during the war.

Meanwhile in London, Elizabeth was gradually preparing for her departure a few days later. Making last-minute purchases and gradually sorting things out to pack.

Eventually her day of departure, 28th August, arrived and she headed for Victoria and boarded the 'Golden Arrow' for Paris. Whilst the family had stayed the night in Paris, Elizabeth was going straight through to Arras. The French 'Fleche D'Or' was due to arrive at Gare du Nord around 5.30 PM French time, and she had a three-hour wait in Paris, after getting to the Gare de L'Est, a short distance from the Gare du Nord.

Elizabeth arrived in Arras at 11 PM that night and was met by her brother Brian; after greeting her parents she immediately went to bed, tired after a full day of travelling. The following day the whole family moved on to Rheims for another week.

The city had been greatly damaged during the war, particularly the cathedral, which was still in the process of being re-built.

Their hotel was another small family hotel not far from the Place Royale, the principal square of Rheims, very central. Elizabeth and her mother arranged to have several trips to the local vineyards whilst Brian and his father, after hiring a car, were visiting the battlefields along the Aisne valley, where Tom Austell had been first blooded in 1916, and the scene of the American first attack at Chateau Thierry. Tom and his father returned to Rheims on the 2nd of September.

Brian left on 3rd September to return to England for the start of the school year whilst Elizabeth and her parents moved on to Metz the next day. At Metz they visited the battlefields around Verdun, where the French army had made a stand immortalised by the famous phrase of General Robert Nivelle, often incorrectly attributed to Marshal Petain – "Ils ne passeront pas" – they shall not pass.

The main fighting took place between February and December 1916, and the area still bore the scars of the battle, and there were large graveyards everywhere attesting to the numerous casualties.

They stayed in Metz for three days and then moved on to Strasbourg. Tom Austell had arranged a trip whilst in Strasbourg around the Black Forest area of the Rhineland, partially to satisfy his wife and partially for Brian's sake and his German language studies. Unfortunately, Brian had had to leave; nevertheless, they'd carry on with the trip.

The hotel they were in was another small family hotel, and there were a mixed bag of tourists staying there, including two young Englishmen who had been visiting the battlefields and were on their way to Germany. The Austells went out for a meal to a small restaurant near the centre of Strasbourg, and coming back into the hotel Tom and Elizabeth stopped in the bar for a nightcap before going to bed, Mary Austell went on upstairs to the bedroom to write one or two postcards to relatives.

In the bar were the two Englishmen they had heard earlier at the concierge's desk. Elizabeth and her father were sitting at a small table, and one of the Englishmen went up to the bar for another drink. On his way back he picked up Elizabeth's light cardigan which had fallen off her chair and stopped to talk, his friend joined them.

On Friday, 26th August, David Coulter put in a telephone call to Group Captain Thompson to find out if he had any last-minute instructions. Gerald Thompson said there had been no further developments and wished them a safe journey with the admonition not to take any risks, drop everything if the situation warranted it.

The following Monday in great spirits, David Coulter set off very early in the morning to drive down to Hereford to pick up Tom Wadsworth and then travel on to Dover. The drive down from Chester took three hours, and he collected Tom Wadsworth at 5 AM and then took the road out of Hereford, which would eventually get them to Dover in the late morning to board the ferry.

The trip across country to Dover was uneventful, traffic was light most of the way and they arrived about eleven in the morning leaving David Coulter's car in the cavernous warehouse to be lifted onto the ferry. They then joined the other passengers going through the Immigration formalities prior to boarding.

Once on board they left their light luggage in the cabin and went back on deck to see if they could see their car loaded on board. Although the watched the loading of some of the cars, either they had missed theirs or which they found out later some had been loaded at the stern whilst they'd been watching the loading forward.

Promptly at 1 PM the ferry cast off and headed out through the harbour entrance for the two-hour trip across to Calais.

The trip across was smooth and the Channel sea reasonable calm, but only to be expected at that time of year, a month later might be different, with the seasonal September gales starting.

At Calais they collected their car, a slow process because of the paperwork, and eventually arrived at their hotel on the outskirts of Calais at around 7.30 PM.

Next morning, they set off on the poor French roads for Arras via St Omer, Bethune and Lens, areas of severe fighting for the British Expeditionary Force during the war, stopping off at places en route that Tom Wadsworth wanted to see in relation to the war. Some of the areas still showed signs of the intense fighting which had taken place over the four years of the war, although a lot had been done to repair the damage in the countryside; nevertheless, in places the outline of the trenches could be clearly seen, along with shell holes and pieces of discarded equipment.

They eventually arrived in Arras around 4 PM and settled into their hotel.

In the morning they left their hotel around 10 AM, travelling via Cambrai to Le Cateau. Cambrai was the scene of the first major tank battle of the war, where the British for the first time employed a mass tank formation but failed to exploit the breach made in the German lines. The tactics used in that attack were similar, except for the use of artillery in the place of aeroplanes, to the tactics that Tom Wadsworth and David Coulter were practising and their units developing and those which the German Condor Legion were using in Spain during the current Spanish Civil War.

The terrain at Cambrai had been well chopped up by artillery over the months prior to the attack, although a softening up barrage of artillery was not employed immediately prior to the attack, as was the custom. Even so the use of a large number of tanks took the Germans completely by surprise and large sections of their front lines were destroyed and a penetration of several miles made, which was failed to be held because of lack of support troops.

The two men had difficulty in finding a hotel in La Cateau and eventually ended up in an inn on the outskirts of the small town. The following day was spent trying to trace the route of the retreat from Mons and stand of the British troops. Very little remained to be seen of the battlefield, basically because the ground had been cultivated since and the trenches the British had dug had been very shallow, the forerunners of the deeper trenches used by both sides later.

The following day they moved to Chateau Thierry and the surrounding district, the scene of the American Army's blooding in July 1918, spending two days there.

The American infantry had attacked without the benefit of the artillery softening up the enemy prior to the attack, as had been the custom throughout the war to date, and this took the Germans by surprise. It allowed the American infantry to make major gains of ground in what had been up to that date a static area.

Moving on the two men travelled towards Strasbourg, stopping off for one night in Nancy. In Strasbourg they stopped in a small hotel, where by chance they met up with the Austell family.

Joan Healey and Hans Van Dyke collected their tour members from the Cunard R.M.S. Antonia in Southampton and travelled with them on the boat train up to London, depositing them for a first night stay in their hotel in the Strand. The tour members had their first night in London to settle down, and the tour proper started the next day with a visit to the Tower of London, followed by a visit to Windsor Castle. That evening after dinner in their hotel, Hans Van Dyke and Joan Healey gave the party a briefing on the points of interest expected to be seen on their tour around Europe.

The tour had a slight change in transportation arrangements. The original idea had been to travel by train across to Brussels and collect a bus there. The worsening political situation had caused Edward Smith, the owner of Bluebird Travel, to re-arrange the arrangements, and the bus was to be picked up at Calais also when returning, instead of travelling by train from Paris the bus would be kept and they would return to Calais in it. The trip down the Rhine by boat was cancelled. Travelling on the bus gave them the flexibility, should war break out, of being able to head for Calais at any time and not depend on the railways to return. Rail schedules would be disrupted, cancelled or utilised to mobilise troops.

The tour party consisted of elderly Americans. Most had English roots, a few had French ancestors and one or two were of German origin. In deference to the age group of the party, the mileage between stops was kept at roughly 100 to 150 miles.

The party, totalling 30, had originated in the mid-west of the United States and had boarded the Cunard liner in Montreal, Canada, a favourite port for mid-western Americans to use. The trip down the St Lawrence River to the Atlantic through the Straits of Belle Isle between Newfoundland and Labrador, roughly 1000 miles down the picturesque river, was considered as being one of the high spots of their trip.

The following day the tour party saw the 'changing of the guard' at Buckingham Palace in the morning, followed by a free afternoon to shop, Joan Healey taking a few of the ladies to Harrods.

The Germans in the Sudeten lands of Czechoslovakia had begun talks with the president of Czechoslovakia to try and resolve the issue between them. The British Government had recalled their ambassador to Germany for consultations, and Sir John Simons had made a statement regarding the British position in the event of Germany attacking Czechoslovakia. The position appeared to be stabilising, and when Hans Van Dyke talked to Edward Smith that evening, they agreed the tour could continue but they would monitor the position.

Coming from the telephone Hans Van Dyke met with Joan Healey in the bar of the hotel, she looked enquiringly at him as he walked to their table in the corner.

"What did Mr Smith say, Hans?"

"We continue. The position doesn't look too bad. Both sides are talking at the moment. After all, this tour has nothing but Americans on it, I've a Dutch passport as well as my British one, so I'll just be a Dutchman. But should war breakout or appear imminent, you leave me and head for the border and transport to England; you're English, I can play the Dutchman and no one will be any wiser."

"But we're only in Germany for part of a day, that's the loop through Freiburg and the Black Forest, if need be, I can meet you in Switzerland should it look as if war was about to happen. You'll need help with the tour to get them back. I understand from reports that people are returning now from Europe, cutting short their holidays. Those additional people, combined with the normal early September returning tourists' peak, will clog the Channel ports."

Hans nodded in agreement. "I wonder how those two young men are getting on; they were due to be in the frontier area around this time."

"Two young men?"

"Yes, you remember? I think they were both something to do with the military."

"Oh, yes. One was Air Force, the other a soldier, both reservists. Maybe they've gone back."

Hans thought for a moment, then said, "I think the British Government has called up some reservists but not all. It's certainly put the Royal Navy on a wartime footing, calling up the Reserve Fleet units, but I'm not too sure what the Army or the Air Force have done."

The following morning the party boarded the train in Victoria station and travelled down to Dover, boarding the steamer for Calais.

As they disembarked at Calais, they were confronted by a large crowd of people, all returning holiday makers trying to get back to England. They boarded their bus; the original intention had been to give them refreshments after immigration procedures whilst waiting for their baggage to be off-loaded. The refreshment facilities were crowded with tourists, some of whom it appeared had spent the previous night there, trying to get a place on one of the cross Channel ferries.

Some of their party were dubious after seeing the crowds that they should continue, and some became a little agitated, Hans Van Dyke, with his usual unperturbed self, calmed them down and promised them that their return was assured.

The journey to Brussels from Calais through Dunkirk, Ostend, Bruges and Gent was about 120 miles, the first part along the North Sea coast and the scene of heavy fighting during The Great War. At Ostend the coach turned north-east towards Bruges, Gent then Brussels, delivering them to their hotel, 'The Mayfair', on Boulevard de Waterloo.

The first night dinner had been arranged in one of the many small restaurants off the Grande Place, and the following day a guided tour around the battlefield of Waterloo for some whilst others went with Joan Healey to see the lace-making fraternity.

Shortly before leaving Brussels the next morning, Hans said he heard on the radio that the Germans were mobilising their troops, but he understood the British prime minister was flying to Germany to see Adolf Hitler to try and avert any war.

Hans talked again with Edward Smith before they left; he'd spoken to him the night they arrived in Brussels, acquainting him with the scene at Calais. Edward Smith had every hope that the prime minister would be able to resolve the issue with Hitler and authorised them to continue and to only turn back if their tour party demanded it.

The trip to Paris from Brussels was about 120 miles, via Mons and Le Cateau, the scene of heavy fighting during the opening phases of The Great War in 1914 by the small but very professional British Expeditionary Force.

They arrived at their hotel in Paris, the King George V in Avenue George V, a hotel much beloved by Americans, first opened in 1928 by an American and regularly used by most well-heeled Americans ever since.

Their first night was a quiet night with dinner in the hotel; the following day they were given a private tour of the palace of Fontainebleau, lunch in a small restaurant nearby, followed by an afternoon baroque recital in what had been the chapel of Marie Antoinette in the palace. In the evening they were taken to a performance at the opera.

The next day firstly was taken up by a visit to Notre Dame Cathedral and then the Louvre, the afternoon was left free for shopping, followed by a quiet night in the hotel.

The following day they left for Rheims, staying there one night and then onto Strasbourg, arriving there on the 8th of September. Strasbourg was full of French troops on their way to the Maginot Line. Hans spoke to Joan very disparagingly of the standard of discipline amongst the French troops and their drunkenness.

"Of course, Joan, these are garrison troops for the Maginot line and not the first-class frontline troops, which I hope are in better shape than these men."

They were to stay there one night and travel to Geneva via the Black Forest area of Germany, entering Switzerland at Basel, travelling to Berne for a one-night stop via Solothurn and then onto Geneva for two nights.

The crossing into Germany was to be made shortly after leaving Strasbourg at Kehl on the Rhine, a place which had changed from German to French rule, then back to German rule several times in its chequered history.

They left Strasbourg early on the morning on the 9th of September to travel the 120 miles to Solothurn in Switzerland via the Black Forest area of Germany. The evening before Hans had talked to Edward Smith again on his assessment of the situation between Germany and Czechoslovakia. Edward Smith authorised him to proceed through Germany. Edward Smith thought that whilst there was a lot of unrest in the Sudetenland of the Czech Republic, the matter would be resolved by negotiation, not war. To be on the safe side, they should miss Geneva out and return to Paris via Colmar and bookings would be made for them at the Hotel Imperial.

Hans had also discussed the situation with Joan Healey and offered her the option of travelling through France to Basel whilst he took the party via Germany to Basel. Although they were only going to be in Germany for part of the day and war didn't appear to be imminent for that day, he felt the Germans were so unpredictable that the mere sight of a British passport might upset them. He was going to use his Dutch passport at the border; he'd obtained visas in both his British and Dutch passports to visit Germany in view of the political situation before they had left England. Also as they had left England, he had produced his Dutch passport to have it franked as leaving England. The French and Dutch governments had a reciprocal agreement that visas would not be required by their respective citizens travelling in either country.

At the French border crossing, point troops were very much in evidence in support of the French immigration officers. Joan Healey, as usual, took the party's passports to have them franked as leaving France but on return to the bus, handed each one of the tour party their own passport. The German authorities demanded that each member of a group should present himself at immigration for examination on entry.

Leaving Germany also required each individual to present himself separately to an immigration officer, because of the ban on members of the Jewish community leaving Germany.

Whilst the German immigration officers were very polite, there seemed to be an air of menace about the Immigration Hall. The green of the immigration officer's uniforms was in contrast to the black uniforms of the S.S. men, who seemed to be overseeing the passport examination.

Nevertheless, their tour party was allowed to proceed after they had all been examined and Hans had given details of their route to the S.S. officer in charge of the proceedings.

Boarding the bus again, Hans explained that they would be using the old road to get to Freiberg and Basel. There was a new road called an Autobahn, sections of it were partially completed and when finished, it was intended to connect Frankfurt to Basel with a high-speed road limited to vehicles which could travel at over 40 miles per hour. It had been commenced in the early 1920s with private funding but had been taken over by the German Government in 1933.

Hans went on to explain their first stop was to be at Offenburg, at the mouth of the Kinzig River Valley, where the Kinzig River flows out of the Black Forest. The town itself dates back to 1100; the most notable feature was the Jewish Bath House, a medieval structure reputed to be haunted.

Then he said it was intended that they would stop in Freiburg for lunch, a city on the western edge of the Black Forest on the Dreisam River. The city is bordered by the Black Forest mountains Rosskopf and Bromberg to the east and Rosskopf and Tuniberg to the south. To reach the city from Offenburg, they would be travelling through the western edge of the Black Forest. From Freiberg they would travel south to enter Switzerland at Basel.

He cautioned the party, if they should pass any military installations on their journey, to be careful not to appear to be taking photographs, to keep their cameras out of sight. The German authorities were very strict and didn't allow photographs to be taken of anything remotely considered military. When they reached Freiburg and disembarked for lunch, if they were approached by anyone in uniform, they should comply with whatever the person said and not argue and leave any discussions with the relevant person to him or Joan.

They then moved off, moving away from the Rhine River and travelling alongside the Kinzig River towards Offenburg. Once through Offenburg, they ran alongside the rail track in parts, often coming out of the dense woodland to get glimpses of the Rhine below them and seeing the construction work on the new Autobahn. They were often having to pull off the road by direction of the military to allow convoys of army vehicles to pass them; therefore, a journey which should have taken about an hour took them two hours to complete before they eventually entered the suburbs of Freiburg and finally the Munsterplatz.

The party disembarked, and Hans explained that the red building opposite to where they parked was the Historisches Kaufhaus, a building constructed between 1520 and 1530 and once the centre of the financial life of the region. The Gothic Cathedral, with its towering spire, was constructed between 1200 and 1530 in red sandstone.

A farmers' market took place every day and the square was full of farmer's stalls.

As Joan Healey looked around the square, this being her first time in Freiburg, to her surprise across the square through some of the farmers' stalls she saw the young man from Chester, David Coulter, and presumed his companion with him was the other young man he said he'd be travelling with; she waved to David Coulter, trying to catch his attention.

Hans was talking to the driver of the coach, arranging a time of pick-up, prior to taking the group to the little restaurant where lunch had been arranged for them.

Joan walked through the group to Hans.

"Hans, I see those two men from Chester across the square there. I'll just go over to them. I'll meet you in the restaurant; I'll not be long."

Hans nodded and turned back to the driver.

Joan walked across the square to David Coulter, who looked surprised when he saw her coming towards them.

Chapter Nine

When William Foulkes finished work on the Friday night, he cleaned up and waited in the canteen of the Filton factory for his contact.

There were a group of about 30 people of the works' darts team and supporters travelling on the coach to the Gloucester factory. Judging from the chatter on the bus, most of them knew people in the Gloster Aircraft Company, either from previous darts matches or had actually worked there at one time or another.

Foulkes recognised the risk he was taking in visiting the aircraft works, but he was desperate for more money and hoped to get some information to give him a bargaining position with the Germans. He'd met a woman, a few months earlier, a lot younger than himself – whilst he was 50 she was in her mid-30s – and he was trying to impress her. This was costing a lot of money, and she'd recently suggested he should buy a car to take them out in at the weekends.

When the coach arrived at the Hucclecote site it turned in through the gates and went around the back of the factory buildings, eventually stopping outside a low wooden building marked 'canteen'.

Everyone disembarked and went inside; they were greeted by a similar number of people, and the whole party then adjourned to a smaller room with a temporary bar down at one end. Apparently, alcoholic beverages were not allowed on the site, with the exception of functions such as the darts match.

Looking around the group from the Gloster Aircraft Company, William Foulkes was relieved to find that he didn't see a familiar face amongst them. The three people he had seen there at the time of his visit were the foreman of the maintenance section, the clerk from the personnel department and the boy who had taken him to the maintenance department.

The game started and both groups settled down to have a very convivial evening. The evening was well underway when his contact in the Bristol group brought across a man and introduced him as one of the foreman from the Gloster Aircraft Company. The man was about the same age as William Foulkes, and Foulkes went and bought beers for both his contact and the foreman.

"I understand you had an unfortunate experience here trying for a job?"

"Yes, I seemed to more or less get the brush off; at least I didn't hear from them, although they promised me an offer. The man interviewing me was a little bit hostile for some reason."

"That's a bit strange, we're so short of qualified people, we're taking on part-qualified to fill some vacancies."

"I thought it would have been easy. Maybe I said the wrong thing."

“Let me have your name, and I’ll make sure you’ll get a letter.”

Foulkes wrote his name and his address down but deliberately misspelt his name and street address. He spelt the name as ‘Ducks’ and the street address he gave as Turton Street instead of Burton Street, but the same house number. The foreman promised he’d look into it and make sure that he received a letter.

Foulkes then suggested to the foreman that maybe they had a full quota of people at that time and were looking for unskilled people. The foreman said he didn’t think so, apart from their normal output of Gloster Gladiator planes, they were getting tooled up for two special planes. One was for the new Hawker Hurricane fighter, a monoplane developed by their parent company Hawker and part of the new breed of fighter aircraft for the Royal Air Force, anticipated to go into production in a few months, early 1939. The second aeroplane was a very special plane built to suit a special engine, but he didn’t know much about it, it was all very hush hush.

Foulkes then suggested that because they were getting new designs to manufacture, maybe that was why he hadn’t heard from them, they were awaiting a definite date to commence production. The foreman didn’t think that was so, because they knew when they’d be going into production for both aircraft; unfortunately for Foulkes, he didn’t elaborate any further, and Foulkes daren’t ask any more questions regarding the special aircraft.

Thinking about it Foulkes thought that if the Hawker plane was going to be produced in early 1939, the other plane couldn’t be far behind, and that was good enough to pass on to the Germans.

The evening seemed to be a success and the Gloster people won the match.

The following morning the foreman, as good as his word, visited a contact in the Personnel Department and recounted the story as he’d received it from Foulkes, as how this man, a very experienced engineer, had tried for a position at Hucclecote and hadn’t heard anything after being promised a letter. He thought that Foulkes was the sort of person they should be taking on, an experienced man and from the age group that wouldn’t be called up into the military should war break out, which was highly likely as everyone knew.

The Personnel clerk took the details from the foreman and said he’d look into it. Checking the records of offers made to people, the clerk couldn’t find anyone of that name. He told the foreman that no such person had been interviewed within the last few months with that name: there must have been an error somewhere along the line, either the name was wrong or the man had been interviewed somewhere else.

The foreman decided that somewhere along the line there was an error; the man must know his own name and must have known where he’d been, otherwise why would he have come with the darts team; therefore, the Personnel Department had made a mistake in their records. The next time he saw the man from the Bristol Aeroplane works, he’d ask him just to make sure he’d got the right name, then follow through again with the Personnel people, although it was the man himself who’d written down the name.

The following day he received a telephone call from his contact in the Personnel Department, who told him he'd checked with the street directory for Bristol and there was no such street as Turton Street. The nearest he could get to it was Burton Street. The foreman thought it all mystifying and decided to forget it.

Charles Ferguson, the MI5 controller for the West of England, had just talked to Robert Wilson, the inspector in the Special Branch, over a matter of a group of people who'd just arrived from Germany and whose documents were being checked out. Then he asked him if there had been any fresh developments in the Bristol aircraft investigation.

"No, sir. I'm about to pull my men off the case until we get a better break, such as one of those letters giving us a better clue."

Charles Ferguson stared into space for a short time then said, "You know my policy, Bob. I don't interfere in any investigation that's ongoing, except when I think a new direction is required. I was talking to that Group Captain, what's his name?"

"Thompson, sir."

"That's right. He said they were going to manufacture the airframes for the new aircraft at the Gloster Company. Now that's not that far from the Bristol Company, a matter of 40 miles. Maybe the man is somehow linked with the Gloster Company and Germany is trying to mislead us into believing he's with the Bristol people, or it could be an out and out error. The MI6 information was said to come from Bristol, whilst I realise the MI6 informant has been very accurate in the past, it doesn't mean to say he's got it right this time, he may have got a little mixed up between Gloster and Bristol. Why don't you have your men pay a visit to the Gloster factory, ask a few questions, they may turn something up that will give us a clue."

Later that day Inspector Robert Wilson telephoned Sergeant Anthony Rudd, his man in charge of the Bristol investigation.

"Tony, the chief thinks that there maybe a little confusion by the Germans between Bristol and Gloster; he thinks that we should pay a visit to the Gloster factory at Hucclecote, just on the outskirts of Gloucester. Talk to their personnel people about new hires and also their current staff."

"OK, Bob. Can't be any worse than what we've so far turned up here. I'll go tomorrow with one man, and if it looks promising, I'll call in others."

The following morning Anthony Rudd discussed his instructions with Paul Hodge, security manager for the Bristol Aeroplane Company, who agreed to telephone his opposite number at the Gloster Aircraft Company and advise him that the Special Branch officers would like to visit.

Paul Hodge duly telephoned Thomas Williams, security manager for the Gloster Aircraft Company, who groaned when he heard of the visit.

"We've only just received the official notification that the jet engine project is under the Official Secrets Act and these people want to visit. I suppose it's to check out our security procedures."

“No, Tom. They’re looking for someone who might be passing on information to the Germans. Apparently, there’s someone in this area up to no good, and they’re trying to find him or her but they think it’s a him.”

“Most of our people have been with us for a good number of years, we’ve had a few new hires but not that number, and anyway the Personnel people will give them the details. They better come next Monday.”

“I think they’d like to come tomorrow, if that’s OK by you?”

“All right, I suppose so, I better alert the Personnel Department, they’ll need to see the records.”

Paul Hodge passed on the agreement for a visit to Sergeant Rudd and a rough outline of his conversation. Tony Rudd laughed.

“I guess he thought we’d get in the way around the place.”

The following morning Anthony Rudd, with another man, set off early for the Gloster factory at Hucclecote.

On arrival they were shown into the office of Thomas Williams, the manager for the security.

After a brief discussion about the threat of war and various aspects of how the security of the factories would be affected, Tom Williams took them to the Personnel Department.

In the Personnel Department they discussed the number of new employees with the manager and said they’d like to examine the new employee files. The manager then handed them over to the clerk responsible for new hires and left them to it.

The first couple of hours turned up nothing, nearly all were men or women with open backgrounds and nothing to indicate anything peculiar. The clerk they were with – a very helpful woman – had brought them some coffee, and they were sat there discussing things in general. The woman said they’d had a funny thing a few days ago and recounted the episode of the bad name and address.

Tony Rudd asked her to go over the story again; she said that one of the foremen had brought this name and address to her he’d received the night before from a man who said he’d been given the brush off after applying for a job. According to the foreman, the man’s credentials were impeccable and he should have been employed. The name and address didn’t appear in their records, which although manually kept were in perfect order; she’d then checked the street address, and there appeared to be no such street in Bristol where the man said he lived.

Tony Rudd asked to see the foreman, and the woman telephoned the foreman, who agreed to see them. Tony Rudd didn’t think it was going to lead them anywhere, but it was worth looking into, if only just out of curiosity, and it was the Bristol connection that made him delve a little further.

The woman sent them with a youth to the foreman’s office on the shop floor; he was a man in his fifties and had worked for the Gloster Company all his working life.

Tony Rudd asked him to go over the story in his own words.

The foreman said there'd been a darts match arranged between themselves and the people with the Bristol Aeroplane Company, a more or less regular event because of the interchange of workers over the years.

One of the foremen from Bristol had mentioned a man who was working there who'd applied for a position at Gloster but felt he'd been given the brush-off for some reason or another and asked would he see him.

He did this and when he talked to the man, found he was the ideal sort of person they were looking for and got him to write his name and address down so he could find out what the Personnel Department were playing at. He'd checked with personnel later and found the name didn't match their records nor did the address. A rum thing if ever there was one.

"Did the man ask any questions about their aircraft?"

"Not really other than general questions about the work."

"Did he say who interviewed him before at Gloster?"

"No, we didn't discuss it."

"Who's your contact at the Bristol factory? The man who brought this other fellow along?"

"A man called Tim Smith; I've known him for years and worked with him years ago. Solid as the Rock of Gibraltar."

Anthony Rudd left the foreman and walked slowly back to the personnel department. Whilst the affair was a bit odd, the man hadn't really acted suspiciously apart from giving a false name and address and that could be attributed to an entirely different reason other than espionage, the fellow might have form, a prison record maybe. Why disturb him; they must have passed over him when they examined the Bristol records as clean.

Nevertheless, when driving back, he thought a talk with the man might help and resolved to get this Tim Smith to show him the man.

That evening he recounted his experience at Gloster to his superior, Robert Wilson, who agreed it was odd but to walk carefully. Interview this Tim Smith man by all means but don't move on the other fellow until his background had been re-checked in the Bristol Aeroplane Company records.

The following morning, he first telephoned the Bristol Aeroplane Company and arranged to meet with Paul Hodge, their security manager.

Meeting him he recounted his experience at the Gloster factory and the man Tim Smith had taken there. Paul Hodge telephoned the Personnel Department, giving the name 'Ducks' and the street as Turton Street. They came back after about an hour and said no such person was on their books.

Immediately, Anthony Rudd wondered if this Tim Smith was the man they were looking for and he was trying to insert an agent into the Gloster factory to gain knowledge of the jet plane programme. That this 'Ducks' was the agent and the two were working in cahoots with each other. Tim Smith being the agent the Germans had referred to in their communications, which would account for the information the Germans were receiving regarding the Bristol production.

He voiced this opinion to the security manager, Paul Hodge, who then called up the Personnel record for Tim Smith. On receiving the record, Paul Hodge examined it closely and shaking his head, passed it over to Anthony Rudd.

"I can't see him being an agent, Tony. He's been with us since the days of the British Colonial Aeroplane Company in 1911, apart from three years of war service. He could have stayed here, but he volunteered at the age of 31 in 1915. He served in France and Egypt and came back in 1918 and has been with us ever since. No, we need to look for someone else."

After examining the file, Tony Rudd agreed. "The file's pretty impeccable, but I've seen stranger things happen in this game. He could be short of cash and sold himself to the Germans or he could have been a sleeper for some reason. I think from the evidence we have, we'll give him a closer look and his affairs."

Later that day Anthony Rudd telephoned his chief in London, Andrew Wilson. After a short wait, he was put through to Andrew Wilson.

"Sir, Rudd here. This gets murkier and murkier…" Andrew Wilson cut in.

"What gets murkier and murkier, Tony?"

"This Tim Smith and the other man. We checked, or at least tried to check, the records for the other man and he doesn't exist on the Bristol Company Personnel records. So this Tim Smith was trying to insert a man into the Gloster Company as a man from Bristol and the man isn't from there. Tim Smith's records with Bristol Aeroplane Company are impeccable; he's been there for years, a thoroughly trusted man."

"What do you recommend?"

"We give Smith a 24-hour surveillance party for a while and see if he contacts the German Embassy, either by mail or in person."

"OK. Go ahead; keep it up for a month."

William Foulkes sent a letter to German Embassy, stating he had important information and wanted a meeting with his controller and payment. The letter was intercepted, copied and sent on.

A watch was kept on Heinz Kern but he didn't meet with anyone and the same with Tim Smith in Bristol.

Tim Smith stayed in Bristol and appeared to be epitome of a British artisan type. He lived in a semi-detached house on a housing estate in the Westbury Park area of Bristol. A keen follower of Bristol City football club and out at the ground every weekend. He had a wife and three grown-up children, only one of whom was at home, and usually spent his Friday nights at the local public house, where he seemed to be well-known.

In the meantime, William Foulkes received a letter at his letter drop, telling him to visit London and go to a public house on the corner of Rochester Row and Vauxhall Bridge Road at midday on the next Saturday and someone would contact him there but not Heinz Kern.

The message also added that he was to bring any information he had with him. Payment would only be made on the exchange of information.

A few days previously Heinrich Haslop had telephoned Wolf Landsberg, the Abwehr section head for the United Kingdom in Berlin, and asked him how the search for information for the British jet engine was proceeding. Wolf Landsberg was unable to give him any further information because of the temporary closing down of the contact in Bristol due to the British activity looking for a spy.

Heinrich Haslop said the Admiral would not be pleased and said the Admiral had had requests from Reich Marshal Herman Goering wanting to know how far the British had got with their project. This wasn't true, Gruppenfuhrer Diemer had requested the status of the jet engine information, but also Haslop wanted to ginger up his people, have a firm date then use it to spread confusion with the hierarchy in Berlin.

Wolf Landsberg, in turn, had telephoned Heinz Kern in London on a secure line and had asked him the same question.

Heinz Kern had replied he'd obeyed standing orders that as soon as he suspected counter-espionage activity, he was to stop any on-going projects, therefore had discontinued contact with their man in Bristol. Wolf Landsberg ordered him to make contact again and obtain the latest position but to be very careful.

Heinz Kern decided that he was still being followed by the British, so the contact should be made by a junior member of the Embassy staff, making a straight exchange of cash for information but with the strict instructions, if there wasn't any information, the cash hadn't to be handed over.

The member of the Embassy staff who was making contact with Foulkes knew him by sight, having been given the task previously of shadowing Heinz Kern when he had met with Foulkes a few times before.

William Foulkes caught the very early bus out of Bristol to enable him to be in position prior to midday. The bus took him into the Victoria bus station, and he walked slowly down Buckingham Palace Road and then cut through Victoria railway station onto Vauxhall Bridge Road until he reached where Rochester Row joined. He walked past the public house; the time was 11.00 AM, a little early for his meeting, so he carried on until he reached the Vauxhall Bridge and idled away half an hour looking at the water traffic on the Thames.

Going back to the public house, he ensconced himself in a corner of the public bar with a half pint of bitter and a newspaper.

Shortly after midday a large blond youngish man put his head around the door from the lounge bar next to the public bar and looked about the room. His eyes lighted upon William Foulkes and he walked across to him, holding out his hand and greeting him in passable English very quietly.

Foulkes heaved himself from the bench he was sitting on and got the German a half pint of bitter, which the German sipped distastefully.

He spoke quietly. "You have the information for me?"

Foulkes nodded and reached into the inside pocket of his jacket and pulled an envelope out, first looking around the bar to see if anyone was watching. He had prepared a sheet of paper giving a date in 1939, when he said the first flight of the jet aircraft was scheduled to take place, along with details of the airframe, as much as he could remember from what he'd seen on his original visit to

Hucclecote, together with the details of the scheduled manufacture of the Hawker Hurricane monoplane fighter.

The German opened the envelope and glanced at the information, then in turn handed a fat envelope to Foulkes, who checked the contents and found there was one hundred pounds in pound notes, a sizeable sum.

"We will be in touch, Herr Mulroney," the German said quietly, using Foulkes' alias.

Foulkes nodded.

Foulkes finished his bitter and stood up, shaking the German's hand, walked out of the bar back towards the Victoria bus station.

The German sat there sipping his beer, waited half an hour and got up, leaving the bar. Outside he hailed a taxi, telling the driver to take him to the Piccadilly Hotel, where he walked through the foyer to the Grill Room and was shown a table. He was pretty sure he hadn't been followed and after eating lunch returned to the embassy, where an impatient Heinz Kern awaited him.

Heinz Kern opened the envelope and had a look at the one page contents, then quickly drafted a message to Wolf Landsberg, sending it to the communications room, where it would be encoded and sent by radio to Berlin.

In Berlin later that day, Wolf Landsberg received the message and telephoned Deputy Director Haslop, giving him the date.

"Did this originate from our contact in Bristol?"

"I would assume so, although Kern's message didn't say so, it just said he had received a report."

"Speak to Kern and ask him the origin, then see if we can get a cross-check from somewhere. I don't want to circulate this until we have another source to confirm it."

Haslop replaced the receiver and sat pensive at his desk, he then picked up the telephone and asked to speak to Gruppenfuhrer Diemer. When connected, he said,

"Gruppenfuhrer, I've received an unconfirmed report that gives April 1939 as the scheduled date for the first test flight of the British jet aircraft. I've requested a cross-check, if possible. They must be close to that date because we also have some details of their airframe the engine will be fitted into."

"Can you send me a memo?"

"I'd rather wait until I have some sort of confirmation."

"When do you expect that?"

"I can't say for certain, I hope it will be soon."

"Good, let me know as soon as possible."

Heinrich Haslop then put a call in to the aide of Field Marshal Von Brauchitsch and advised him that the British would be testing their jet aircraft in April next year, seven months' time. The Luftwaffe would be testing sometime this month, September, giving them a head start on the British. The Fuhrer might be tempted to back the jet project instead of the rocket project at Peenmunde. The aide thanked him and said he would bring it to the Field Marshall's notice immediately.

In his office Heinrich Haslop smiled to himself, thinking that a little bit of in-fighting would start and delay both projects, giving the British time to at least match the German progress.

Wolf Landsberg sent a coded cable to Heinz Kern, asking him to try and cross-check the date of the jet aircraft flight given by his Bristol informant.

On receipt of the cable, Heinz Kern sat in his office and wondered what he should do. Foulkes was his most likely agent to find anything out about the jet engine project; the others were not even in the area and certainly not as technical as Foulkes. He had two in the Liverpool area and three in Scotland. His London area agents had all been either deported or had disappeared very mysteriously. He wondered if there were any Jewish people he could lean on and blackmail into helping him.

He'd liked to have gone down into the area himself to see if he could make contact with a sympathiser who might be able to help but daren't in case he was labelled '*persona non grata*' and requested to leave the country. If he made a mistake like that under the present climate in Germany, he would be at the best shunted off to rusticate in a quiet corner of the Abwehr or at the worst sent to a concentration camp to be liquidated.

He contacted one of his people in the Liverpool area, who was working in an aircraft factory over on the Cheshire side of the River Mersey, the man lived and worked near Chester, to see if he had any information regarding the jet engine project, but he came back with a negative answer and didn't even seem to know what he was talking about.

The other man in the Liverpool area was an Irish building labourer, who worked for a large civil engineering company which was building new airfields and expanding existing ones. The man was totally non-technical and of low intelligence but was a useful fount of information in regard to the location of British airfields; however, not the man to send on a mission such as the jet engine project.

His people in Scotland were too far away to ask to travel down to the south of the country and to try and gain information.

Heinz Kern was beginning to feel trapped and desperate; he was aware that Wolf Landsberg would be contacting him again soon because this British jet engine project, for some reason, was very important to the hierarchy in Germany.

He sat at his desk, idly thumbing through the 'Flying Now' magazine, when he came across a paragraph that he thought might get him off the hook. The paragraph was at the bottom of a page on the inside, tucked away neatly below a nearly full page spread on gliding. It said that the development and production of gas turbine engines was now covered by the Official Secrets Act and accordingly, the magazine was unable to report any further developments unless sanctioned by the Air Ministry.

The editor had put this in because the magazine had always given a lot of coverage on the subject, and he felt for the magazine to suddenly fall silent needed an explanation.

Heinz Kern immediately drafted a secure cable to Wolf Landsberg, telling him that the jet engine project in England was now under of the Official Secrets Act and to have anyone probing for information was extremely risky and could result in the death penalty for anyone caught. He would re-check with his original informant and obtain from him the source of his information.

Wolf Landsberg discussed the confirmation problem with Admiral Canaris' deputy, Haslop, who reluctantly agreed that if the source was reliable, it would have to do.

Landsberg then sent a cable to Heinz Kern, asking him to find where and whom had his agent obtained the information from.

Heinz Kern in turn wrote to William Foulkes, wanting to know where he'd got his date from and how reliable was the source.

After receiving Heinz Kern's letter, William Foulkes didn't reply for several days; he wondered at the origin of the request for the source of his information. Very rarely in the past had the Germans asked that question. He had deduced early in his search that the information regarding the jet engine project was very important to the Germans, but surprisingly it wasn't the technical details they were asking him to obtain but the timing of the flight trials, which meant the Germans were on a similar track and were really wanting to know if they were ahead or behind the British development. That, in turn, meant it was the German Air Force behind the request and the head of the Air Force was Herman Goering, a close associate of Adolf Hitler, the Chancellor, so if it was he who was pushing for the information, then the information would be worth a lot more money.

The problem he had was that the date he'd given them was a figment of his imagination, and he wondered how he could produce something the Germans would believe.

On his way to the Bristol Aeroplane Company canteen each day, he passed the incinerator plant, and quite often there were large square baskets of waste paper from the office waiting to be incinerated and left under a sheltered awning. It gave him an idea that might help him authenticate his date. Quite often the incinerator operator was absent, and during the middle of the morning the area was pretty deserted; close to the incinerator building was an electrical substation for the Bristol factory.

He got another letter from Heinz Kern demanding an immediate answer to his first letter, and the following morning Foulkes went across to the Bristol factory with a bag of tools and opened the door of the substation. Leaving the door open, he walked across to the baskets of waste paper and started to search through them for a clean sheet of headed paper, complete with the Bristol logo on it, or a sheet with very little writing that had been discarded for some reason. Although he didn't find a sheet completely blank, he found several sheets with very little writing, which he took.

That afternoon he finished work early and in the centre of Bristol went into a stationers and purchased some carbon paper for a typewriter, some correction fluid called Liquid Eraser for use on typed words and some sheets of paper the same size as the Bristol Aeroplane factory paper.

Later that evening he visited a neighbour whom he knew had a typewriter and borrowed it, saying he wanted to produce a decent-looking C.V. for himself.

Then working very slowly and carefully on one of the sheets of paper, carefully erased the three words of an address someone had typed then discarded the paper; the paper was slightly creased but that suited his purpose. Examining it under a very harsh light, he decided it was good enough for his purpose.

Using a sheet of the paper he had purchased as a top sheet, he put the Bristol sheet underneath with a sheet of the carbon paper in between, so he'd obtain a carbon copy on the Bristol paper.

Dating it five weeks ago, he typed a 'Top Secret' memo purported to come from the Director of Flying Testing, advising that coming into force from the 1st March, 1939 until the 31st May, 1939 a low-level flying ban plus a ban on the use of the Gloster airfield. This was because tests were scheduled to take place of a new aircraft designed by Gloster using a new type of aero engine. The ban should not be discussed with anyone not involved in flying.

Foulkes examined his final product and decided with a few smudges and more creases, the document looked like good carbon copy of an original document.

He then hand-wrote a letter to Heinz Kern, asking for a meeting at the same place and the same time the following Saturday, in response to his request, and for more money.

Saturday found William Foulkes waiting in the same bar for the German to turn up.

The same German appeared, and William Foulkes went and got him a half pint of bitter and came and sat down opposite the German.

"You have some information, Herr Mulroney?"

"You have some money?"

"Yes, but I need to see your information first."

Foulkes hissed quietly through clenched teeth. "Money first. I risked my neck for this, and I'm giving you good information. I think Kern has a cheek asking for a confirmation of something I told him. I have always turned up accurate info. I don't need you people, the Russians would pay better."

The German's face was impassive and flat and his eyes contemptuous.

"We will be quite happy to turn you in, Herr Mulroney, if you don't co-operate. Give me the information now, I mean now."

Foulkes reluctantly handed over the envelope containing the forged document. The German opened it and read the contents.

"You said in your previous letter sometime in April, this says March to May."

Foulkes could almost see the wheels in the German's head turning.

"Yes, don't you understand, they've closed off the area for three months. The test is bound to be in the middle, which is April."

The German still looked doubtful. "So this is all you have?"

"That's enough. I had to take a big risk and search their waste paper baskets for it."

"Where did you get the previous information from?"

"From that same letter, which I kept."

The German reached into his inside pocket and handed an envelope to Foulkes.

Foulkes opened and did a quick count. Fifty pounds this time, but considering the Germans were getting a bit suspicious, he decided not to complain.

Foulkes then stood and shaking the German's hand, left the bar. The German waited for half an hour, then took a taxi back to the German Embassy.

Inside the Embassy, he handed the envelope over to Heinz Kern, who in turn looked at the memo.

"Is this all he had?"

"Yes, Herr Kern, he said that because they'd closed the area for three months, the test was bound to take place in the middle, April, and that was how he arrived at April for the first report you had."

"Did you pay him?"

"Yes, Herr Kern. I felt that he'd fulfilled his side of the bargain."

"Mmmmm, I suppose this will have to do. I'll talk to Berlin."

Kern telephoned Wolf Landsberg on the secure line.

"Landsberg, Bitte."

"Herr Landsberg, in regard to the confirmation of the British jet flight, I have a copy of a top secret memo sent out by the Director of Flight Operations at the Bristol aircraft factory, advising his people that the Gloster airstrip will be closed during March to May for testing a new aircraft and engine. This looks like a good confirmation. Do you want to see the memo?"

"No, keep it and bring it over when you next return to Germany. Where did you get the memo from?"

"My agent in Bristol. The same one who originally gave us the news."

Wolf Landsberg then put the receiver down, closing off the conversation.

He walked down the corridor to Deputy Director Haslop's office and requested to see him. After checking with the Deputy Director, the secretary signalled for him to go in.

Haslop indicated he should sit and continued writing for about five minutes; he then put his pen down and looked up expectantly at Wolf Landsberg.

"Yes, Wolf, you have something important?"

"Yes, Herr Director, Kern in London reports he has a copy of a British memo which confirms that the date for the British trial is sometime in April next year."

"What's the origin of the memo?"

"I think it came via the original agent, the one who first gave out the news of the test."

"That sounds like someone marking their own book, as the English say. Whilst I'll accept it, I have my reservations, but we'll use it to convince the Gruppenfuhrer."

Chapter Ten

Elizabeth Austell and her father Tom Austell had pleasant few drinks with the two Englishmen they had met in the bar of the hotel in Strasburg that evening, and next morning Elizabeth stopped to talk to them as the two settled their hotel account. She was walking back to her room through the foyer of the small hotel after breakfast and had left her parents at the breakfast table when she saw them at the desk.

"You two away this morning?"

David Coulter answered her, "Yes, we're hoping to go through Karlsruhe and on to Stuttgart to see the home of the mad king Ludwig but also a hunting lodge near Boblingen, the scene of a great scandal before The Great War. I came across it in a book and as we were going near there, I thought a visit would be interesting. When are you going?"

"I think we're here until the 10th of September, then we go to Colmar and Paris. But I think we're doing a trip into Germany the day after next, just to have a look at the Black Forest."

"We should be in Freiberg in the Black Forest on the 9th or 10th, we may see you. We'll watch out for you that day."

"I'll look forward to it. Have a safe journey. Goodbye."

David Coulter and Tom Wadsworth set off in their car, heading towards Karlsruhe. They crossed the frontier into Germany at Kehl and were questioned by the German Immigration Officer as to the reason for their visit and their intended route.

David Coulter showed him the map given to them before they had left England by the Automobile Association, marked on it was a recommended route. The route ran along the German side of the Rhine to Karlsruhe, then turning east to Pforzheim and on to Stuttgart, a distance of about 80 miles.

The Immigration Officer also asked where they intended to stay in Stuttgart and their reason for going there. Again David Coulter showed him the list of recommended hotels given to them by the travel agent in Chester, with the Graf Zeppelin Hotel marked with a star. He also showed him a book on Ludwigsburg and the surrounding district, explaining he was interested in the history of the place and his friend was a surveyor and keenly interested in architecture and why buildings, particularly old palaces, were located in certain places.

The dark-blue uniformed Gestapo officer sitting with the immigration officer listened with interest at first and then lost interest, muttering to the immigration officer, "Student tourists."

The officer stamped their passports and wished them a safe journey, and the two men set off in high spirits towards Karlsruhe.

On the 40-mile trip to Karlsruhe they were passed, going in the opposite direction, by several convoys of German Army lorries, some with soldiers on-board and others with the back flaps down, concealing the contents. About ten miles from Karlsruhe, they were pulled off the road by a police car, which had come up behind them very fast, and had their passports examined and were questioned as to where they were going. The police were in the black uniforms of the Security Police; the two friends guessed it was because their car had English registration plates and so was easily spotted as an English car. Just on the outskirts of Karlsruhe, they passed a group of grey-green tracked army vehicles towing very low trailers, each with a tarpaulin covered tank of some sort on it.

After they had passed them, Tom Wadsworth remarked to David that the German Army appeared to have learnt its lesson and was transporting the tanks by trailer. When they'd invaded Austria last year, so many of their tanks had broken down, very few arrived in the Austrian capital to make a show of strength.

In actual fact, the group the two saw were an experimental battleground recovery unit to be used to rescue tanks from a battlefield, refurbish them and send them back into battle.

The two were able to miss the centre of Karlsruhe and using part of the newly constructed autobahn, they were able to turn east and travel towards Pforzheim.

On leaving Pforzheim, they took a wrong turning and ended up ten miles south of Stuttgart at Sindelfingen. They stopped on the outskirts of Sindelfingen, asking a policeman directions for Stuttgart; before he gave them directions, he first asked for their passports and where they were going to stay.

As they headed north out of Sindelfingen, travelling towards Stuttgart just out of the town, they saw signs pointing to the airport (Stuttgart Flughafen).

Stuttgart lay in a valley and the hills around were covered in vineyards, the road from Sindelfingen dropped down a steep twisting hill into the centre of the city. Their hotel, The Graf Zeppelin, was located on Bahnhof Strasse, opposite to the railway station, and they found parking for their car at the rear in the hotel car park.

On checking in for two nights, they gave their next destination as Freiburg in the Black Forest area of Baden-Wurttemberg. As they waited for the lift, David Coulter saw a man in plain clothes – who had been sitting in the foyer – walk across to the reception desk and speak to the clerk, who turned the hotel register around so the man could read it. David guessed he was checking on them for some reason, maybe just because they were tourists; that coupled with the questioning the policeman in Sindelfingen had given them, he realised that the briefing Josef Mecklinger had given them in London was true. Germany was a very much policed state, and he also realised they would have to be very careful out at the airport.

The following morning after breakfast, the two men went for a walk around the shopping area of Stuttgart, more to discuss in private and in the open air their plans for the two days they were in Stuttgart. They were very conscious now of the amount of surveillance the Germans had in place and were not sure that there wouldn't be some form of microphone in their hotel room or they wouldn't be overheard in the hotel public rooms such as the lounge.

David Coulter was of the opinion they should move out to the airport on a scouting expedition that morning, then go back later in the day, making sure that they weren't followed. They didn't expect they would be followed but had to make sure. Not that it mattered to a great extent, they would adopt the cloak of being tourists, after all the German Third Reich wanted the foreign currency tourists brought. David Coulter also said that they should go out the next day as early as possible, assuming the Germans would do any aircraft tests early to take advantage of the still early morning air.

The two men walked back to their hotel, and David approached the hotel reception for directions to reach the Magyarhof Hunting Lodge at Maulesruhle. The clerk didn't seem to have heard of the hunting lodge but directed them how to get to Maulesruhle and told them to ask there.

David Coulter and Tom Wadsworth, after leaving the hotel car park around 5 AM, missed the turning for Leinfelden, the nearest place of any size to Maulesruhle, and ended up on the Sindelfingen road again. They were able to take a turning, which took them to back to Leinfelden, but wasted half an hour of their time.

The two aircraft promised by the Heinkel factory at Warnemunde to be delivered by the end of June failed to materialise until nearly the end of July; consequently, the whole programme was set back a month. When they came to fit the engine into the airframe, they found the airframe had been designed around the second generation of HeS Turbo jet; not that there was a great deal of difference between the second and third generations of engine, but some of the holes for the securing bolts had to be re-positioned, causing a further delay.

To cover himself, Klaus Brendel made sure he sent a report to Gruppenfuhrer Diemer cataloguing the list of delays and errors, none, of course, were due to him.

Therefore, it was mid-August before the engine and the airframe were married together satisfactorily and the engine tested in situ in the plane in the newly built special hangar. This was reported to the Gruppenfuhrer, who had been almost daily telephoning Dr Brendel for progress reports and exhorting him to speed up the process. Dr Brendel was moving as fast as he dared, knowing that a mistake which might cause a delay could also cause him to be relegated to the backwaters of the Reich Development Authority or even worse, a summary dismissal.

He wasn't very happy with the engine tests, it showed a tendency to run faster for no apparent reason, which if it did in the air, would be fatal for both the pilot and the plane.

Meanwhile in Berlin, Gruppenfuhrer Diemer was doing his best to sabotage the work of Field Marshal Von Brauchitsch and the field marshal's Peenmunde

Project by spreading false information regarding the reliability of the rocket-assisted munitions. The consequences were that both projects became subjected to delays. Admiral Canaris' deputy monitoring both projects through their network was highly amused at the fact that both organisations were fighting each other and he didn't have to do anything to cause delays.

By the end of August, Klaus Brendel was satisfied that they could proceed with the outdoor stationary tests just prior to having it taxi around the perimeter track. In the last week in August, the He 178 was pushed out onto the concrete apron in front of the hangar and the pilot Sturmbannfuhrer Max Dietz climbed into the cockpit. He'd already familiarised himself with the controls of the plane in the hangar, but this was the first time he was going to control the plane and engine himself, as opposed to the engineering people.

Dr Brendel and his team watched as Max Dietz gave the signal to the ground mechanic to start the engine; after a few coughs, the engine roared into life and he settled it down to a steady hum as he waited for the instruments to tell him the engine had reached its operating temperature.

Once the engine reached the correct operating temperature, he slowly moved the throttle forward and increased the power, then brought it back down again, shutting the engine off and climbing out of the cockpit.

"It seems to be operating well, Herr Doctor, I think we can move to the test bay and try more power."

The engine intake was in the nose of the plane and the exhaust outlet at the very rear, the thrust from the jet engine exhaust was tremendous, and so to limit the effect of these gases, Dr Brendel had a special bay constructed to take the shock of the gases from the exhaust and limit the noise.

Dr Brendel gave the orders to the ground crew, and the plane was pushed into the bay. Once again Max Dietz climbed into the cockpit and the engine re-started, this time he increased the power to the halfway mark, letting it run for about ten minutes before shutting it down to the idling mode.

Dr Brendel and one of his team climbed onto the wing to watch the instruments as the engine ran at idling speed and every five minutes or so, Max Dietz would run it up.

After about an hour of this, Dr Brendel gave the order to shut down the engine and after letting it cool off, had his team examine it.

The following two days they did the same thing, until they were satisfied that the engine was performing well, and Dr Brendel gave the clearance to start the taxi trials along the runway.

By the end of the first week in September, Dr Brendel was able to report to Gruppenfuhrer Diemer that the engine and aeroplane had performed well taxiing along the runway, that Test Pilot Max Dietz was happy, and they expected to make their first flight shortly – which would be a series of hops along the runway prior to taking-off and making a circuit of the airfield.

Towards evening of the final day of the runway taxiing, the test pilot was taxiing the aircraft back along the taxiway, a concrete road parallel to the runway, and glanced to his right across the perimeter road to the trees beyond and thought he caught the reflection of the sun on what – in after thought – were field glasses. He stopped the plane outside the hangar and climbed out, Klaus Brendel's team took charge of the aircraft, and he walked slowly across to the pilot's changing room. It wasn't until he'd stripped his flying suit off and had changed into his Luftwaffe uniform that he realised the significance of the field glasses. Someone was watching the airfield and the tests of the jet plane, maybe taking photographs.

He quickly walked to the office of Erich Linhard, Chief of Security, but the man wasn't in his office, so he went out onto the apron in front of the hangar and asked where the security people were. Fortunately, their patrol vehicle came into view after completing a circuit of the field.

He reported his suspicions to the sergeant in charge, who immediately drove to the section of the perimeter fence where Max Dietz thought he'd seen the glasses.

The sergeant and the man with him walked up close to the perimeter fence and peered into the trees but found no one or anything that looked at all suspicious. Then, driving back to the main entrance of the factory, went out onto the road around to the place on the other side of the perimeter fence, but other than a series of wheel tracks, most of them old in the dirt where vehicles had pulled off the highway, found nothing else. They returned and reported to Max Dietz that there appeared to be nothing or anyone in the trees but that they would report his concerns.

The following morning Erich Linhard received their negative report on his desk; he read it but didn't attach much importance to it, he thought it might have been the reflection of the setting sun on a car windscreen.

That same morning Max Dietz, the pilot, was talking to Klaus Brendel prior to going to the aircraft and mentioned the incident. Dr Brendel looked a little startled and reached for his telephone, asking Erich Linhard to come to him. Dr Brendel's concern was not that a foreign agent might be watching but someone from Field Marshal Von Brauchitsch's office might be spying to make a report on their progress to the Field Marshall.

Eric Linhard appeared at his doorway.

"Linhard, Sturmbannfuhrer Dietz tells me he thought someone has been watching our tests, I thought you had assured me that the security was good on that part of the perimeter."

"Ja. Herr Doctor, I've just seen the report myself. I'll put a vehicle on the outside as well."

"Linhard, I want everyone caught in those trees to be arrested and brought here. I don't care what they are doing or who they say they are; everyone, do you understand me?"

"Ja, Herr Doctor, perfectly." Erich Linhard clicked his heels as he spoke and then left the office.

"You know, Dietz, these country people around here have no sense of the importance of our project and that man Linhard is a prime example. Earlier this year, I pointed out to him the weakness of the security due to that patch of trees but he just ignored it."

Then he and Max Dietz went on to talk about the proposed programme of short hops down the runway for that day. They agreed that he would take the aircraft and move down the runway to take it off the ground a few feet, then back down again, each time returning to the hangar. This he should do four or five times, after which the design team would again check it out, and if all was well, he would then do a low level circuit of the airfield. Then in the afternoon, he would make a half an hour's flight in the area west of Stuttgart because it was sparsely populated and less people would see it.

Gerhard Schmitz, a bread deliveryman from the bakery in the village of Birkach, had just made a delivery to the Heinkel factory canteen and was leaving the factory. As he neared the main gate, he caught a glimpse of a strange aircraft near the hangar. He was an avid aviation buff and had served in the Luftwaffe for his compulsory military service. He was therefore curious when he saw this aircraft; it didn't seem to have a propeller, just a big hole in the nose, no place to fit a propeller. After he'd turned onto the Neuhausen Road returning to Birkach, he pulled off into a group of trees and sat watching this strange aeroplane. He first thought the ground crew must be going to fit an engine into the hole in the front, but that sort of operation was normally done in a hangar, and then realised it wasn't really large enough to take an engine. It already seemed to be filled by strips of something running from the outer rim to a hub in the centre, rather like a turbine. It was a high-wing monoplane, with what looked like a fixed undercarriage, a most peculiar-looking plane.

Eric Linhard walked back to his office cursing the jumped up jackanapes he'd just left and called his second-in-command in.

"Willhelm, put together another motorised patrol and get them to circle the airfield on the outside of the fence, and tell them to pay particular attention to that patch of woodland on the Sindelfingen road. If they find anyone in there, it doesn't matter who they say they are, bring them in for questioning. The good doctor says someone was spying on his machine yesterday. Off you go, man, and get it underway now, quickly."

Erich Linhard's second-in-command walked quickly to the security office and called two men, giving them instructions to take a vehicle and patrol on the outside of the perimeter fence and bring in anyone they find parked in a position from which they can see the airstrip. Taking a small Volkswagen truck, the two men drove out through the gates onto the Neuhausen–Sindelfingen road turning towards Neuhausen. As they approached the group of trees between the road and the perimeter fence, they spotted a small van parked by the side of the road and pulled up alongside it. One security guard got out, whilst the other covered the driver of the van with his Luger.

The security guard on the road walked around to the driver's side of the van and opened the door.

"Where are you from? What are you doing here? Papers please." Holding the door with one hand and stretching the other towards the driver.

"I'm Gerhard Schmitz from Kubel's bakery in Birkach. I'm on my way back, I've just been to the Heinkel factory and saw that aircraft over there and wondered what it was, I did my service in the Luftwaffe, but I never saw anything like that."

The guard examined the man's identification papers and confirmed who he was; he turned to the other guard, who was still in the Volkswagen.

"These papers check out. He seems clear."

"That's not what our orders are. We are to take anyone back we find."

"Yes, but this man is a bread deliveryman. It's stupid to take him back. We don't know who else is in these trees, there could be other people."

The driver of the Volkswagen turned to the deliveryman.

"Have you seen anyone else here?"

"No, but I've not long arrived. I've only just left the factory."

"We better take him in and come back." The security guard standing by the van walked around to the opposite side and climbed in beside the deliveryman.

"Go back to the factory." The deliveryman started the van and turned, following the Volkswagen, which had already turned and was going in direction of the factory gates.

Arriving at the factory gate, the Volkswagen turned again, allowing the van to pass and stop just inside the gate. The security guard and van driver got out and went into the guardhouse.

"Telephone the chief and tell him we found this man in the trees watching the new aeroplane. We'll go back on station." He walked back out to the Volkswagen, and they moved off towards the Sindelfingen road and the trees. They stopped where the short drive from the factory joined the Sindelfingen road, and a small low slung saloon car passed in front of them, going towards Sindelfingen.

"See that. That's an English car. I wonder where he's been." The driver said as he turned the Volkswagen towards Neuhausen.

"Probably a tourist setting off for his day. Take it slowly passing the trees, so we can see if anyone is there."

The driver moved the Volkswagen very slowly while passing the fringe of trees.

"I think we need to search on foot, in some of those areas there the trees and scrub is pretty thick." The driver slowed almost to a stop by an area where tyre marks on the sandy soil seemed to indicate a vehicle had moved off the road. The driver was about to say something when his partner impatiently said.

"Don't be silly, Jens, we'd see their vehicle. They'd need one to get here and would have to leave it by the roadside. Come on, drive up there, there's nothing here. This is all the other patrol found yesterday; just a few wheel marks."

The driver moved the Volkswagen along at a faster pace towards the eastern end of the airstrip.

Later that morning after fruitlessly circling the airstrip regularly, they returned to the security office once they saw the jet aircraft moved back into the hangar.

The sergeant in the office told them that Herr Linhard wanted to see them and to go to his office.

Erich Linhard looked up as the two men entered.

"Bit of a wild goose chase? Nothing out there to indicate someone was spying?"

"No, sir. No vehicles other than the bread deliveryman. Several vehicles passed but no one stopped."

"Did you look in the bushes to see if there were any traces of someone being in there watching?"

The driver started to say something when the other man cut in. "No sir, we searched thoroughly, there were some tyre tracks, but they were just off the road as if someone had pulled in, but they were old."

"All right, dismissed."

The two men went out, and out of earshot of the office started a furious argument.

"I told you we should have looked on foot. You lied in there."

"What's it matter, he'd have sent us out again, and I'm hungry, I want my morning break. There was nothing there in the trees."

"We don't know. After our break, we'll go out again and see."

The two men took their break and telling the sergeant that Herr Linhard wanted them to have a look in the trees again, went back onto the Sindelfingen road, slowly driving along until they reached the place where they had seen the tyre tracks earlier. Pulling off the road, the two then left their vehicle and followed the tracks into the trees. It could be seen a vehicle had been driven between the trees at an angle to the road of about 30 degrees and stopped behind a thick patch of scrub, which would have shielded it from the road. It was also shielded from the runway by another patch of heavy scrub and anyone wanting to see the activity on the runway would have had to get closer to the chain link fence of the perimeter.

There wasn't much to be seen near the perimeter fence, a few scuff marks in the sandy soil, which could have come from anything.

"Nothing to indicate that these tyre tracks were part of a spying mission, Jens, they can't see the runway from here, so it was probably a couple having sex, a nice little hideaway for it."

Back at the factory Erich Linhard telephoned Dr Brendel and reported his men had searched everywhere on the other side of the perimeter fence and hadn't found any trace of a spy. Maybe the pilot had been mistaken and had seen that sun reflecting off something else other than a pair of field glasses.

The two men returned to the factory for further instructions.

Meanwhile, Erich Linhard wrote up a report for Dr Brendel, giving details and emphasising the age of the wheel tracks and dismissing the idea that someone was spying. The flicker of light that the pilot had reported as a reflection from some field glasses; in his write up Erich Linhard passed off as a reflection from some glass. There were a few broken bottles in that area and as the aircraft moved down the runway, a shaft of light from the early morning sun could have glanced off a shard of glass.

Dr Brendel received the report later that morning, after reading it, he telephoned Erich Linhard and ordered him to keep the patrol on the outside during the period the aircraft was out on the runway each day. Eric Linhard was to liaise with the flight office for a schedule.

Dr Brendel's problem was although he half believed the report Erich Linhard had sent him, he also wondered if Field Marshal Von Brauchitsch's people were spying. The thought didn't cross his mind that there could be a foreign agent spying on him and his work. He also threatened that if there was someone out there and Erich Linhard's men didn't flush him out, he'd personally see that the man guilty of missing him was sent to a labour camp.

Following the telephone call from Dr Brendel, Erich Linhard called his men together and gave them a briefing on the importance of the jet plane project but also on the need for tight security around the perimeter fence. Any breakdown in the fence security would mean that the personnel guilty of being slack could be shipped off to a labour camp. Whilst he didn't spell it out plainly, every one of his men knew what sort of camps these labour camps were and the brutality of the guards who ran them. Most of them knew someone who had been sent to the camp and had not returned or if they had returned, had been very close-mouthed about their experience.

Erich Linhard was also aware personally that if he could, Dr Brendel would have him dismissed. He and the good doctor had not got on from the very start; whilst he was very conscientious in his approach to the security of the factory, he had refused several requests of the doctor for various measures to be implemented such as racial background checks on the employees to weed out anyone of Jewish origin. He was also aware that he'd have to comply with such requests possibly in the future, but until the hierarchy of the factory proper ordered him to do such things, he was ignoring the doctor, thus incurring the doctor's enmity.

He'd been through the Great War as an artilleryman, rising to the rank of sergeant (unteroffizier) and didn't like the way Germany was moving under Adolf Hitler, but also realised he daren't even breathe a word of his thoughts even to his wife. His brother had emigrated to the United States immediately after the war had ended and was always trying to get him to join him, but Erich Linhard had left it too late and now wouldn't be able to get permission to leave, such was the restrictive regime under the Nazi Government.

Later that afternoon Erich Linhard contacted the flight office and found there was to be an early morning flight the next day, following the taxiing tests up and down the runway. He immediately set up two motor patrols for outside the perimeter fence and one inside, this latter one was the usual security patrol.

First light in mid-September was about 5.30 AM and dawn about 6 AM; the test was scheduled for the stillness of the early morning, to take place commencing 7 AM and an anticipated take-off around 8.30 AM. The aircraft's planned flight was to first circle the airfield at a low altitude, and then land; if all was well, it would take off again for a short flight to the west of Stuttgart for the duration of about half an hour. Nothing fancy would be tried at this time, and any aerobatics would be done later after further checks.

Erich Linhard decided he would be available in the guard-house on the gate and ordered the outside patrols, one circling the airfield clockwise, the other counter clockwise, to report to him each time they passed the gatehouse.

The patrols were to commence at first light and continue until the aircraft was back in the hangar, anticipated to be around 9.30 AM. Each circuit of the airfield would take approximately half an hour, longer if they stopped to check on someone, with strict instructions that if anyone was found in the trees, they were to be brought in for interrogation.

That morning Erich Linhard overslept, cursing a bad alarm clock, he hastily dressed and made his way to the gatehouse. Consequently, he entered the gatehouse shortly after seven, as one of the patrols was leaving through the gate, having reported in for the first time after a circuit of the airfield, one turning to the right and the other to the left. His man inside the gatehouse saluted as he entered.

"All quiet, Joachim?"

"Yes, sir, very little activity."

"How about the road outside?"

The road could be just seen from the gatehouse.

"Very few vehicles. A few trucks earlier, two autos, a big Mercedes and a small sports-type both passed about ten minutes ago but that's about it. The patrols have just reported in and have seen nothing."

"Did any of the vehicles stop, do you know?"

"Not that I could tell, sir. I think they all carried on."

The first circuit both patrols made had produced nothing, and it had been only just getting light, the aeroplane was not out of the hangar, so both patrols paid little attention to the undergrowth around the airfield.

The aircraft was now out of its hangar, and the pilot was warming the engine up ready to move off.

The patrol Erich Linhard had seen leaving and had turned to the right towards Neuhausen was the same patrol that had gone out the previous day, Jens and his friend Carl. As they approached where the fringe of trees started, they reduced speed and slowly travelled along the road, looking into the trees and undergrowth, slowing down still further as they approached the area where they had found the tyre marks the day before.

Carl was driving and kept his eyes on the road whilst Jens watched the scrub and bushes. They passed the position of the tyre marks and moved past the clump of trees and bushes where the thought the vehicle had been concealed. Jens couldn't see anything and said so. Carl glanced back via the driving mirror; the road bent slightly and as he glanced in the mirror, he caught a glimpse of something other than bushes.

"There's something there, Jens," he said, stopping their vehicle and climbing out, taking his Luger from its holster as he did so, then walked back slowly along the road, moving into the bushes towards the spot where he had seen something. Jens in the meantime had joined him, looking around as they walked back.

As they moved behind the tree and bushes, they could see a small low vehicle hidden behind the wall of bushes. Reaching the vehicle they saw it was empty.

Carl at the front of the car looked down. "This is an English car, look at the number plate."

Jens went around to the rear and saw the small square number plate. He looked about and signalled to Carl to be quiet, listening.

They could hear nothing other than the roar of the jet aeroplane warming up. He moved around to the front of the car and whispered to Carl.

"Whoever it is will be by the fence, come." He walked quietly towards the fence along the clear ground between the small trees. Carl followed a few steps behind him, watching their front intently, both with their Lugers in hand.

They'd gone about 20 feet and a small portion of the fence was in view, behind a small bush close to the fence they saw a crouched figure sighting a camera towards the airfield hangar, obviously taking a photograph of the aeroplane.

Jens leading was about to call out when he heard a thud, accompanied by a groan behind him, and the next thing he was conscious of a bang on the back of his head and blackness.

Carl, lying on the ground in a haze, was vaguely aware of someone taking his belt off and binding his hands behind his back, then felt something strapped over his mouth. He tried to focus his eyes but could only make out two figures moving past him out of his line of sight and that he had a blinding headache.

Erich Linhard took the report of the other security patrol on their first return to the gatehouse.

"Did you see the others?"

"Yes sir, they were stopped by the trees about a quarter of a mile up the road." The man pointed towards the right. "They must be searching the trees."

"Mmmm, that was where the report of the observer could have been located. All right, make another circuit, anything suspicious, let me know. Pay particular attention to where the old Bernhausen road used to be. I know it's now closed but someone might get there. It's easy access."

"Yes, sir." The two men left.

Erich Linhard waited another half an hour, and the second patrol had not yet reported back after their first circuit. He wondered what they were doing; it shouldn't take this long to search a belt of trees.

He heard the roar of the jet engine and looked out of the gatehouse window in time to see the jet aircraft slowly start to move down the runway and gradually lift into the air, but when a few feet off the ground, the engine flamed and then there was a loud explosion with bits of metal from the inside of the engine flying out. The aircraft dropped back onto the runway sharply and the left-hand undercarriage wheel collapsed, causing the aircraft to spin around and then come to a shuddering halt, with one wing partially torn off.

The second patrol came in again and reported all clear.

“Did you see anything of the other patrol?”

“No, sir, we thought they must have completed the circuit and were in here.”

Erich Linhard sensed there was something seriously wrong. He’d not been a policeman for a few years without having a gained a sense of things when they weren’t working to plan.

He sent the second patrol back out and telephoned his office, ordering his second-in-command to send a vehicle and two men to him at the gatehouse. On its arrival he got into the vehicle and ordered the driver to turn towards Bernhausen and stop when he reached the trees on the right-hand side. This the driver did, looking up the road, Erich Linhard could see it was clear for about a mile, so where was the other patrol.

Ordering the men out, he formed them into a line across the trees from the road to the perimeter fence and ordered them to walk slowly towards the other end of the treeline.

“The patrol vehicle should be here somewhere, if not, we may find the men.”

Slowly, the men walked as best they could, trying to keep a straight line through the undergrowth. Erich Linhard walked on the road, keeping pace with his men. The line reached the other end of the tree plantation without finding anything, neither vehicle nor men.

He stood on the road; his men were grouped a short distance away and wondered where on earth the patrol had got to when the second patrol arrived from the opposite direction.

“Have you seen anything of the other patrol?” As he spoke, he heard the jet engine roar again and then suddenly go silent.

Whilst he stood, he heard one of his men call, turning he saw the man pointing down the road and he shifted his gaze. On the edge of the road, about a hundred yards away, was a man in the dark uniform of the Heinkel Security Force.

Erich Linhard and his men ran towards the man, and as they got closer, could see he was hatless, a bloody smear across his forehead and his hands appeared to be held behind him.

As they neared the man, Erich Linhard called out: “What happened? Where’s your vehicle?”

The man Carl didn’t seem to hear, and his eyes were unfocussed and glassy; his trousers started to fall around his knees and he stood looking stupid, trying to focus on the sound of Erich Linhard’s voice.

Two the men grasped Carl’s shoulders and one pulled up his trousers whilst a third unstrapped the belt from Carl’s wrists behind his back. Someone gave Carl a drink from a flask of liquor, he seemed to pull around, and his eyes rested upon Erich Linhard.

“I’m sorry sir, we were attacked from behind and knocked out and fastened up. Jens is still in there.” He gestured with his head towards the bushes, and Erich Linhard motioned to one of his men to go and look. The man eventually dragged out an inert Jens and laid him on the road, trying to bring him around.

“Did you get a look at these men?”

“No sir, but their vehicle was an English-registered small car.”

One of the men from the second patrol volunteered the information that an English-registered car had passed them travelling towards Sindelfingen shortly before they had turned off the Neuhausen road, about half an hour ago. Two occupants, the driver a young man, sandy-haired, but they couldn’t see the other man properly other than to see he was male.

Carl had recovered enough to confirm that a sandy-haired young man was taking photographs of the airfield just before they were attacked.

Erich Linhard left the group after giving instructions to his men to bring the two patrol men to the gatehouse and raced off to try and have the car apprehended somewhere around Sindelfingen.

Chapter Eleven

David Coulter and Tom Wadsworth, after missing a turning, eventually made it to Leinfelden and into Echterdingen and then on to the Heinkel factory; with their late start and then getting lost, it was early evening by the time the two men made it to the Heinkel factory.

Driving past the main gate of the Heinkel factory towards a town named Neuhausen, they came to a group of trees which seemed to shield the runway from the road. David pulled off into the trees and found a spot which was shielded from both the road and the runway.

The two men climbed out and crouching, crawled through the undergrowth to the chain-link fence. David had a pair of field glasses with him and as they reached a point where they had a clear view of the airstrip, an aircraft was taxiing along towards the hangar, which was on their right side.

They had never seen one like it before, the aircraft was moving along but didn't have a propeller. The nose cone appeared hollow and the aeroplane emitted a strange high-pitched whistling sound as it moved easily down the runway towards the hangar. David had already examined the aircraft through the binoculars and cursed himself for not having the camera with him. The aircraft, by now, had reached the hangar and the pilot switched the engine off for it to die down. The pilot climbed down and the ground crew swarmed over the plane. One man stood back a little on the concrete apron and shouted orders up to the rest of the ground staff.

David caught his voice as he shouted up to the crew to get the nose cover on and the aircraft under a tarpaulin wrap, then move it to the hangar and that a test was scheduled for early tomorrow morning about seven.

David pulled at Tom, who was lying alongside him, and slowly the pair made their way back to the car and moved off out into the road, turning to head back towards Stuttgart.

"Well, what about that, Tom. I am sorry I didn't have my camera with me, we could have taken a photo and then headed back to France tomorrow."

"We can come back tomorrow, but at what time. We'd need to make a guess."

"No, we don't. I heard the chief of the ground crew say they were up for an early test tomorrow at seven, which makes sense if they're going to fly it. They'll use the still morning air to get the best and safest result."

"That's fine. We've a built-in excuse for leaving the hotel early. We're going to Freiburg anyway. We leave the hotel, go to the airfield, you get your picture and we then go on to Freiburg."

They drove back to Stuttgart and as soon as they entered the hotel, booked an early wake-up call, telling the clerk they wanted to leave early because they were driving to Freiburg and wanted to stop on the way at Freudenstadt and have a look at the famous spa there. Freudenstadt was roughly midway between Stuttgart and Freiburg.

Next morning they left the Graf Zeppelin Hotel before six o'clock, just as it was getting light, and drove up the hill towards Stuttgart airfield and the Heinkel factory. On the way up Tom Wadsworth expressed a concern he had about passing the gate of the factory to get to their viewing spot,

"It's a bit dodgy, Dave, to pass the gatehouse too often. These Krauts watch everything and there aren't that many cars on this road, let alone an English one."

"I take your point Tom, so OK, whilst I get the photo, you stay a little to the side, and if someone tries to collar me, you jump him."

Tom Wadsworth laughed. "It'll be just our luck to get a twenty stone six-foot-six German policeman making the collar." Both men laughed, more out of nervousness than humour.

They arrived at the spot they had been at the night before and concealed the car again. Whilst David Coulter went to the hide-out near the fence, Tom moved slightly to the side, into some thickly grown bushes. Looking around he found a pretty solid lump of a windfall to use as a club.

David Coulter looked at his watch and saw the time was a few minutes before seven o'clock, he glanced towards the aircraft hangar and with Teutonic thoroughness, the doors were opening on time, ready for their seven o'clock start.

The jet aircraft was moved out onto the concrete apron, and David could see the pilot was already inside the cockpit.

The strange whistling sound started, then a sharp crack and the sound intensified turning into a roar. The aeroplane started to move, and David took a quick snapshot of it just as it started, then he turned to where he thought Tom should be and was surprised to see a figure slumped on the ground immediately behind him and a second figure in the act of falling, with Tom standing behind the figure with what looked like a club ready to hit the man again.

The man fell and lay inert, Tom nodded to David and said something but David couldn't make out what he said because of the noise of the aeroplane moving down the runway. Then there was an explosion from the direction of the runway but the two were too occupied to look.

As David watched Tom bent down and opened the man's jacket, then undid his trousers' belt, taking it and fastening his hands behind him, as he did it he motioned to David to the same with the other man. They finished and David went back to his position near the fence, the plane was stationary on the runway with men running towards it and a fire tender alongside it. Smoke curled up from the engine and the noise had ceased. He took several shots of the plane; in the meantime Tom had dragged and rolled the two inert bodies under a bush.

"Come on, Dave, we can't hang about, these two will be missed and someone will come looking."

David was fascinated by the plane, which previously had left the ground a few times, up into the air a few feet then dropping down but was now stationary, obviously it had been in trouble. It was lying with part of the undercarriage collapsed.

David reluctantly left his post and followed Tom back to their car; as they neared it, they saw the German car parked on the road.

"We better get that out of sight, Dave; otherwise, it's a dead giveaway that something is wrong if someone's searching for those two comes past."

David Coulter thought quickly and had a better idea.

"Tom, you drive my car, I'll following in their vehicle; once through Sindelfingen, stop at the first secluded spot you see. We'll change number plates with this thing and ditch it. Those two back there will have our number plate and the whole of Germany will be looking for an English car with an English number plate. At least this will give us a breathing space." Then after a silence added, "I hope."

Tom saw the logic and ran to their car; the two vehicles sped off in the direction of Sindelfingen, taking a chance and passing the Heinkel factory gates again.

Sindelfingen was about five miles from the Stuttgart airfield, and the road to Boblingen and then onto Freudenstadt branched off just before the town.

David signalled to Tom with his lights just after leaving Boblingen and they stopped.

"We can't go to Freudenstadt, they look for us there. We told the hotel we were going there. Let me look at the map. Just a minute."

David looked at the map, he saw that the quickest way to the French frontier was via Freudenstadt, but he was sure they would look for them there or somewhere along that road. He decided they should keep on this road and head for Freiburg and cross over after Freiburg to Colmar on the French side.

Whilst David had been looking at the map, Tom had been scouting around. They had stopped near a wooded section of the country, with a narrow track leading off into the forest; just after leaving the main road the track crossed a small bridge over a dry stream bed, which obviously in winter would be full of water. It looked an ideal spot to hide the Volkswagen, the way down was fairly steep but negotiable by a car; they could get the vehicle under the bridge on the dry stream bed; at a cursory glance no one would see it, and it certainly couldn't be seen from the main road.

He put it to David, who immediately agreed and they drove the two vehicles along the short distance along the track about 50 yards from the bridge, where they could get the Volkswagen down into the dry bed of the stream and then drove the Volkswagen along the dry stream bed to under the bridge. Then David took his toolkit out and unscrewed the number plates from the Volkswagen. Taking his off then substituting the German plates for his own but unable to make the screw holes match, he used some wire he had to fasten them on.

Tom used a branch to scrub out the marks of the Volkswagen as it had been driven along the stream bed; he also covered the marks made by the car as they had moved it off the track into the bed of the stream. Fortunately, it had been fairly dry over the past few weeks, and the marks could be covered by a lot of the fallen leaves, which at a cursory glance looked as if they had fallen naturally.

The two then set off again towards Schramberg, actually heading directly for Switzerland. The railway ran alongside the road and after a while, both men wondered if they should abandon the car and take the railway. After a discussion they decided against it, thinking the Germans would watch the rail connections with both France and Switzerland closely. The first place of any size they would come to was Herrenberg, a small town of about 3600 inhabitants according to their guidebook, and where they would normally have turned off for Freudenstadt and on to Strasbourg.

The turn-off for Freudenstadt was the other side of the town, the town itself was made up of typical German black and white half-timbered houses; some looked as if they went back to the Middle Ages.

They went through the town and passed the turn-off for Freudenstadt, as they did, Tom looked up the road and saw that there was a roadblock a few hundred yards up the road, manned by what looked like the military but he couldn't tell.

"There's a roadblock on that Freudenstadt road, military by the look of it."

A short time later David, who was driving, said, "Don't look now, but I think we are being followed."

"By whom?"

"Either a German army motorcycle with sidecar or police, I'm not sure which, can't see clearly what their uniforms are, they're wearing some sort of grey overall, but the passenger has a gun."

"Coincidence, do you think? Going the same way as us?"

"No, they're dropping back. I think they read the number plate and saw we are a German car."

"It paid off then?"

"I think so, but we better push on as fast as possible but without attracting any attention to ourselves. If we don't get sighted soon, they'll start casting a wider net."

"What do you mean, Dave?"

"For them to have put up a roadblock on that Freudenstadt road means that someone must have seen us turn towards Sindelfingen and worked out we were trying to head for the frontier to get to Strasbourg and therefore, put a roadblock just out of Herrenberg. They are also looking for an English car, that's why the motorcycle came after us; they spotted us going past the turn-off and gave chase, then saw that we had German number plates on. If we don't get sighted soon, they'll start to look in a wider circle. Not necessarily on any road to the frontier, they may think we're going to lie low somewhere. Secondly, the Volkswagen we hid could be found at any time or they may circulate the number plate numbers and so if it turns up on an English car in one of these villages, the local policeman will try and collar us. I'm not too sure how efficient the German police system is in circulating information in circumstances like ours."

"Do you think those two men I hit were badly hurt?"

"No, I think the fact I've got photographs of their aeroplane will be enough for us to be shot."

"Do you really think so, Dave?"

"We'll be classed as spies. They shoot spies here. In UK we hang them. Either way, it's a dead end." They both laughed, although they knew it was no laughing matter.

Their big test was the town of Rottweil, a fairly large town and obviously dangerous from the point of view that they could be stopped at any time if news had gone ahead of them. Rottweil was roughly ten miles ahead of them; there they should branch off towards Schwenningen, a further ten miles on. From Schwenningen they had 40 miles to go to Freiburg through the heavily wooded Black Forest country.

They were now entering the outskirts of Rottweil and were slowed down by what looked like farm traffic, old cars and horse-drawn carts. On reaching the centre of the town, they saw that the market square was full of gaily coloured stalls and a farmers' market in full swing. Moving slowly through the confusion, they saw several policemen in their green uniforms and semi-military personnel in their dark blue uniforms with their swastika armbands. None seemed to be looking for any one in particular but trying to sort out the tangled traffic; eventually, they moved through the square and out towards the suburbs, looking for their road to Schwenningen, which they almost missed. Once clear of the town they were able to increase speed, most of the traffic going the other way towards Rottweil.

The road to Schwenningen climbed upwards and eventually, they reached the top of a fairly steep hill and levelled out along a plateau, before dropping down towards the built-up area of Schwenningen. The town seemed to be in two halves, separated by the plateau, and seemed larger than Rottweil. David slowed down and pulled into the side of the road by a small café near to a group of houses. Tom looked questioningly at him.

"How come, don't we need to push on?"

"Yes, but I wanted to have a look at the road ahead if I could; where it goes into the built-up area down there." Pointing at houses they could see about half a mile ahead down the valley, which appeared to be the start of the town proper.

"Why?"

"If word has gone on ahead of us, they'll try and stop us before we get into the built-up area; you know, just on the outskirts."

David took the field glasses from the car and stood looking down the road, examining closely as far as he could see. Although there wasn't much traffic on the road, a few motor vehicles, farm carts and one or two trucks, there appeared to be a stoppage just out of sight, where the road disappeared between the houses. David thought it was either a set of traffic lights or some other traffic control or a roadblock of the police searching for them.

He went back to the car and Tom looked at him.

"See anything?"

"Yes, there seems to be a stoppage down beyond the houses but if it was the police looking for us, they wouldn't be stopping everyone, would they? They'd be looking for an English car and two men in it. So that has to be a traffic control of some sort. Shall we take a chance?"

"Yes, I agree they'd only stop motor cars and not everyone."

David set off again, following the road down into the town; as they neared the house, they saw the stoppage was actually a policeman directing the traffic at a cross-roads. They both breathed a sigh of relief and actually got through the junction quickly, the policeman not even giving the car a glance.

Leaving town the road started to climb up through the dark forbidding trees on either side, which turned the road into a gloomy cavern.

"I know why this place gets its name, Black Forest," Tom remarked.

"I agree, it is gloomy. Y'know, I think we'll not get any sort of roadblock until we reach Freiburg."

"What makes you say that?"

"At Freiburg, according to the map, we can go either way to get to a frontier crossing, either north to Strasbourg or south to Basel and Switzerland. So they'll block the entrance to Freiburg just the same as they blocked the road to Freudenstadt; that is if they think we've come this way, and we've no way of finding that out until we hit a roadblock."

"How about trying to get in touch with a consular official somehow? Remember what they said in London. Have we got a contact number?"

"No, if you remember, they said to act like normal tourists and ask for consular assistance."

"But we didn't envisage a situation like this, did we? Nor did they."

"Well, it can't be helped. We're in trouble up to our armpits, and we have to get ourselves out of it. These Krauts won't let us near a consul if they get us. We'll just disappear."

In London Aubrey Evans, of MI6, received a coded cable from the MI6 man in the Berlin Embassy, marked 'Urgent. Pass to addressee immediately'.

It told him that the Germans were looking in the Stuttgart area for two Englishmen wanted in connection with an attack on two security men from the Heinkel factory.

Aubrey Evans hastily put a call through to Group Captain Thompson.

"Gerry. Looks as if our two wandering boys have got themselves into a bit of trouble."

"Have you had word from Germany?"

"Yes, a cryptic cable from our man in Berlin. The only info I have says that the Krauts are looking for two Englishmen in the Stuttgart area wanted for an attack on some Heinkel security personnel. I'll try and get a better handle on it."

"It surprises me that our two would attack anyone but stranger things happen. They were specifically told to keep out of trouble."

"In Germany these days it's difficult. I'll keep you informed, and I'll try and get someone to locate them. See what we can do to help. If they are in trouble, they'll try and head for the French or Swiss frontiers, which means they'll be in the Black Forest area. We've no one down there, but leave it with me."

Aubrey Evans thought for a while, his nearest man was in the Düsseldorf area, and he didn't really want to put him in a position where he'd be exposed. He wondered if the French desk had anyone close to the frontier that could help. He picked up the telephone and asked for Pierre Roberts.

"Pierre, Aubrey here. We've a slight problem developing in Germany, Black Forest area, and wondered if you had anyone in the Strasbourg area that might help."

He listened in silence for a moment.

"OK. If you can think of something or someone that might be of assistance, I'll be grateful."

Later that day Aubrey Evans received a second cable from Berlin, telling him the two men had apparently been found close to the perimeter wire of the Heinkel factory and in getting away from the security men had injured one of them.

Aubrey telephoned Gerald Thompson and gave him the details. Gerald Thompson thought for a few minutes, then said,

"I would say they saw something they shouldn't have, which was why the Germans had the security men about the place on the outside of the wire."

"I think you might be right, Gerry. I'm still trying to get help to them but haven't succeeded so far."

In the Heinkel factory Erich Linhard had raced back to his office and immediately telephoned Dr Brendel but was unable to reach him; the good doctor was outside watching the take-off of the aeroplane and by then experiencing a feeling of horror when the engine malfunctioned, knowing he'd be the scapegoat, his mind wondering how he could avoid been blamed.

Erich Linhard looked at the map of the area pinned up in his office. The Englishmen, if that's who they were, would head for the French frontier now they had been spotted. The quickest way would be Freudenstadt, about 40 miles south west of Stuttgart, the turn-off for the Boblingen road was about 30 miles west of Sindelfingen.

Erich Linhard telephoned the police in Sindelfingen and spoke to the Chief there, a man he had known for many years. Giving a brief outline of the attack, who he thought it was had made the attack and where he thought they'd be going, he asked for the two men in the English registered car to be apprehended, making sure they found a camera which he thought had been used.

The Police Chief in Sindelfingen in turn telephoned the police in Freudenstadt who, to cover himself, alerted the local Gestapo office. Then he sent a police sergeant and three men to set up a roadblock close to the turn-off for Sindelfingen near a village called Herrenberg. The Gestapo inspector S.D. for the district, Reinhold Muehler, took his assistant with him and joined them at the roadblock. The inspector decided this was a high profile case, and he wanted to be seen leading. The police had brought a motorcycle and sidecar with them. They watched the traffic, only looking for an English car; nothing came through, then the Gestapo man thought he saw an English car pass by at the road junction, travelling towards Rottweil. He ordered the motorcycle patrol to catch up with it and stop it.

The patrol returned after three-quarters of an hour to report although it was an English vehicle, it had German licence plates on it. They sat and waited.

After half an hour nothing had turned up other than a few private cars and trucks, Reinhold Muehler decided that either the Englishmen had turned off somewhere or had passed unseen on the Rottweil road. He decided to check the time the Englishmen would have left the vicinity of the Stuttgart airstrip and check the direction they were seen to go in. Taking his assistant, he drove towards Boblingen and Sindelfingen on the Stuttgart road, watching all the time the traffic coming in the opposite direction for an English car. He stopped at the first inn he found just outside Boblingen and bullied the proprietor into letting him use the telephone.

After a torrid time with a telephone operator, he finally got through to Erich Linhard at the Heinkel factory and asked him when the incident had taken place. He was given details of what had happened, including the taking of photographs, and in what confirmed direction the Englishmen had last been seen going, the make and colour of their vehicle. He was given the time of nearly three hours ago, the Englishmen had been thought to be going towards Sindelfingen, but no one had actually seen them go that way, although an English car had passed the Gate House in that direction around the time of the incident. The car sighted previously and that morning was a dark-coloured, low, English sports vehicle, possibly an M.G., but a complicating factor in the incident was that a Volkswagen patrol vehicle was missing – it had been the one the two security officers had been using prior to the attack.

Reinhold Muehler then telephoned his headquarters in Freudenstadt, telling them it was his intention to follow the possible route taken by the Englishmen, passing the turn-off for Freudenstadt and continuing on towards Freiburg; that his office had to alert their office in Freiburg to watch for an English car thought to be travelling towards them. The clerk who took the message misunderstood the instruction and telephoned the police in Freiburg instead of the Gestapo office.

Following his connection with his office in Freudenstadt, to cover himself, he also telephoned his headquarters in Ulm, advising them of the incident and emphasising the nature of the information they had and would be taking out of the country. The Ulm office ordered him to stop them at all costs and said they would be putting out a full alert to cover the whole of the Black Forest area.

Reinhold Muehler set off to chase the English car seen going past the Freudenstadt turn-off.

As he drove along he worked out that if the attack took place around 7.00 AM and they were sighted passing the gates of the Heinkel factory half an hour later but didn't pass the Freudenstadt turn-off until 9.15 AM, a journey of only about half an hour, they had stopped somewhere for three quarters of an hour as a minimum, possibly an hour. They had stopped to ditch the Volkswagen, take its plates, fix them on their car and then set off again. Smart, clever people but not smart enough. He cursed the patrol that hadn't stopped the English car on the Rottweil road when it chased it, even though it had a German registration.

As he raced down the Rottweil road, he warned his assistant to keep an eye open for the Volkswagen, possibly dumped in a field, although he thought they'd have hidden it somewhere in one of the clumps of woodland which were frequently on either side of the road. Neither he nor his assistant saw any sign of the Volkswagen between Boblingen and the Freudenstadt turn-off, which they passed without making any contact with the roadblock personnel other than noting they were still there.

Reaching the small village of Sulz, he pulled off the road and went into the small inn. Using the telephone he spoke to his headquarters in Freudenstadt again and found they had spoken to the police in Freiburg but not the Gestapo office. The police were alerting their police stations along the Freiburg to Rottweil road to stop and hold the occupants of any English cars on the road. He corrected that and said it should be any English car, even if registered in Germany. He also said they should have alerted the Gestapo office in Freiburg and to do so immediately.

He set off again at a high speed, although traffic was starting to be heavy and he was slowed down considerably by trucks, mainly army convoys.

In the meantime, David Coulter and Tom Wadsworth had passed through the little town of Neustadt with its lovely old market square, which they negotiated with difficulty because the weekly market was that day and the farmers from the district were just unpacking their carts and trucks.

They were still following the rail line running close to the road, shortly after passing through Titisee, about five miles from Neustadt and about 12 miles from Freiburg, David suggested they tried to get something to eat at the next small village. Tom agreed and at the next village after leaving Titisee, just before the road bridged the rail line, they pulled up in front of the small bakery of a hamlet. It consisted of a few houses, two or three shops, one of which was the bakery, and further along the main road was what looked like a group of farm buildings. Both men got out to stretch their legs and looked around, and then David went into the bakery to buy fresh rolls and anything else it sold. Tom leaned on the car, looking back along the road they had come along, idly watching the odd truck pass along with a car every now and again, when he heard a voice. Turning he saw standing by the front of the car a dark-green uniformed policeman, wearing the traditional flat-topped shiny peaked helmet of the police force, addressing him in German.

Earlier that morning Guenther Solaro, a young police officer from the Freiburg district, currently stationed in the village of Welden on the Freiburg to Rottweil road, received an urgent telephone message from his headquarters in Freiburg, warning him to watch the road from Rottweil for an English car which possibly could be passing through his village between then and mid-afternoon. The make wasn't stipulated but should an English car be sighted, it was to be stopped and the occupants held, reported and kept until officers from the Gestapo arrived to question them.

Cursing his luck, he had intended to go hunting wild pig that day with a farmer friend from one of the local farms. He'd already breakfasted and quickly put his jacket on, grabbing his hat and saying goodbye to his landlady, he walked out into the street. He wandered up and down the highway, calling in to the few shops and saying good morning and sampling the sweet rolls in the bakery, keeping his eye on the traffic.

He thought the message he'd received was the usual stupid instructions he was prone to get from the headquarters in Freiburg. How could he stop a moving motorcar if the occupants were determined not to stop? He could make a roadblock of farm carts and make vehicles slow down but as this was one of the main routes to the frontier with France, he could see how popular that would be with the numerous military vehicles using the road because of the current political situation, and also party officials used the road a lot. He was standing by the railway bridge when he saw a car pull in and stop in front of the bakery. He walked back towards it and the closer he got to it, he realised it wasn't a German make of car.

Could this be the English car that had dropped into his lap? Visions of promotion swam before his eyes for apprehending the fugitives.

Walking closer he saw it had a German registration plate on the front and felt a sense of disappointment, although he still wasn't sure of the make of the car. A young man was standing leaning against the car, looking the other way up the road, and as Guenther stood by the front, he asked him his nationality and for his papers. The man turned and stood looking at him, making no move to reply.

As he repeated his question, a sandy-haired man came out of the bakery bearing some wrapped loaves, and so Guenther, whilst undoing the flap of his gun holster and putting his hand on the butt of his gun, repeated the question, looking at him.

The man walked towards him and reached into the inside pocket of his jacket whilst holding out the wrapped loaves to Guenther, who instinctively grabbed at them with both hands. The man said something in English to the other man and at the same time kept pushing the loaves at Guenther so that Guenther had to step backwards. As the bakery cellar flap was slightly raised up off the street, pedestrians were protected either end of it by a low railing, Guenther fell backwards as he caught his heel tripping over it, throwing the loaves in the air to one side and winding himself as he landed flat on his back.

He took a little time to recover his breath and to sit upright and was just in time to see the car go out of sight over the rail bridge, dropping down as the road dipped into a valley.

Guenther raced back to his small office at his lodgings and telephoned his Freiburg headquarters, reporting an English car had stopped in his village, that the occupants had attacked him and were going towards Freiburg. The 'attack' was reported in the local Freiburg newspaper the next day but the inhabitants of Welden and the district had a laugh over the so-called attack. One of them had witnessed it, and the story circulated that Guenther had been attacked by a loaf of bread.

The police headquarters immediately set a roadblock up at Zarten, on the Freiburg-Rottweil Road, about three miles from the centre of Freiburg.

As David Coulter came out of the bakery, he saw the German policeman standing asking Tom Wadsworth for his papers and what his nationality was in German. The policeman turned as he heard the bakery door open, saw David and walked towards him. David's first thought was to stand his ground and pretend to be German, then he remembered Rebecca Wurtz, his German teacher's admonition before he'd left that he could never pass himself off as a German.

He pushed the bread at the policeman as he pretended to reach for his papers, at the same time calling to Tom to get into the car quickly. The policeman instinctively stepped backwards and caught one of his heels in the lip of the cellar flap, which caused him to fall backwards flat on his back.

David jumped into the car and pressed the starter button. Fortunately, the engine caught immediately, being still warm from their journey, and he slipped it into gear and took off down the road and over the rail bridge. Tom looked back as they breasted the rail bridge, seeing the policeman starting to stand up.

David then said, "They've obviously sent word on ahead and guessed we are headed this way when we didn't show up in Freudenstadt. We need to get off this road, that policeman will send word ahead of us."

They drove on for about a mile with the railway still running alongside the road down a river valley heavily wooded on either side. David spotted a turn-off across the railway to the left. Tom looked questioningly at him as they turned onto a level crossing and reached a dirt track the other side of the rails but running alongside the rails, obviously used by the rail engineers to service the railway line.

David then looked for a turn-off into the trees so he could stop and look at the map.

"We need to get off that road, I know it goes where we want, but we must find another way. They'll have a roadblock up ahead somewhere. This track is used by the railway people, and they may have a way off to the left to join another road into Freiburg."

David found a small clearing that gave them cover, the main road still running close to the rail lines. He opened his map and studied it, looking for a route off to the left, but found nothing. Tracing the railway along the road on the map, he saw where the railway crossed under the road again to go over to its right-hand side. It then veered away from the road by almost a mile into the forest behind a hill. There was what looked like a track off immediately behind the hill, which ran due north then turned west to a small town called Denzlingen. From there they could run due south to Freiburg.

They turned back onto the track again and set off as fast as the surface of the track allowed. They came to the place where the road crossed over again, then just before a place called Zarten the railway moved off into the forest, veering north. David stopped the car again after turning off the track into a small clearing. Tom again looked questioningly at David.

"I want to see where there's a roadblock, if there isn't one in that village, then I'm going in to get some food. You wait here with the car."

David crossed over the rail track and walked carefully through the trees to where he could clearly see the road, then stopped and cautiously crawled forward to the edge of the woodland, peering towards the road. Looking down the steep slope he saw the Germans had a roadblock just on the outskirts of the village. It looked to be manned by a mixture of police and men in dark-blue uniforms. They were checking all vehicles and pedestrians as well. He walked back to where Tom was, after carefully crossing the rail line again.

"The roadblock is just out of the village, come, we better try up north."

The moved down the track until they came to the junction of the track with one which turned north, as the map had indicated. Shortly after they had joined it and started to travel north, they found a small wooden hut at the side of the track in a small clearing. David stopped the car and Tom tried the door which opened, so they went in. The hut was being used by railway maintenance crews as an equipment store but also a rest room. There was a coffee pot and mugs, some coffee grounds, a stove which used a gas cylinder, and a partially used loaf of bread, a little stale but not too stale. They quickly made coffee and shared the dry bread, not very filling but better than nothing, then moved on towards Denzlingen.

Half an hour later they emerged out of the forest to find the main Karlsruhe to Freiburg rail track below them and the beginnings of the small town of Denzlingen about two miles away to their left.

Meanwhile, Reinhold Muehler, after a frustrating trip which had necessitated taking some hair-raising risks in passing other vehicles, had reached the village of Welden. Before leaving Rottweil he'd telephoned the Gestapo office in Freiburg for news and had been informed the fugitives had been sighted at Welden but the local police had been unable to apprehend them. A roadblock had been established just outside Freiburg at Zarten, so far with no result.

He stopped in Welden and asked at the bakery where the police station was located. The proprietor eyed his uniform with respect and coming outside with him, pointed to where Guenther Solaro could be located. Before Reinhold Muehler could get back into his car, Guenther came running down the street to him and saluted when he reached him.

"Are you the policeman who was attacked by the Englishmen?"

"Yes, sir. They assaulted me and then they drove off in the direction of Freiburg."

The bread shop proprietor snorted when he heard the word 'assault'. He laughed.

"He pushed a loaf of my good bread into his hands, and then this fool tripped." Reinhold Muehler could see there was a certain amount of animosity between the two locals and didn't want to get involved in a local feud, so kept quiet.

He turned and got back into his car and headed off towards Freiburg.

Chapter Twelve

Heinrich Haslop decided to hot things up in London and was able to send a message via the British Embassy in Spain to MI6 saying that the Germans were still receiving information from the Bristol area regarding the first flight of the jet aircraft at Gloucester.

The information was passed on to the MI5 controller for the West of England, Charles Ferguson, who in turn contacted Inspector Robert Wilson.

"Ferguson here."

"Yes, sir."

"I've had word from our mystery man in Germany that jet engine and plane information is still reaching Germany. Have you had any further developments on that investigation with the surveillance on that Bristol employee?"

"No sir, I think the man's as clean as the driven snow. I understand we've had information that an Irish name from this area has been contacting the Embassy again and asked for a meeting. Now our guess is that the meeting took place. This man Smith never went near any German Embassy official. The German Embassy, as you know, has a 20-mile restriction on movements and Smith didn't leave the Bristol area to meet with anyone."

"Mmmm, what do you recommend?"

"I talk to him and ask who he tried to introduce to the Gloster factory."

"Do it. Whoever you get then, check them out thoroughly if it warrants it. It could just be something entirely innocent. Warn him before you discuss details."

"Yes sir, I'll do it tomorrow."

Charles Ferguson terminated the call and put a second call in to Group Captain Thompson.

"Gerry, Ferguson here."

"Yes, Fergie, what can I do for you?"

"We've had another message from our source in Germany. He says information is still coming out of the Bristol area. Wilson is going to try another tack tomorrow. Have you had any information at all?"

"No, not on that. My two men in Germany seem to be in a bit of trouble, but Aubrey Evans is seeing what he can do."

"If Aubrey can, he will, a good man. I'll keep you posted on this. 'bye."

The following morning in Robert Wilson sent a message to his sergeant in Bristol, Anthony Rudd, that he would be arriving at Bristol Temple Meads station that morning at eleven.

A message was also sent to Paul Hodge, security manager at the Bristol factory.

Tony Rudd met him and drove him out to the Bristol factory. On the way there Robert Wilson explained that information was still coming from the Bristol area but he, Robert Wilson, agreed that this man Smith was clean. Therefore, they needed to interview him and ask who it was he was trying to introduce to the Gloster factory.

On arrival at the factory, they went straight to the office of the Security Manager.

Tony Rudd introduced Robert Wilson and the three sat down whilst Robert Wilson briefed them on his mission.

"I think you are both aware that information has been sent out of this area by someone to Germany. We have been looking for him or her and so far not had much luck. The only clue we think we may have is a false name given to the Gloster aircraft people by someone your Tim Smith was trying to introduce to work there. We think your Tim Smith is clean, we've been watching him for a month now and nothing has surfaced, which leads us to confirm our suspicions of him."

Both Tony Rudd and Paul Hodge nodded in agreement. Robert Wilson went on.

"I think the time has come when we ask Tim Smith who he was with that night. Then do an in-depth investigation of that man. So let's have Tim Smith in and talk to him."

Paul Hodge stood up. "I'll go and see the Personnel Manager and get it set up. It's his area and I have to handle it through him."

The other two waited after Paul Hodge had gone.

"Do you think that this is the man Mulroney, who writes to the German Embassy, sir?"

"Maybe, it's the only lead we have so far, so we must follow it."

Paul Hodge came back with a man of about 60 and introduced him as John Timpson, the Personnel Manager.

"I've sent word to Tim Smith to come to see us on a personnel matter," he said.

They chatted amongst themselves regarding the darkening situation in Europe whilst they waited, then agreed on the way they would handle the interview. Eventually, a woman opened the door and ushered in a grey-haired man in overalls.

"Come in, Tim, sit down." John Timpson indicated a chair facing the desk, behind which Robert Wilson, the Special Branch inspector, and Paul Hodge sat. Tony Rudd was sitting to one side and John Timpson took a chair and sat next to Tim Smith.

Paul Hodge opened up the proceedings.

"Tim, we are about to discuss with you something which is highly confidential, and you cannot talk about it with anyone, not even your family. You understand?"

Tim Smith looked a little uncomfortable as Paul Hodge made his statement but nodded in agreement.

He went on. "These two men are from the Special Branch of the police," indicating Robert Wilson and Anthony Rudd.

Tim Smith looked at them. "Yes, I was aware of him," he pointed to Tony Rudd.

Robert Wilson, as agreed between them, took over.

"Mr Smith, for several months we've been aware that someone in this district, that is the Bristol area, possibly connected with the Bristol Aeroplane factory, has been passing confidential information to possible enemies of this country. I think most of you have been aware we've checked through the Personnel Records to see if we can find a clue which would lead us to this person. So far without luck. We're not even sure that this person is working in the Bristol factory, although the information being passed to Germany would indicate so. We have received some information via another source, which gives us another lead and may be of importance, and we think you can help. You follow?"

Tim Smith looked puzzled. "If I can, I will."

"Good man."

Tony Rudd now took over the proceedings.

"Tim, you took a man with you when you went to a social night to the Gloster Aircraft people a little while back, I think you told the Gloster people he was looking for a job, but had been rejected. That so?"

Tim Smith thought for a moment. "Yes, that's the fellow that's working for the Bristol Corporation, doing some electrical work outside for the expansion programme. He's been there a few months and they use our canteen. That's how I met him. He'd applied to work at Gloster but said he hadn't heard back from them. I said I'd introduce him to someone who could maybe help him. I don't know what happened after that. I introduced him to the Foreman Fitter there, who was in their darts team."

"What's this man's name, Tim?"

"Bill, but I think his surname is Folks, I'm not too sure. I only see him in the canteen. He sits with us most of the time but lately, I think he's been moved to another job. I haven't seen him for a week or so; he's maybe working for the Gloster people by now. He was keen to go there, he'd got family trouble and needed to be closer to Cheltenham."

Tony Rudd looked across at Robert Wilson. "I think that's a big help, don't you, sir?"

"Yes." Robert Wilson looked at Tim Smith. "Mr Smith, thank you for your information. I caution you again not to discuss this with anyone, especially Mr Folks. He's obviously not the man we are looking for, and we wouldn't want him upset. Thank you."

John Timpson took Tim Smith out with him as he left.

The others looked at each other. Tony Rudd was the first to speak.

"What do you think, sir?" speaking to Robert Wilson.

"On the face of it with the odd information this man has given to the Gloster people, if it is accurate, I think he's worth having a closer look at. I wonder where he is now. I didn't ask for a description, we can get that later if we need it. If he is the man whom we are looking for, it's an explanation why we didn't turn him up looking through the company records."

"How do you mean accurate?" Paul Hodge spoke.

"Well, the information, name and address were given to that foreman at night during a darts match. Maybe he misheard, so I think we need to go carefully. Can you check the arrangements made with the Bristol Corporation about the use of the canteen and where the work force is now? Make up some story about some tools or something."

Paul Hodge nodded. "Give me a little time; I'll get back to you possibly tomorrow."

"Talk to Tony here, I'll be back in London."

The meeting broke up with Tony Rudd taking Robert Wilson back to Temple Meads station to board a train for London, Paddington station.

On the way to the station, Robert Wilson warned Tony to be careful during his interview with the man working for Bristol Corporation. "If he is our man, his name certainly won't be Mulroney, that will be a pseudonym, and he'll lie to you for sure, so you should doubly check everything out, every avenue."

Tony Rudd had worked with Robert Wilson for about five years and had not known him to ever be wrong when he sensed something about a person and he obviously sensed something about this man.

After the other two had left, Paul Hodge went to John Timpson's office.

John asked him how he thought the other two had reacted to Tim Smith's story.

"Oh, they believed him, and I think they have let the matter go. By the way what was the arrangement for the Bristol people to use our canteen? A bit unusual isn't it, particularly with all these new aircraft we're working on."

"No, we usually do accommodate people like that, there's so much activity going on with the new factories, it's handy to keep in the good books of Bristol Corporation and if we get a problem they help us out."

As if out of curiosity, he dropped another question. "Who were they?"

"Some electricians, I think, they were putting in a new substation for those two aero engine factories going up across the road."

"Have they finished?"

"I believe so, I think they finished last week."

With that he left John Timpson's office and went back to his own. There he checked his local telephone book and established where the electrical department was located for the Bristol City Corporation.

Anthony Rudd left Robert Wilson at the Temple Meads railway station and returned to the Bristol Aeroplane Company's offices and joined Paul Hodge.

"What have you got in mind for the investigation of this man Folks or Ducks, whatever his name is and his address?" Paul Hodge asked.

"Bob Wilson feels that there might be something phoney about this man, so he wants him checked very thoroughly. If he is the man Mulroney, he'll have a watertight alibi and a good solid background, and we'll need to check everything very carefully and not take his word for anything. Secondly, we don't want to startle him so that he takes off. I suggest you approach the Bristol Corporation; if I do, it will immediately set tongues wagging, whereas the Bristol Aeroplane Company has dealings with them on a regular basis."

"If we can identify the man, could you arrange surveillance of him with your people?"

"No problem. Look, why don't you approach the Corporation pretending some tools have been found and do they belong to their men? With luck you might see him or at least learn what his proper name is. Have they moved off the site yet?"

"So I believe, but I'll check it out. When I saw John Timpson earlier, he said they had."

"OK. The story is this, some tools had been left near the site, the civil works contractor said they weren't theirs, and they were brought to the Bristol aircraft factory because whoever brought them thought they might have belonged to your people. As security manager they eventually ended up with you, and you are trying to trace the owner.

"Bit thin but it might work, particularly if I say they look like personal tools rather than the sort a contractor would provide for his men."

The night before the Austell family were due to go on their day trip through the Black Forest to Freiburg and back, they received word from the tour company that because of the political situation the French bus company had cancelled the trip. The tour company had managed to arrange at the last minute train reservations the following day, if they were interested, at no charge to themselves.

The train trip would go from Strasbourg to Offenburg in Germany, where they could pick the local train from there to Freiburg through some very pretty Black Forest country. This would put them in Freiburg mid-morning. Then at 5 PM they could pick a train up in Freiburg, which would take them to Basel in Switzerland. In Basel they could change trains again and be in Colmar by 8 PM. The trip was such that a Swiss visa wouldn't be necessary because they were not staying in Switzerland, merely transiting through.

Arrangements would be made for them to stay in Colmar instead of coming back to Strasbourg and thus, their scheduled return to Paris wouldn't be changed, the only change being the return to Strasbourg. The tour company also agreed to pick up any extra costs incurred in the hotel in Colmar, again because of the political situation, the only rooms the tour company could get were in the Imperial Hotel, a hotel of a slightly higher standard than the one in Strasbourg. Most of the hotels in Colmar were filled with French army reservists on their way to the Maginot Line bases.

The Austell family (Mary, Tom and Elizabeth, brother Brian having left them) talked it over and agreed they would go on the train and spend the night in Colmar.

They boarded the train early next morning and after a stop at the frontier for immigration inspection, the train moved on, and they disembarked at Offenburg, with about a half hour wait for the Freiburg train. They noticed the station seemed full of soldiers, apparently all waiting for the same train as themselves.

They had about half an hour to wait, so Elizabeth thought she'd go and see if she could find a kiosk with chocolate or something. She walked down the platform and was about to enter the refreshment kiosk when she was stopped by a group of rather drunken soldiers speaking to her in German. As she tried to go around them, one stood in front of her speaking; she turned to go back and he moved quickly, standing again in front of her. His comrades all thought it funny and laughed, the soldier was still asking her something and moved closer to touch her, drunkenly leering at her.

She looked wildly around for an escape and all she could see were these drunken soldiers. A voice cut in loudly, and the men straightened up like ramrods, two other soldiers pushed their way roughly through the crowd, an officer and a non-commissioned man. The non-commissioned officer barked at the drunken crowd, who stood stiffly to attention looking straight ahead; the officer spoke to them in icy tones, then turned to Elizabeth, speaking in English,

"Fraulein, may I apologise for the actions of these drunken oafs on behalf of the German Army? These men are just barbarians and not fit to wear the uniform. Allow me to accompany you."

He spoke again quietly, his man barked an order, and the group parted to allow them to pass through, he escorted her to the counter and asked her what she was seeking, then in German asked the rosy-cheeked girl behind the counter. Elizabeth had time to study him and saw a pleasant-looking man slightly older than her, blond hair and blue eyes, taller than her, wearing a grey uniform with a cross at his throat and a few medal ribbons on the left-hand side of his chest.

After she had paid for her purchases, he walked with her out of the kiosk, the soldiers still standing outside with the other man standing in front of them. As they passed the man, her protector said something to the other man, she caught the name Erhard but the rest was in German, and as they walked down the platform to her parents, he walked behind them.

Her protector chatted as they walked, asking her about her visit and where she had been. They reached her parents, who looked questioningly at her; she turned to the officer, who saluted her father and introduced himself as Hauptmann Carl Zuicher of the Panzer Grenadiers. He bowed and clicked his heels as he kissed her mother's hand and stood talking with them.

The local train came in and he escorted them on-board, the train was packed mainly with soldiers. His man moved some soldiers from some seats in the open-plan carriage so they could sit down together, the Hauptmann sitting with them next to Elizabeth.

The train stopped at Lahr, midway between Offenburg and Freiburg, and more soldiers joined the already packed train. At Lahr two policemen had joined the train also and were examining the identity papers of all civilians on the train. When they reached the Austell family, they examined their passports and spoke to them in German.

Their new-found friend answered for them, after the men had moved down the train, he explained that the two policemen were checking for two Englishmen who had apparently assaulted some German security men and were thought to be trying to make their way towards the French border.

The crowds at the Freiburg station were chaotic, mainly German army men making their way to their units, so within the station groups of men were standing around, waiting to see someone from their unit with transportation.

The family disembarked and said goodbye to the German officer, but not before Elizabeth had given him their address and telephone number, telling him should he ever get to London, he was to look them up. He saluted them and walked off with the non-commissioned officer.

The Austell family made their way to the station entrance and found the door well-guarded. Every civilian's papers were being examined and all males were questioned by men in the blue uniform of the security police.

Once outside the station Elizabeth consulted a guidebook she had brought with her and started to lead the family to various places of interest.

Paul Hodge, the Security Manager at the Bristol aircraft factory, checked with the Personnel Department in regard to the Bristol Corporation workmen and found they no longer used the canteen facilities. He then telephoned the Bristol Corporation offices and was directed to a location in the Ashton Gate area of the city, not far from the Bristol City Football Club ground.

The place looked like a maintenance depot of some sort, and he went into the office. Explaining who he was, he was taken to the office of the manager, who in turn called in a foreman of the electrical section.

Paul Hodge then told his story about the tools and the Bristol City workmen who had been working close by and using their canteen.

The foreman said that would be Bill Foulkes, Tom Jardine and Dave Evans, who were all out on various calls at the moment. They were the only qualified electricians he had sent to that job. He'd ask them next day and then give him a call. Paul Hodges took a note of the names, making sure he got the spelling of Foulkes correctly.

Paul Hodge took his leave and went back to the Bristol factory. He telephoned Sergeant Tony Rudd of the Special Branch and gave a brief outline of his visit.

"I think our man is this Bill Foulkes character. His name is similar to Ducks or Folks, could be a corruption of his name during the darts match."

"That wouldn't account for his address being incorrect."

"Maybe that's another corruption. Y'know, noise with people talking."

"Darts match, no, everyone is very quiet. Too many corruptions, one maybe but two…highly suspicious. Probably he's hiding something, maybe he's got form, but somehow I think you're right, he sounds like our man."

"Yes, now I wonder if the Gloster people have any record of a Foulkes. He said he'd tried there before, so they might have an address."

"Then again he may not have, but I agree it's worth a try."

Paul Hodges telephoned John Timpson and asked him to speak to his counterpart in the Gloster organisation and ask if he had had any application for employment from a man Foulkes and could he give an address. He was to say it was a follow-up to their visit there a week or so ago when they had reported a corrupted name and address.

This he did and the Gloster people came back and confirmed they had had an application from a Foulkes and the address was 69, Burton Street, Bristol. They had made the man an offer but hadn't heard any more and assumed he'd found work somewhere else.

Paul Hodges telephoned Tony Rudd with the information, giving the address.

"I'm betting this man gave a false name and address just to cover his tracks. His story about having difficulty in getting employment was a cover. He wanted to get into the Gloster factory and ferret for information on the jet programme. I wonder why he didn't take the job when offered if he really wanted to get there. Odd. Anyway, the street is Burton Street not Turton Street but the house number is the same."

"OK Paul, I'll talk to Bob Wilson, Special Branch at Scotland Yard, and get approval to put full-time surveillance on this character, I'll also check whether he's got form, which could account for his attempt to conceal his whereabouts."

Paul Hodges received a call from the Bristol Corporation saying that all three men confirmed the tools at the Filton job weren't theirs. He suggested they try one of the other contractors working on the new factory wiring and gave him three names of electrical contractors.

Tony Rudd telephoned his superior in London.

"Sir, we think the man working for the Bristol Corporation sounds to be our man."

"Which man, Tony?"

"Sorry, sir, I was jumping ahead. We checked with the Bristol Corporation using the gag that there were some tools found, electrician's tools. They came up with three names of people working on that site. One was a man with the name of Foulkes, which sounds very much like Folks. Secondly, we checked with the Gloster people and although they didn't have a previous enquiry from a man named either Ducks or Folks, they did have one from a man called Foulkes – they made an offer but didn't get a reply. So it looks as if we've found our man. What I'd like to do is put full-time surveillance on this man and check his background before we interview him."

"Sounds as if he might be the one. I agree, let's watch him for a while, then we can make a search should we find anything in his actions that are suspicious."

Satisfied, the two men talked details of the surveillance operation to be mounted against William Foulkes.

William Foulkes was followed and watched day and night, but nothing seemed out of place as an English artisan. He'd been working for Bristol Corporation for 15 years, lived with his maternal grandparents, both dead now, in a small semi-detached house in a respectable suburb of Bristol, had adopted their name when in his early twenties, born in South Africa to an English woman.

His father, Hans Van Doork, was a Boer killed in the Boer War, and his mother died in an English camp in South Africa where, as part of the family of a fugitive Boer, she was being held. He'd been brought up by his grandparents, who had always lived in Bristol and not Cheltenham but he could have relatives in Cheltenham.

Although he wasn't married, he was currently involved with a woman several years his junior; had recently purchased a second-hand car but that wasn't unusual for a person of his level of occupation. His lifestyle didn't indicate he was receiving money from any source other than his salary.

Discreet enquiries made with his employers indicated he was a conscientious and reliable worker, often sent out on unsupervised projects. He had been recommended for a more senior position but so far the Bristol Corporation had been unable to offer him any advancement.

At the end of a month Andrew Carter, one of the Deputy Controllers of the Special branch in London, during the course of the monthly review of activities, brought up the subject of the search for the spy in the Bristol area.

Robert Wilson gave him a brief outline of the position on the surveillance of William Foulkes and the negative results so far.

"It looks as if this man is in the clear, Bob. What's your opinion?"

"Nothing has turned up so far. The man is clean so far, no suspicious movements. We don't think he's been alerted to the surveillance. The only thing we have to go on is the man's odd behaviour with the Gloster personnel people, coupled with the information coming out of Germany. This could be explained by him getting restless in his current job and looking around, then getting the idea Bristol Corporation might be going to promote him and getting cold feet when that other man introduced him to someone in Gloster. Hence the phoney name and address."

Andrew Carter looked pensive for a moment.

"From reading the reports, when he told that man Smith he wanted to work at Gloster, it was because he had family problems in Cheltenham, when it doesn't look as if he has any family there. Now that's a discrepancy that needs explaining. I think you've got the right man, so leave the surveillance running and dig around a bit more. Mark my words, something will turn up."

"Yes, sir."

William Foulkes, when asked about the electrician's tools, thought it a bit odd. The country was just coming out of a severe depression and times were hard, most electricians or any tradesman for that matter, mechanic and carpenter, would look after their tools carefully. So although the story might be true, he casually asked who at the Bristol factory had asked the question and was told the Security Manager.

This immediately put him on his guard; he remembered being told they were checking the records there for someone.

He wrote to Heinz Kern, telling him he had to lie low for a time, because the security people were searching for someone and he wasn't sure whether he was under surveillance or not.

Privately, he cursed the situation, he needed more money to keep his girlfriend quiet, she was a demanding young woman and although he'd bought this car to drive her about, she wanted to go out most nights to a music hall or theatre.

So William Foulkes decided not to go near the newsagent to see whether the German Embassy had another task for him in case they did an investigation into the newsagent's background.

In Berlin, Deputy Director Haslop read the reports of the incident at Stuttgart and it confirmed in his mind that the English were doing what they, the Germans, were doing with the English engine and trying to find out where the jet engine programme had reached. He was more than happy when he saw the report of the malfunction of the engine and hoped the information would reach the English but to make sure, he would drop a line about it also. Secondly, he made sure that a copy of the report landed on the desk of Field Marshal Von Brauchitsch, the leader of the anti-aircraft missile program, with a note from himself attached indicating that this setback could put the German programme back by about a year, which meant an alternative should be sought to counter the British lead.

The Field Marshall noted this and increased his lobbying of Hitler.

The Deputy Director also wondered who the two men were that the Gestapo were busy trying to find in the Black Forest area, they might be English Service personnel. He contacted the man in charge of that area in the Berlin Headquarters, asking if he had an update on the situation.

The man told him that there had been no further developments since the report late the night before, which indicated the two men had disappeared somewhere close to Freiburg. His man also told him that the Gestapo had taken charge of the operation to apprehend the two men. The German civil police were working under the direction of the Gestapo.

The man said the German police and Gestapo were concentrating on the frontier with France between Kehl, opposite Strasbourg, and Breisach, opposite Colmar on the Rhine, where there were crossings to France.

Haslop, from memory of that area and from the direction the men had taken, was of the opinion that they were going to make for Basel and the crossing there. It was far easier to get into either Switzerland or France from Basel. The men would calculate that the German security forces would seal off the closest routes to France from Stuttgart and therefore, would go for a more distant route to use, although fraught with a longer period of danger before reaching the border.

Deputy Director Haslop didn't want these two men caught, he wanted the English to be aware of the stage the German jet engine programme had reached. If the English programme was behind the German, it would spur them on, and if they were ahead, they would also push to keep their lead ahead of the Germans.

He sat there wondering how he could assist their escape without rousing any suspicions.

He telephoned the section head for the area to come to him. One couldn't trust the telephones anywhere these days to retain any confidentiality.

When the man arrived, he asked him if they had anyone in the Freiburg area and in the Basel area. The man confirmed they had three men located in Freiburg and two men down near Basel. He then gave orders that the Abwehr men should watch for the two Englishmen and not under any circumstances let the police or Gestapo know what they were doing. If they spotted them, do not contact them but immediately report back to him, Deputy Director Haslop, personally, using the code word Stuttgart. They would be given further orders, but under no circumstances were they to allow their knowledge of the men's whereabouts to reach the police or Gestapo. This is an Abwehr operation for the security of the state and either Admiral Canaris or himself would make any decision.

The Abwehr organisation generally had no love for either the police or Gestapo, particularly the Gestapo because of its increasingly intrusive presence into all aspects of life in Germany, and the police because of their increasingly subservient attitude towards the Gestapo. So the instructions given by Haslop were faithfully passed on by the Section Head to the men in the field. This was passed as a 'confidential director's order' that the operation to find the two Englishmen was an Abwehr operation, and they were not to give information to the police and Gestapo unless personally authorised by Admiral Canaris or Deputy Director Haslop.

Haslop again telephoned the area section head, asking him to bring a large-scale map of the area as well along with the latest reports.

In his office Heinrich Haslop had a mapboard on one wall and got the man to pin the large-scale map of the Freiburg area up. Questioning the man, the Deputy Director found that the two Englishmen had last been sighted at Weldon, a small village. Finding the place on the map, he traced the route through to Freiburg along the road and found that there weren't any turn-offs running south, so these men had to go to Freiburg before turning south.

The latest report his man had was that a Gestapo operative who was following them up the road had reached the roadblock at Zarten, and the men hadn't gone through the roadblock so they must have turned off somewhere. Looking again closely at the large-scale map, Haslop noticed that there was a parallel vehicle road following the rail line, a dirt service road, and just before Zarten – where the railway turned into the forest – this track followed the rail line, and as the rail looped around to meet with the road again, there was another track running off it to the north, which met the Manheim Basel rail line that passed through Freiburg at Denzlingen.

The track was a service track used by railway engineers and maintenance crews so that they could stop and leave their vehicles without hindering traffic on the highway. If the Englishmen were using this track, they wouldn't meet the roadblock and those manning the roadblock had missed the significance of the track.

Turning to the section head, "Where in the Freiburg area are your men located?"

"One man is in our office all the time, currently one man is near the roadblock but hasn't yet identified himself to those manning the roadblock. He's in a café close by. The other is still in the office awaiting orders."

"Good, pull the man back from the roadblock and have him hang about the Munsterplatz. They'll end up there, there's a farmers' market every day, they'll want food and will try and buy it without attracting attention, and a lot of foreign tourists go there so they wouldn't attract attention. All he has to do is look for an English car with German licence plates. The other man is to go immediately to where the road from Denzlingen meets the houses of Freiburg and to watch that road. He may be too late but he might see the English car on his way there. Tell him to watch. Pass those instructions now. Go, man."

"Yes, sir." The man scuttled off.

After the man had gone, Haslop sat thoughtfully at his desk. How could he help those two men without attracting attention to himself or the Abwehr organisation? Not the least of all, how could he pass orders down to subordinates – who would assist the men – without having one of these subordinates reporting him to the Gestapo?

Secondly, as long as what he did furthered the cause of saving Germany from the destruction the policies of Adolf Hitler would wreak, his conscience would be clear. His actions were not traitorous, he was working for the benefit of Germany. He was aware there were forces within Germany who were seeking to remove Adolf Hitler from power, who believed, like he did, that Adolf Hitler and the Nazis were not good for Germany.

A thing that puzzled him was why were there two men? The information these men obtained by visually sighting the jet plane could have been obtained by one man. Therefore, the English were using amateurs, people who legitimately could be in the area and had been tasked to check the airfield but had unfortunately panicked when caught in a compromising position near the airfield. For the English to do this must mean one of two things, either they had lost a professional agent in the area recently and their information had dried up, or they never had an agent there in the first place. But they had enough information to know there was jet engine activity at Stuttgart and send these amateurs in, so the second explanation that they never had an agent there was highly unlikely.

The question of how the men came to be in the area was immaterial to helping them get out with their information, but until the men were located, there was nothing he could do. Once the men were located, he could then take action of some sort, although he couldn't think of what he would be able to do.

Chapter Thirteen

As David Coulter and Tom Wadsworth emerged from the forest not far from the main Karlsruhe-Freiburg railway line, David stopped the car at the edge of the trees before crossing the farmland between the trees and the railway. Tom looked questioningly at him.

"Tom, I've been thinking, and I think we ought to put our English registration plates back on the car and dump the German plates. They've served their purpose and got us this far. I don't think here anyone will link us with the fracas at Stuttgart if we have English plates on our car.

"There's nothing incriminating in the car except for the film in the camera. We take that out and hide it, put in a new film and we take a few pictures of ourselves and places, leaving some film to be used. We can present ourselves as English tourists and act full of indignation."

Tom cut the wires holding the German plates on and quickly put back the English plates and screwed them on whilst David took the German plates into the woods. Using one as a spade, he dug a shallow hole, put the plates in, covered them with soil and spread some leaves over to conceal the fresh earth.

Then David wound the camera film forward and took out the roll of film, inserting another in its place, he took a couple of shots of Tom with the valley below as a background; giving the camera to Tom, he posed against the same backdrop and Tom took a couple of shots. They already had about three rolls of films with innocuous shots taken previously around Germany and France. David took the incriminating roll and inserted it into the hollow handle of the wheel nut spanner, sealed the end with insulation tape to make it look as if that end of the handle had had the tape on to give a user a non-slip grip, then put the handle back with the spare tyre.

Dropping down along the track they were on, they joined the track alongside the railway and travelled along it for about two miles to the small town of Denzlingen, where they were able to cross the line and get onto the main road.

They had to wait for about ten minutes before they could turn onto the main road because of a long convoy of military trucks travelling north, away from Freiburg. Traffic travelling towards Freiburg was relatively light, and the outskirts of Freiburg soon came into view.

"I think we ought to look for a farmers' market. All these German towns have them, and we can buy food without attracting attention to ourselves, especially due to the fact that this area is very popular with tourists." Tom agreed. "I'm starving. Where's the Rhine from here?"

"About ten miles due west." David waved his hand towards the right. "According to the map, we shouldn't see the Rhine until we get close to the Swiss frontier, about 30 miles south of here."

The traffic became a little dense as they neared the centre of Freiburg, mostly due to the narrowness of the streets and a goodly number of horse-drawn military carts.

"You know I'm surprised that this German Army has so much in the way of horse-drawn transportation, considering the way they toot about their armoured units and new Blitzkrieg tactics, Tom."

"From what I've read in some of our military journals, something like 70 per cent of the German Army relies on horse-drawn transport for logistics. The mechanical transport is only available for the elite armoured units. Even some of their artillery is horse-drawn, although they're mechanising very quickly."

They had now reached the main square of Freiburg and decided to try and park in a side street and walk back to the square, the Munsterplatz or Cathedral Square. They managed to get a spot very close to the square.

"Bring the camera, Tom, we need to look like a couple of tourists," said David.

Parking and walking into the square, they saw it was filled with stalls selling a great variety of produce, including ones with hot and cold food. They quickly bought food and wolfed it down and then stood looking about.

To David's surprise he saw Joan Healey waving to him as she made her way through the farmers' stalls in the square.

David walked across to meet her. "Now isn't this a surprise meeting you here. I thought you'd be long gone through Strasbourg.

David laughed. "No, it's a long story, we were forced to make a detour, but it's nice to see you. Where's your party?"

"They've just gone to get some food in a restaurant. Are you here for long?"

"No, we've just stopped for a bite and must be off."

Just then Tom came across to them.

"David, I…"

"Tom, this Joan Healey from the travel agents' office in Chester. She's with a party of tourists. Joan, meet Tom Wadsworth, my travelling companion."

"Pleased to meet you, Joan. Look, David, there's a character over there showing a lot of interest in us. He came from the direction of our car and was looking around the square. I think he's looking for us."

David turned and looked behind them but saw nothing untoward.

"Which man?"

In the meantime, Joan was intrigued by the exchange. "What have you two been up to?" she said, laughing.

"It's not really funny, Joan. The police are looking for us, and we have to get to the frontier quickly." David thought quickly and wondered if he should and decided to take a chance.

"In the car, Joan, I've a roll of film which I need to get back to England. I can't explain what's on it but if we get caught and they find the film on us, we'll be in trouble. I hate to ask you but could you take it back to England for us whilst we race for the frontier at Basel? Then if we're stopped, we'll be clean."

Joan looked a little dubious. "I ought to ask, Hans. Can I do that? What size is the film?"

"Thirty-five millimetre. It's from a standard Leica."

"That's all right then, I've got one of those with me. It'd look silly if I was carrying a roll of film for a camera I didn't have. Can we talk to Hans?"

"Yes, I don't see a problem." Then turning to Tom, "Can you see that man?"

"Yes, he's over by that veg stall, pretending to look at some cabbages."

"OK. You walk over to that end of the square. I need to go back to the car and get the film."

He turned back to Joan. "Where will you be, which restaurant?" Joan pointed. David nodded.

"You go to Hans; I'll get the film and see you there, OK? Tom, off you go, look as if you're going to leave and go somewhere, then I'll meet you at the car in about ten minutes."

Tom moved off quickly towards the far end of the square, Joan had already left and David turned and walked slowly back to the car.

The German Abwehr agent was in a dilemma, who should he follow? He opted for Tom, for the other man looked as if he was going back to the car, and so he went after Tom. As soon as the German went after Tom, David quickened his pace and raced for the car. Opening the boot, he quickly got the film and went back into the square towards the restaurant and Joan. The German was nowhere to be seen.

David walked into the small restaurant and stood by the door. Hans Van Dyke and Joan Healey saw him and leaving their table, came across to him. David backed into the small foyer, which was empty, the attendant having gone with a party of people to seat them.

"Joan has said you're in a spot of bother. What happened?"

"My friend and I were in the Stuttgart area; we saw a strange plane and took a few photos of it. The Germans saw us and are chasing us. They had roadblocks just out of Stuttgart, but we avoided them and they have one just outside here to the east. I think they think we're heading for France, but we're going for Switzerland. Anyway, I have this roll of film and wondered if you could take it, then should they catch us, we can pretend to be innocent tourists."

Hans stood for a second or two, thinking of the problems, then agreed.

"I can put it amongst my rolls of film." He explained that on each trip they took photographs of the group in various places in case some of the group missed taking photos. They usually used about five or six rolls of film. "We'll meet you in the Hotel Imperial in Colmar, on Avenue Foch tonight."

"If we don't get back, give it to a Group Captain Thompson at the Air Ministry, otherwise I'll pick it up in Colmar." As if saying goodbye to Hans, he palmed the roll to Hans as he shook his hand.

He walked out of the restaurant and across the square to their car, finding Tom standing by it.

The Abwehr agent followed Tom across the square and lost him somewhere in the crowd; cursing, he thought he better report the sighting of the two Englishmen to his office and get further instructions. He crossed back over the square to a small restaurant, where he knew he'd be able to use their telephone. He glanced inside from the foyer and saw a party of Americans eating with their tour guides, a big man and a young woman.

Using the telephone, he reported into the office, saying he'd located an English car with two Englishmen in it near the Munsterplatz but the car had English registration plates on it, not German. He needed instructions, should he continue to search?

The Abwehr field agent and the agent in the office debated whether he should report the English vehicle he'd found or should he continue searching? They finally decided to report it.

In Berlin, the Abwehr Section Head for the area took the call from their Freiburg office and went to see Deputy Haslop to report the find.

Deputy Haslop listened to the report and decided that it must be the same English car and they had changed the number plates. Maybe they weren't amateurs after all or astute amateurs. He ordered that they were still to watch for another English car with German plates. His assessment that the Englishmen had changed the plates back again he kept to himself.

By the time this had been relayed down the chain and the field agent left the café, the Englishmen had disappeared. The Freiburg office passed this information back to Berlin.

Inspector S.D. Reinhold Muehler arrived at the Gestapo office in Freiburg, knowing that the Englishmen had turned off somewhere along the road from Rottweil but after the village of Welden, where they'd had the run-in with that stupid policeman. Asking where the local inspector was, he found out the man was in Berlin for a few days, so as he outranked everyone in the office, he immediately took control, calling for a large-scale map of the area.

He spread the map out on a desk and traced their route from Rottweil to the village of Weldon and then from there to the roadblock at Zarten. There weren't any turn-offs, either left or right, that they could have used to get them to the French frontier. There were turn-offs but they led to isolated villages and ended there at each village.

He was still puzzling where they could have got to when one of the local men suggested that they had used the service road of the railway to cut across to the main Karlsruhe Freiburg road and had then carried on to the Breisach crossing of the Rhine to Colmar on the French side. The crossing was only ten miles from the road.

Reinhold Muehler looked at his watch, if that was the case, they had ample time to make the crossing, but he was aware that the crossing was covered by the local police supported by the Gestapo and they should have been apprehended.

He asked for someone to check with the police at the crossing to see if they had been sighted. The reply came back negative. He sat at a desk and pondered where they could have got to; he was certain they hadn't come up the Rottweil highway as far as Zarten. They hadn't gone to Breisach for the crossing, so if they had used the railway service road, and that looked likely, they would come out of the forest on the Karlsruhe road but which way did they turn, north to Karlsruhe or south to Freiburg?

It had to be Freiburg. They'd headed this way and most likely intended to cross further upstream at the next crossing, which should be Neuenburg, and after that Basel, or to give the crossing its German name, Weil Am Rhine.

In Stuttgart at the Heinkel factory, Dr Klaus Brendel, the project leader of the jet engine team, looked at this incident two ways. One way was that it was an opportunity to get rid of Erich Linhard, Head of Security, whom he felt was not suited by temperament to be in the position he was in, and he was not hard enough. Secondly, he could use it as an excuse to explain any further delays in the programme, citing caution so as to avoid discovery by England and France of the progress made or lack of progress in the jet engine project.

He telephoned Gruppenfuhrer Gerhard Diemer, giving him an outline of what had happened, the possible taking of photographs and the fact the culprits had not yet been apprehended due to the incompetence of the local security organisation and those in Southern Germany. He emphasised with indignation the English would be aware of their progress by this incident and the incompetence around it.

The Gruppenfuhrer seized on any opportunity that came his way to denigrate the Gestapo, because like the majority of the German military hierarchy, he felt the Gestapo was gaining too much influence at the expense of the military. This situation was to change later, when the high command wouldn't dare voice any criticism of the Gestapo, but at the present they still could.

So he telephoned a contact point in the office of the Sicherheitspolizei, who had control over the Gestapo, giving details of the incident and complaining of the lack of enthusiasm by the security forces to apprehend the perpetrators of the incident and the compromising of a project vital to the survival of the Third Reich.

They, in turn, contacted the Gestapo office in Freudenstadt to talk to the inspector, eventually tracking him down to the office in Freiburg.

Inspector Reinhold Muehler took the call in the absence of the local inspector S.D. and listened to the icy tones of his superior, Wilhelm Altein, Gestapo head in Berlin for Wurtemburg Province, South West Germany, ordering him to apprehend the culprits at any costs, recovering the film and bringing the culprits back to Berlin for trial. Should they escape out of Germany, he was to go after them, recover the film and liquidate them before they could pass the information on.

The whole incident had been escalated out of all proportion to its importance, when the fact was that once in the air, the aeroplane could be seen by many.

Inspector Muehler put the telephone down and cursed the fact he happened to be in the position he was in because the inspector of this office was in Berlin at this time. He could see one of two things would happen, either he would apprehend the culprits and gain accolades for his efficiency and devotion to duty or fail and be condemned for incompetence and made an example of by being buried in some punishment post somewhere to rot for the rest of his days.

Urgent action was needed by him.

So having thought it out, he decided to take the Basel road, and speed was essential. Leaving instructions for the office to contact the police and Gestapo at Neuenburg and Weil Am Rhine to apprehend the occupants of an English car with German licence plates, he took off with his assistant down the road to Basel, driving with scant regard for other road users.

As he was leaving the outskirts of Freiburg, he passed a bus carrying a load of tourists, little knowing that the incriminating film he was chasing was actually being carried on that bus.

When Deputy Director Haslop received the information that the English car with English plates had gone, he guessed they'd be heading south, either to the Basel crossing or Neuenburg a little further north.

He sent for the Section Head again and adopted the attitude that the first car sighted, now that it had gone, might end up at either the Basel or the Neuenburg crossing. If the occupants were apprehended, it might confuse people, making them relax their guard, allowing the real culprits to escape and also create an international incident which should be avoided at all costs. The Section Head should alert his men in the Basel area to the possibility that there was another English car travelling the same road and containing people not involved in the incident. One of his men should be left at the Basel crossing, with the other sent to Neuenburg. They should pass this information on to the Gestapo operatives at each place.

The Abwehr agents at Weil Am Rhine and Neuenburg made contact with both the police and Gestapo men at the frontier posts and advised them that an English car with English licence plates was possibly coming and was not the car everyone was watching out for, the one they should look for was one with German plates. The Gestapo operative at Neuenburg was a little sceptical of the information and was going to apprehend anyone in an English car, unless he had instructions from his own office, but the volume of English cars had increased, and the police pointed out the massive increase in English cars during the last few days would make his task impossible, so they just looked for an English car with German plates.

Another problem the Gestapo office in Freiburg encountered in attempting to intercept the fugitives was that although on the 30-mile stretch of old road between Freiberg and Basel there were several small villages and towns with a police presence, the newly completed autobahn avoided these population centres. Whilst the police were alerted along the possible route, the fugitives could be using the autobahn and the slender resources of the police couldn't cover both the autobahn and the old road.

The Gestapo headquarters in Berlin (Sicherheitspolizei), having been brought into the case, now took an active part in trying to find the fugitives, telephoning their offices and operatives along the German frontier from

Karlsruhe down to Weil Am Rhine, demanding to know the situation and whether they had any news.

The political situation was not good, and English tourists were fleeing the country in great numbers. On the German frontier between Luxembourg in the north down to Karlsruhe, all roads and rail links were choked with English, French and American tourists, all trying to leave prior to the outbreak of war. Therefore, there were a large number of foreign cars and the frontier police, assisted by the Gestapo, were more or less overwhelmed and only looked for an English car with German licence plates.

The frontier between Karlsruhe and the Swiss frontier was not too bad, but an abnormal number of foreign cars started to pass through. The flow of foreign cars through the frontier at Weil Am Rhine had increased. Although it was the main through route for English tourists from Austria and Czechoslovakia, a lot of them had opted for the shortest route, which went across at Neuenburg. The frontier police and Gestapo noticed an increase in the number of English cars at Weil Am Rhine and whilst the Gestapo operative had been prepared to apprehend any one in an English car, he soon found he was swamped by English cars and gave up the idea, so started to look for an English car with German plates.

David Coulter and Tom Wadsworth, shortly after leaving Freiburg, saw a sign on a road leading off to the right stating 'autobahn'. They took the turning and ended up on the newly constructed autobahn between Karlsruhe and Basel and commenced to make good time. They also noticed an increase in the number of foreign cars on the road, mainly Italian and Swiss, apart from a high percentage of German army vehicles.

They also noticed a high proportion of English and French cars on the opposite side of the autobahn, after they had passed the turn-off for Neuenburg in other words people going for the frontier crossing there.

"I hope the crossing at Weil Am Rhine isn't packed, otherwise we might be caught, Tom."

"I agree, although a little bit of confusion might help us."

As they neared the township of Lorrach, the traffic started to slow and eventually, they were crawling along at a snail's pace. The main road from Austria joined the autobahn just a little west of Lorrach and traffic feeding in from that road caused the slow-down.

Inspector Muehler was not having much better luck, he'd made good time and, like David Coulter, had cut onto the autobahn to make better time but was caught up in the traffic snarl up about ten miles behind the fugitives, even though he had commandeered a policeman to stand on the running board of his big Mercedes and wave and shout at the other vehicles to get out of his way.

At the frontier crossing post all occupants of vehicles had to fill out a departure card and have their passports stamped. The volume of vehicles gave the frontier guards a nightmare, and confusion reigned with some vehicles slipping through without completing the formalities. One of the biggest problems was the buses with 30 or more passengers at a time.

The crossing was regulated by a pole across the road and normally was swung up in the air for each vehicle, but because of the volume, the pole had been left at 90 degrees to the road, leaving a clear passage.

David Coulter and Tom Wadsworth arrived eventually at the frontier, filled out their cards and had their passports stamped. They returned to their car and started to move slowly off in the stream of traffic and passed under the pole.

In Stuttgart Erich Linhard had been doing some old-fashioned detective work and eventually, after visiting two or three hotels, arrived at the Graf Zeppelin. He had worked out that the Englishmen – he assumed they were English because an English car had been sighted twice near the Heinkel factory – must have been staying in the Stuttgart area and would have been in a hotel. Talking to the hotel manager, he identified the two as a David Coulter and a Thomas Wadsworth and obtained their passport numbers. They had checked out of the hotel that morning very early, saying they were going to Freudenstadt; without leaving the hotel, he telephoned the Gestapo office in Freudenstadt with this information. This office telephoned the information to their office in Freiburg, who in turn telephoned the frontier posts at Weil Am Rhine, Neuenburg, Breisach and Denzlingen to apprehend the two men giving their names.

In the frontier office at Weil Am Rhine, Frontier Guard Ruediger Vocht took the call and as he listened to the man at the other end of the line, he noted the names down, then spoke to the Gestapo man in the office.

"Here, Gerhard, this is your department, not mine. The names of the two Englishmen we're looking for are here." He handed the man the paper with the names on. "Stop looking for an English car with German plates, all we need is these two. You better look through those cards there and see if they are amongst them. I'll check the sheets the girls have typed up and the cards they are typing from now." Inside the next office three girls were transferring the details from the cards onto large manifest sheets.

"Don't bother," the Gestapo man called out, holding up two cards. "They've just gone through." He went to the three men manning the counter who were accepting cards, checking details and stamping passports.

"Do any of you remember these two? They've just gone through."

The men shook their heads.

The Gestapo man raced outside but confusion reigned, with cars, buses, trucks all trying to get across the frontier, people streaming in and out of the office. The majority of cars were English, so he walked back slowly, knowing that he would probably be held as the scapegoat for the escape of the two men.

He telephoned the office in Freiburg to report the men had crossed the frontier into France ten minutes prior to the telephone call being received. He'd actually no idea; it could have been as the call was being received, but it sounded well and might help to save his skin.

Ruediger Vocht decided to see it his French counterparts could help, although he was very pessimistic, but it was worth a try, particularly if he branded them as criminals.

As the Gestapo agent was going out of the German frontier office, David Coulter and Tom Wadsworth were going through the French immigration formalities across the frontier.

As they stood at the counter, a German frontier guard came into the office and spoke to the French immigration officer.

"We've been told to hold two Englishmen wanted for a criminal act in Germany. Here are the names. Have you a record of them entering France recently through this post?" knowing it was likely they had got through only a short time ago.

Jacques Foulot, one of the French immigration officers, was actually holding the passports of David Coulter and Thomas Wadsworth when the German spoke to Marc Augier, his superior.

The French frontier posts along the Rhine had been alerted by a special request emanating from the British Embassy to assist the two men, should they appear at the frontier.

Marc Augier looked at Ruediger Vocht, who had taken it on himself to check whether the two men had actually made France or were they still locked in the pile of traffic outside. The distance between the French and German posts was about a quarter of a mile, which Ruediger Vogt had traversed on a bicycle because of the traffic confusion. The Frenchman made a show of looking at some papers, then went across to Jacques Foulot and quietly asked him if he'd seen these two men, holding the paper given him by the German. They both looked at the two passports, then at the names, then at the men the other side of the counter. Jacques Foulot quickly stamped the two British passports and handed them back, and the two men disappeared out of the door.

Marc Augier went back to the German and said that the two men had gone through a short time ago and would possibly be down the road to Mulhouse or somewhere in France.

Ruediger Vocht returned to the German side of the frontier and reported to the Gestapo agent the two Englishmen had got away and were in France. The office had also been warned that Inspector Reinhold Mueller was somewhere in the crush of traffic and would be with them shortly.

The volume of traffic seemed to be slackening a little, although it could be just a temporary lull. The amount of traffic coming from France into Germany was considerably less than the other way due to the travel restrictions placed on German nationals by the German Government, so there were fewer to return.

Reinhold Mueller arrived about an hour later, his Mercedes had several dents and scratches on it, where he'd forced his way forward regardless of whom he'd hit. He and his assistant went into the immigration office, leaving the police officer with their car, and asked for the officer in charge. Both men, as usual with Gestapo agents, were in civilian clothes but proffered their identity cards for inspection and having seen the immigration officer at the counter, called to Ruediger Vocht and the resident Gestapo man.

Ruediger Vocht explained that about an hour or an hour and a half ago they received a telephone call giving the names of the two men needed for questioning but it had been too late, the men had passed through into France.

He also said the Gestapo office in Freiburg had been informed. He gave the names of the two men to Inspector Mueller and also that he'd checked with their counterparts over in France and the two men had gone in the direction of Mulhouse.

Remembering his instructions that if the two men escaped into France, he was to follow, he telephoned his office in Freudenstadt to have someone meet him at Breisach on the frontier with his and his assistant's passports, complete with French and English visas and to call at their respective homes and get a change of clothes for an overnight stay in France.

He hadn't at that time the slightest clue which way the men had gone, other than the report they'd gone in the Mulhouse direction. As it was now early evening, he guessed they'd either stay in Mulhouse or Colmar for the night and try and make contact with England by telephone, which would be rather difficult considering the number of English tourists all trying to contact relatives to advise they were now safe in France.

Therefore, he asked his office to also have their agents in Mulhouse and Colmar start checking on hotels to see if they were there, paying particular attention to Colmar.

Reinhold Mueller and his assistant turned back and drove through the thinner traffic along the autobahn towards Breisach, about 30 miles away. They soon hit more heavy traffic and the going was very slow.

It was almost midnight when eventually Reinhold Mueller and his man reached the French immigration office in Neuf-Brisach on the French side of the Rhine opposite Breisach.

Here they were regarded with suspicion by the French immigration men, to find two Germans amongst the crowd of British, American and French people fleeing Germany rather than be caught up in a war was surprising.

Their occupations in their passports showed that they were civil servants, and they maintained they were going to the German Embassy in Paris to do an audit of the financial books and then on to London. They were travelling by car, because due to the political situation the trains were all full with people returning to England, France and other countries.

The French authorities reluctantly let them go and notified their headquarters in Paris that they thought that two members of the German Secret Service had entered the country and gave their names and motor vehicle number.

Colmar is in Alsace and was part of Germany from the 1870s until 1918, when it was taken back and given to France. The town and area were riddled with German sympathisers, and the Gestapo had built up a network of people to work on their behalf in the area. The Gestapo headquarters in Berlin alerted several of these to check out the hotels in Colmar and Mulhouse for the two Englishmen. If found, they were to advise the two agents arriving some time during that night at the safe house in Colmar located on Rue De La Fecht.

The agent who eventually found the two Englishmen was Hubert Mayr, actually an Austrian who had joined the Gestapo a few years before but because of his nationality had been sent to the Alsace region, where it was thought he wouldn't excite suspicion being an Austrian.

He'd been given the task of checking the better class of hotels and eventually got to the Imperial Hotel on Avenue Foch.

He walked into the foyer around midnight and greeted the concierge, a man whom he knew had leanings towards Germany, and asked him if there were many English staying here. The man said the place was full of them, also Americans, including a party of Americans on a bus tour. Hubert Mayr said he was looking for two young Englishmen who were travelling by car; the concierge said there were several who fitted the bill but if he had names, he'd check at the front desk for him.

Hubert Mayr wrote the names down and the concierge went over to the front desk and after about five minutes came back and nodded to Mayr. "Yes, they're staying here, arrived about ten, room 315. Up on the third floor."

Hubert Mayr, very pleased with his information, had a quick look at his watch and saw the time was now two in the morning, so decided he would go to the address on Rue De La Fecht later, around seven that morning, but in the meantime get a little sleep.

He duly presented himself at the consulate house on Rue De La Fecht. He was shown into a back room, where two plain clothes men were sitting. Both looked in their late twenties and whilst one was a blue-eyed, blond-haired, fresh-faced man, slightly on the beefy side, the other – who looked slightly older – was a slim, dark-haired hard expressionless man with a menacing air about him.

"You have found the two Englishmen, Herr Mayr?"

"Yes, sir. They're in the Imperial Hotel on Avenue Foch, about a quarter of a mile away from here; room 315."

The man reached across the table, on it was an opened street map of Colmar. "Show me."

Hubert Mayr leaned forward to show him. Just then the door opened and someone called out. "Telephone, Berlin, Herr Muehler."

The Sicherheitspolizei office in Berlin was in turmoil. Abwehr Deputy Director Haslop had carefully dropped information in various departments in Berlin that the Gestapo had allowed two known foreign agents to escape into France with vital information. This was compounded by Field Marshal Von Brauchitsch telephoning the Sicherheitspolizei office and wanting the latest information on the whereabouts of the two spies and asking when were they going to be captured. Eventually, it came to the ears of Herman Goering, who had his aide start asking for information.

The whole episode was starting to get the smell of a witch hunt, and the key participants were scrambling for cover in a panic.

The Gestapo chief, Wilhelm Altein, responsible for South Western Germany, could see himself being blamed and snarled at his assistant to get Inspector Muehler on the line immediately.

His hapless assistant first tried the Freudenstadt office and unfortunately, got a woman clerk who thought he'd last been heard of in the Freiburg office, so he tried there and found he'd gone into France. Consequently he telephoned the house in Rue De La Fecht but found Inspector Muehler hadn't reached there.

Chapter Fourteen

The Austell family, under daughter Elizabeth's guidance, visited the Munsterplatz and the Historisches Kaufhaus, the marketplace building built in 1532, and the old city hall built in 1559 with a painted façade. After lunch they took a taxi ride out to the Arboretum Freiburg-Gunterstal and had a wander around, finally returning to Freiburg Hauptbahnhof or railway station for their train at 5 PM to take them to Basel.

In the station Elizabeth saw her parents seated safely in the waiting room because they had about half an hour before their train arrived. She went off to find an English newspaper, if possible, to see if she could get an update on the political situation.

She was looking at the papers on display in the newspaper kiosk when she heard a voice.

"Good evening, Elizabeth. We meet again." She turned and it was the German officer from their encounter earlier that day.

"Hello, Carl, I was looking for an English newspaper but I can't see one."

Carl Zuicher spoke to the proprietor in German, and the man shook his head. Carl turned back to her. "I'm afraid you're out of luck."

"Anyway, it's nice to see you again. Are you travelling somewhere?"

"No, I'm here to meet a detachment of my men. Erhard, my sergeant major, is gathering them together, and I spotted you over here. Where are your parents?"

Elizabeth explained she had settled them down to wait, their train was not until 5 PM and they were going to Basel, then back to Colmar. He expressed surprise because there was a direct route through Breisach to Colmar from there but the route to Basel was very pretty.

They stood talking, enjoying each other's company, before he looked at his watch and said she ought to go and collect her parents for the train. He walked with her back to them and insisted on seeing them onto the train but not before Elizabeth had her parents take a photograph of him with each of them by the train. She took his home address in Ulm and said she'd send copies of the snapshots to him.

The journey to Basel was uneventful, and they didn't have any problems changing trains. Arriving in Colmar shortly before 8 PM, they taxied to the Imperial Hotel. They had their dinner and had just left the dining room, crossing the foyer, when the two Englishmen they had met in Strasbourg came in the doors from the street. The two crossed the foyer to the reception desk, and Elizabeth overheard them, as she and her parents passed behind, asking if there were any vacancies.

Elizabeth and her parents waited for the lift, an old-fashioned metal-caged affair that looked as if it had been put in at the turn of the century. As they waited a party of Americans came through the doors and moved to the counter to check-in, marshalled by a tour guide, a big grey-haired man assisted by a young dark-haired girl. Elizabeth noticed she spoke in familiar terms to the two Englishmen, who had stood slightly to one side to allow the Americans to the counter.

The girl had joined the two men, and Elizabeth heard her ask if their transit through the frontier had been without incident. The noise of the Americans at the reception counter drowned out the reply of the men, and the lift arrived and she and her parents went up to their rooms.

In London that evening, Group Captain Gerald Thompson waited in his office for news of the two men in Germany. Earlier in the day he'd talked to Aubrey Evans, the MI6 section head for the Stuttgart area of Germany, and had been told from the information they'd received the two men were still at large. According to the scanty information received, all the border post between France and Germany from Karlsruhe down to Basel or Weil Am Rhine had been alerted on the German side to look for an English car with German licence plates containing two Englishmen.

Through the good offices of the French MI6 section head, via the British Embassy in Paris, all posts on the French side of the frontier had been alerted and requested to render assistance, if need be, to the two men.

Around midnight, just when Gerald Thompson was thinking about going home, his telephone rang and Aubrey Evans came on the line at the other end.

"They've crossed into France, a bit dodgy. Apparently, they made the border at Basel just ahead of the Germans who asked the French for assistance as the two men were actually in the French immigration office completing formalities. The French did the right thing, surprisingly."

Gerald Thompson left the building for home, leaving instructions that any call from either David Coulter or Tom Wadsworth was to be routed to his home, regardless of the hour.

When David Coulter and Tom Wadsworth arrived on the outskirts of Colmar, they stopped at the first café they saw and asked how to get to Avenue Foch, they wanted the Imperial Hotel. Following the directions given by the obliging proprietor, they eventually arrived at the Imperial Hotel. Leaving the car outside, they went in to the desk and asked for rooms. The clerk shook his head and in poor English said they didn't have a vacancy, and with a Gallic shrug said there were a lot of people travelling.

They turned away, standing a little to one side and wondered what to do when Joan Healy and Hans came in through the door, marshalling their tour group.

Joan came across to them whilst Hans sorted the rooms out with the clerk at the desk.

"Hello again, did you manage the frontier formalities without any problems?"

David grinned. "I think there were too many people trying to get out of Germany for them to pay a lot of attention to us. No, we didn't have a problem. But we have one here, there aren't any vacancies, and we need to talk to London on the telephone as soon as possible. There's nowhere else open, so we need a hotel where we can get at a telephone for a call to London. Probably all the hotels are as full as this one."

"Let me talk to Hans and see if he can get you a room. These hotels always keep one or two spare for emergencies."

Hans Van Dyke finished getting the tour party their rooms and came over and joined David, Tom and Joan.

"You boys got through all right, I see. Any problems at the frontier?"

David laughed. "No, I was just telling Joan, there was such a tangle of traffic, English and French vehicles, that I think the Germans had their hands full. They didn't even look hard at us."

Joan cut in. "Hans, they have a problem. They need to contact London, everywhere is closed and the hotel has just told them they haven't any space left. They need a telephone. Is it possible you might be able to do something here, so they can use their room as a base whilst awaiting their call? All calls to England will be delayed; everyone will be trying to contact England just to let relatives know they are safe, apart from military calls, which will get priority over the telephone network."

Hans turned and looked at the reception desk, there still was quite a few people trying to get rooms.

"Wait here and I'll see what I can do. I know the manager here very well." With that he moved off, crossed the foyer towards the side of the desk and to a door. He tapped and went inside. The other three stood waiting.

"Do you want your film back now, David?"

"No, keep it for the time being. I won't need it until we get to London, although they may give me other instructions when I talk to the people at the Air Ministry. Let's leave it for the time being."

As they watched, Hans came out with another man and they went to the reception desk. The man went around to the side and behind the desk and spoke with one of the two clerks there. They conferred for a short time, then the man came back to Hans. Hans waved to David, who went over to the two.

"David, Monsieur DuPont has kindly found a room, it's only small but will meet your needs. Give him your details."

David and Monsieur DuPont went into his office, and David gave details of himself and Tom. Monsieur DuPont warned him that there was a five-hour delay, if not longer, on getting calls through to England due to the heavy volume of traffic. David thanked him and went back to their little group.

"All fixed, thank you, Hans."

"What room are you in?" asked Joan.

"Room 315. He said it wasn't large, and there would be a five hour or more delay in any telephone calls to England."

"That's the same floor that we are on." She turned to Hans. "David says he doesn't want the film back immediately, but wants to telephone London first."

Hans nodded. "Probably the best. They may have sent people over here to look for you."

"You mean they're likely to chase us in France?"

Hans laughed. "My friend, this part of France has changed hands numerous times over the centuries between France and Germany, and the Germans will have no compunction whatsoever in following you here or using some of their sympathisers in this area to get back whatever is on those film of yours, even killing you in the process. So be careful and lock your door. By the way, where is your car?"

"Just across the street, over there."

"If I were you, I'd move it around the back somewhere, that way if you have to, you can go out the back way and get away quickly."

"If there is a five hour or more wait to get a call through to England," David Coulter looked at his watch, "it's now ten here, that would make it three in the morning. I think we stay here tonight, book the call early tomorrow and wait until we get through. Then head off for England."

Hans shrugged. "As you wish, but if I were you, I'd try and get away as early as possible tomorrow, but anyway, move your car now to the back."

Tom Wadsworth went out to the car; he had to search several streets before he found a spot just at the rear of the hotel, where a man was pulling out. He parked and returned to the other two, having been away about 15 minutes. Hans had gone and David was with Joan. To David's unspoken question, Tom nodded. "Not a lot of room but I managed, just at the rear."

The three went up together, parting as they got out of the lift, agreeing to meet for breakfast the next morning.

Sergeant Anthony Rudd of the Special Branch had stepped down the checks on the Bristol personnel files but had left a man there just for appearances' sake. He read the surveillance reports in regard to the man Foulkes, and they appeared to show the normal activities of man in his position. No outward display of having money to throw away, no meetings with any suspicious characters and certainly no meetings with any of the German Embassy staff. He stayed in the Bristol area during the week, going to places where his employers sent him; at weekends he met with a woman, and they spent time together going out to theatres and public houses but not at any time did he go anywhere near Gloucester. Secondly, the man also never went near Cheltenham, where he'd previously said he had family.

After reading the reports he gave the matter a lot of thought and wondered if he should approach Robert Wilson, his superior, and ask him for permission the talk to this man Foulkes.

In London, Andrew Carter, Deputy Controller Special Branch, had telephoned Robert Wilson, Anthony Rudd's immediate superior.

The two men talked over one or two current cases, including one of some bombings by the IRA in Manchester. Andrew Carter had noted the name Mulroney in the reports regarding the Bristol area and asked if Robert Wilson thought there was any connection with the IRA in Manchester.

"No, sir, I don't think so. I think this name is just an alias for communication purposes."

"How is the Bristol case proceeding? Anything concrete turned up yet?"

"Not yet, sir. We think this man Foulkes is our man but so far he hasn't put a foot wrong."

"Have you interviewed him yet?"

"No, sir. We haven't anything to go on to even speak to him, other than his story doesn't really stack up, but the coincidences could be explained and we didn't want to frighten him."

"Well, somehow according to MI6, information is still leaking out of Bristol. I think you ought to find a reason for speaking to him and it might make him break cover. You've nothing to lose."

"Yes, sir. I'll go and see Tony Rudd and see if we can cook something up."

The information came from the German Unknown's latest note sent to the Lisbon Embassy and passed on immediately to MI6. It also contained the information that the German jet engine had failed in its latest test. The informant had come to the conclusion that the English had lost their operative or operatives in the Stuttgart area, which was their reason for sending in the two men the Gestapo were chasing. He, therefore, thought he ought to give them any information he could in regard to the German progress just to spur them on.

Immediately after Aubrey Evans of MI6 received the information in regard to the jet engine, he passed it on to Group Captain Thompson. This was on the morning immediately prior to David Coulter and Tom Wadsworth's crossing into France the next night. He still hadn't had any word from them and wondered what had happened. He telephoned Aubrey Evans.

"Interesting information in your note about the engine, Aubrey. The usual source, I suppose?"

"Yes, Gerry, I wonder why he sent that? The information about the leak in the Bristol area is pretty standard info that we usually receive, but we have never had information in regard to progress Germany is making in the development of weapons. If he's as high up in the Nazi organisation as we think, he'll be aware of the ruckus your people created in the Stuttgart area and maybe guessed what we are after."

"Sounds likely, incidentally, I haven't yet made contact with those two as yet. I thought I might have heard overnight but didn't."

"I wouldn't worry too much. Communications are pretty bad from France. Everyman and his dog are trying to tell relatives they are safe and well. That coupled with the movements of the military, and you have a fairly chaotic communication picture."

"Yes, I suppose so."

"Also Gerry, the Berlin desk received information that there is a fight going on for funding between the missile people led by Field Marshal Von Brauchitsch and the Luftwaffe, led by Gruppenfuhrer Gerhard Diemer. This failure of the jet engine might tip the balance for Hitler to favour the missile people rather than the Luftwaffe and slow the programme down."

"That surprises me. I have always thought that Hitler favoured the Luftwaffe because of Herman Goring, and he never liked or trusted the army because the generals never supported him during his early years. Any idea how far they are with their missile programme?"

"No, not really, what we have is old and some of it is a bit like that American character in their pulp fiction, y'know Flash Gordon. Anyway, Gerry, I'll try and get some information for you in regard to your two people. But seriously, their missile programme is still in its infancy and a long way off anything concrete, Von Brauchitsch is pushing it like mad because it's an army programme. A matter of prestige with him, not tactical advantage over an enemy."

"Thanks, Aubrey. I'll talk later."

Putting the telephone down, Aubrey Evans walked down the corridor to his opposite number on the French desk of MI6.

The man's secretary said he was free and Aubrey knocked and went in. Anthony Bright looked up as Aubrey came in and waved him to a seat; he was on the telephone and completed the call almost immediately.

"Yes, Aubrey. What brings you to Frog land?"

"Aubrey laughed. "The usual confusion in France but more so with all this war talk going on."

"Yes, it all looks a bit dicey, and I was in the last show and I think the Krauts are spoiling for another go. They never forgave us for the Versailles Treaty; that's one of the reasons they love Adolf, he's regained most of what they lost through it."

"Well Tony, we had an operation going in Germany; the R.A.F. wanted us to find out about the German jet engine programme. We lost our man and Group Captain Thompson, he's the R.A.F. Intelligence man for engines, with our agreement, sent in a couple of amateurs to fill the gap. Nothing spectacular, just to gain a little information; they got spotted and went for the border and apparently got through safely. But we haven't heard from them. We think they are in or near the Colmar area somewhere. Can you help?"

"Ah, that was the info I received earlier and passed on about the two making the crossing."

"Yes, I had talked to my French counterpart as soon as I heard there was a problem, and he had the borders monitored, and strange to say the French border people did the right thing when the men crossed."

"A rare occurrence with the French; but only if it suits their purpose, not what's best for anyone else. I have a contact in the Colmar area, but I think it'll be like your men trying to get news to you, all the lines will be overloaded because of the political situation, but I'll try. Who am I looking for?"

"A David Coulter and Thomas Wadsworth, both reserve officers, one Air Force and one Army. They'll be in an English car, a maroon MG, registration VY 4069, although they did have some false German registration plates on at one stage, so your man should look for either English or German plates."

Anthony Bright scribbled the details down. "Leave it with me, Aubrey, and I'll see what I can do."

Aubrey Evans went back to his own office and telephoned Gerald Thompson.

"Gerry, Aubrey here. I've had a word with our French desk; they think like I do, all we can do is play the waiting game because of the communication problems. He has a man in the Colmar area and is going to try and get in touch with him, but he's not very hopeful."

Reinhold Muehler, in Colmar, felt a cold feeling in the pit of his stomach at the call to go to the telephone. He knew it would be Wilhelm Altein, his superior in Berlin, and he would want to know if he'd had any success yet.

He walked to the next room, leaving Hubert Mayr, and picked the handset up.

"Sir, Muehler speaking."

The icy tones of his superior came over the line. "Have you found them yet and carried out your instructions?"

"We've located them, sir, here in Colmar, and I'll move in now."

"You bring them back to Germany for interrogation. We need to know how much they saw and to whom they passed the information on to, you understand? Anything less will be considered a failure.

"But I understood I was to obtain the film then liquidate them. This is French territory. It will be difficult."

"Didn't you hear me? Anything less will be considered a failure in your duty."

"Yes, sir, I understand." The telephone went dead.

Reinhold Muehler went back into the other room and stared blankly at the wall. It was now 7.45 in the morning, and he had to act quickly before the Englishmen set off on the road again. Thinking, he decided reluctantly to call back Wilhelm Altein and ask if he could interrogate the two Englishmen here, get the information required, then liquidate them. He turned to Hubert Mayr, "Get me Berlin on the phone." Hubert Mayr picked up the phone and tried to get an operator to place the call but the lines were busy. He turned to Reinhold Muehler and shrugged.

"The lines are all busy, Herr Muehler."

Again Inspector Muehler looked at his watch, now it was 8.15, he couldn't wait, he had to go after them now, once they moved away from Colmar he'd never find them. Thinking his alternatives, he decided that he had to get them now, bring them here before he tried to get them back to Germany anyway, by which time the lines might not be so congested and he could talk to Herr Altein.

“We need weapons and take us to this hotel, Mayr.” Mayr opened a drawer in his desk and produced two Luger pistols and shoulder holsters. The two on the other side of the desk checked them and taking their coats off fitted the holsters on and put the pistols in place, then put their coats back on. Gesturing to Mayr to go, Inspector Muehler and his assistant, Gerhard Gruppe, followed Hubert Mayr out to their car. He directed them to the hotel, and they parked their car in the street about a block away.

“Look for their car, Gerhard; it should be close to the hotel. Mayr, you come with me.” He walked up the front steps and into the hotel foyer. A desk was over on the far wall directly in front of him, to the left a lift cage. A clerk was behind the desk with a man and woman standing in front of the desk.

The clerk behind the desk glanced up at them but then turned back, giving his full attention to the couple who were obviously checking out.

To his right was a double-door entrance to the dining room, which he walked across to intent on having a look there first. He’d no idea what the two men looked like. He reasoned that when they entered the dining room, the maître d’hôtel would ask for their room numbers to book the meal to that room, so he needed to see the maître d’ first or the list which would be on the high desk just in the entrance to the room.

Stopping at the entrance he looked into the room, which was fairly large, and saw a number of the tables were occupied but mostly by older people. Over by the window at the far end were two young men with a girl. The reports he’d received of the young men he was looking for hadn’t mentioned a girl with them, so he continued to scan the room. He couldn’t see anyone to match the description of the men he was looking for and so was about to turn away when the maître d’ appeared at his elbow and spoke to him.

“Monsieur, may I help?” He spoke in French.

Inspector Muehler answered in French. “I was looking for two young men, Englishmen. I’m from the tourist bureau in Freudenstadt, friends of theirs were wanting to contact them to let them know they are safe. I understood they had checked in at this hotel and as I was passing through Colmar on my way back to Germany, I was asked to pass the message on; the telephones being as they are at the moment, everyone wanting to telephone.”

“Have you tried the desk, monsieur?”

“Yes, they said they hadn’t checked out yet and suggested I try here.”

“Their names and room, monsieur?”

Thinking quickly Inspector Muehler gave Jackson and Stafford the only two English names he could think of on the spur of the moment and said he didn’t know their room. The maître d’ turned to the book on the desk and opening it ran his finger down the list of people he’d had through that morning for breakfast.

Inspector Muehler looked over his shoulder and saw that a Coulter and Wadsworth of room 315 were the last on the list and had been placed on table 8. He looked around and worked out that the two men with the girl were on table 8, so the girl was maybe just an acquaintance. He had a good look at them so as to recognise them again, by which time the maître d’ had turned to him.

"They haven't been here, monsieur."

"Sorry to have troubled you. They must have left." Inspector Muehler turned and walked away, followed by the hapless Mayr. Muehler led the way out of the hotel and stood on the pavement outside, waiting for Gerhard Gruppe to return with news of where the car was parked.

He didn't have to wait long before his assistant returned with news the car was close to the rear of the hotel.

After giving it a little thought, Inspector Muehler decided to wait close to the car, to try and bring them out of the hotel would be courting trouble. Judging from their actions in Germany, they would immediately guess what was likely to happen if physical coercion was tried and any subterfuge was out of the question, he and his people weren't equipped for it, such as fake uniforms or papers.

"Gerhard, show me where and then come back to the front here in case they leave this way, although it's unlikely." Then turning to Mayr, "You wait here until Gerhard gets back, then join me at the rear."

Gerhard Gruppe took Inspector Muehler to the rear of the hotel, where he had found the car and left him. Muehler looked about. Unfortunately, it was a cul-de-sac ending at the hotel yard entrance. Either side of the road were tall houses and no sign of anywhere he could wait. To loiter by the houses would attract attention and anyway, he would stand out like a sore thumb and warn the men. The cul-de-sac joined the road at the end at a 'T' junction, there was a little traffic and people walking across the top but again, nowhere to wait inconspicuously. Both corners of the cul-de-sac were vacant but if it was like Germany, the kerbside either side of a junction had to be kept clear for three metres.

Then whilst he was thinking, his eyes wandered over the rear of the hotel and he saw a fire escape running up the side of the building at the rear. Mayr could wait with the car on the street corner whilst he and Gruppe went up the fire escape and got them. He was pondering the problem when Mayr turned the corner, so he up walked to meet him.

"Mayr, what's the rule here in France about parking in a street near a corner?"

"I've no idea, Herr Muehler."

"Go and get our car and bring it here."

He thought regardless of the rule, if he parked the car on the corner pretending they had trouble, any official wouldn't bother them too much and he could leave Mayr with the car.

Whilst Mayr went for the car, he walked around to the front and spoke to Gruppe.

"Come inside the hotel with me and I'll show you our quarry, they are in the dining room, over by the window with a girl. Wait in the hotel until they leave and go upstairs to their room and come around to the rear and tell me."

He took Gruppe into the hotel and went to the door of the dining room, the maître d' was there and recognised him from before.

"Ah, still looking for your friends, monsieur?"

Her Muehler nodded and stood inside with Gruppe, who glanced across where the three were and nodded to Inspector Muehler, and they turned and walked out. The foyer had seats scattered around, and Gruppe took a seat facing the door of the dining room.

Inspector Muehler then left and went back around to the rear. Mayr was waiting with their car, and Inspector Muehler ordered he should wait on the corner with the bonnet up and pretend to be doing something in the engine.

He then studied the fire escape in detail. The hotel had five floors above the ground floor, and at each floor level where it met the fire escape, there were double doors to facilitate people leaving the building quickly. Their quarry, being in Room 315, would be on the third floor.

Tom Wadsworth and David Coulter had met with Joan Healey as pre-arranged the evening before and had gone in to breakfast together. Before leaving their room, they had spoken to the clerk on the desk, and he had put them in touch with the concierge in order to book a telephone call to London. After they had gone up to their room the previous night, they discussed whether they should try for the call then or leave it to the morning. The prospect of having to stay awake until the early hours was not appealing, so they decided to put it off until the next morning. They had booked the telephone call on waking at six and had been told that there was a four-hour delay.

They met Joan in the foyer and the three moved to the dining room. Over breakfast Joan asked if they had made contact with England yet.

David answered. "No, we have a four-hour delay in the call, or so the concierge said, and we booked it at six this morning and it's now 9.30, or at least almost, so I think it should be coming through anytime." He turned to Tom. "I think we better get up to the room for the call." Then turning back to Joan, "What time are you leaving?"

"I'm not too sure. We were supposed to be in Geneva, but our schedule had been disrupted by this wretched crisis. Hans is trying to get things straightened out, because we need to be in Paris by the 11th and back in England on the 17th, the party has to join the Cunard Ascania on the 20th. Come on, I'll go up with you. Do you want the film now?"

"Yes, I think so. I can't see anyone coming into France after us."

"I'll see Hans and get it for you, and I'll bring it to your room."

The three walked out into the foyer and to the lift. None of them noticed the blond man get up and walk out as they left the dining room.

Joan left the two men after the lift had dropped them on the third floor; her room was to the right and theirs to the left.

Gerhard Gruppe saw the three leave the dining room and hurried out and around the back of the hotel. He saw their car on the corner with Hubert Mayr peering into the inside of the engine and Inspector Muehler standing about 50 feet away towards the hotel.

"They've gone upstairs, Herr Muehler." Inspector Muehler looked at his watch. "We'll give them ten minutes and then move in, using that fire escape," pointing at the structure going up the wall. "We will also come out that way. You take the men and I'll go for a camera if there is one there. Mayr can wait here with the car."

He turned to Mayr. "Stay here with the car, keep the engine running."

The two men moved off towards the courtyard of the hotel; they cautiously entered, watching the entrance to the hotel kitchen but all was clear. Swiftly mounting the fire escape, they climbed to the third floor. The door was locked but it took Gruppe only a few minutes to pick the simple lever lock and get the door open and then they got into the corridor.

Inspector Muehler checked the numbers on the room opposite and saw it was 320 and the one next to it was 319. So room 315 had to be the fourth one down the corridor towards the lift.

The two men walked to 315, and Reinhold Mueller knocked on the door and at the same time took out his Luger.

The sandy-haired man opened the door and Reinhold Muehler pushed in, pointing the gun at the surprised man, the other man in the room was standing by the bedside table.

"Now don't do anything silly, otherwise you will get hurt," Reinhold Muehler said in heavily accented English and repeated it in German.

The two men stood watching the two Germans very warily.

"We would like you to come with us. We will walk out of here as if we are friends and go to the fire escape at the end of the corridor and down it into the street. You will walk with me," he pointed to David. "Your friend will walk with him. We will shoot if you try anything funny. You understand?" he repeated his English instructions in German again.

David looked at Tom and nodded.

"Now before we leave, where is the film?"

"What film?"

"The film you took of the aeroplane in Stuttgart."

The man looked mystified and looked across at his friend, and then shrugged his shoulders.

"We don't have a film of an aeroplane, the camera is over there, and our films are with it in that small bag. Search us, and that's our luggage over there, search that. I don't even know about any aeroplane in Stuttgart. Anyway, who are you to hold us up and question us?" he reached for the telephone.

Inspector Muehler waved the gun muzzle. "No, no, my friend. Don't think about it." Inspector Muehler decided to get these two back to their base and force them to tell him where the film was hidden, which it obviously was, otherwise the man wouldn't have told him to search. It may be in their vehicle somewhere. He picked up the camera.

He spoke rapidly in German to Gerhard Gruppe, "Get your man moving out and I'll follow, quick we need to get these back to the house and find out where the film is."

The party moved out into the corridor and turned towards the fire escape. As they walked towards the door, Joan Healey came around the corner further along behind them and stopped as she saw the group. Tom and David with a blond and a dark-haired man going in the direction of the fire escape, which was in the opposite direction to the lifts. She stopped and drew back around the corner.

Originally when Joan left the two boys, she went to Hans Van Dyke's room and tapped on the door. When he came, she said she'd just left David and Tom and they said they'd take the film. Hans walked across to his small bag where he kept the films and rooting amongst them came back with the roll of 35mm film, giving it to Joan. Joan was about to leave when he spoke,

"I've checked with Ed Smith, he says the situation is a lot calmer now, but we are to stay here for part of the day and then go on to Rheims. So I think we'll give our charges the morning off and let them do as they please. What do you think?"

"Suits me," Joan replied. "Let me take this to the boys, and I'll come back and we can then round up the party." With that Joan made off to the boys' room to the other side of the lifts, and as she turned the corner towards their room, she saw the little scenario of the two being escorted to the fire door.

She watched them out and then turned, going back to Hans.

As the party moved out towards the fire door and as Reinhold Muehler closed the room door, the telephone rang, but Muehler didn't hear it.

The concierge let the telephone ring in room 315 for about five minutes, and then spoke to the caller at the other end.

"I'm sorry, monsieur, there is no answer."

There was a silence as he listened to Group Captain Gerald Thompson at the other end, then he said,

"He booked the call, and I saw him go up to his room with the other man, but I've no idea what has happened."

He listened again. "Yes, monsieur, this is the Imperial Hotel on the Avenue Foch, Colmar, and as soon as I see him, I'll tell him." Putting the telephone down, he turned to a person at the desk wanting details of trains.

Chapter Fifteen

Robert Wilson, a Special Branch police inspector, following his discussion with Andrew Carter, the Deputy Controller, gave the matter of flushing William Foulkes out into the open a lot of thought. It would have to be done carefully in case the man was legitimate and innocent. Anthony Rudd, the sergeant in the Special Branch in Bristol, was sure they had the correct man sending the information to Germany.

He decided to go down to Bristol and go over the various interview information with Anthony Rudd.

Arriving in Bristol, he went straight to Anthony Rudd's office; he'd already warned him of his visit.

They sat and discussed William Foulkes over a cup of coffee.

"What does Inspector Wilson think we should do?"

"He says like all policemen, Tony, dig around, something will turn up if the man isn't on the level. We have a number of items which lead us to suspect him.

"One, he claimed he had family problems in Cheltenham and that was his reason for wanting to work in Gloucester, and he doesn't have any family in Cheltenham.

"Secondly, that address he gave in that darts match was a phoney, very similar but non-existent, and he is not in the Gloster Company files but William Foulkes is there.

"Thirdly, he never replied to the Gloster Aircraft Company offer for some reason. It's my bet he only wanted to get into the Gloster factory to see what was going on in the way of aircraft production.

"Fourthly, our information coming out of Germany indicated that detailed information of the Bristol aircraft production was being sent back to Germany, and it could have only come from someone in the factory, and he had access to the Bristol factory via their canteen."

"What do you suggest, sir?"

"I think we may talk to various people involved again before we get him in, to make sure our facts are straight. The way we get him in is to get all three Bristol Corporation men who worked on the substation project in on the basis that because of the Official Secrets Act we are doing background checks on people who will in the future be involved in building activities where work of national importance is going on. Bit thin, I know, but the best I could think of. People have been aware we have been looking into the personnel files in the Bristol factory but not the reason why, I hope. To strengthen the story, we could even ask the Bristol Corporation for any others that at some future time who could be involved in similar areas."

"I think we should start in the Gloster area first and then come back to Bristol. I'll set it up."

The two men met with Tom Williams, the security manager for the Gloster Aircraft Company, the next day. Robert Wilson opened up the proceedings.

"Tom, we were wanting to go over the details of that man who applied for a job here but apparently according to your personnel records never did, although a man of a similar name and address did. Could we talk to the foreman and the personnel clerk again, just to check we have the correct information?"

Tom Williams agreed and had the two people involved brought in. Both confirmed their earlier statements and that the name and address had been written down on a paper. The foreman remembered the man writing it down, and the personnel clerk remembered the paper the foreman brought in. She hadn't kept the paper, and neither of them could identify a photograph of William Foulkes when shown it. They also cited a copy of the letter sent to William Foulkes offering him a job at the Gloster factory and sent to his address in Burton Street.

After a discussion with the woman, she telephoned the labour exchange who had sent Foulkes to them and fortunately, spoke to the clerk who had handled Foulkes. The man remembered that Foulkes wanted to move to the Gloucester and Cheltenham area because of the ill health of his parents. A further discrepancy.

They then checked with the foreman at the Bristol Aeroplane Company and confirmed his story about the darts match and how William Foulkes had talked to the foreman at the Gloster factory.

Anthony Rudd then telephoned and made an appointment with the head of personnel for the Bristol City Corporation, the first stage for interviewing William Foulkes.

In London, Gerald Thompson, Group Captain R.A.F. Intelligence, put down the receiver of his telephone after the abortive call had come through from Colmar. He thought it a bit odd that David Coulter would go to the trouble of booking a call and not be there when the connection came through; he pondered a while and then decided to talk to Aubrey Evans.

"Aubrey, I had a call from one of our men, it was from the Imperial Hotel on the Avenue Foch, but when they tried to connect me to the room, there was no answer. The odd thing is that he'd booked the call, as one has to, and he'd been warned the approximate time it would be through. It seems a little odd to me."

"I'll talk to our French people and see if they can check on that hotel. Leave it with me, Gerry."

Anthony Rudd and Robert Wilson met the Personnel Manager for Bristol City Corporation the following day, after they had been to the Gloster Aircraft Company.

Robert Wilson introduced himself and then cautioned the man under the Official Secrets Act and explained they had been searching for a while for a German agent who is believed to be in the Bristol area and particularly with a connection to the Bristol Aeroplane Company. They had been through the personnel files of the aircraft company without any success in finding any likely suspect.

He continued that they understood that the Bristol Corporation had men working in the proximity of the aircraft company and even had men working on the premises, was that correct?

The personnel manager said he wasn't sure but it was possible; that he would need to check with various departments such as electrical, sewerage, and the like.

Again Robert Wilson cautioned him and suggested he use some sort of subterfuge to obtain the information from the various departments and that the subject of why the information was needed could not be communicated to anyone outside of the room they were in.

The Personnel Manager said that from time to time they did do surveys of likely requirements for labour over and above the present force, and the reason why that labour would be needed, the location of the current labour force also had to be given to justify any increase. Therefore, it would be comparatively easy to obtain a list of projects and people either at or in the vicinity of the aircraft company. They would need to give him time, maybe three days, so they agreed to meet in three days' time.

They met again in three days, and the personnel manager said they had two projects going on at the present time in that area. They had had three, all connected with some factories being built for the Ministry of Defence under the armament expansion programme. One had been completed, which was an electrical substation job, the others were ongoing, one was in connection with the sewerage, the other with an access road. Currently no one was working actually on the Bristol Aeroplane Company's premises, and they hadn't had anyone there for a couple of years. The sewerage project employed 16 men; the access road employed a similar number, and he had their personnel records there for inspection.

Anthony Rudd said that was strange because the Bristol Aeroplane people had said some of the Bristol Corporation employees had been using their canteen but weren't now, so it sounded like the project that had been completed. Anyway, they'd have a look at the personnel records he had there.

This they did during the course of two hours, asking the odd question as a cover-up. When they completed the examination, they asked about the substation project and who were the people on it. He telephoned the manager of the electrical department and confirmed his men had been using the Bristol Aeroplane Company's canteen and that it was not unusual for that to happen. Three men were involved, Bill Foulkes, Tom Jardine and Dave Evans. Currently, they were working on various jobs, except for Bill Foulkes who had just taken three days off.

The Personnel Manager produced the necessary records, and the two Special Branch men had a look at them and agreed that as they were all long-time employees, there wasn't anything to rouse suspicions but maybe they could help to identify someone asking questions.

Robert Wilson then said he'd like to talk to the three men, was it possible to see them but rather than upset them and tell them the police wanted to talk to them, could they be called to the personnel office on some other matter as a cover?

The Personnel Manager didn't see a problem in that and it was arranged when Bill Foulkes came back after his break the three would be brought in at different times to the personnel office separately. He added that he'd telephone Robert Wilson when he had the three men ready for an interview.

Gruppenfuhrer Gerhard Diemer returned to his office in the impressive Luftwaffe HQ building on the Wilhelmstrasse in Berlin. He was fuming, he had just spent a very uncomfortable half an hour in the Reich Chancellery, first with the Fuehrer and Herman Goring and then a further half an hour with Herman Goring in another office. He had been asked to explain exactly what was happening in the Stuttgart area in regard to the jet engine. Firstly, why were two spies allowed to penetrate the security, secondly why was the programme so far behind schedule and then subject to a further setback of a total failure of the engine during tests? He detected the hand of Field Marshal Von Brauchitsch in the whole business of having the Fuehrer briefed in detail of their failures. He telephoned Klaus Brendel in Stuttgart to vent his anger on the project leader of the engine team.

Brendel, trying to cover himself in turn, tried to move the blame to Erich Linhard, head of the security.

"Herr Brendel, the failure of the engine was nothing to do with security. Additional funding for the project was dependent on the early success of the engine. I made it quite clear to you when I visited you a few weeks back. The Fuehrer is now favouring the Von Brauchitsch rocket project in Peenmunde. I hold you personally responsible for this failure," with that he slammed the telephone down and sent for his assistant to see if they could find a competent man to replace Brendel. He completely overlooked the timescale had been set by himself with a total disregard as to whether it could be met.

In another office along the Wilhelmstrasse, Deputy Director Haslop was chuckling to himself when the news that Reich Marshal Goring and Gruppenfuhrer Diemer had met with the Fuehrer, at the Fuehrer's request to discuss the jet engine project. He was certain that it was the result of the information he'd fed to Field Marshal Von Brauchitsch a few days earlier. He also guessed what sort of meeting that had been and the result, which would throw further confusion into the engine project. The two Englishmen appeared to have got away, certainly into France with the news, no doubt the Gestapo would follow them, but it was a little late to stop the information reaching the English Air Ministry ears. He also thought that Diemer will try and correct the position and therefore, he expected a call from Gerhard Diemer demanding more information on the English jet engine position.

He picked up his telephone handset, when the operator came on he was put through to Wolf Landsberg, the section head for England.

"Landsberg, have we had any more information regarding the progress the English are making on their jet engine?"

"No, sir. You may remember the last information we had was just prior to the English authorities searching for an informant in their aircraft establishment in the Bristol area. Heinz Kern's man has had to lie low until the searching stops."

"Mmmm, the English will never give up searching, you better contact Kern and tell him we need more information, something definite, and he better set up something to work around the English authorities."

"Yes, sir. I'll send a cable immediately."

The following day Heinz Kern in the London German Embassy, Carlton House Terrace, received a coded cable from Berlin. After de-coding he read the contents several times, wondering how on earth he was going to fulfil the demand. Firstly, his one and only man had to keep quiet until the English finished searching; he had no others he could draft in to get information. Secondly, he didn't have a means of communicating directly with the man anyway, other than the newsagent 'drop'. The cable suggested he work around the English authorities with someone else, but he hadn't got anyone else in the area. He had two people in the Liverpool area of England and three in the Glasgow area of Scotland.

He sat there wondering about it and turning over in his mind the possibilities such as him taking a chance and going to Bristol to see William Foulkes, a risky trip because he was restricted to the London area and if he was followed and caught, two things would result – he would be expelled from the country and Foulkes would be arrested. He was pretty sure that if Foulkes was being ultra-cautious, he wouldn't go near his mail drop, so it would be useless writing there; he also didn't have a telephone contact point. He decided the only course he had left would be to write to Foulkes at his home address. Dangerous only if the authorities were intercepting mail at his home address, and he was pretty certain the authorities weren't aware of Foulkes' existence, although searching for an agent.

He decided to write directly to him, contravening the Abwehr regulation of only handling an agent through a mail drop or personal contact.

Heinz Kern then searched though his cupboard, where he kept a supply of stationery bearing various fictitious letterheads and matching envelopes. He selected one for a non-existing engineering company, although very similar to a very well-known large company, then typed a letter asking for information from Foulkes in reference to his enquiry about a car engine replacement. After typing he slipped it into a matching envelope. In a second plain envelope, he enclosed a small sum of money as a sweetener, knowing Foulkes would be aware of where the money came from. In the letter he suggested that Foulkes called at their offices in Vauxhall Bridge Road, and offering a time and date two weeks ahead.

Foulkes arrived back home from his being down with his girlfriend in Cornwall, and amongst his mail he saw the two envelopes. One with the logo of an engineering company he'd never heard of and the other a plain envelope.

The plain envelope contained 25 pounds and nothing else, the engineering company envelope contained Heinz Kern's easily interpreted request for information on the jet engine programme, giving him a meeting time and place two weeks ahead.

Whilst the request gave him an immediate problem because he didn't have any further information, he did have hopes of getting something later. He'd deliberately gone to Gloucester as many weekends as he could with his girlfriend; fortunately, she liked the place and whilst it wasn't anywhere the size of Bristol, she quite liked the pubs and the two small theatres. It was expensive taking her there but he'd still have to take her somewhere. He'd made sure the pubs they visited were in the region of the Gloster factory in the hope of meeting someone who worked there. He struck lucky on about their third visit to a small pub close to Hucclecote, where the Gloster factory was situated. There was a new housing estate, parts still being built between Gloucester and Hucclecote, and in the village near the housing estate his girlfriend started to talk to a man and woman, sitting close to them whilst he was up getting fresh drinks. They were both about the age of his girlfriend and after talking with them for the rest of the evening until closing time, agreed to meet the following week on the Friday. The man had mentioned he was in the assembly section of the aircraft factory.

They met the following Friday in the same pub, the two women seemed to get on very well together, and William Foulkes made sure he and the man did the same. The man didn't own a car and so William Foulkes and his girlfriend agreed to collect them the following Saturday and take them on a picnic to Weston Super Mare, a seaside town south of Bristol.

William Foulkes realised that the Germans would be expecting him to meet with them in London with information, so he penned a note using his alias in it. He said he was unable to deliver the package at that time, a later date would be more suitable.

Heinz Kern interpreted it that Foulkes was requesting more time to deliver some firm and better information. He immediately sent a coded cable to Wolf Landsberg in Berlin, repeating the message from Foulkes.

The deputy director seemed satisfied when Wolf Landsberg reported Kern's message.

In London, the letter from Michael Mulroney had been intercepted and whilst it was obvious that Mulroney was going to meet with someone, the rendezvous place and time obviously weren't available. The letter was addressed to Heinz Kern, so surveillance on him was doubled. They were pretty sure he knew he was being followed around, so a second covert team was put in place to monitor his movements as well as leaving the first team there. He'd be too busy watching the first team to be aware of the second.

In Bristol when William Foulkes reported back after his three days off, his foreman said he and the other two men who had been and were likely to be working on the Bristol Aeroplane site again and in that vicinity on substations would be needed to be vetted by the police for national security requirements.

The whole Bristol Aeroplane site was now covered by the Official Secrets Act. The Personnel Manager had agreed previously to use a different story, but having given it some thought, he telephoned Robert Wilson and communicated his idea with him and received the clearance to go ahead and use that line.

William Foulkes was working on a substation in the Clifton area of Bristol when his foreman told him to call in at the Personnel offices to meet with the police, who wished to interview him for clearance under the Official Secrets Act. He was to be there in the afternoon, and the other two men were there in the morning.

William Foulkes first wondered if they were specifically targeting him and then remembered the other two also had to go. He was a little uneasy, turning over in his mind the search they made at the Bristol aircraft factory and that they could be still there for all he knew. He searched his memory for anything that could give him away and wondered if they knew about the trip he'd made to the Gloster factory. Thinking about it, he decided if the opportunity arose, he'd mention it before they did and in his mind he put together a story.

After lunch he went back to the Personnel Department and gave his name in to the girl on the reception desk. She led him to a room off the corridor behind her and said the police would be along shortly. The room was furnished with a desk, three chairs behind it and two in front and a couple of filing cabinets in the corner.

He'd not been in there long when three men came in, one he recognised as the Personnel Manager, the other two he guessed were the police, one a man in his mid-forties, the other a younger man, mid-twenties. They took their place behind the desk

The Personnel Manager opened up and explained that because of the political situation certain areas were considered to be areas of 'national importance' and covered under the Official Secrets Act and all personnel likely to be using or working in these areas had to be vetted.

The older man opened up first, he had produced a pad and from where he sat on the other the other side of the desk William Foulkes could see it had an official logo in the right-hand top corner and a series of printed lines, each one ending with a series of dots across the page, he guessed they were questions to be asked with spaces for the answers

He was asked his full name, date and place of birth, his parents' names, brother or sisters, etc. the usual questions one would expect in a security vetting.

The Personnel Manager left shortly after they had started, and he was left with the two men on his own.

He was asked by the younger man how long he'd been working for Bristol Corporation and was he happy there?

He gave them the number of years and said he was happy enough, although he'd like a promotion if he could have one but at the moment prospects were not good. He'd applied for work at other places, aircraft factories and the like, but although he'd had offers none had really tempted him. A few months ago he'd applied to the Gloster Aircraft Company and had been interviewed but hadn't received an offer. He said then whilst working on the substations near the Bristol Aeroplane Company he'd gone with the Bristol people to a darts match at the Gloster factory and talked to a foreman, who made a note of his name and had promised to see what had happened to his application.

At that time, he was particularly interested in working there because he had sister in Cheltenham who was having a difficult time with her marriage, and he thought if he worked at Gloucester he would be closer to her than being in Bristol. She'd since returned to South Africa. When asked for her name, he said she was using the name of Foulkes like himself. He hadn't heard from her since she'd gone back but was expecting a letter any day, she had said she was returning to Johannesburg.

But he'd heard nothing from the foreman at Gloster and guessed the man had forgotten his name or to ask the Gloster Company personnel department.

He'd stop looking for a change for the time being and hoped they wouldn't pass this information on to the Bristol Corporation personnel manager.

They asked him a few more questions about his interests and friends; whether anyone had approached him for information when he was working near the Bristol factory and then dismissed him.

After he'd gone, the two Special Branch men sat there and discussed his answers

"He sounded very plausible, sir," Tony Rudd said.

"Mmmm, I agree but there was something about his answers on the Gloster Company application which didn't sound right to me. I wonder if he did have a sister in the Cheltenham area, he told the Labour Exchange people his parents weren't in good health. Maybe she was there as well. Convenient she's gone to South Africa. I even wonder if he has a brother and a sister at all. We'd need to check in South Africa, if possible. The 1931 census showed only himself and grandparents living in that house in Bristol, no others, that doesn't mean there weren't any somewhere else. His mother died when he was a baby, therefore any siblings would be older than him and could have flown the coop as it were. His grandparents have since died."

"I think we should check, sir."

"I agree. I'll set the wheels in motion when I get back. It'll take a while. You know what the mails are like these days."

After he'd left the two policemen, Foulkes laughed to himself. His story sounded very plausible, and he hoped he'd have deflected any suspicions.

On the train on the way back to London, Bob Wilson kept going over the interview they had had with Foulkes. Something kept nagging him about it, and he couldn't place a finger on that part of the man's testimony that didn't sound right.

He had a meeting with Andrew Carter, the Deputy Controller, the following day over another matter, but shortly before he left Andrew Carter's office, Andrew Carter asked him how the investigation was going. Robert Wilson brought him up to date on the interview and their findings.

"Keep trying, Bob. If you're sure of the way you're going, keep at it. Follow your instincts. You've been long enough a copper to know that somewhere in that interview that man let himself down and gave the game away."

"I'm checking out the sister story to see she if has a visibility on the South African scene. Most people travel via Union Castle Line to South Africa, although there are quite a number leave from the Continental ports. He said he thought she was going to Johannesburg, so I've written to the police there to see if the name Foulkes is in the area. They're pretty clued up, the police there, and have methods of tracing people so they might come up with something."

"As I said, Bob, keep trying. If you shake enough trees, something always falls out."

The following weekend Foulkes and his lady met with the two from Gloucester, and he drove them out to Weston Super Mare. They had a wander around the pier, tried their hands at a couple of the slot machine games, before returning to the car for a picnic lunch the two ladies had jointly fixed. After lunch, whilst the ladies fixed themselves up to be comfortable, Foulkes and the man chatted about their respective jobs. Foulkes gradually and carefully brought the subject around to aircraft, talking about his experiences at Fulton and the aircraft there. The man was one of those who are desperate to show off their knowledge and asked Foulkes if he knew that some aeroplanes could fly without propellers. Foulkes carefully said he didn't think that was possible. The man said they were making one at Gloster, the engine was made somewhere else and they made the airframe. Foulkes said it was a little hard to believe. He assured him it was possible, and they already had five airframes ready and were awaiting the engines. There had been a problem with the engines, but he thought it had been ironed out now and were expecting the engines to be delivered anytime. The engines made the plane very heavy, so the runway had been strengthened to take the weight. He didn't have any idea when a flight test was going to take place, but it must be soon because of the runways.

Foulkes didn't think it could be that close because concrete needed time to cure before it could take heavy weights, from his experience anything from one month to three months. Thinking about it later, he guessed they weren't going to have a test flight for at least three months. The date was getting closer to the date he'd given to the Germans, which he'd made up. So he thought he'd stick with that date, lending authenticity to his previous report, which he suspected someone in Germany doubted, maybe Kern's boss.

His problem now was to get this information to the Germans and get money in return. He wrote to Kern asking him to suggest to him a rendezvous or contact point of some sort. Kern again wrote in the name of the engineering company and said their representative would meet with him to discuss his engine replacement, and he would be in touch later.

Kern then sent a letter to one of his people on Merseyside to call in at the German Embassy and apply for a visa for a visit to Germany, which would be refused. The man, an Irishman, Anthony O'Brien, lived in Chester and called at the consular part of the German Embassy and applied for a visa. He was told to wait and then was called in to an office for an interview. Here he met Kern, who explained they had a problem with their operative in Bristol. He was to contact the man and receive an envelope from him, which he was to send to the German Embassy; in return he was to give him the envelope which Kern handed over. Kern gave him Foulkes' address and told him to contact him in the name of the engineering company under the guise of which Kern had been writing to Foulkes. If asked by anyone other than Foulkes who he was, he was to say he worked for that engineering company as a sales representative and was following up an enquiry by Foulkes. Kern provided funds for the trip.

Foulkes prepared a letter giving the details, confirming his earlier date for the proposed flying trials, the runway strengthening and the name of the man he'd met and who had given him the details.

About a week later he received a letter from O'Brien suggesting a rendezvous in the Bristol Temple Meads forecourt car park, asking for the car registration for Foulkes' car. He was to leave the message on the car seat and go inside the station, leaving the car unlocked.

The Special Branch men detailed to follow Foulkes followed him into Temple Meads station; O'Brien switched the envelope after Foulkes had gone into the station. The Special Branch follower saw Foulkes go to the enquiry desk, obviously to make an enquiry about a train and then go back to his car and thence home, none the wiser to the switch of documents.

A letter to the embassy was intercepted from 'Michael Mulroney', asking if the information sent was satisfactory.

Special Branch Inspector Wilson realised that if it was Foulkes, he'd found a way of receiving from and getting information back to Kern by a means that was not visible to them. He'd been under surveillance during the period and hadn't posted one letter. Actually, Foulkes had slipped the letter to Kern into the outgoing Bristol Corporation mail from the office.

Wilson also had a message back from the Johannesburg police stating they had been unable to trace anyone with the name of Foulkes, had they any more information which could help them?

Turning it over in his mind, he wondered if Foulkes' sister had gone back to using the family Afrikaner name and wondered if he could find that out. He telephoned his sergeant, Tony Rudd and brought him up to date on the German Embassy messages and Johannesburg police's answer.

"I was wondering, Tony, have we Foulkes' Father's name anywhere?"

"Yes, sir. Just a minute whilst I get the file out. Yes, here it is, Johann Van Doork."

"Good man, I'll try them with that. The girl may be using that surname."

He hung up and drafted another letter to the Johannesburg police, asking if they had any trace of a woman under that name, and secondly, would their birth records show any offspring from that family? The woman had been detained in a concentration camp and had died, but her son had been brought up in England and there was supposed to be a daughter of the same family.

He finished the draft of the letter and whilst waiting for it to be typed, sat thinking about the interview with Foulkes. There was something in that interview which rang a bell, but for the life of him he couldn't put his finger on it. At the moment their surveillance of Foulkes hadn't turned anything up and with the activity still taking place in the German Embassy, Foulkes was beginning to look clean.

In Bristol Anthony Rudd also sat thinking about the interview, he hadn't felt there was anything amiss other than he thought the man was a little too glib. The information he'd just received from Robert Wilson would seem to indicate that Foulkes was in the clear.

Robert Wilson telephoned him again.

"Tony, I been thinking. The only way that the German Embassy could get in touch with Foulkes would be via the mail. Can we have a check of the mail being received at Foulkes' home address, and secondly, check with Bristol Corporation, their personnel people, to see if employees use them as a *post restante*. Also along those lines, anywhere in his daily routine, has he ever called off anywhere where he could pick up mail?"

"Yes sir, I'll get on to it immediately."

In the German Embassy, Heinz Kern had heard nothing back from his superiors and so guessed the information he had sent had been acceptable.

Chapter Sixteen

David Coulter and Tom Wadsworth walked slowly out of the fire escape door and stood on the platform as one German went down and waited until they were all down, and then led the way across to a car parked at the entrance.

"Get in." The two of them climbed into the back along with a German and the other two got into the front, one turning and watching them, one in the back with them. The car seemed to travel up a lot of old streets, eventually coming out into where there were a lot of more modern buildings and stopped in front of a tall building older than the rest. The German in the back with them got out and stood in the street and beckoned David and Tom out. Meanwhile, the other German had gone to the door of the house and opened it. The German with them motioned them forward into the house, his hand suggestively in his coat pocket, sensing that David was looking to make a run for it. He hissed, "Don't try, Tommy. I'll shoot."

Once inside the house they were put in a small room off the hall. The room was furnished with a settee and two armchairs, along with some small coffee tables – one set between the chairs and the other two either side of the settee. David went across to the window and tried to lift the sash, without success. Tom picked up one of the small tables and tried to wrench one of the legs off, firstly without much success but on his third table a leg came off easily. It made a good truncheon.

Outside Reinhold Muehler looked at the camera and saw the reel still had five shots left; he called to Hubert Mayr after winding the film back and taking it out.

"Mayr, do you know a trustworthy photographer who could develop these films for us?"

Hubert Mayr shook his head. "Not here, sir. The nearest would be across the border in Germany. I don't even know of a photographer here."

Muehler thought for a few minutes, then turning to Gerhard Gruppe pointed to the films.

"We need to know what's on these films, and if they got a snaps of the plane. We better have them in one at a time. Bring that ginger-haired one in first, he seems to be the leader."

Gruppe produced his pistol and walked out into the hall across to the room where they'd put the two Englishmen.

After seeing the party go out through the fire door, Joan Healey went back to Hans Van Dyke's room and tapped on the door. Hans called, "Come in."

Seeing it was Joan, he said, "I was about to call you. I think we ought to get on our way now, say in about an hour. Tell the party."

"Hans, I've just seen the two boys being taken out through the fire door at the end of this corridor."

"What do you mean, taken out?"

"They were with two other men. Do you think they were Germans? If they were friends, they'd have gone out through the foyer, but they went out through the fire door."

Hans heaved himself up out of the chair and for such a big man moved rapidly out into the corridor past Joan and walked swiftly to the boy's room and then to the fire door. He looked out and all seemed quiet; through the glass panel of the door he could see into the courtyard below and out into the street beyond. Nothing moved, whatever had been there had gone. He walked back to room 315, the boys' room, the door hadn't been closed properly, so he went in. Their luggage was still there along with clothes, as yet not packed.

As he stood there the telephone rang, and he hesitated at first then picked it up.

"Hello." The cultured English voice came through over the very bad line.

"That you, David?" Thinking quickly, Hans guessed that this might be David Coulter's contact in England, somehow connected to the camera film.

"No, David Coulter is not here, but I am a friend of his. My name is Hans Van Dyke, I am a courier for the agency he and Thomas Wadsworth used in Chester to plan their trip. By coincidence we have arrived at the same hotel, at the same time. We did meet them in Germany also and carried out for them an item you were interested in. You are Group Captain Thompson."

"Yes, how is it you are in his room?"

"My assistant, Miss Healey saw them being escorted away from here by two men, they could only be the men who were looking for them earlier, if you get my meaning."

"I do. What do you suggest?"

"I have a party of tourists I need to get to the Channel coast. We must leave here no later than midday." Hans looked at his watch and saw it was 10.30. "I'll try and find out where they are, but it will be difficult. These people will try and take them back to where they've been, so you should try and get the French to watch at the frontiers. You understand?"

"I do, thank you. I'll have someone contact you as soon as you land in England."

"He should ask me how Holland is at this time of year. This as a means of identification. You understand?"

"I do Mr Van Dyke. Thank you. Should you find out about their whereabouts, call me on this number, night and day, Central 60800," with that Gerald Thompson hung off.

He turned to Joan. "Round up the group and tell them we leave at midday. Get hold of our driver and tell him the same thing and get yourself ready as well. We have to get to Rheims today, to enable us to reach Calais tomorrow in time for the night crossing. I'll see if I can find out where our young friends have got to and who with."

Leaving Joan, Hans went down into the foyer to the telephone booth and picking up the phone, asked the operator for a Colmar number.

The number he telephoned was that of the local police, when someone answered, he asked for Inspector Guy Fontaine.

After he'd hung up, Gerald Thompson picked the phone up again and asked to be put through to Aubrey Evans of MI6.

"Aubrey, Gerry Thompson."

"What can I do for you, Gerry?"

"Not too sure if you can." He quickly gave Aubrey the gist of his talk with Hans Van Dyke.

"So you see, Aubrey, they'll try and take them across into Germany or silence them in Colmar. Van Dyke more or less told me he had the information the two boys had collected and would bring it across to us. We need, firstly, to make sure the Krauts can't get across the border with them, and secondly, to find out where they are being held.

"OK, I think speed is of the essence. I'll talk to Anthony Bright of the French desk for that area. Leave it with me."

The two men hung up, and Aubrey Evans walked down the corridor to Anthony Bright's office. Walking into Anthony Bright's secretary's office, he nodded to the closed door leading to the inner office.

"He free?"

The girl nodded. "Yes, Mr Evans, I think so, let me make sure." Lifting her handset she pressed the intercom button and spoke into it.

"Mr Evans is here, Mr Bright." A silence, then she turned to Aubrey, "Go in, Mr Evans."

A grey-haired 50 or so year old man sat behind the desk, he waved to a chair in front.

"Sit down, Aubrey. What's the problem? Those two amateurs you've got on the loose on the French frontier?"

"Yes, Tony. Looks as if the Krauts have nabbed them. Can we get the frontier alerted and also find out if there's a German base in Colmar, y'know a house or somewhere?"

"Difficult the Colmar bit, but the frontier I can get sealed. The two heavyweights that crossed earlier have been identified as Gestapo, a Reinhold Muehler, a nasty bit of work, and a Gerhard Gruppe, not much known about him." Let me talk to my French counterpart, he doesn't like Muehler, evidently had a run in with him somewhere, so will be only too pleased to have a go at him."

Anthony Bright picked up his telephone and speaking in French to his secretary asked her to get Philippe Dauchez for him. He waited a few minutes, then spoke rapidly in to the telephone in French, nodded a few times, spoke again and then hung up.

"Fixed, Aubrey, but the Colmar bit will take a time. I'll place a call, but it's still pretty chaotic with the telephone to that area. Leave it with me, and I'll give you a call as soon as I talk to the man."

Aubrey took his leave and went back to his own office and telephoned Gerald Thompson.

"Gerry, the frontier is fixed but Tony Bright is trying to reach his man in the Colmar area to find an address. I'll call as soon as I have news."

Hans Van Dyke waited until they had put him through to Inspector Fontaine's office and was answered.

"Guy, my friend, Hans Van Dyke. How are you, long time no see. Do you think we'll be tackling the Boche again?"

"Hans, nice to hear from you. No, I don't think either side is ready, but we will in the future have to tackle them. This man Hitler won't stop with the Czechs. He needs expansion, apart from raw materials. What can I do for you?"

"Bad as that, eh? Look, I have a slight problem. Two young friends of mine were in Germany and got into some sort of scrape and fled to here, but the Germans came across after them and have taken them here in Colmar. Have you any idea where the Boche has his consulate, because I think that's where they'd go?"

"Yes, it's on Rue Napoleon just where it joins Rue de la Paix just outside the old town. What are you thinking of doing?"

"I thought I might go along and see if I can't cajole the Boche into releasing them."

"Unlikely. Would you like some unofficial official help?"

"It might help, Guy. It's very good of you."

"Not at all. Anything for an old comrade in arms." (They'd both fought together in the Great War, when Hans had been attached as an interpreter to a French unit fighting alongside a British unit.) I'll come to pick you up. Where are you?"

Hans gave him the hotel name and agreed to be outside in ten minutes.

He then turned to Joan. "If I'm not back by 11.30, you take the party on to Rheims, I'll join you either there or in Calais. Don't worry, I'll be all right."

Joan looked a little startled, she'd never handled a party before by herself, but then she shrugged, there's a first time for everything.

"You said before we'd leave at midday and midday it will be."

Hans could see she had her mind made up, so he gave a short laugh. "As you say, midday."

Hans was waiting outside as the large Citroen police car pulled up alongside him and Guy Fontaine, a 41-year-old slightly balding Frenchman in police uniform opened the passenger door. As Hans got in, he saw there were two other uniformed policemen in the back.

"Good morning again, my friend. I brought some reinforcements to help. A show of strength, as it were."

Taking a route through the old town the car raced off, its siren blaring clearing the way, and pulled up outside a tall white-walled old house on the edge of the old quarter.

In the consulate David and Tom heard the key turn in the lock, and Tom hastily moved behind the door as it was opened slowly. David saw the blond German in the doorway, a gun in his hand, he beckoned David out. David walked towards him as if to go out as Tom swung the door into the German; the German sensing the door was closing, half turned to it, and David grabbed his arm pulling him into the room. As he came in, Tom moved from behind the door and slammed the chair leg hard on his head, the German went down with a thump.

David reached down and took the gun from the German's hand, and he and Tom dragged him into the centre of the room. The German lay inert and blood oozed from an abrasion on his head where the table leg had landed, showing through his short-cut blond hair.

"He's not going to wake up for a while, Tom. Let's get out of here, see if we can find the other one, the dark one, he looked the most dangerous."

They cautiously opened the door and moved silently into the hall. The door directly opposite was partially closed and David heard a voice speaking German, telling another man, called Mayr to see what was keeping Gruppe.

David motioned for Tom to get the other side of the doorway whilst he stayed on his side, pantomiming for Tom to hit someone coming out.

Hubert Mayr came through the doorway out into the hall, and Tom hit him hard with the table leg as David caught him falling, letting him down gently.

David heard the dark man call out from the room, asking what had happened, then the sound of someone walking across the polished oak floor.

The dark man came through the door, and David pointed the gun at him, telling him in German to put his hands up. The dark man started to put his hand into his jacket, David swung the gun up to his head and the man stopped, watching David warily.

"Take his gun, Tom, it'll be in his jacket, probably under his left arm. Be careful, don't get between me and him, otherwise I won't be able to kill him if need be." The German obviously understood English because his eyes flicked to Tom and back to David to see their positions.

David smiled, saying in German. "Don't think of it, friend, I'll kill you."

Tom carefully reached and opened the German's coat and found his Luger stuffed in his trouser waistband.

"Take the gun, Tom, and see if there are any more in that back room and bring them here." To the German he said, "Turn and kneel, then undo your belt, take it off and drop it behind you on the floor, then put your hands behind your head." David moved and kicked the belt away; watching the other man Tom had knocked out come to and sit up, he motioned for the dazed man to follow suit, kneel and take his belt off.

Tom came back with three people, two women and one man, all looking a little scared.

"Can't find any more, David, there may be some upstairs."

The man wasn't wearing a belt but had braces on, suspenders the Americans call them, and David made him take them off and hold his trousers up.

"Put them in the room they had us in, Tom. You," he touched Reinhold Muehler with his foot, "stand up and go with them." They herded the group into the room they had been in; the blond-haired German had come around slightly and was sitting up holding his head. Once the group was inside, David and Tom backed out, closed and locked the door.

In the hall was a small side table, David had seen the dark-haired German put the keys to his car there and walked across to pick up the keys.

"Come on, Tom, before we have any callers, I think this is the German Consulate." The two dashed out and getting into the car moved off down the road. David tried to remember how to get back to the hotel and after several false turns, stopped and asked a passer-by, who directed them.

They arrived back at the hotel as the tour bus containing Joan Healey and her group moved off on the start of its journey to Rheims.

Quickly racing upstairs, they grabbed their already packed bags and quickly went back down to the foyer to check-out. Whilst Tom was completing the formalities, David asked the other clerk if the American group had left. The man said they had gone not five minutes ago and were expecting to stop the night in Rheims at the Hotel Splendide on Rue St Thierry. David asked if it was possible to get a booking there for themselves, and the clerk said he would make a reservation for them via the telegraph. "Rest assured, monsieur, it will be done."

Once Tom had completed the checking-out process, they made their way to their car in the rear, leaving the Germans car outside the hotel.

Once in their car David took the wheel, and Tom consulted the map, giving David directions for getting out of Colmar to Epinal and then Bar-le-Duc to Rheims.

Hans Van Dyke and Inspector Guy Fontaine looked at the building they had stopped in front of, it looked deserted and hadn't a car in front of it, which they had expected. Both men, along with the two uniformed policemen and Guy Fontaine, pressed the doorbell. They waited five minutes, then Guy motioned to the two uniformed men, pointing to the door. "Break it."

The one gendarme, a beefy six-foot-three man put his shoulder to the door and heaved, it gave way and opened up into a hall with a group of five startled people looking at them. One man was dabbing an abrasion on his head.

"Against the wall," Guy Fontaine spoke in German; the two Gendarmes with him unholstered their pistols and waved them around. The group complied and stood in a line.

"Where are the two Englishmen you kidnapped from the hotel this morning?" Guy asked, speaking again in German.

"What Englishmen?" A voice asked from the side and a dark-haired imperious German came from a door further along the hall. "Do you know you are violating protocol by trespassing on German territory?

Guy looked at this German and used a very vulgar expression, "B*** Sh**. This is just a consulate and is not covered by diplomatic immunity. Get in line with the others."

Guy Fontaine turned to Hans.

"Go and search, take Jacque with you." One of the gendarmes moved to the side of Hans, and they set off to search.

A quick search of the building didn't reveal any trace of the two men. Guy, in the meantime, had been looking at the blond German with the bruised and broken head and another of the Germans was looking a little seedy also. He quickly put two and two together and guessed the Englishmen had probably broken loose somehow, roughing up a couple of the Germans in the meantime.

When Hans came back, he took him to one side and quietly said, "Hans, I think your two men have broken away somehow, have a look at that blond German. He's been belted by something, sure as eggs are eggs, it wasn't by one of these."

Guy beckoned the other German to one side and asked him. "How did the Englishmen get away?"

The German started to say. "They…" then shook his head and said he didn't know anything about any Englishmen. Guy smiled, that trick always worked.

"Come Hans, let's go. Your boys are away down the road." They were about to walk out when the dark-haired German spoke.

"Inspector, I wish to report a stolen motor vehicle. It was taken from the front of the building not long ago. I want the culprits apprehended."

Guy smiled. "What is the registration and description, monsieur?" The German gave a description of it and the registration. Guy wrote them down said he'd have the details circulated.

The party reached the hotel and as they stopped in front of it, Guy burst out laughing. "Look, Hans, we've found the missing car. There it is and with the keys in it."

The two men went into the hotel and across the foyer to the reception desk, and Guy asked in rapid French whether Monsieur Coulter and Monsieur Wadsworth had checked out; the clerk told him they had gone about an hour ago and Monsieur Van Dyke's party had left shortly before. He'd made a booking for the Englishmen at the same hotel as Monsieur Van Dyke's party, as the Englishmen had requested.

"Hans, your party has left, so now why don't you take the German's car that's been conveniently left outside and go to Rheims? I'll withhold reporting it stolen until later today, and by the time it is circulated around the country you'll be well ensconced in Rheims. You can drive, can't you? You might even catch your party up somewhere along the route. Those Boche will be a little inconvenienced without a car."

Hans thought about and smiled, then looked at Guy. "Are you sure you won't be in trouble should the Boche report you?"

"I'll make sure any report comes to me, I can easily lose it, and in any case, they'll think the two Englishmen have taken the car."

"OK, I'll just check that my luggage has been taken and then I'll take their car."

"I'll wait here, good friend, until you are on your way."

Hans went up to his room and saw all was clear, his baggage had gone, and went back down to Guy. The two men parted outside, and Hans set off for Rheims driving rapidly and hoping to catch up with the bus somewhere along the way. If they stopped for lunch, which he knew was scheduled to be at Bar-Le-Duc, he might stand a chance and then he could ditch the car in some other place other than Rheims to again confuse any search party.

Taking a few risks as he drove, he reached Bar-Le-Duc around 2 PM and headed for the restaurant close to Saint Etienne Church in St Pierre Square, where the party were booked in for their lunch. Outside the restaurant he saw the tour bus, and Joan Healey marshalling her charges for the final leg to Rheims then Paris. He pulled in behind the bus and walked around to the door. Joan Healey beamed as she saw him.

"Hans, how on earth did you get here so quickly?" She looked at the big Mercedes car he had arrived in and rolled her eyes. "Whose car is it?"

Hans laughed. "By courtesy of the French police and the German Gestapo." He quickly went on to recount the search for the two men and the result.

"Have you seen any trace of them? I believe they left very shortly after you did."

"No, the traffic wasn't too bad, but I wasn't looking for them. I expected you to bring them somehow."

By now all the party were in the coach, and the driver was looking expectantly at Joan and Hans.

"Let me ditch this car in a quiet spot and I'll be with you." He was about to move it when he thought that this spot was as good as anywhere and so he turned back to Joan.

"Let's go, I'll leave it here." He and Joan boarded the coach and signalled the driver to go.

In the meantime, approximately 30 miles to the south-west of Bar-Le-Duc in Vitry, David Coulter and Tom Wadsworth were sitting in their car having a quick snack before setting off again. They were surprised that they had not caught up with the coach that Joan Healey and party were travelling on. They assumed they would take the N4 route and then turn onto the N44 to Rheims through Chalons, so when they reached Ligny they had turned onto the N4. The fact they hadn't caught them was not bothering them, as they hoped they'd be in the same hotel in Rheims.

In London, Anthony Bright, section head in MI6 for the frontier area of France, was talking to Aubrey Evans, section head for the Stuttgart area.

"Aubrey, I've heard from my man in the Colmar region. He'd made a few enquiries at the police headquarters and rumour has it that had been some sort of fracas at the German Consulate and one of their inspectors was involved, sounds like something to do with two Englishmen allegedly kidnapped. The Germans deny any knowledge of anything about two Englishmen. He's not sure of the details, although a German car has been reported missing. Sounds like your boys are certainly having a great time with the Krauts."

"I'll talk to Gerry Thompson at the Air Ministry and see if he's got any news. Did the men involved get away?"

"According to my man, yes they did, and it looks like in the German's car."

Aubrey Evans put a telephone call through to Group Captain Thompson at the Air Ministry.

"Gerry, Aubrey Evans. Tony Bright says his man is reporting an incident involving your two in Colmar." He went on to give a brief outline of what he'd just heard. Then he went on, "Have you heard anything?"

"No, but I think that ties in with the information I gave you earlier and that Dutchman, Hans Van Dyke, may have been successful in helping them. He sounded pretty resourceful, I must keep him in mind."

"He's more in my field than yours, Gerry."

"I agree. The big question is where will the boys head for next? I think it might be Paris. Do you think you could alert your man in Paris? Secondly, do you think the Krauts will chase them?"

"If the Krauts think they haven't been in touch with London, yes, they will try to silence them and get back that information, although the Dutchman has it but they don't know that, so they will try with your boys."

"All I can do is wait for them to get in touch. It's this damned crisis with the Germans and Czechs that's causing chaos to the telephones. They're bad enough normally but add a few thousand more people trying to get through to England and it collapses. Incidentally, I understand that the P.M. is flying to Germany tonight to see if he can resolve the situation."

"He should forget it and go for war; this fella Hitler just wants trouble. We'll have to clobber him sooner or later. Better to be sooner."

"We're not ready by half, Aubrey. We need at least another one, if not two years, as far as this service goes, and I understand it's the same with the others, the army in particular."

"That doesn't surprise me, Gerry. The army are like a lot of dinosaurs; all body and very little brain. It's shameful the way the cavalry regiments dominate their thinking. Cavalry went out when machine guns and tanks came in. Even a good infantry regiment with rapid firing of rifles could defeat a cavalry charge these days. Look at what went on at Mons in the last show, the infantry fired so rapidly that the Germans thought they had machine guns. We still have cavalry regiments who are fighting a last ditch battle to keep their horses. But the Krauts aren't ready either from what I hear, just a lot of bluff."

"These young people like Wadsworth and Coulter and their unit commanders are thinking properly but the entrenched diehards in the War Office and in my service as well, I must admit, can't think beyond their own patch."

"I agree, Gerry; anyway, if I can pick anything up, I'll give you a call."

"I'll do the same."

In Colmar at the German Consulate house, Reinhold Muehler was holding a council of war following the departure of the French police. His assistant

Gerhard Gruppe had managed to stop the bleeding of his superficial head graze. Muehler was lecturing them on the alternatives available, always at the back of his mind was the thought of his fate if he failed or if Wilhelm Altein in Berlin, the Gestapo head for this area, deemed he'd failed.

"We can either go back to Germany and report a failure, and you are all aware of what that will mean, or try and follow the Englishmen and even if we don't stop them contacting their superiors in England, we can liquidate them for violating German security. My decision is that we try and follow them. Mayr, have you an idea where we can obtain transport?"

"Ja, Herr Muehler, we have my car. I am allowed a vehicle and one is also provided by the German Diplomatic Service."

"We need weapons. Have you anymore?"

"Ja, Herr Muehler, in that cupboard over there." He pointed to a corner cupboard in the hall.

Muehler walked across to it quickly, opened the door and saw there were two Lugers plus ammunition and took them out, giving one to Gerhard Gruppe.

Reinhold Muehler then asked if they had any suggestions how to start looking for the men. Hubert Mayr looked thoughtful, then said, "I have a contact in the hotel; these men may have left a forwarding address, which will lead us along the path they took."

"Good, Mayr, let's go to the hotel and see this contact of yours. Where are the vehicles?"

Mayr led them to the back and in the yard were two Mercedes; one with German registration plates, the other with French.

"Take the French-registered vehicle. It would be dangerous to use a German registered car in these times."

The three men piled into the vehicle with Hubert Mayr driving and headed back to the hotel, pulling up in front of the door. Hubert Mayr got out, leaving the other two behind and went in to see the concierge he knew.

The man informed Mayr that the two Englishmen had left about two hours ago and were going to Rheims and had requested his assistant to book them into the Grande Hotel on Rue St Thierry.

Mayr went back and informed Reinhold Muehler.

Muehler told him to get in the car and Mayr refused. He had a legitimate reason for staying, but more importantly, he could see that it was highly likely they would be detained by the French authorities either before they accomplished their task or immediately afterwards. He was also aware that if they didn't achieve the results required, they would be punished should they return to Germany, and he wanted no part of failure.

Muehler didn't argue with him but made a mental note to give him a bad report when he returned to Germany, although he understood why Mayr was refusing to accompany them and the knowledge made him furious.

Muehler put the car in motion, leaving Mayr standing on the pavement outside the hotel. Before leaving the precincts of Colmar, he stopped at a filling station to obtain road maps covering the trip to Rheims.

He drove very fast, with complete disregard for anyone else on the road, but was careful to keep an eye out for any gendarmes that might be operating along the highway. He followed the route taken by the American party of Joan Healey and arrived in Rheims six hours later, covering the 180 miles at an average speed of nearly 30 miles an hour, which at times meant he'd been travelling at 60 miles per hour. The time now was seven o'clock in the evening and it was growing dark. On the outskirts of Rheims they got lost and had to ask the way, eventually arriving at the hotel on Rue St Thierry at eight o'clock.

They sat outside discussing how they should tackle the problem and finally decided to try and get rooms first in a different hotel. Further down the street they located a small hotel and were able to get rooms there, paying advance using the excuse they wanted to leave very early and try and make the German-French frontier, they were worried about the political situation. The proprietor was a little suspicious of the two Germans but as they seemed to be in a hurry to get back to Germany, didn't think a lot about it.

Hans Van Dyke and Joan Healey arrived at the Hotel Grande shortly after six and got their party settled in their various rooms. Then the two of them went into the bar for a drink after cleaning up and changing.

They were there when David Coulter and Tom Wadsworth arrived. The bar was situated just off the foyer, with large double doors opening onto the foyer, and so they were able to watch arrivals and departures whilst having a drink.

As David and Tom walked in, Joan got up and walked out to meet them.

"How are the two of you?"

"Good, thank you, where's Hans? Is he with you?" Joan nodded and pointed in the direction of the bar.

"OK, let's get checked in and we'll come over." The boys went off and Joan returned to Hans. After Hans had joined the party at Bar-Le-Duc, he'd filled Joan in on – as far as he knew – the boys' fate and his theory of their breakout.

"They're coming back down."

The two boys joined Joan and Hans after about 15 minutes and ordered up drinks for themselves.

"Now you two, what happened after the Germans took you?" Hans asked.

David filled him in on what had gone on in the German Consulate and how they'd left the car outside the hotel after taking it.

Hans laughed. "Well, with the connivance of the French police, I took the car and caught up with Joan in Bar-Le-Duc about 60 miles from here, where the car is now resting. I hope the Germans don't have another one. But seriously, have you boys told anyone where you were going?"

"Yes, we told the clerk in the hotel to book us in at the hotel you were all staying in."

"Which means the Germans will know where you are and if they follow, will be able to find you, so be on your guard. Have you spoken to anyone yet in England?"

"No, not yet. We've just booked a call."

In England Aubrey Evans received a call from his man in Colmar that the two Englishmen had gone on to Rheims, so he passed on the information to Aubrey Evans, who in turn passed it through to Gerald Thompson.

In Berlin, Wilhelm Altein screamed at his secretary to trace where Reinhold Muehler was, whilst not far away Deputy Director Haslop was chuckling to himself when he received a report of the happenings in Colmar and the fact that that the two Englishmen appeared to have got clean away. A fact he would exploit to the full to hang a little discredit on the Gestapo.

Chapter Seventeen

The morning Joan Healey had been left to shepherd their party and take them onto Rheims, Elizabeth Austell was looking out of the window of the hotel in Colmar. Her room was at the rear of the hotel on the fourth floor. Her room was at an angle to the fire escape, and she saw the Germans and the two English men leave the hotel. She wasn't aware they were Germans, although she didn't like the look of them. One man had gone on ahead and waited at the foot of the escape until the other man and the two Englishmen arrived at the bottom.

It almost looked as if the Englishmen were being escorted off the premises, strange, and it was also a strange way to leave the hotel. She watched as they walked out through the big doors of the gateway and along the street until they all climbed into a big car. She was uneasy; it somehow seemed to have an air of menace about it. She thought about contacting the other English girl who seemed to be very friendly with the two men, but on second thoughts decided it was the general air of uncertainty that was upsetting her.

Their train was not until two in the afternoon and was taking them direct to Paris for an overnight stay. As she packed her suitcase, she wondered about the two Englishmen and those two men with them, but then with her activity of seeing to her parents put it out of her mind.

She later went down to the foyer to tell the concierge that their cases were ready to be moved from their rooms and was in time to see the two Englishmen leaving the hotel through the front door and so guessed the little episode she had seen that morning was not as sinister as she thought it might have been.

As she was checking herself and her parents out, she asked the clerk if he had heard any news of the Franco-German situation, and he told her that Mr Chamberlain had flown to Germany the evening before and was meeting with Herr Hitler that day but the French Government were calling up more reserves. Unless Mr Chamberlain could agree some sort of settlement within the next week, there most certainly would be war.

As she went back to their rooms to collect her parents, Elizabeth thought that given a week's grace they would be home, they expected to be home within the next three days.

In London, England, Robert Wilson, the inspector in the Special Branch tasked with finding the possible German spy or collaborator in Bristol, had received a reply from the Johannesburg police in response to his enquiry relating to the family of Johann Van Doork.

The Johannesburg police said that there were six Van Doorks in that area and two in Cape Town, the only one that fitted the information he had sent was a

Johann Van Doork, a farmer from near Krugersdorp who had been killed during the battle of Colenso, married to an English woman, Mary Elizabeth Foulkes in 1887, one child from the marriage, a boy Wilhelm, born 1888. The woman had died in 1900; there was no trace of what had happened to the boy.

The report pleased Robert Wilson; it confirmed more or less that the story of the sister and parents in Cheltenham was part of a cover-up. It blew a hole in Foulkes' story; the noose was tightening around the man, and they almost had enough information to call him in for further questioning.

Robert Wilson telephoned Anthony Rudd and gave him the information he'd received from the South African police and asked him if he'd pursued the enquiries with the Bristol Corporation and questioned if had he managed to get a check of the mail being delivered to the Foulkes home.

Tony Rudd said he'd spoken to the Post Office Investigation Branch in Bristol, and they had promised to have the mail deliveries monitored but so far he hadn't received any reports. The surveillance still hadn't turned anything suspicious up, did Robert Wilson want it kept on? Obviously, the man was too clever an operator to be caught out by surveillance, and the German Embassy were not giving anything away either.

A few days later the first results of the mail survey came in, with all mail delivered having originated from out of the Bristol area or another area other than London.

In Germany, Deputy Director Haslop was sitting thinking how he could turn up the heat a little on the major players in the jet engine saga and take a little heat off the two Englishmen currently fleeing across France, presumably being chased by the Gestapo. The lives of the Englishmen was not a thing he thought about, all he was really interested in was that the English got the information as to where the German jet engine programme had reached, and he wondered how he could confirm the delivery of the information to the English authorities. If the English had received the German jet engine position, there may be an increase in activity in the English jet engine camp, so he thought he'd get his man to ask the question.

He telephoned for Wolf Landsberg, the London section head, to see him, and when he arrived, he asked for the latest situation on the English jet engine project. Wolf Landsberg said he would need to get their man to try and find out; that they had had nothing since the confirmation of the dates previously given by Kern.

A coded message was sent across to Heinz Kern asking the question, which in turn gave Heinz Kern a problem.

Heinz Kern was pretty sure that William Foulkes would be unable to provide much further information on the English jet engine project until the English had started to take a major step forward. All they would be doing at the moment would be still experimental; he was sure that as soon as there was a major movement, William Foulkes would inform him because Foulkes needed the money. So he turned over the alternatives in his mind; he could try and contact Foulkes and ask the question, he could compose an answer himself or he could do nothing until they pressed him again.

The problem was resolved by the Gestapo operative in the embassy, Paul Muller, who read all communications to and from the embassy. He asked Heinz Kern what he was doing about the request from Berlin for information regarding the English jet programme. Kern said he was getting in touch with his operative in the Bristol area but that he had to be careful because the English were watching.

Kern cursed the Gestapo man and sent a letter to Anthony O'Brien, the Liverpool man he'd used previously to contact Foulkes, telling him to call in at the consulate again to apply for a visa. Kern knew he would have to send some money to Foulkes if he wanted to have some sort of a reply.

When O'Brien called in at the consulate, Kern saw him and gave him the wherewithal in the way of documentation to be a representative of the engine manufacturer. He was to deliver the letter to Foulkes in the guise of a quotation for an engine for his car.

O'Brien contacted Foulkes by letter to set up an evening meeting in a pub of Foulkes' choice, Foulkes also setting the time.

Foulkes replied by letter addressed to the engineering company, which Kern had given for O'Brien to use at O'Brien's mail drop in Liverpool.

The pub which Foulkes selected was one of the ones he used regularly and where he was known. He advised O'Brien to ask the barman for him when he arrived. It was Foulkes' intention to tell the barman after the meeting was over a plausible excuse for the visit.

The Special Branch man tailed Foulkes to the pub and saw him meet with O'Brien and the two men talk. He saw O'Brien give Foulkes a brochure of sorts and after the two men had talked for about half an hour, they shook hands and O'Brien left.

The brochure that O'Brien had handed to Foulkes contained Kern's letter and a small sum of money hidden within the centre pages, the two men had agreed to meet in a week's time at the same pub.

In his report of the activity of Foulkes during his period of surveillance, the Special Branch man reported the meeting but said that the brochure handed over referred to motor vehicle engines, which the Special branch saw as the title of the brochure as he passed their table when he got up for another drink. His assumption was that the man met had some sort of connection to motor vehicle engines and certainly wasn't one of Foulkes regular friends.

Opening the two envelopes at home, Foulkes was gratified to receive the sum of money and then cursed the second envelope containing the request for more information. He knew he hadn't much chance of getting any more other than that from the man he and his girlfriend had met. He had to move very cautiously in asking questions because he knew by now that the jet engine project came under the Official Secrets Act.

He and his girl were meeting the other two the next Friday, so he decided to drop the odd question in the course of the evening related to the project should the opportunity occur.

In Germany, Deputy Director Haslop realised he was asking for something that may take a while to eventuate with the English, even if they had already received the information, but it was worth a try.

In Bristol, Tony Rudd, the Special Branch sergeant, who had been away on other work for a few days, was catching up with the surveillance reports on Foulkes and the meeting in the pub with the supposed car engine representative struck him as slightly odd. Normally, that sort of thing would be done at the garage supplying the engine or at a person's home. After he'd finished reading the report, he went down to the squad room to see if the man who had been on duty at that time was available. He found he was there and asked him about the man, had he seen the man Foulkes had with him before, the magazine was it purely technical? Did he notice which way the man had gone? Did he see him arrive?

The operative hadn't shown a lot of interest in the man basically because he thought he was a salesman selling something to do with the engine of Foulkes car.

Tony Rudd had a word with the sergeant running the surveillance team and in agreement with him was assured they would follow-up on any future strangers that Foulkes contacted, just to make sure they were clean.

Tony Rudd, giving thought to the meeting between Foulkes and the unknown man, guessed that he could be the connection between Foulkes and the German Embassy. According to all surveillance reports, monitoring of his mail and the information reaching the German Embassy, he only seemed to have met the man the once. The possibility did cross his mind that there was a blind mail drop somewhere, although here again the surveillance reports should have turned up something and hadn't. He turned back the old surveillance reports, and the only odd thing that came up was his visit to Bristol Temple Meads railway station enquiry office and yet he hadn't bought a rail ticket or made a rail journey.

The only odd items, and they weren't that odd, in the mail delivered to the Foulkes address were a letter from an engineering company in St Helens, Lancashire, but posted in Liverpool, and a plain envelope posted in Southampton, which appeared to be a holiday brochure of some sort. The people monitoring the mail hadn't opened them, they were only looking for letters postmarked London.

Tony Rudd talked the situation over with Robert Wilson, Special Branch inspector in London, going over the meeting in the pub and the Bristol Temple Meads trip, plus the fact that he was getting his information back to the German Embassy somehow; others must be involved if he was Michael Mulroney.

"I think we should pull him in now, sir. We have enough discrepancies in his story to question him on."

"I agree, Tony, but if he's part of a larger group, and that is what you are suggesting, I want them all. We cannot rely on him to give us any information. Wait and see if he meets the same man again, then we'll have a close look at the other man, if we think he's doubtful, we'll take them and play one off against the other."

"You wouldn't want to wait and see if he sees any others?"

"I don't think so; most of the German operatives have been rounded up. We know their man Kern in the embassy is short of people now, we know there has to be some amongst the refugees that have come over from Europe, but we don't think there are many."

The two talked briefly again and then rang off.

Foulkes and his girlfriend met the man from the Gloucester area and his girl again on the following Friday, whilst the two women had gone to powder their noses together, the man casually mentioned that he thought the Germans were also working on a similar aeroplane to theirs. He'd heard one of the bosses talking to a man who'd come down from London when they were inspecting the unfinished fuselage, and he mentioned the German angle and from what they had said they had more funding, so were going to step up the production, which would mean the project was continuing, whereas before it had been doubtful.

The following Monday Foulkes sent a letter off to the German Embassy with the exaggerated information that the British were accelerating their production of the plane. He also asked for more money for his informant, whom he said was demanding more because of the risks he was taking.

This letter was intercepted and confirmed to Robert Wilson that if Foulkes was Michael Mulroney, he had another method of getting his money, so he passed a message to Bristol that they should be particularly vigilant because Mulroney was expecting more money and it had to get to Foulkes somehow.

Kern, in London, passed the information on to Wolf Landsberg in Berlin, who in turn sent it to Deputy Director Heinrich Haslop.

Heinrich Haslop was misled into believing that the information the two Englishmen had obtained had reached the English Air Ministry and had been acted upon.

Robert Wilson wondered if Foulkes was just making the information up or was there any basis of fact in his report, which would give them a problem because it would indicate that there was someone else in the circle. He decided he should talk to that group captain at the Air Ministry and see if there was any truth in the information Foulkes had sent to the German Embassy.

He quickly thumbed through the file on the Bristol German agent investigation and came up with the name of Group Captain Thompson and it gave a telephone number.

He telephoned and made an appointment to see the group captain the following morning, giving the subject matter he wished to discuss.

The following morning, he was ushered into Group Captain Thompson's office. He'd met him before on a previous case apart from this one.

Gerald Thompson had a healthy regard for this Special Branch inspector and so knew he would be coming with something solid that required answering.

Gerald Thompson stood and shook hands with Robert Wilson, they made small talk until their coffees had been brought in, then Gerald Thompson looked enquiring at Robert Wilson.

"Now, what can I do for you, Inspector?"

"As you are aware, we have been searching for a while for a German agent operating in the Bristol area. We think we have our man, but we want to make sure he's a loner and not operating a ring, because if we pull him in, the rest of the ring will be still out there. He's crafty and from the look of it is a loner but something came up last week which made me think..." He went on to explain the information that 'Michael Mulroney' had sent to the German Embassy and asked was it fact or fiction, showing Gerald Thompson the wording in the letter sent to the embassy.

Gerald Thompson thought for a moment and then turned and picked up his telephone, asking his secretary to get a contact in the engineering branch for him.

When connected he spoke for a while, asking about the progress on the jet engine and its status.

Putting the telephone down, he turned back to Robert Wilson.

"Looks as if your man is exaggerating. The only change there has been is that the Ministry funding has been extended and the project is moving forward, whereas before there was doubt that any more funding would be available."

"Thank you, sir. That makes it a little easier for us. He must be gathering snippets of information from the pubs he visits in the area and is making a guess or deliberately cheating his masters for some extra money."

"What do you propose to do, Inspector?"

"At the moment he's pretty harmless. We have him under surveillance, and although there's a fair amount of circumstantial evidence against him and we think it's enough to pull him in, we may leave him for a while just to confirm he is a loner."

The two men chatted for a while on the international situation, then Robert Wilson took his leave.

Back in his own office, he telephoned Tony Rudd in Bristol with the information he'd received from Group Captain Thompson.

"It certainly looks as if our man is stretching what little he gleans around the place, sir."

"Mmmm, I think he needs money and doesn't like the look of the political situation, so he thinks he'll milk it as hard as he can, because should war break out, his source of money will dry up. He also thinks that he can stretch out such information he receives, because again if war breaks out, he'll never be found out."

"What do you suggest, sir?"

"I think we'll wait a couple of weeks more and then move in. We've enough discrepancies in his story to ask him for a clarification."

That evening Robert Wilson stayed late in the office, going over the evidence they had on Foulkes, the discrepancies and the details of the interview. Reading the interview notes again, it suddenly hit him; the thing that he'd had at the back of his mind and couldn't place. Foulkes explained the difference in his name and address during the interview with the foreman and the foreman misunderstanding and writing it down incorrectly, the foreman was positive that Foulkes had written the information down himself and that was the information on the note he'd given into personnel. The woman in the Personnel Department remembered the note but she had not kept it.

Foulkes had deliberately given a false name and address so he wouldn't be traced as being the man offered a place at the Gloster factory.

Having reviewed the information, Robert Wilson decided to speak to his superior the next morning for permission to bring in Foulkes and charge him; he also realised that if convicted, Foulkes would hang.

The following morning, he went to see Andrew Carter, Deputy Controller, his immediate superior in the Special Branch.

Andrew Carter's secretary, a woman in her fifties, contacted her boss on the intercom and nodded at Robert Wilson for him to go in. Robert Wilson entered the spartan office of his chief, a man slightly older than himself, Robert Wilson was 45 and Andrew Carter was a man of 50. They'd worked together for a good number of years, and each man had respect for the other.

"Morning, Robert. What can I do for you?"

"Good morning, sir. The Bristol German agent investigation, sir. I think we are in a position to bring a man in for detailed questioning, and I would like to have a warrant issued for his arrest, sir."

"Mmmm, I've followed your reports on the investigation, Andrew. I take the man you want to collar is this Foulkes character? Your evidence is a bit thin, I thought."

Robert Wilson went over the discrepancies in the story Foulkes had told them, the non-existent sister and parents in Cheltenham, the dart match discrepancy over who wrote the name down, and the fact he had been in an admirable position to pass on information about the Bristol aircraft machines, which were the subject of intelligence warnings from Germany, whilst working putting in the electrical substation.

"Sounds as if he's our man then, Bob, although a bit thin."

"Yes, sir."

"Have you talked to anyone in MI5 about this?"

"Not for a few months. I didn't have a lot of information then, but I did talk to Mr Ferguson, the MI5 comptroller for the West of England."

"OK, Bob, I'll talk to him and let you know what he thinks and get back to you. Should anything of importance turn up in the meantime, give me a call."

"Yes, sir." With that Robert Wilson took his leave.

When he returned to his office, he put a telephone call through to Anthony Rudd in Bristol and brought him up to date on his progress in London, and also asked him to have an arrest warrant prepared for Foulkes.

"We may have difficulty with the evidence; it's a bit slim, as you say."

"Do it under the 1916 Defence of the Realm Act and bandy the Official Secrets Act around, these magistrates always get excited over the Official Secrets Act. That 1916 Act has never been repealed, and we used on the IRA suspects a few weeks ago. There is a new act being drafted, but it won't be law until later this year or maybe next."

Later that day Anthony Rudd went before one of the local magistrates in closed session and presented the case against Foulkes. The magistrate, an elderly retired army officer, didn't quibble and issued it immediately, such was the atmosphere being generated by the German Sudetenland Crisis and Czechoslovakia.

Anthony Rudd now had his arrest warrant to keep in reserve and use as soon as Robert Wilson gave the go-ahead.

In France, Reinhold Muehler and Gerhard Gruppe, after taking their small suitcases to their rooms, went out and finding a small café in the next street had a meal, sitting over coffee afterwards they discussed how they should tackle their problem. They had to get any film the two Englishmen had taken at Stuttgart and then liquidate them. They certainly wouldn't be able to take them back across the frontier to Germany, even in normal times it would have been difficult, but right now it was impossible because of the political situation. They also agreed they couldn't do anything about them whilst they were in the hotel, firstly they would have to locate their rooms, an impossible task without inside help, otherwise they would arouse suspicion, and then interrogate them.

So they agreed the first thing to do was to locate the Englishmen's car, it had to be somewhere close to the hotel that the Englishmen were staying in, these smaller hotels didn't usually run to a garage, so tourists usually left their vehicles in the street close to the hotel.

They would then wait by the car to capture the Englishmen as they came to collect their car.

They left the café and started to systematically search the streets around the Hotel Grande on Rue St Thierry. They eventually found the car and moved their vehicle close to it. Checking their watches and seeing it was midnight, they decided to go and catch a little sleep, reasoning the Englishmen wouldn't move until after dawn the next day, which was about six.

In London, Group Captain Gerald Thompson had left his office around seven that evening with instructions that any call that came in from the two men in France should be immediately transferred to his home.

In Rheims David Coulter and Tom Wadsworth sat in the bar with Hans Van Dyke and Joan Healey after having had their evening meal with them, discussing their next move. Hans and Joan said they'd be going about ten in the morning, after Hans had talked to Edward Smith, the owner of the travel agency, to see whether they should go to Paris or head straight for Calais. The date was now 12th September and they had to be in Calais for the 17th of September. Paris was approximately 80 miles from Rheims and Calais was 200. The distance from Paris to Calais was also 200 miles.

Around midnight the night porter came across and said that their call had come through and would they go to the booth in the foyer? The pair excused themselves and went to the telephone booth located in the foyer. David picked up the telephone when it rang.

"Hello." The line was very bad, and he could barely hear the voice on the other end but recognised it as Group Captain Thompson.

"That you, David?"

"Yes, sir. Sorry it's taken so long to get…"

Gerald Thompson cut in,

"Don't worry about that, where are you?"

"Rheims, sir. We have the information about…"

Again Gerald Thompson cut in, "Not over the telephone. Make for Calais immediately. I'll have someone to meet you there and also your friend Hans. He knows the identification phrase the contact will use. It's now just after eleven here at night, Monday, and just after midnight your time 13th September, Tuesday, early morning. Try and make Calais today, our man will be there." The phone went dead, David jiggled the receiver cradle without success, then the night porter came on.

"I'm sorry, sir. The connection has been cut; the army want to use the line."

In London, Gerald Thompson guessed what had happened to the telephone connection and was satisfied he'd got the main message through and now needed to organise a contact in Calais.

The two young men re-joined Hans and Joan, and David gave the gist of the short call. Hans looked at his watch,

"It's now 30 minutes past midnight. What do you intend to do? By the way the identification phrase is 'How is Holland at this time of year?' and you'll know the right man has made contact."

David thought for a few minutes, with Calais 200 miles away, even at 30mph on average, which would mean travelling a lot faster at times to compensate for the slower periods, it would take them around seven hours without a break. They needed to be in Calais at the shipping terminal prior to three in the afternoon; secondly, there was the question of a passage back on the ferry. Their booking was for the 17th and they would be in Calais on the 13th, but maybe the Group Captain had something arranged.

The Group Captain had made a note in his mind first thing to talk to his contact to try and get the two a passage that afternoon or at the latest the next day.

David looked at Tom. "What say we check-out as soon as possible and leave immediately, the trip will take at least seven hours, and we need to be in Calais no later than three in the afternoon. We can take a short catnap and a meal somewhere."

Hans cut in. "Also remember, the Germans might still be looking for you. So watch yourselves in Calais. We will still bring back the film, don't worry about it, just make sure you look after yourselves."

Joan Healey said, "Come on then. I'll help you pack." The three went out and up to the boys' room. Hans smiled to himself as they left, thinking that Joan had taken a shine to the Coulter boy.

Leaving Joan and Tom to pack what little they'd taken out of their luggage, David went down to the desk. The normal staff wasn't on the desk, only the night porter, and David explained they needed to get to Calais that afternoon to make the ferry so would like to leave now. The night porter was accustomed to the early departures of guests at times and was fully conversant to the preparing their account. Whilst doing so he made conversation with David, asking him about his ferry booking. David truthfully said he didn't have a booking, but they were being met by a friend who would have the details for either today or the next day.

The two boys left, promising to be in touch when they were back in England.

The Austell family had left Colmar on the 12th of September direct to Paris for one night and then catching the Golden Arrow again to be in England for the 14th of September. Elizabeth thought quite a bit about the German officer and hoped that the political situation would clear and he would be able to come across to England to visit with them.

Once back the two boys moved their luggage down to the foyer. Whilst Tom went and brought the car, David stayed talking to Hans and Joan in the foyer; as Tom came back in, David gave Joan a kiss on the cheek, shook hands with Hans and the two boys left. The time was two o'clock in the morning.

The streets were deserted, apart from the odd military transport, and the boys made good time clearing Rheims.

Their route was through Laon, St Quentin, Arras and St Omer to Calais. They intended to stop in Arras or at least in that area for a meal and a short sleep, although they agreed that the person not driving would sleep during the trip.

Chapter Eighteen

In Rheims Gerhard Gruppe and Reinhold Muehler were awakened by the telephone operator of the small hotel they had rooms in and went down, settled their account and had coffee and croissants before leaving to take up a position close to the place where the Englishmen had left their car. As they walked around to where their car and the Englishmen's car were, Inspector Muehler checked his watch and saw it was just after 5.30 AM, shafts of light were beginning to show in the east, heralding dawn.

David Coulter and Tom Wadsworth had made good time and at 5.30 AM were just the other side of Cambrai, having stopped there to pick up some rolls and croissants and had their flask filled with coffee. They found a spot to park, just off the road amongst some trees, and broke their fast. They settled down to have a few hours' sleep, setting an alarm clock for 8 AM.

Meanwhile in London, Group Captain Gerald Thompson had arrived at his office in the Air Ministry at 6 AM and called Aubrey Evans, knowing he would be in his office early also.

"Morning, Aubrey, Gerald Thompson here."

"Morning, Gerry, I take it you've heard from your two men."

"Yes, they should be in Calais around midday and are going straight to the boat terminal. Have you a man who can help them there?"

"Yes, although it's pretty chaotic the way things are at the moment. Every man and his dog is trying to make it back to England before the storm breaks, as it were."

"Yes, I can imagine. I think the PM is still over in Germany, is he not?"

"So I believe. Rumour has it he's going to try for a deal with Hitler, and the best of British to him. I have a man over there who has a couple of photos of your men, those you gave me a few months ago, and he's aware of the situation so all should be well. I'll contact him immediately."

"Thank you, Aubrey. I wonder if the Krauts are following them."

"I think so, they'll not give up that easily; the two heavies that we know entered France will follow, because if they don't, they'll be held responsible for the two getting away and will be sent to one of those labour camps the Germans have, not nice places."

The two Germans reached their car and when they looked for the English car, found it had gone. Gerhard Muehler could feel the icy hand of Wilhelm Altein, his superior in Berlin, already guiding him to a forced labour camp. A concentration camp where as a failed Gestapo agent he'd be treated far more severely than the usual inmate and their treatment was bad enough, where something like 70 per cent died within the first year.

"They've left early, back to the hotel and wait outside with the car whilst I see if the concierge knows where and what time they went, Gruppe."

At the hotel Muehler went inside and saw just the night porter at the desk and asked him where were the two Englishmen, Wadsworth and Coulter? The concierge told him they had left around two that morning hoping to make Calais that day.

As he was leaving the desk to go out, Hans Van Dyke came out of the lift to sort out the accounts of the tour and saw him and put two and two together that the two Germans would be going to Calais to intercept the two young men. He searched in his briefcase and found the telephone number Gerald Thompson had given him, giving it to the night porter, he asked for an urgent call to be made.

Normally, the night porter would have made an ordinary guest to wait for the day clerks to arrive, which they did at 6.30 AM but he was aware that this man was a very regular guest at the hotel and usually travelled as a tour guide, bringing with him a number of people. So he sat at the switchboard located behind the reception desk and tried the international operator in Paris himself. His persistence paid off, also assisted by the time of the morning when the calls to England were at their lightest, notwithstanding the political situation.

Gerald Thompson took the call. "Yes, Mr Van Dyke, what can I help you with?"

"Group Captain, your two friends left here in the early hours and should be in Calais around eleven this morning, at least that was their target, they intend to get to near Arras and have a rest, then continue. Now I've just seen some German pursuers, who have left now to follow them in hope of catching them at Calais. The problem, as I see it, is that if your two stop on the way, which they intend to, both parties will reach the ferry terminal at Calais about the same time. You should have someone meet them and either get them to a safe place or be prepared to defend them. These Germans will be chasing them to assassinate them, believing that the information has already been passed on to you."

"Thank you, Mr Van Dyke, we'll take precautions. We must meet, give me a call when you get back and we'll arrange something. Thank you."

Gerald Thompson hung up and sat thinking about the problem. Then he dialled Aubrey Evans again.

"Aubrey, Gerry here again. You were right, I've just heard there are two Krauts chasing them and should arrive in Calais about the same time as my two. Will your man be armed, because from what my informant said your man will need a weapon, I think?"

"Mmmm, I'll try and get him again. I've just spoken to him but I never asked him about protection. Leave it with me."

Aubrey Evans telephoned his man in Calais but didn't get an answer, so hoped the man had the sense enough to take a gun with him.

The Germans had made good time, although taking risks and reached outskirts of Calais at two in the afternoon. They got slightly lost entering Calais but after asking for directions, found themselves on the Rue du Nord and in sight of the terminal buildings and rail station. The traffic was heavy heading in the same direction as them, most vehicles were English tourist cars heading for the ferry. Eventually, they found that could make no further progress forward, so Reinhold Muehler left the vehicle and walked towards the terminal building on foot. Gerhard Gruppe was to stay with the car and make progress forward as best he could.

Reaching the terminal building, the German wondered where was best for him to search for the two Englishmen and decided the car ferry offices would be the best. He reasoned the Englishmen would not have a passage booked and would be there trying to get a passage, the problem he had was not knowing when the Englishmen had arrived here in Calais. They had left Rheims around two that morning, the hotel concierge had said, now there were two of them to share the driving, so they could have arrived in Calais anytime from eleven onwards, but they would have to leave their car or stay in it in the line of vehicles, hoping to make the ferry that evening.

So a visit to the terminal building first, and then have a look in the vehicles lined up for the ferry. In the terminal building he found a crowd of people all trying to reach the counter to obtain a passage on the vessel that afternoon, going through the crowd he couldn't see any sign of either of the two Englishmen, so he made his way down to the quayside and started methodically from the front, checking on the vehicles to see if they were in the line-up. The vehicles were lined up three abreast and the ferry hadn't yet started to load, having only just arrived in a couple of hours previously and discharged the small number coming from England. He didn't find them in the queue of cars. So he walked back along the Rue du Nord until he found Gerhard Gruppe and slipped into the car with him. As he did so, Gruppe looked enquiringly at him.

"No sign of them either in the office or lined up to board."

"Maybe they are not coming to Calais?"

"I think it's pretty certain they'll be here sometime. I don't think any other port can handle motor cars, and they did tell the man at the hotel that Calais was their destination." He sat pensive for a moment, then turned to Gruppe.

"I'll watch here. You find a telephone and telephone the embassy in Paris. Try and get a contact here who is reliable who can help should we need to go to England. We can leave the car here and board as ordinary passengers; we stand a better chance of boarding that way, but we need someone to help. If we see them on-board, we can accomplish our task, otherwise we can do it in England."

Gerhard Gruppe left the vehicle and walked down the street, going into the first small shop he found and asked where the main telephone office was located. The proprietor, a surly pot-bellied Frenchman first directed him to the main passenger terminal building on the quay but after Gerhard Gruppe explained it was impossible because of the number of people trying to telephone, the man directed him into the town centre. Finding the office Gruppe asked at the counter if he could telephone Paris, giving the embassy number and telling the clerk that it was the German Embassy number.

The clerk directed him to a booth and after a short while the telephone rang and he was connected, he gave his name and identified he was a Gestapo official. After a discussion with the people in the embassy, having been passed from one to another, he was given a contact in Le Havre, the German representative for the Hamburg-Amerika line, who might be able to help with a contact in Calais.

Meanwhile in the car, although he watched carefully, Reinhold Muehler didn't see any sign of the Englishmen but as he was a fair distance in totally stationary traffic from the terminal, it wasn't surprising.

After a lot of difficulty in finding another telephone, Gruppe then telephoned the name and number given in Le Havre. It was a German Heinrich Siechmann, who seemed at first reluctant to help, but the mention of the Gestapo made him immediately give the name of a Frenchman in Calais who acted as a forwarding agent for the Hamburg-Amerika line, a Philippe Charonnat, and his telephone number, along with his address.

As he walked back to where he'd left Reinhold Muehler and their car, he fortunately passed the street the Frenchman's office was in, so turning into it he found the office halfway along.

The office was on the first floor above a shop; on a board next to the door was a list of shipping lines the man represented, which gave Gruppe a hope that he'd have a little influence in getting them a passage across to England.

The office was at the end of a grubby passage on the first floor, and Gruppe knocked and went in to a fairly large room with two desks in it. The room was in keeping with the building, papers piled everywhere, a grubby carpet on the floor and the windows overlooking the street looked as if they hadn't been cleaned for a long time. A 50 or so year old man looked up as Gruppe entered and said in French,

"Can I help you, monsieur?"

"Possibly, myself and my superior maybe will have to go to England on the next sailing of the ferry. We haven't yet tried to get tickets but from the look of things, it will be difficult. Herr Siechmann in Le Havre said you might be able to help, is that so?"

The Frenchman looked him up and down and then turned away for a moment, looking out through the dirty window and then turned back.

Speaking in German this time, he said, "Herr Siechmann telephoned me a short time ago, and I think I can get two tickets but it will cost a lot of money. Can you pay?"

Gruppe thought *'these French, on the make all the time'*.

Out loud he said he could, and so the Frenchman told him to come back in two hours, which would still give him ample time to board the ferry.

Arriving back at the car, he briefed Reinhold Muehler with the ticket position, and the two sat in the car watching the other vehicles as they gradually moved ahead towards the ferry terminal.

David Coulter and Tom Wadsworth had arrived at the Calais terminal about half an hour ahead of the two Germans. The place was chaotic, with cars gradually becoming grid-locked as the Germans had found it.

Leaving their car a block away from the terminal building, they walked to the terminal office and joined the queue of people at a point just outside the door.

They had only just joined the line when a sandy-haired man in his forties came and spoke to them.

"Pretty rough in there, have you two come from Holland? How are things in Holland?"

David nodded but didn't speak, and the man scarcely moving his lips quietly said, "Follow me carefully."

The man made off slowly towards the right and then turned into a small side street, a cul-de-sac, and halfway down entered a small yard. The two boys followed him, once inside, he closed the small gate behind them and turning held out his hand. In slightly accented English, he said,

"Marc Farjot, you are David Coulter and Thomas Wadsworth? Papers, please." Both of them produced their passports, and he scrutinised them, comparing their photos with one he had produced. Then he nodded and smiled. "Come." He led the way into the back of a small house at the end of the yard and into a lounge room facing the street, a street filled with cars trying to get to the terminal.

"Now, gentlemen where is your car?" They explained where they had left it, and he held out his hand.

"Give me the keys. I need to take it to another place, easier to get at from here. You will need to leave your car here, and I'll get it to you after all this chaos has finished, in about a week. You are too easily identified by the car, and it will be easier to get you on the ferry without the car. The Germans are not far behind you. I'll leave you now and move the car. I'll be back shortly with your luggage." With that he went out, leaving the two boys.

Whilst he was out the telephone in the hall rang twice, but the two didn't move to answer it, judging it would be for him, not him calling them from another location.

He was back in half an hour with another man, a porter and their luggage.

"Now gentlemen, a drink." He produced a bottle of red wine and poured them a glass each.

Sitting down facing them, he produced tickets for the ferry.

"I have you on the ferry in a two-berth cabin. The cabin has been booked in the names of Smith and Jones. No one checks the names against identification unless there is a dispute, and I'm sure there won't be one this time. We'll get you on board shortly before it sails; in the meantime, I have an associate trying to find the two Boche but in this crowd it is very difficult, so if we don't locate them you will need to be careful. Do not leave the cabin until you reach Dover and someone comes to you using the same phrase about Holland."

They told him about the telephone ringing and he nodded. "That will be my chief in England. I'll call him now." He went out, closing the door behind him.

He came back in after about 15 minutes. "I have talked to your Group Captain Thompson, and he agrees that you should not leave the cabin until someone identifies themselves to you using the Dutch phrase. They think the

Germans wish to assassinate you both." The two looked at each other, wide-eyed, and David spoke.

"You mean kill us here on French or British soil?"

The Frenchman nodded. "These two will stop at nothing if they've been ordered to kill you." He held up his hand, the palm facing David, who was about to speak.

"No, don't tell me what you have done or not done. I'm not interested; my task is to get you onto the ferry in one piece." He looked at his watch. "We need to move in about an hour."

In London, Group Captain Thompson, having spoken to Marc Farjot, smiled to himself and made a quick telephone call to Aubrey Evans and Anthony Bright, MI6 section heads for Stuttgart and France, to give them the news. That the MI6 operative in the Calais area had made contact with the two fugitives and had them in a safe house, ready to see them onto the ferry for Dover. He then gave thought whether to meet the ferry in person but on second thought decided to leave it to MI5 in UK. Just in case the Germans had followed them and there was trouble, he felt he'd only be in the way.

He placed a call in to Thomas Wright, the MI5 comptroller for the South East of England, and spoke with him about the possible problem at Dover.

"I'm not sure the Krauts will follow them to Dover, but they might, so I think you should warn your men there that there may be trouble."

"Never mind, Gerry, I've already got that covered; we'll work on the presumption the Krauts will try." The two men talked for a short time and then hung up.

Group Captain Thompson was more than satisfied with the situation; it looked good.

Thomas Wright, the MI5 officer in charge of the Dover area, decided that with all the interest being shown in these two officers, he'd go to Dover himself and lend assistance to his man for the operation. The vessel they were on was scheduled to be in at 4 PM, so checking with his senior man in Dover, he boarded a train and arrived in Dover shortly after 3 PM.

The MI5 office in Dover was in the port area in amongst the freight forwarding agent's offices; a grubby-fronted building of three stories. The MI5 office was on the first floor a small one-room affair, sparsely furnished with a plain light oak wooden desk, five chairs, a small table under the window with a typewriter on it and two wooden low cupboards. The window overlooked the port area passenger terminal. On the desk alongside the typewriter was a pair of high-powered field glasses on a stand.

He walked from the rail terminal to the office and first knocking, let himself in.

The two men in there, both in their mid-twenties, looked surprised as he came in.

"Good afternoon, gentlemen." The two men had stood up when he walked in, and he motioned for them to sit down taking a chair himself.

"I thought I'd come down just to lend you some support. All action I'll leave to you. Do we know if the Germans boarded the ferry?"

The senior of the two men answered. "Yes, sir. We had a call from Marc Farjot in Calais to say our men were on the ferry, and he was pretty sure at least two Germans had followed them on. Apparently, he has a contact, a Frog who works both sides and actually assisted two Germans to get on board. So we know at least two are on-board, our two men have been told to stay in their cabin for the voyage and not move until one of us comes for them at Dover. We have been given a recognition phrase."

"You are armed, I presume?"

"Yes sir. Both of us. I'll go and get the two, and Tom here will wait at the entrance to the cabins, then follow us as we leave. The immigration officers and customs on the shore have been warned we will be bringing two men off. We have a car at the end of the terminal building. We're not too sure who the German are, although the Frogs did pass on to MI6 that two Gestapo men had crossed into France in the guise of being finance people going to their Paris Embassy. It is possibly them, and their names have been passed onto the immigration department here, and we'll detain them because they possibly won't have visas for here. They haven't had time to get them."

"If they're travelling on a diplomatic passport, they won't need them," Thomas Wright observed.

"Yes, sir," just then the telephone rang and one of the men answered. Gave a terse, "Many thanks," then turning to Thomas Wright,

"The ferry is just entering the port, sir, we better get down to the quay." The senior man turned to Thomas Wright, "Would you like a piece, sir?" Thomas Wright nodded and the man went across to the cupboard and took out a small automatic pistol and shoulder holster. Thomas Wright shook his head.

"No, give me the S and M thirty-eight." The man returned the pistol and brought out a revolver and shoulder holster. Thomas Wright took his jacket off and slipped the shoulder holster on, putting the gun in the holster and then his jacket on.

"Let's go," he said, moving to the door. The three men moved down the stairs and walked slowly towards the terminal building as the ferry manoeuvred its side on to the quay. The three men joined a group standing on the quayside consisting of uniformed customs officers and two policemen, a sergeant and constable. Both the policemen looked curiously at the MI5 group, the sergeant nodded to the senior man, then said,

"I'll follow you, sir. Bill here will cover the top of the gangway and stop anyone leaving until you're clear."

The senior MI5 man nodded.

The gangway was lowered down by a dockside crane and the top end secured to the open door in the side of the vessel. This gangway was for crew and shore officials use only, the passengers left by two gangways, which would be placed between the upper deck and the second floor of the terminal building.

The dockside labourers watched as the gangway was slowly lowered into position and then secured it on the quayside. The MI5 party followed the two policemen up the gangway and then moved through the crowd of crew members waiting to go ashore. As the MI5 party moved towards the passenger accommodation, Thomas Wright heard the police constable stopping the crew members from leaving. The small party entered into the passenger accommodation and checked the cabin numbers, eventually arriving at the one the two young men were using. One of the MI5 men moved away and walked back along the narrow corridor and up the stairs at the end. At the top he entered a large open space with an office across from the stairs and took up position at the top, warily and covertly looking around at the group of passengers milling around, trying to spot anyone odd amongst them.

Reinhold Muehler and Gerhard Gruppe sat and waited for the required two hours the Frenchman had asked for, watching the cars edging their way towards the terminal; although most of the cars were English, they didn't sight either of their quarries. At the end of the two hours Reinhold Muehler shook his head. "Come," he said and moved from the car, and the two walked back to the Frenchman's office. At the office the Frenchman produced two tickets for the sailing and then asked for payment, still holding onto the tickets.

Muehler looked at Gruppe and nodded. Gruppe paid and the Frenchman handed the tickets over, saying that they were only tickets and didn't entitle them to any cabin space at all, they'd have to see the vessel's purser on board.

The two Germans moved out and towards the vessel, eventually arriving on board after a scrimmage through a crowd of people trying to board.

Moving down the stairs to the next deck, they found the purser's office stood at the back of a huge crowd, all trying to secure cabin space.

Muehler, who was intending to try and find where the two Englishmen were to be found, waited for a while, then started to push through the crowd.

The purser and his assistant were in the process of telling people that no more cabin space was available, and as Muehler breasted the office counter, the purser shook his head.

"Sir, we haven't any more space available."

Muehler shook his head and smiled and spoke in English, "No, sir. I was trying to locate two English friends of mine." The purser looked curiously at this obvious German from his accented English.

"They were booked on this vessel and had cabin space. Their names are Coulter and Wadsworth. I lost sight of them in the crowd on the quayside but I know they boarded."

Again the purser looked at the German, then produced his manifest of passengers in cabins.

After he'd skimmed down the list he looked up and shook his head. "Neither of them are listed. You must be mistaken; they're not even on the supplementary list."

Muehler looked a little mystified for the benefit of the purser but knew now they were there under different names but daren't suggest it. He thanked the purser and made his way back to Gruppe.

"I think they're in a cabin under a false name, but we better look around just in case. Then we'll get them when they try to leave the vessel."

The two men moved off through the crowd of milling passengers, eyes searching all the time. They had reached the rear of the vessel shortly before it sailed, and Muehler looked over the side to the forward part of the ship. Only one gangway was in position prior to sailing and as he watched, he saw a group of three come out of the terminal building and make their way to the sole remaining gangway. The two Englishmen were there accompanied by another man and disappeared into the bowels of the vessel. There was no way he could get down to where they were in time.

He called Gruppe and told him what he had seen, and the pair made their way forward without a lot of hope and rightly so, they searched several times but eventually gave up, hoping to see the disembark at Dover.

"We need to shoot on sight, Gruppe," Muehler said as they sat watching the crowds milling about the deck. The trip across was smooth, and the vessel eventually slowly moved through Dover harbour. Gruppe and Muehler stood on the upper deck close to where passenger gangway would be grounded, looking down at the quayside. As they watched, Muehler saw a small group of men, three in civilian clothes and two in uniform with helmets on, obviously police men, join another group of uniformed men as a gangway was lowered down and placed in position. The three civilians could have been immigration officials but as the formalities were conducted in the terminal building, he didn't think so. They could be shipping line officials, but he suddenly doubted it when he saw some more civilians at a wide doorway on the upper level, his instinct kicked in and he guessed they were the reception committee for the two Englishmen. He gauged the distance from where he stood to the lower gangway and knew it was too far for an accurate shot for either himself or Gruppe with handguns, neither of them were any sort of marksmen at a distance. They needed to get closer, because he again guessed neither of the two Englishmen would be going with the ordinary passengers through immigration. The other factor which swayed him was whilst he was willing to sacrifice his life for the Fuhrer and Fatherland, he also wanted some chance of living to fight another day. To shoot from the ship was stupid unless they could manage to merge into the milling crowd of passengers, which would give them a chance to plead ignorance of the affair in the case of a detailed examination of all the passengers, which would undoubtedly take place.

He and Gruppe moved back into the vessel and found some stairs leading down below, following the milling crowd of crew members, they found themselves in sight of the open door in the side of the ship which they had seen from the upper deck and saw just moving off the bottom of the gangway were the two men they wanted, accompanied by three civilians and a uniformed police officer. As they watched, the party disappeared into the terminal building.

They tried to follow but were stopped by a uniformed policeman at the head of the gangway and directed politely to the upper deck and the passenger gangway.

Thinking about it as they walked up the companionway to the passenger gangway, Muehler decided to go to the German Embassy in London and seek assistance, apart from talking to his superior in Berlin. He guessed by now the Englishmen had passed on the information they had obtained to a higher authority, so now his mission was to be one of pure revenge, killing them. He shuddered at the thought of having to report failure to Wilhelm Altein in Berlin, but he would have to do it prior to obtaining assistance from the staff of the German Embassy in London.

In London, after Inspector Robert Wilson had left his superior Andrew Carter, Carter picked up the telephone and called Charles Ferguson, the MI5 controller for the West of England. He briefed him on Robert Wilson's information and suspicions. Charles Ferguson was silent for a minute, then agreed that although their evidence was a little thin, they should get the man in for questioning, but he also suggested that Group Captain Thompson should be informed as well.

William Foulkes was currently working at an electrical substation in the south of Bristol and whilst he worked he was thinking about what he should do. A few days earlier he had become aware that he might be under surveillance and had confirmed it the previous day.

The same man who seemed to be loitering outside the Bristol Corporation Depot he spotted close to the substation.

He tried to think what sort of a mistake he'd made for them to suspect him and wondered if he could rectify it. Then thinking about it, he came to the conclusion that it was possible for the German Embassy, in the shape of Heinz Kern, to have informed on him, trying to get rid of him with his usefulness over. He realised that if he was arrested, he was a candidate for hanging; espionage for a foreign power was a capital offence.

By the end of the day, he had decided the only course he had open was to do a runner, but where to? To get anywhere on mainland Europe he needed visas for the various countries, although if he could get to the Channel Islands, he could get a day visa for a visit to France and instead of coming back, he could stay over there and try to get to South Africa, his birth place, from Marseille or with luck move to Italy and Genoa, where he knew vessels left for South Africa. Once in South Africa, he'd move up north to the Belgian Congo or one of the other European colonies

The house he lived in had been his grandparents' and was rented; he paid the rent monthly and was paid up to the end of the month, three weeks away.

So that evening he packed a small suitcase with enough clothes to last him a week. He had a small stash of money, a few hundred pounds, enough to get him onto the Continent and then to South Africa. He had a passport and didn't need a visa for South Africa and was aware he could purchase a transit visa through France on arrival over there. The other thing he felt was in his favour was the confusion generated by the current political situation; controls were bound to be sloppy. Earlier that day he'd purchased a copy of the Lloyd's Shipping Gazette, which covered the movements of ships worldwide, and saw there were several cargo ships carrying a few passengers out of Marseilles that week bound for either Cape Town or Durban. He kept his car in one of a bank of garages at the rear of the group of shops several hundred yards away in the next street.

He wondered if they kept the surveillance on him during the night and decided to leave very early via the back lane to his car. To do this he needed to climb over a neighbour's fence, but if he left early enough, the chances of anyone seeing him were remote.

That evening, in Bristol, Special Branch Sergeant Anthony Rudd decided to pick up William Foulkes for questioning the following day, so he briefed the local inspector and had a uniformed constable instructed to accompany him to make the call. The Special Branch only had William Foulkes under surveillance during the daytime hours; their man usually arrived close to Foulkes' house shortly before the Foulkes left for work. They had been only interested in his contacts and therefore, once he looked settled for the night, they left him alone.

Around four that morning Foulkes quietly prepared himself some breakfast, put a sandwich together to take and left the house, walking down his garden and climbing his back fence, thence through a neighbour's garden and over his back fence into the lane at the back, cursing the man's noisy dog. He made his way in the darkness, although it was just getting light, to the lock-up garage he kept his car in and moved the car out, fastening the door behind him with a stout padlock.

He then headed south out of Bristol towards the ferry terminal for the Channel Islands at Weymouth.

Chapter Nineteen

Anthony Rudd collected the uniformed police officer at 6 AM and continued on to William Foulkes' house. The Special Branch officer assigned to watch had been briefed to be there early, around 5 AM. The three officers went up the short path to the front door of Foulkes' house and rang the bell. No one came and after five minutes Rudd sent the uniformed constable around rear. The man came back and said the back door was locked but no one was about. Rudd looked at his watch and saw it was nearly seven o'clock, he turned to his Special Branch man.

"What time does he usually leave for work?"

"About seven, so he should be around."

Rudd thought quickly. "You two wait here whilst I find a telephone." Walking quickly he made his way to the group of shops and a telephone booth he knew was there. Reaching it he telephoned Robert Wilson in London.

"I think our bird has flown the coop, sir. He doesn't appear to be at home, to enter I need a search warrant."

Charles Wilson's reply was a flat decisive, "Go in and I'll cover you with a warrant later."

Anthony Rudd raced back to the house and with the aid of a lock pick opened the front door, and the three men entered.

A quick search of the house revealed that Foulkes had gone, everything was neat and tidy, and his clothes appeared to be there. In a drawer of the kitchen dresser Anthony Rudd found a bundle of papers, sitting at the kitchen table he proceeded to examine them. In the meantime the Special Branch constable searched the small lounge room sideboard for more paperwork.

Anthony Rudd detailed the uniformed officer to visit the houses on either side, using the spurious excuse that a relative of Foulkes had been hurt in an accident, to see they knew anything of his whereabouts.

The Special branch officer searching the sideboard found letters from a Heinz Kern but with no originator's address on them, but the envelopes were addressed to a Michael Mulroney at a poste restante.

The uniformed officer came back, and one of the neighbours said his dog had been very agitated around four that morning but he'd looked out and saw nothing.

Leaving the uniformed man in the house, Anthony Rudd and his man went back to their office, and he reported to Robert Wilson that he was sure that Foulkes had done a runner and certainly early that morning. He also reported on the letters, which Robert Wilson said would be from the Abwehr man in the German Embassy and Anthony Rudd was to send them up to London. Robert

Wilson said he would put out a warning to all ports with a connecting ferry to European ports to be alert and to have Foulkes apprehended should he show.

Robert Wilson gave the order to send a 'restrain if found order' to immigration staff at all the Continental ferry terminals and in particular, the Irish ferries. Robert Wilson thought Foulkes would try for the Irish Republic because the extradition treaty between the two countries had lapsed in 1937, when the Irish Free State changed to the Republic of Ireland, cutting itself off totally from UK. The new treaty was not yet in place but still in the process of negotiation. The ferry to Jersey from Weymouth was ignored, because it was thought he'd not try there, Jersey being part of the UK.

Robert Wilson also put in a request to Andrew Carter, Special Branch deputy controller, to have Heinz Kern declared 'persona non grata' and deported because of his connection with Foulkes, evidenced by the letters.

In the meantime, William Foulkes had reached Weymouth and caught the morning ferry to St Helier, Jersey, leaving his car in the Weymouth Municipal car park in the town, purchasing a ticket at the last possible moment. Whilst at that time in the morning there were only a few cars there, he was aware it would fill up during the day, offering at least 24 hours of concealment and more if the council employee was careless.

Reaching St Helier, he booked a ticket across to St Malo leaving that afternoon and reached St Malo at 5.30 PM. He then applied for a transit visa across France to Marseille at the immigration office and left for Paris on the late evening train, hoping to catch a train to Marseille the following day.

In Paris he checked into a small hotel in the Montparnasse district and the following morning caught the train down to Marseille, arriving at the Gare St Charles. There he was able to get lodging in a small boarding house in a small street just off Rue de Lyon, close to the docks, and decided the following day to look for a berth on a vessel for South Africa.

That evening, after supper in the boarding house, he was talking to the proprietor and mentioned he was trying to get to South Africa. He told him his sister was ill and he hadn't a lot of money, so was looking for a cheap trip and had been working in France as an electrical fitter in Paris. The proprietor suggested he tried get a berth on a ship sailing down to South Africa, working his passage, and gave him the name and office address of a man who supplied replacement crew for foreign ships.

The following day Foulkes called at the office, a seedy place not far from his lodgings. The office was in a dingy building on the ground floor. Foulkes entered and spoke to the girl behind the desk, in reasonable English she told him to sit down and went into an inner office, coming out again shortly afterwards and beckoning Foulkes to go in.

The fat swarthy man behind the desk asked Foulkes what he wanted, and Foulkes explained he needed to go to South Africa because of his sister and although he was prepared to pay for a cheap passage, his landlord had suggested he first discuss it with this man. The man's eyes narrowed and then said for a small fee he could probably get him a berth on a ship, in fact there was one there at the moment, a small cargo boat wanting crew to replace some who had jumped ship. The vessel was a tramp steamer registered in Liberia, and the wage paid wasn't much. If he was interested, the man would put his name forward and his qualifications but couldn't promise anything. Foulkes was to come back the next day.

Foulkes went back the next day, and the man said he'd got him a place as an assistant to the electrician on the vessel but his expenses had been more than he thought. He'd already weighed up Foulkes as a man on the run from something, either a woman or the police. He said Foulkes would need to be registered as a seaman and have the correct paperwork. Foulkes said he'd been robbed shortly after arriving in Marseille; the man said he could help but it would cost extra.

Eventually, after three days, Foulkes was signed on the Liberian vessel SS Timbro, registered in Monrovia, Liberia, as an electrician's assistant, using the name Michael Mulroney.

He'd used the name Michael Mulroney, because when he was getting his seamen's papers and had told the tale of having been robbed, he was asked if he had anything with his name on it and he had with him an old envelope with the name Michael Mulroney, the envelope had originally contained money sent by Heinz Kern.

It sailed shortly afterwards for Cyprus to pick up some fruit destined – along with timber already loaded – for Jeddah, Saudi Arabia, and from there was due to go to Bombay before Durban. He thought he might be able to write to Heinz Kern in the embassy to give him a contact point when the vessel made it to Bombay, and he would also ask for some more money. He could post the letter in Cyprus and maybe get a reply at Durban.

In London the day Foulkes sailed from Marseille, Andrew Carter, the Special Branch deputy controller, Robert Wilson and Anthony Rudd met in London to discuss where they should go next. Andrew Carter opened the proceedings with a brief résumé for the other men's benefit of where they were. Heinz Kern had left UK, no news had turned up at any of the ferry ports as to the whereabouts of Foulkes. After discussing where Foulkes could be, Anthony Rudd said he didn't think he was in the Bristol area, he'd had the police looking for the car for the past week after Foulkes first disappeared. His girlfriend hadn't seen or heard from him since he'd gone.

Andrew Carter looked a little thoughtful, and then asked Anthony Rudd,

"You say his car is missing. It means if he has left the country, the car must be somewhere close to a ferry port. He'll have used it to get to his exit point. He may not have left the country but as what he was doing carries the death penalty, he'll try and leave, I'm sure."

Robert Wilson thought for a moment, then said, "I can't see the immigration people missing him, he'd need a passport plus the visas for the relevant country he was going to, although with France he can get one at his point of entry, just as the Frogs could get one here. It's a reciprocal agreement." He turned to Anthony Rudd,

"He's got a passport, hasn't he, and is that missing from his house?"

"Yes, sir. We checked with the passport office in Bristol, he was issued with one four years ago. We didn't find it amongst the paperwork at the house."

Andrew Carter spoke again. "The car is the key. Circulate the number to all forces and have them search. A car should be easy to find, there's not that great a number around at the moment, and get the various ports to pay particular attention to car parks near their ferry terminals."

This time the message went out to all police forces in the country to watch for the car, particularly in a car park; Liverpool and Holyhead were specifically given a request for a priority search because of their proximity to Ireland and since they had Irish ferries.

Police Constable William Taylor, of the Dorset Constabulary, was on his usual round of visiting. This included various pawnshops in the town and lost property offices at the railway station and municipal offices, delivering the latest police list of things people had stolen from their homes or reported lost and called in at the municipal offices in Weymouth. He handed the list in to the usual clerk and stood chatting about the Saturday football match between Weymouth Town team and a team from up north. He was about to leave when the clerk laughed and said, "You haven't had a car reported missing, have you?"

William Taylor said, "No, have you found one?"

The clerk replied. "Well, there's one in our car park on Mons Street, you know down by the quay. That's locked every night; it's really a visitor's car park. It opens early and closes around midnight. The attendant reports a car has been left there for over a week. It looks as if it's been dumped, maybe stolen."

"Have you the number?" the clerk fished in some papers and came up with a foolscap-size sheet and ran his finger down the writing and gave the car registration to Constable Taylor.

"Hmm, that's a Bristol registration. I'll check it when I get back." He then left on his rounds and got back to the police station later that day.

The following morning, he remembered the car in the car park and spoke to the sergeant on duty.

"Sarge, there's a car looks as if it's been dumped in the town car Park on Mons Street. Here's the number, I wonder if it was on any list as stolen. It's a Bristol reggie."

The sergeant looked at the number, then reached for a clip-board and scanned it; he turned the page and stopped.

"This is being searched for. Not stolen but the Specials Branch at the Met are very interested in it. I better see the inspector."

In London later that morning, Andrew Carter telephoned Anthony Rudd. "Tony, you better get down to Weymouth. Foulkes' car looks as if it's turned up in the car park there. Weymouth, that's a Channel Island ferry port, he's gone over there. He should be easy to find there."

"Maybe not, sir. You can get day trips across to France from there. He'll have used that route to get on the Continent and from there I bet he's heading for either Ireland or somewhere else that doesn't have an extradition treaty with the

UK. He's just trying to throw us off the scent. He's cunning. But I'll have the bastard and have him topped."

"Now Tony, you're not judge and jury, that's not your function. All you do is to find and present the evidence."

Anthony Rudd took himself down to Weymouth and met with the superintendent in charge, explaining why they were after the car. He examined the car but nothing gave him any clue as to where Foulkes had gone but it had to be St Helier and Jersey.

From Weymouth he telephoned London and got permission to proceed to Jersey, returning to Bristol he packed an overnight bag and went back to Weymouth. In the meantime, at Weymouth the police had checked with the ferry office, showing a photograph of Foulkes, but neither of the two clerks there could remember him.

In St Helier he made contact with the local police, who then started to visit the local boarding houses and show a photograph of Foulkes. In the meantime, he visited the offices of the Malo-St Helier Ferry Company to see if he could turn up anything there.

They were, by agreement with the French and British authorities, required to keep manifests of passengers who took advantage of the day trips to France. Here he struck lucky; approximately ten days before a Michael Mulroney had purchased a trip across to France on the scheduled afternoon trip the day after Foulkes disappeared from Bristol. Anthony Rudd then telephoned Robert Wilson in London.

"Looks like he's using the name Michael Mulroney, sir." He went onto explain what he had found and asked should he go over to St Malo and see what he could find there? Robert Wilson said no, he'd talk to Andrew Carter first and then go from there.

Andrew Carter ruled that it should be handed over to MI6 and let them follow through on it, rather than bring him back as a minor player, he could be interrogated wherever he ended up and then a decision would be made as to what was to be done with him.

Andrew Carter made a formal application to MI6 and handed over what they knew of Foulkes a.k.a. Michael Mulroney, and where they believed he was heading.

Andrew Carter telephoned Group Captain Thompson, prior to the official report being issued, and gave him advance warning of the contents.

"It looks like the German source in Bristol has slipped the net, Group Captain. We went to pick him up and he'd gone early that morning, we tracked him down to Weymouth and then across to France via Jersey. I've handed the relevant documents over to MI6 to follow up in France. But I doubt whether the Frogs will co-operate to any great extent."

"No chance he was warned?"

"Other than he may have spotted he was under surveillance and decided the game was up. The other premise is that he may have thought the political situation was about to blow up and wanted to be clear of UK before the inevitable happened. I'll keep you informed should we get any more news."

"What's MI6 going to do should they find him?"

"My recommendation was to interrogate him wherever they find him, then let their superiors decide what should be done. I don't think extradition will be one of the alternatives."

The group captain realised what Andrew Carter was saying and, knowing how MI6 operated, didn't say anything other than to thank the Special Branch man for his information, mentally noting to ask Aubrey Evans informally to let him know of any further developments.

He later spoke with Aubrey Evans.

"Aubrey, I've had Carter from the Special Branch bring me up to date on their search for the German informant from the Bristol area, and I understand he's slipped the net. He's now in France, obviously trying to go somewhere from there. It crossed my mind that he could be useful in passing a load of dud information to the Germans in regard to our progress with the jet engine. They were searching for information, as you know."

"Yes, Gerry, that had also crossed my mind as well. We've turned a few lately, so I'll bring it up at our strategy meeting tomorrow. If we can find him, we can offer him the choice that he either he works for us or we liquidate him then and there. That's an offer he won't be able to refuse. The German Abwehr contact in the embassy has been sent back. The poor devil is either in a punishment posting somewhere or the Gestapo have him in their clutches. If we bring him back, it will fit into the picture with Kern gone and a clamp down on in the Bristol area by us, so any delay in his contacting the embassy won't be unusual."

"I'll leave it with you, Aubrey. Let me know when you require any misinformation."

"It won't be me, Gerry. It'll be MI5, I'm not too sure who, but they'll be in touch. I'll keep you informed as to our search for him." The two men closed the call off.

The hapless Heinz Kern had been met at the German border and taken from the train on the instructions of the Gestapo head responsible for the embassy safety and immediately taken to Berlin. Deputy Director Haslop was unable to obtain any information of his whereabouts until after the Gestapo had forced him to take poison and then delivered his body to his family.

There followed a stormy meeting between Admiral Canaris and the Gestapo official over the action, and the Gestapo man blamed Kern for compromising the operations at the embassy and said as such he was a traitor. Canaris was powerless to do anything.

The admiral made arrangements to send another man to the embassy and instructed him to try and make contact with Kern's agent in the Bristol area. He should be able to find some sort of documentation leading to him in Kern's files at the embassy. The admiral was unaware that the agent in question had done a runner.

The Admiral was being asked almost daily for reports of the progress of the British jet engine and had staved them off by saying his man in the embassy had been compromised and he was in the process of putting another one in his place.

The MI6 operatives in France tracked Foulkes from his arrival in St Malo and his transit visa taking him to Marseille. After discussion with London, it was decided to check the shipping departures following his possible arrival in Marseille and see the destinations and then check the crew muster lists lodged with the register of sailors at the Marseille port office.

It was painstaking work, 55 vessels had left Marseille in the two weeks following his estimated arrival in Marseille. They checked for both Mulroney and Foulkes, not being sure which name he would use. After a three-day search, they found a Michael Mulroney had left Marseille on a Liberian vessel bound for Cyprus and then Bombay, its ultimate destination being Durban.

The port in Cyprus was Famagusta, and a quick check showed they would miss him there but could get him at the Suez Canal, when the vessel reached Port Said on the Mediterranean.

On arrival the vessel was boarded there by a detachment of Egyptian police, acting under British Embassy instructions, and Foulkes taken to the consulate in Port Said. Here the MI6 operative for the area gave him the alternative of returning back to England as a passenger on the next British Royal Mail steamer under escort or taken out into the desert and shot. Understandably, Foulkes took the passage back to England to be met by Special Branch officers and held in custody until formally charged with espionage, before being remanded in custody by a magistrate in a closed session at Bow Street.

He'd not written to Kern from Cyprus, as he intended to do, they had only been there for 24 hours and no shore leave had been granted.

He was interviewed by MI5 operatives and offered the choice of working with and under the direction of them, supplying information to Germany that they would give him, or be hanged as a traitor. He agreed to work for them.

He was then lodged in a safe house in Berkshire, along three other turned German agents, although they were all kept separate from each other and coached on how to make contact again with the German Embassy.

Foulkes was given a certificate on hospital paper of a private hospital just outside Birmingham to send to his employers, the Bristol Corporation, plus a note to say his sister was seriously ill and he wished to take two or three weeks off and was sorry he hadn't been in touch before. I also said that his sister had been taken to hospital after a serious accident, and he needed to stay with her a little longer.

The new Abwehr operative arrived at the embassy, but after checking through the files of Heinz Kern, couldn't come up with a contact point for the man in Bristol and hadn't any idea who he was or what his name was.

He'd been at the embassy for a week when a letter arrived, addressed to Heinz Kern, postmarked Bristol from a Michael Mulroney, giving an address asking for more money before he'd give any more information.

The Abwehr man sent a coded cable back to Berlin to Wolf Landsberg, the Abwehr section head for England, asking for instructions. The letter from Mulroney also said that he was no longer under surveillance and that the authorities seemed satisfied he was clean and he could come up to London for a meeting if need be. Mulroney had also enclosed a cutting from the local Bristol paper, which gave details of an Irish labourer who had been arrested in connection with the leakage of information in regard to the Bristol Aeroplane Company.

Deputy Director Haslop, after discussing it with Admiral Canaris, was at first suspicious and then accepted the story and seemed comfortable with Wolf Landsberg's recommendation. This was to send the man from the embassy who had met with Foulkes before, along with a second man following him, to make doubly sure Foulkes was not under surveillance.

A letter was sent back to the Mulroney poste restante, giving a time and date of a meeting at the public house in Pimlico.

Upon receipt, MI5 swung into action, on the day prior to the meeting a team of telephone engineers arrived and started to work at junction box opposite to the pub in Rochester Row, with a second team further down the road. A team were also working at the junction with Vauxhall Bridge Road, supposedly telephone engineers.

Foulkes was briefed what to say and ask for more money before he could obtain and supply any more information; he needed the money to pay people in Bristol, no money, no information could be obtained.

Foulkes turned up at the same pub in Rochester Row and ordered a half pint of bitter, at the appointed time the same beefy German came in and sat down opposite him. Foulkes got up and got him a half pint and then asked about some money, putting a newspaper on the table between them. Whilst they were sitting there, an MI5 man came in and ordered a drink, going to sit at a table further down behind the German's back, finished his drink quickly and walked out. He'd seen enough of the German to be able to follow him with a team when the German left.

Positioned in the post office van opposite to the pub door was a man with a camera, who would take photos of the German as he came out. The MI5 man waited with him to identify the German when he exited the pub. The 'O' of the post office logo could be moved from the inside to give an aperture, which the camera lens could be aimed through to take a photo without the subject being aware it was being taken.

The German said he'd report back to his superiors and they would be in touch.

The man who had followed him and covertly watched the rendezvous then followed Mulroney back to the Victoria Bus Terminal and waited until Mulroney boarded the bus for Bristol.

He reported that Mulroney was not followed and had returned to Bristol.

The relationship with the embassy was resumed, Foulkes feeding false information back as and when required by MI5 and 6.

Foulkes was allowed back to Bristol and returned to work for the Corporation, living in the same house. He physically reported to an address in Chelmsford one week and was given information from time to time to pass on to the German Embassy via the mails, receiving payment to his poste restante.

In Germany, Abwehr fed the resultant information into the system. When war broke out his contact ceased, and Foulkes was allowed to continue to work in Bristol for the Corporation.

Before the war ended, he committed suicide.

On the Cross Channel Ferry at Dover the two Gestapo men were fuming, they were in a line-up of passengers going through the immigration controls, with the knowledge that their quarry had left the vessel half an hour before them.

Reinhold Muehler, the senior man of the two, was fully aware that his superior in Berlin would no doubt have something nasty in store for him if he couldn't report success in liquidating the two Englishmen. As he waited he weighed up the pros and cons of not telephoning Wilhelm Altein, his superior until he'd killed at least one of the Englishmen. One of the main stumbling blocks was the fact he needed to ask for assistance from the German Embassy in London in finding the men; the Gestapo men in London would need to get approval from a higher authority in Germany before they would lift a finger.

The two men reached the front of the queue and presented their passports and arrival cards to the immigration officer. The man looked at the cards and the two passports, and then stood and took their papers to another man standing behind the row of desks. The two immigration officials conferred, looking across at the two Germans as they talked. The obvious senior man nodded and came back with the other man.

"Will you come this way, sir? We won't be a moment." He led them back across the room to an office and ushered them in. Muehler decided to try and bully his way past the Englishman, so started to say. "Why are we being held like this? The Englishman listened to him and then replied,

"You're not being held anywhere. We need to ask a few questions."

"We need to catch the boat train, and if we don't, we'll hold you responsible."

"Yes gentlemen, I understand. Tell me why are you coming to England?"

"We are both with the German Finance Ministry and proceeding to our embassy in London to do an audit. Discrepancies have shown up, and we need to check with the staff."

"But our information is different. We think you come from the Gestapo office in Freudenstadt; that certainly isn't the German Finance Ministry, is it now?"

Muehler cursed to himself, the man was well-briefed, so he looked indignant and thought quickly. "Our passports say we are civil servants, and it so happens that the Freudenstadt office of the Geheime Staatspolizei was the last place we audited."

The man replied in very fluent German. “If you say so, Herr Muehler.” He stamped their two passports and handed them back. “You are free to leave.”

The two Germans made their way down to the railway platform and boarded the train, but first walked the length of the train, searching for the two Englishmen. Muehler went off to the bureau de change to exchange some German marks into sterling and then found a telephone booth. Ringing the German Embassy, he ordered the resident Gestapo man to meet them at Victoria on arrival, and after a discussion with him, told him to bring with him the location of the British Air Ministry. He’d thought that the train would be in London before a car carrying the two Englishmen arrived and assumed because of the nature of their assignment in Germany, they would be Royal Air Force personnel and would be taken to the Air Ministry for debriefing.

Having made enquiries before he boarded the train, Muehler found the train journey would take 95 minutes for the 70 odd miles, a car would take nearly two and a half hours.

On the way up in the train, they had a compartment to themselves, and Heinrich Muehler discussed the proposed action with Gerhard Gruppe. They both were to shoot at the two men, he would take the one with the sandy hair and Gruppe was to take the other man.

Gruppe protested, saying that they would be apprehended and face the death penalty in England, they were not on diplomatic passports. This gave Muehler something to think about; the two men would have obviously passed on the information and therefore, to kill them in public was a little stupid and as Gruppe said, could lead them to being executed themselves.

In the Immigration Office, the senior official who had interviewed them telephoned the MI5 man in Dover with the information that the two Gestapo man were on the London train, obviously going up to their embassy. They were claiming to be audit clerks going up to the embassy to do some work, the senior one had admitted being in the Gestapo Freudenstadt office but said it was for audit work. The MI5 man said he would pass it on and thanked him and immediately telephoned London to advise the two were on the boat train.

David Coulter and Tom Wadsworth were on their way to London by car with an armed escort consisting of the MI5 Dover man and driver.

The driver kept an eye on the vehicles behind him and saw nothing that gave him cause for alarm. They had one stop on the way up to London.

In Rheims Hans Van Dyke had received instructions to continue onto Paris with the group and then make for Calais to meet their original scheduled crossing date of 17th September. Joan Healey wondered if the two had succeeded in avoiding their German pursuers, and Hans seemed unperturbed about it, saying he was sure they were all right.

Chapter Twenty

The car carrying David Coulter and Tom Wadsworth arrived in London and dropped them at the MI6 offices, where they were met by Group Captain Thompson and Aubrey Evans.

The two gave a résumé of what had happened and what they had seen at Stuttgart airfield. David did most of the talking, saying that the security had been tightened up from the time they were there first to when they went back the second time.

"We did tell you not to get into any trouble but just to observe," this from Aubrey Evans. "You were very lucky to get away the way you did. Where's the film now?

David then recounted their meeting with Hans Van Dyke and Joan Healey in Freiburg and how they asked for help with the film. Aubrey Evans laughed, turning to Gerald Thompson.

"Amateurs, Gerry, you can't beat them for improvisation." Turning back to the two, "Don't you two realise you could have had the whole lot of those innocent tourists locked up and created an ugly international incident?"

The two boys looked a little sheepish and David said, "But if we'd have been caught, we would have looked in the clear, and at that stage they were looking for us the other side of Freiburg. Also either way, it gave you two chances of having the information instead of just one with us."

"Now when is the party back in England?"

"They have a booking on the ferry for the 17th, unless of course they have difficulty in getting on-board due to the number of people wanting to return."

Gerald Thompson looked at Aubrey Evans, "I think we better make sure they make that ferry."

Aubrey Evans nodded. "Yes, I'll alert my man in Calais." He turned to David again,

"Where are they now?"

"In the King George V Hotel in Paris. They should have arrived."

"OK, I'll get word to them and make contact to make sure they make the ferry on the 17th."

Gerald Thompson stood and the two young men did likewise. "Thank you, Aubrey. We'll get back to the A.M., and you two can write up a full report on your sightings of the jet plane. Then, go to the hotel in Russell Square. I'll find a car for you to use until your car is brought across from France later."

The two Germans arrived at Victoria and were met by the current Gestapo operative from the embassy with a car. This arrival was noted by the man MI5 had sent to Victoria and he confirmed they had gone to the embassy.

The two young men sat down with a stenographer in the Air Ministry and gave an account of their experience from the time they arrived in Stuttgart to their arrival back in the UK. They then proceeded to the Imperial Hotel in Russell Square, a hotel they had stayed in on their previous visit.

Neither the Air Ministry driver nor the two young men noticed they were followed to the hotel by two men in a small Morris car, the sort often seen in England then. After they arrived at the hotel and checked in, one of the men followed them in and waiting with them at the reception desk made note of the rooms they had been given. To cover himself he asked about the availability of rooms for the following weekend as the two young men left the desk to go upstairs.

He then went back to his companion in the car, gave the information to him and went back into the hotel to sit with a newspaper in the foyer. The car went to the German Embassy.

The two young men had an early evening meal and then went up to their rooms, intending to have an early night. Group Captain Thompson telephoned them before they left to warn them that two Germans had followed them over from France, so they had to be on their guard. He would give them a call when he knew what the Germans were doing there.

In the German Embassy the driver of the vehicle from outside the hotel gave the details of the rooms the two men were in to Reinhold Muehler.

He and Gruppe then discussed their next course of action. He'd just had a stormy telephone conversation with his superior Wilhelm Altein in Berlin and been told that he was required to do as he was ordered – liquidate the two Englishmen as an example of the long arm of the Third Reich for those who transgress.

Both Reinhold Muehler and Gruppe were aware of the last time they had tried to take the two Englishmen and hesitated to shoot them in an English street, knowing the penalty would be death. They couldn't see a way of making a clear getaway if they shot them in an English street.

Gruppe came in with a suggestion; neither of them were using diplomatic passports, so their movements were not restricted – as with diplomats – to a 25-mile radius of the embassy.

They could track down their quarry to where they actually lived and could liquidate them there.

The Abwehr operative was tasked with finding out where the two men lived and their home addresses, it could be a military installation somewhere. Muehler didn't think that they were civilians, possibly reservists, but he was sure the English wouldn't send two civilians on a mission like that.

The following morning the Abwehr man went to the hotel to see who was behind the reception desk and who else he could find. He found the two

Englishmen had already left, and the clerk refused to give him a forwarding address, saying he could leave a message with him and he would see it sent on.

So he searched for a European of some sort, either a German refugee or one from one of the countries close to Germany; the hotels in London were full of them due to the threatening political situation in Europe.

He would first try and bribe then and if that failed, depending who it was, would see if he could threaten them with the idea of mistreatment of relatives by the authorities in the country where ever they came from.

He was in luck; the waiter serving in the lounge was originally from the Saar area of Germany. The Abwehr man put it to him he was wanting the home addresses of two of the guests from the previous night, he said he'd met them the previous night and had promised to see them before they had left but had missed them. The waiter looked a little dubious at first but when the Abwehr man flashed a five-pound note, the waiters eyes glistened and he told him to come back that afternoon and he'd meet him in the pub across the square on the corner.

Later the Abwehr man was able to give the home addresses of the two Englishmen to Muehler.

One was near a town called Chester, a village called Christleton, and the other near Hereford, a village called Much Birch. Checking the map, Muehler decided to go to Chester first, then down to the Hereford location the same day, and carry on to the Cross Channel ferry at Weymouth, picking up a hire car at Dieppe and driving back to Germany non-stop.

That morning Group Captain Thompson telephoned Aubrey Evans and said he debriefed the two young men and the information was a little disturbing, showing that the Germans were well ahead in the jet engine field.

Aubrey Evans went on to say that they had the other party covered and would discreetly shepherd them back to England, although it was doubtful that the Germans would have any idea of the valuable package they carried.

They then discussed the two Gestapo men, who as far as they knew, were still holed up in the German Embassy. Gerald Thompson, who had thought about it overnight, then expressed his fears to Aubrey Evans,

"I'd like a better handle on the activities of those two thugs who followed our two. I'd hate them to have a go at our boys, who are babes in the wood as far as this sort of thing goes."

"Where are your two, Gerry?"

"Gone home. I gave them instructions to leave this morning, and I presume they have gone. I could check. I'll telephone them and see if I can warn them."

"Mmmm, good idea. I'll also have a word with my counterpart in MI5 and see if we can watch the two Germans. Leave it with me. The problem is they aren't on diplomatic passports, so can go where they like; on the other hand, we can treat them like any other person who breaks the law and they will not have diplomatic immunity.

"They wouldn't have our boys' addresses."

"Easy enough to find out from the hotel, Gerry."

Later that day he telephoned Group Captain Thompson and told him they were going to have the two Germans followed night and day. They were still in the embassy, the MI5 embassy watcher hadn't seen them leave, although the Abwehr operative had been seen to go and return twice.

The next morning the two Germans were seen to leave and were followed to a car hire firm in Charing Cross Road. They hired a car and drove back to the embassy, to be seen a short time later leaving putting their suitcases into the car and driving off.

The Special Branch at Scotland Yard had been alerted as to possible action outside of London, and a team was quickly organised to follow the Germans. They were given orders to take them alive, if possible, but not to hesitate to shoot if there was any danger.

It was obvious after a short time the Germans were headed up north, along the A5 to Shrewsbury. There they stopped overnight, leaving next morning up towards Whitchurch along the A41 to Chester. They picked a small hotel just outside Chester for the night.

In Paris Hans Van Dyke had taken the morning off whilst Joan Healey took the group to the Louvre, he was catching up on some paper work in his room when the telephone rang. He was expecting Edward Smith to call. The voice on the other end spoke in French but the opening phrase was the one he'd been told to expect, "How are things in Holland?"

The person said he'd be contacted at Calais and to make sure he arrived with his group in time to make the ferry. Their passage was guaranteed.

That evening Hans met a courier with another group whom he knew, and the man gave him some horrific tales about the chaos at the ferry terminals with the numbers of people trying to get back to England.

After their short stay of three days in Paris, Hans Van Dyke made sure the party left early to enable them to reach the Calais terminal in good time. Their itinerary originally had them leaving on the morning ferry from Calais but due to their changes along the route, their ferry was in the afternoon. They arrived at the Calais terminal to find chaos, as Hans had expected. Hans left the party on the coach outside the coach company's office about half a mile from the terminal and was about to walk to the terminal building, as he stepped onto the pavement, he was approached by a man who used the phrase again. He introduced himself as Marc Farjot and motioned for Hans to return on-board the coach and follow him on.

He guided the driver around some backstreets, eventually arriving at a gate further down the port from the ferry terminal. Alighting, he went through a small gate at the side and the main gate opened shortly. Marc Farjot beckoned the coach through and the gate was closed behind them.

Getting back onto the coach, he instructed the driver to go down the quayside to a large shed or warehouse-type building.

"You people should go through the door there," pointing. "Wait inside and I'll meet you in a moment after I've arranged to have the baggage taken on-board."

The party went inside the cavernous warehouse, and he joined them shortly, leading them to a cargo lift and taking them up to the next floor. On that floor they joined other passengers going through the immigration procedures and then boarding.

The vessel left on time. On their arrival in Dover, they were contacted again, and prior to leaving on the boat train to Victoria, Hans was taken to an office, where he handed over the reel of film given to him by the two boys. He was also given a telephone number to make contact with a Gerald Thompson when he was free.

They saw their group to their transatlantic vessel, the Cunard R.M.S. Antonia, and then left for Chester to report to Edward Smith.

The four Special Branch men followed the two Germans to the small hotel in Chester that evening and waited until they had obviously retired for the night. The hotel the Germans had picked, unfortunately, was such that the Special Branch men couldn't get a room. The street outside was not conducive to waiting in to watch the hotel. They noted where the Germans' car was parked and were able to find a position to watch it. Early the next morning, the two Germans came to their vehicle and drove off, heading towards Christleton, where David Coulter lived. They stopped in the village, obviously to ask for information, and proceeded to the house. The difficulty the Special Branch team had was keeping them in sight without arousing suspicion because of the lack of traffic on the road. The two Germans stopped opposite to the drive to David Coulter's house, the Special Branch team car following was forced to drive past and stop out of sight further down the road. One of the men walked back to the bend, as he did so he was in time to see the Germans turning their car and disappearing back towards Chester.

He ran back to their car and they turned also, speeding back. They reached the junction of where the Christleton road joined the Tarvin-Chester Road and turned towards Chester, hoping to catch them up.

The Germans, instead of turning towards Chester – which was to the left – had turned to the right, heading towards Tarvin. On reaching the outskirts of Chester, the MI5 car stopped where their second car was located but the occupants hadn't seen the German car go past. After conferring, the two groups decided one group would go into Chester and stake out the work place of David Coulter whilst the other group went back and staked out the house. This they were able to do by sitting in their car in Christleton village with the drive of the house in view.

The Germans' idea was to find a small village not far along the road from Christleton but had to drive into Tarvin and so passed their time there, having a lunch of sandwiches at a small inn. Late in the afternoon, they drove via country lanes to join the A41 on the other side of Christleton and then found the turn-off for Christleton to try and get to the house from the rear.

The two Germans had decided earlier that there wouldn't be any guards anyway on the house; the getaway from Christleton would be better than the office or street in Chester. They didn't want to enter the house and wait there for him, because they weren't sure who was also in the house.

There was a shrubbery close to the house, using that as cover they could shoot him as he left his car, but to get to it they would need to approach from the side or rear. To go up the drive one would be in full view of the house. Turning off the A41 towards Christleton village, they saw the house backed onto a field, which would be ideal for them to use to enter the shrubbery at the side of the house and watch the drive. They decided that Gruppe would wait with car whilst Muehler did the shooting.

They stopped the car on the lane leading to Christleton village from the south, and Gruppe waited as Muehler got out and climbed over a fence, walking along the edge of the field behind to the house. He reached the boundary of the house's garden, where it joined the field boundary, the shrubbery butted onto the field, and he was able to leave the field and into the fairly thick shrubbery around the house.

Moving towards the front of the house, he took up a position where he could see the driveway in front of the house and saw one car there. He cursed and wondered if the Englishman was back; as he watched, an older man came out of the house, going to the car took something out of it, then went back into the house. So he decided that that would be the Englishman's father and he settled down to wait.

The two Special Branch officers waiting in Christleton village, with a good view of the entrance to the Coulter driveway, waited but so far nothing suspicious had happened. Then the senior of the two, who was looking at a map of the district, turned to his companion,

"I wonder if there's easy access to the rear of the house. Whilst I would expect these Germans to blunder in through the front, they may have other ideas, particularly if they have sighted us. Have a walk down the lane there towards the main road and see if you can see much of the house from the lane."

The second man left the car and walked towards where just through the village the road forked, one fork going to the A41 main road, the other back into the country. As he turned down the fork leading to the A41 and rounded the bend, he stopped. About two hundred yards further on was the Germans' car, he quickly moved to the side to be shielded by some of the hedge. He could only see one person in the car, which meant the other German must be somewhere else. He quickly walked back to their car and reported it to the senior man.

"He'll either be in the house or holed up where he can get a shot at someone in the drive. My bet's the drive, too many unknowns in the house; otherwise, he'd have the other man with him to keep them quiet."

"The shrubbery is a bit thick and it would be an easy shot to get someone getting out a car."

"We have a telephone number for Coulter's office. Give him a bell and get him to get to our people and have them come here. In the meantime, we'll take the Kraut out in the lane."

The second man went off to the public telephone box outside the village post office and came back after five minutes.

"OK. They were in the office, Coulter has just left and they were about to follow. I talked to George and told them to come here outside this pub."

"We'll take him this way. We drive to the car, I'll get out holding this map and ask for directions, you get out and go to the passenger, side and I'll wave my piece at him from the driver's side."

They drove off and turned towards the A41, pulling up parallel to the German car. The senior man got out and went around to the German driver.

Gruppe saw the car pull up and a man get out, holding what looked like a map, and walk around to him. Gruppe dropped the window, as he did so, the passenger door opened and another man bent to get in. Gruppe reached for his shoulder holstered gun, but the man outside tapped on the window with the barrel of a large revolver, shaking his head and beckoning him out. Gruppe got out and started to complain. The man on his side told him to shut up in German and started to pat his body, quickly finding his gun.

"Naughty," before he could even start to complain again, the two men quickly handcuffed him with his hands behind his back and pushed him into their vehicle. Whilst one man did this, the other opened the bonnet of the Germans' car and took something out, obviously immobilising it.

Both his captors got into their car and drove down onto the A41 and U-turned to come back up the lane again back into Christleton Village. They stopped and U-turned again outside the post office, and one climbed into the back with Gruppe.

"Where's the other man?" this in German. Gruppe remained silent. The man alongside him smiled, and Gruppe heard him cock the pistol and felt the muzzle against his knee. "Where is the other man?" Gruppe decide that discretion was the better part of valour; he didn't want his knee damaged.

"In the shrubbery at the top of the drive." The two nodded, just as the other half of their team arrived, pulling up behind them. The senior man got out and walked to the other car.

"We've got one here, the other is apparently in the shrubbery at the top of the drive, waiting to ambush anyone arriving. Their car is immobilised just down the lane."

"Can we see the German from the drive gateway?"

"Don't know, but I shouldn't think so. That shrubbery is all rhododendron, privet and laurel, very thick."

Just then a car came past and turned into the Coulter drive.

"That's the Coulter boy. Didn't you warn him?"

"He'd already left. We didn't know what the situation was. How could we?"

The senior man started to run towards the driveway, gun in hand. The other two quickly got out of the car and followed. The senior man reached the driveway and started up it, calling out to David Coulter, who was just getting out of the car, bending down to pick something up and then straightening up.

He half turned and looked at them, seeing three men running up the drive, then heard a crack and felt a pain in his left shoulder at the same time, the shock of which seemed to throw him down against the open door of the car, hitting his head against the top of the car door frame, momentarily stunning him, causing him to fall further.

He vaguely heard more bangs, the tinkle of breaking glass and shouts and then a voice said, "Keep down, Mr Coulter. Stay there." A hand in the middle of his back held him down; the pain in his shoulder didn't seem too bad.

Reinhold Muehler in the shrubbery saw the car turn into the drive and guessed it was the Englishman, he watched as it stopped, the driver got out and then bent and reached inside to get something, a bag with a broad strap. He was momentarily distracted by three men who came into sight, running up the drive and calling out. The Englishman at the car turned as the men shouted and Muehler took a quick shot, the angle was bad for him, he saw the Englishman fall to the side and guessed he'd hit him somewhere. One of the men running up the drive loosed a shot in his general direction, which cut some leaves off the bush near him. One man ran towards the car, the others coming towards him, so he loosed off a couple of shots in their direction, making them dive for cover. He looked at the car and could just see a figure on the other side through the passenger window, so he sent a shot crashing through that window, then turned and moved quickly back towards the field and their car.

The three Special Branch men running up the drive heard the first shot and saw David Coulter fall, one ran to him and crouched beside him, the other two continued up the drive, heard shots fly past obviously aimed at them and dived down into the shrubbery to their left.

One speaking, quietly asked, "Can you see him?"

The other shook his head. "No but I think he's in the bushes about level with the car. I'll work around to the side and come in behind him; you stay here."

The man with David told him to stay there as a shot crashed through the passenger window of the car, missing both of them. There was a silence for about five minutes, then they heard one of the men calling out, "He's gone for their car."

David and the Special Branch man stood up. David felt his shoulder, it seemed all right, bruised but there was blood on his neck when he took his hand away. The Special Branch man looked at his shoulder and neck. "You've got a slight wound to the back of your neck, here hold this." The man took a handkerchief from his pocket and pressed it against where David's neck was bleeding. He then picked up the gas-mask satchel that David had leaned into the car to get earlier on arrival and laughed. "This saved your life." He showed David the misshapen solid brass adjustment buckle on the shoulder strap of the satchel.

"That first bullet ricocheted off this buckle and creased your neck. You were lucky."

Muehler saw his shots had missed and knew it was only a moment before the others would get him. He slipped back through the bushes to the field and raced down the edge to the fence, scrambled over and got to their car. Gruppe wasn't there, he looked wildly around and couldn't see any sign of him. Pulling open the door of the car, he saw that the keys weren't in it.

His mind skipped through his options, he could surrender and face civil charges, he could go for the main road and hope to hi-jack a car or shoot it out here.

He decided to face civil charges in the hope the German Embassy would do a trade for him. He put his gun on the ground and stood by the car with his hands in the air.

A man came out of the field cautiously as another man walked slowly down the road towards him, gun in hand.

"Game's up, Fritz," the first man said as he motioned Muehler to back away from his gun and then turned him around to handcuff him.

"Come, let's get back." The man roughly prodded Muehler in the back towards the man coming down the road.

The pair were taken back down to London and kept incommunicado for two weeks and interrogated, but being minor Gestapo thugs, they didn't really know much. The German Embassy daren't make too much of their disappearance because of the nature of their mission and so after preliminary enquiries about the whereabouts of two German nationals, which of course the British authorities disclaimed all knowledge of unless more specific information was available as to where they had travelled to, couldn't help.

After a consultation between the Special Branch and MI5, it was decided to ship the two back to Germany, knowing full well what fate awaited them there. They were taken and handed over to the French, who took them to the frontier.

In Germany, the Peenemunde Rocket programme was given priority over the fighter plane, and consequently, a weapon with which the Germans could have dominated the skies was delayed until it was too late to have any major effect on the Allies' bombing programme of Germany.

The first flight of a British jet fighter took place in 1941, and the first operational fighter was used in late 1944, a few weeks after the first German operational fighter was used.

The German Heinkel project was not continued, instead firstly, in late 1943, the Messerschmitt Me 163 was produced but the high-grade fuel required became unavailable through Allied bombing. Work was concentrated on the Me 262, which required a lower grade fuel, but due to further delays, was not available until late 1944.

The 610 Auxiliary Squadron was re-trained as a fighter squadron, first equipped with Hawker Hurricane single-engine planes and later with the famous Spitfire. David Coulter kept in touch with Tom Wadsworth, although their joint military operations ceased. Tom Wadsworth and David's sister eventually got married and so they became brothers-in-law. David Coulter married Joan Healey on the outbreak of war in 1939.

The Austell family arrived back in England on schedule from Paris on the 15th of September.

Mr Neville Chamberlain thought he'd secured an agreement with Adolf Hitler after visiting Germany three times, but the document eventually proved worthless.

Elizabeth Austell heard from the German officer, Carl Zuicher, they had met on the railway station, after she had sent a copy of the photo taken in Germany. He visited them in London twice between October 1938 and August 1939, and Elizabeth went over to Germany in May 1939 and met his family and spent a month there. They talked of marriage, but he wanted to wait to see how the political situation developed and hoped it would settle down. The last she heard from him was a letter written in late August 1939, when he was over on the east side of Germany on the Polish frontier.

She first considered joining Princess Mary's Nursing Service, which served the R.A.F., but on second thoughts she joined Queen Alexandra's Nursing Corp for the Army and remained unmarried throughout the war, serving first in France. Evacuated through Brest at the fall of France, she then went to Egypt, following the Eighth Army via a hospital ship. Returning to England after being wounded at Salerno, after the sinking of the hospital ship, she joined a casualty clearing field hospital, and went to France on D Day serving in Europe.

She often thought about the German, Carl Zuicher, and was determined to try and find him after the war, hoping he survived it.

It is not known whether it was Admiral Canaris or Heinrich Haslop who kept passing information during the war, obviously any channels were limited by then. Both Canaris and Haslop were replaced at the insistence of Himmler in February 1944, placed under house arrest and executed in April 1945.

Carl Zuicher, the German officer, fought in Poland, France, North Africa, and in the late stages of the war in Italy, often thinking about Elizabeth Austell and determined, if he survived, to find her, wondering at times when he was fighting the British if she was somewhere close on the other side. Every time he was in a position to interrogate captured British medical staff, he would make enquiries about her. He never ever received any firm news of her, except in North Africa, when at a captured British casualty clearing station outside of Derna in Libya, he was interrogating some wounded prisoners with a British medical officer, whom he had insisted accompany him. After they had finished, he asked, as was his usual way when he ran into captured hospital staff, if he knew her. The man thought he did in a Cairo military hospital, where he thought she was a theatre sister.